MIRAGE

Camilla Lackberg is a worldwide bestseller renowned for her brilliant contemporary psychological thrillers. Her books have sold over 40 million copies in over 60 countries and have been translated into 43 languages.

www.camillalackberg.com

Henrik Fexeus is one of Sweden's most sought-after lecturers and a prize-winning mentalist. He has done astounding psychological experiments on SVT and TV4 and became a household name in 2007, with the debut book *The Art of Reading Minds*. Fexeus's books have won several prizes, sold over 2.5 million copies and are translated into more than 40 languages. Henrik made his debut as an author of fiction in 2017, with YA novel *The Lost*, the first part in his critically acclaimed Final Illusion Trilogy.

www.henrikfexeus.se

Also by Camilla Lackberg

PATRICK HEDSTRÖM AND ERICA FALCK SERIES
The Ice Princess
The Preacher
The Stonecutter
The Stranger (previously titled *The Gallows Bird*)
The Hidden Child
The Drowning
The Lost Boy
Buried Angels
The Ice Child
The Girl in the Woods
The Cuckoo

FAYE'S REVENGE
The Gilded Cage
Silver Tears

MINA DABIRI AND VINCENT WALDER TRILOGY
Trapped
Cult

SHORT STORIES
The Scent of Almonds & Other Stories

Also by Henrik Fexeus

The Art of Reading Minds
The Art of Social Excellence

MINA DABIRI AND VINCENT WALDER TRILOGY
Trapped
Cult

MIRAGE

CAMILLA LACKBERG & HENRIK FEXEUS

Translated from the Swedish by Ian Giles

Hemlock Press,
An imprint of HarperCollins*Publishers*
1 London Bridge Street
London SE1 9GF

www.harpercollins.co.uk

HarperCollins*Publishers*
Macken House, 39/40 Mayor Street Upper
Dublin 1, D01 C9W8, Ireland

This paperback edition 2026

1

First published by HarperCollins*Publishers* Ltd 2025

Copyright © Camilla Lackberg & Henrik Fexeus, 2023
Published by agreement with Nordin Agency, Sweden
Translation copyright © Ian Giles 2025

Originally published in 2023 by Bokförlaget Forum, Sweden as *Mirage*

Camilla Lackberg & Henrik Fexeus assert the moral right to be identified
as the authors of this work.
Ian Giles asserts the moral right to be identified as the translator of this work.

A catalogue copy of this book is available from the British Library.

ISBN: 9780008464325 (PB)

This novel is entirely a work of fiction. The names, characters and incidents portrayed
in it are the work of the author's imagination. Any resemblance to actual persons,
living or dead, events or localities is entirely coincidental.

Typeset in Minion Pro by HarperCollins*Publishers* India

Printed and bound in the UK using 100% Renewable Electricity at CPI Group (UK) Ltd

All rights reserved. No part of this publication may be reproduced, stored in a retrieval
system, or transmitted, in any form or by any means, electronic, mechanical, photocopying,
recording or otherwise, without the prior written permission of the publishers.

Without limiting the exclusive rights of any author, contributor or the publisher of
this publication, any unauthorised use of this publication to train generative artificial
intelligence (AI) technologies is expressly prohibited. HarperCollins also exercise their
rights under Article 4(3) of the Digital Single Market Directive 2019/790 and expressly
reserve this publication from the text and data mining exception.

1

FOURTEEN DAYS TO GO

Niklas ate slowly, gazing at his family on the other side of the dinner table. It was only December 17th, which meant it was a little too early for his liking to put up the Christmas decorations, but he and his daughter had decided to make a start now. There were small white porcelain Father Christmases adorning the table and the room was illuminated by the warm glow of the Christmas tree lights. They had realized that a spruce might be a little tired-looking by Christmas Eve if they brought it inside now, so they had hung the string of lights above the table and were using it instead of the normal light.

His daughter was wearing a knitted jumper with flashing red and green LEDs enmeshed in it, while he had donned a bright red Christmas tie in honour of the meal. His suit was ash-grey, just as always. There were limits to this madness.

He raised the fork to his mouth loaded with another bite of grilled pineapple glazed with ginger, chilli and honey. As it happened, he didn't believe that fruit belonged on a dinner plate, but his daughter loved pineapple. She probably preferred it to the juicy Kobe beef. Oh well, that would leave more for him.

The others at the table were just as occupied with their food as he was, which was why they didn't seem to notice the way he was looking at them. That was fortunate – he probably looked rather daft, but he couldn't help that. For want of a better description, he felt at ease. This was a new feeling, although in the end it hadn't taken much to achieve it.

It hadn't taken a dazzling career – even though he was exceedingly successful.

Nor had it required a magnificent apartment on Östermalm's Linnégatan, although he really did appreciate the home he and his daughter shared.

All it had taken was for the three of them to sit together at the table.

The assassination attempt he had faced six months earlier – the one that had even made it into the pages of the tabloids – was consigned to the past. Of course, he still required additional protection. That would probably remain the case for at least another six months, until his employer was totally reassured, but he'd had a protective detail for so long that he thought of them as family.

Family.

That was what it was all about. His daughter was sixteen and on the way to becoming a woman, and he thought he'd done a pretty good job of teaching her about the world. Of course she sometimes said she hated him, but that was doubtless just a teenage thing. And sitting opposite him was his ex-wife. If he had been told six months earlier that the two of them would be spending time together like this he wouldn't have believed it. Not remotely. But the cliché was true – time healed all wounds. And now here they were like the archetypal modern family, eating Christmas dinner many days too early and managing not to hate each other. They had even given each other Christmas presents.

A lump formed in his throat and he looked out of the window so that neither of the other two would see that his eyes had filled with tears. The snow was falling softly and prettily in the darkness outside. The world looked picture-perfect. And the same was true of his life at this very moment. For the first time in years, he felt no tension in his shoulders. There was no incipient headache.

A buzzing noise from the hall indicated that someone was ringing the doorbell. His daughter looked up from her plate in surprise.

'Who's that?' she said. 'It's Saturday. You promised you wouldn't work tonight because we were going to have Christmas dinner.'

'I've no idea,' he said truthfully, rising from his seat. 'It couldn't be for either of you, could it?'

His ex-wife and daughter both shook their heads.

Niklas went into the hall, heading for the front door.

'If you've booked a Santa then you're in big trouble,' his daughter called from the kitchen.

Whoever was ringing the bell, it would be someone that the security detail in the street had admitted after a thorough security check. That they hadn't called in advance indicated that this was not someone he needed to be prepared to face. A high-resolution screen on the inside face of the door showed him who was on the outside: a man wearing a bicycle helmet, with a red star across his chest. There was also a dusting of white snow on his shoulders. A messenger from Not Just Mail. That explained it.

'Yes?' Niklas said as he opened the door.

'Niklas Stockenberg?' the man said, slightly out of breath as he proffered a small black envelope. 'Here you go. Message for you.'

The envelope was unmarked. Niklas frowned as he accepted it and turned it over. It didn't say anything on the back either.

'From whom?' he said, looking up.

But the man was gone. He'd started running down the six flights of stairs back to the street and his bicycle as soon as he had handed over his consignment. He was probably already late for his next delivery.

Niklas closed the door and opened the envelope to find a piece of white paper within. As he pulled it out he realized it was a business card – and a luxurious one at that. There was no name on the card. Instead, there was something that looked like a number. It was a large eight with the bottom half coloured in. Beneath that there was a phone number. The card was otherwise empty.

Niklas frowned. He didn't recognize the symbol and the phone number was unfamiliar to him, but something at the back of his mind immediately told him that he knew what it was. Told him it was a message he'd been expecting for many years but had hoped he would never see. He'd suppressed the expectation of its arrival and forced it out of his life – and he wasn't ready for it now, either.

Then again, it might just be an advert, he thought.

There was only one way to find out. He pulled his phone from the inside pocket of his jacket and dialled the number. His hands were shaking.

An automated recording of a female voice answered after three rings.

'Hello Niklas Stockenberg. We hope you have been satisfied with our services during this period which has now reached its end. You have … fourteen days … one hour … and … twelve minutes … left to live.'

He clutched the phone tightly, as if trying to crush the very message that it had delivered. His throat constricted. He could no longer breathe. The room began to spin and he had to place a hand on the wall to support himself and avoid falling over.

Laughter came from the kitchen; his daughter and her mother were amused by something.

Niklas fell to his knees on the hall runner. It was a good job he'd bought one that was so expensive and thick, otherwise it would have hurt his knees, he thought. He screwed his eyes shut and tried to focus his thoughts. He had known this day would come. He had known for a long time. But he had refused to think about it. He had hoped he would be spared – after all, it had all been such a long time ago.

'Where've you gone, Dad?' his daughter shouted. 'I'm warning you: if you're putting on a Santa Claus costume then I'll alert the media.'

He once again supported himself against the wall and stood up slowly, clearing his throat several times and trying to fill his lungs with air so that he wouldn't tremble too much. Then he went into the kitchen.

When the two women at the table caught sight of him, they immediately stopped laughing.

'Who was it?' his daughter said in horror. 'You look like you've seen a ghost.'

His ex-wife stood up.

'Sit down before you take a tumble,' she said, pressing him down onto a chair.

She placed a hand to his brow.

'It was no one,' he said. 'Wrong door.'

'You're soaked in sweat. Have you had some kind of funny turn? Are you taking any medication? Should we call an ambulance? Talk to me, Niklas.'

He turned his head and tried to smile at his daughter.

'It's nothing to worry about, Nathalie,' he said. 'I just had a dizzy spell.'

Nathalie looked askance at her mother. Niklas removed his ex's hand from his shoulder and held it briefly.

'Thank you Mina, but there is no need for an ambulance,' he said. 'It'll soon be over.'

The snow falling outside was no longer soft or pretty. Instead, it was cold and inexorable, isolating him in a prison of winter. He couldn't move; he couldn't get away.

There was nowhere to escape to.

In two weeks' time he would be dead. He, who still had so much unfinished business. He gazed at Mina, opened his mouth to say something, then closed it again. Had he done all that he could for them? Had he been a good father to Nathalie? Would they miss him? What would they say at work?

Nathalie's jumper continued to flash merrily at him in shades of red and green.

He really did not want to die.

The business card fell from his hand onto the floor and he left it there.

Niklas let out a deep sigh and stroked his chin.

The last twenty years had been good. Very good, in fact. But just as he'd told Mina: it would all soon be over.

In fourteen days, one hour and twelve minutes. Although it was probably only ten minutes by now.

2

Vincent was lying on the floor of his dressing room at the Scala Theatre in Karlstad. He had turned off the ceiling light, leaving only the lighting around the make-up mirror illuminated. The warm bulbs framing the mirror were one of the few things that resembled the stereotypical idea of being behind the scenes in a theatre. It was probably no more than the result of lifelong conditioning by Hollywood, but he thought the lightbulbs around the mirror were both beautiful and romantic.

The show had ended an hour earlier. His crew were in full swing onstage, de-rigging a flight of stairs down from the dressing rooms and green room above. The set, the props and a not insignificant quantity of lighting gear needed to be disassembled and loaded into two large lorries. They always brought in local muscle to assist with the loading work, and his tour manager Ola Fuchs was a legend in the Swedish showbiz world, but it still took almost three hours for them to finish their work. What people didn't know was that Vincent's two hours of glamorous entertainment required at least seven hours of decidedly unglamorous set-up and strike carried out by a large number of people. Every night.

He carefully adjusted his posture on the floor. The linoleum floor covering beneath him was incredibly hard. He glanced up at the sofa and realized he should have opted for that instead, but it was too late for that now. All he could do was to keep lying where he was.

The Scala Theatre was full of odd – and thus uncomfortable – numbers. The ceiling above the stage was five metres high. He would have preferred six. Suspended from the ceiling there were seventeen fly-bars to which the lighting and set could be attached. That wasn't a good number either. Five and seventeen made twenty-two, which was two twos. Better. What was more, two plus two made four, which was the total number of performances he was scheduled to give at the Scala on this tour.

His costume was on a hanger. He'd worn the three-piece suit today, even though it was the final show before Christmas. Three pieces. Bloody hell. The thought hadn't crossed his mind. The suit had meant that he'd been dripping in sweat by the time the performance was over, so he had stripped down to nothing but his T-shirt and underpants as soon as he reached the dressing room. It might make him look a little less dead if someone barged in, as opposed to lying there on the floor in his full stage attire. He smiled to himself. You learned from your mistakes.

A loud bang from somewhere beneath him made him start. It sounded like something had been broken. Vincent could make out Ola's profanities all the way up here, but he'd learned long ago that it was better ignoring some things. Early on in his career, he'd tried to help with the set-up and strike for his shows. He'd heard about stuck-up performers who never lifted a finger and cared about nothing but their own performance, and Vincent didn't want to be like that. But he'd quickly realized that he was just in the way. It was a better solution for everyone involved if he steered clear until they were done – and that meant he had at least another hour lying on the hard floor before the lorries were fully loaded. That was lucky for him, given that his headache had returned with full force. On the table beside him there was an empty water glass with white grains visible on the inside of the vessel. Aspirin. For some time now, he'd been sustaining himself on painkillers – preferably ones with caffeine in them. He considered taking another, but concluded it probably wouldn't make any difference. Instead, he screwed his eyes shut and sighed as he waited for the headache to pass, or at least to dissipate a little. On previous tours, he'd usually only been tired afterwards. His thoughts had perhaps been a little sluggish. The headaches were new. They'd started after his performances around six months earlier. It hadn't been long before they'd become a permanent feature. Sometimes they were more palpable, sometimes less so, but they were always there. Aching. Disruptive. He could no longer even remember what it was like not to have a headache.

He had refused to believe that it was a sign of ageing, since he was still a few months shy of fifty. Besides, his performances were no more strenuous now than they had been before. That left two possibilities. It was either a brain tumour or it was psychosomatic. He was sceptical about the former given the absence of any other symptoms. But if the headache was self-inflicted then what on earth was he playing at? Was he trying to tell himself something?

He wished, as he did so often, that Mina were there. She would probably have had a good answer. Following the events of the previous summer centring on Nathalie and Nova, they had only managed to see each other a handful of times. On the one hand, they'd both been busy with their respective lives – Vincent preparing for his new show and Mina working on new investigations – and on the other hand the threshold for seeing each other still felt pretty high unless it was on police business. But when they did get around to seeing each other, it was always too fleeting. It was never enough. The headache was milder whenever he was with her, while the shadow that had dwelled within him for so long stayed beneath the surface.

Her team of police detectives had received a renewed vote of confidence from the top brass, which meant that Mina was generally busy working. And on those few occasions when she wasn't, Umberto of ShowLife Productions had conspired to schedule Vincent's tour dates so that they clashed with Mina's leave with almost sadistic precision. It was as if her boss and his management were in cahoots to keep Vincent and Mina apart.

Then there was that other thing, too. The riddle in his study at home that he didn't dare mention to her, the one that made it no easier to meet up. Now that he came to think about it, it might be the source of this headache. He had, at any rate, devoted more and more thought to it during the autumn – without managing to solve it. All he knew was that he was well-advised to take the threat it posed seriously.

Whoever had sent the first message to him six months ago was clearly a person of great patience. Vincent didn't want to trouble Mina with that. He would have to sort it out by himself.

Nevertheless, he hoped at the end of each performance to find her there waiting for him in the wings, just like the very first time they had met in Gävle. Of course, she never was. She had her life, he had his. And the fact remained: they saw far too little of each other.

However, since the end of the summer he'd been able to spend far more time with his family than before. He'd been on crutches thanks to a broken foot, which had meant he'd been unable to appear onstage for months. Instead, and for the first time ever, he'd been at home every evening – and every day for that matter – just the way his wife Maria had always wanted. Still, it had turned out after just a few days that she wanted that rather less than she had thought. Even the kids had started to wonder suspiciously why he was constantly at home.

And the shadow within him had begun to stir.

So no one had been happier than his family when he resumed touring. Since then, he had been working double time, often doing two performances a day. The trick was to keep busy, not to dwell on things it was pointless to think about.

He gazed up at the ceiling. Could brain cells burn out? Was it actually possible for him to damage his brain through overuse? Probably not. But he was going to look it up anyway, because in that moment as he lay on the floor in the Scala Theatre in Karlstad, that was how it felt. He sighed, closed his eyes and added the headache to the long list of things he wanted to talk to Mina about.

3

Akai walked determinedly along the metro station platform. He had long since learned that provided you looked like you knew what you were doing, no one would ask any questions. The bright yellow hi-vis vest he was wearing was also doing its job. To the weary eyes of passengers at this time of night, the vest paradoxically made him invisible. He was just one of the people who worked on the metro. Pay no attention to him … That he was there to work was of course true, in a way. It was just that it wasn't in the way the people around him assumed.

He reached the end of the platform and opened a small barrier while taking care not to show his face to the ceiling-mounted CCTV camera. Just a regular service technician on his way to do a job. Nothing more. But it was lucky that the rattle of the spray canisters in his bag couldn't be caught on camera.

The barrier led in turn to a staircase that descended from the platform and into the tunnel. He didn't really like being in the tunnels – it was far too dangerous. The new trains were much quieter than the old ones, which meant that the risk of accidents had increased for those artists who continued to enter the tunnels.

Anyway, he had long since moved on in his own artistic expression. Graffiti was for amateurs. His work focused on poster art and stencilling. A retro nineties look. Sure, it wasn't the same since the identity of his idol Banksy had supposedly been revealed, but Akai thought he was taking it to a new, cutting-edge level. His previous exhibitions in Stockholm's old town had confirmed that theory. It was almost shocking what people were willing to pay for his works without even knowing who he was. Akai was merely his nom de plume – just like Banksy, he had no intention of telling people his actual name. His identity was to remain a mystery to the art world.

Once he had proceeded a few metres into the tunnel, he switched on his headlamp. The tunnel had been built wide enough to enable work crews to move about without risking being too close to the tracks. He knew the technical room was not far ahead. It was the room where his friend's girlfriend, a metro technician, often worked. Akai had promised his friend that he would give her a birthday present by decorating the entire room. The plan was to surprise her in the morning when she entered the room and wasn't confronted with the usual concrete. Instead, she'd be entering a forest. Trees and shrubs would be covering every single wall, and in their midst there would be a troll family in the style of John Bauer. It was going to be amazing.

He passed an earlier painting of his in the tunnel. It depicted several of his own friends. Someone had daubed *Sussi was here* across the face of one of his friends. Bloody vandals.

The gravel crunched beneath his feet. The door to the technical room swam out of the gloom, captured by the lamplight. He side-stepped a large heap of gravel and then came to a halt. Something was off. He turned back towards the heap of gravel. It was so big it almost reached waist height. There was nothing strange about there being gravel down in the tunnels – there was all sorts of stuff down there. But there was something white protruding from the mass in several places. The white was reminiscent of something he'd seen in a movie, although he couldn't quite place it. He brushed some gravel aside before taking a quick step backwards when he saw what it was.

Bones.

Someone must have put them there as a sick joke. That was the only explanation. But what animal had bones that big? When he tugged at one of the bones to extract it, the gravel began to shift and the stones on top cascaded away to reveal more. A skull smiled grimly at him in the glow of his headlamp.

A human skull.

Akai had no idea whether he screamed or ran first, but he definitely did both.

4

THIRTEEN DAYS LEFT

Mina stared at the sandwich on the plate in front of her in fascination. She really had made progress. In the past, a sealed yoghurt would probably have been her only feasible breakfast option. Now here she was, eating a sandwich that could have been exposed to just about anything. *And* she had enjoyed dinner at Niklas's the night before, even if it had been unpleasant when he'd become so dazed. But Nathalie had reassured her that it was not a common occurrence and he had recovered quickly. Mina hoped he would take her advice seriously and see a doctor this morning.

Dinner with her daughter and ex-husband … Life really did take the most inscrutable of paths sometimes. She would have been lying if she had claimed her way through life had been straightforward. Instead, she and Nathalie had performed a dance more akin to the cha-cha-cha – taking two steps forward and one step back. Yet it had still meant that they had slowly progressed to where they were now. A point where they could eat dinner together as a family – all three of them.

Mina took a bite from her open sandwich, savouring the combination of butter, cheese and pepper on the dark, almost treacly slice of bread, fully aware that she might as well be eating a slice of cake for all the nutritional goodness it offered her. Then again, it was Christmas.

She wondered how Vincent would be celebrating. With his family, of course. But would it be a big Christmas with all the extended family, or would it be a more leisurely occasion? She felt a pang of something but dismissed the idea that it might be jealousy. She missed him. They had only been in touch on a handful of occasions since he had saved Nathalie's life in the summer. There were several reasons for that. For one thing, neither of them was much good at small talk. For another, Mina had been in the thick of it as she slowly worked to foster her fragile relationship with her own daughter. Peder's death had also left a void – a necessary distance mandated by grief.

She felt her eyes sting as she thought about her late colleague.

Then there was the trifling issue that she had no idea what they meant to one another. She thought about Vincent more often than she was prepared to admit to herself, but he had a family. And a very jealous wife. Mina didn't want to cause a furore.

Instead she'd buried herself in her work, and that had been her excuse for not seeing him.

In an attempt to stop thinking about it, she forced herself to focus on the breakfast show chattering away on her TV. The singer-songwriter Niklas Strömstedt was in the studio to perform his Christmas classic 'Light a candle'. Triad? Wasn't that the name of the band he'd been in when he'd penned the single? She desperately tried to recall who the other two men had been, but was only able to summon the images of Orup and Anders Glenmark, who had been in another band with Strömstedt. The opening bars began to play against a backdrop of lit candles, and she felt herself reluctantly being drawn into something resembling the Christmas spirit. She actually hated Christmas. Her childhood Christmases had been anything but peaceful. By the time she'd moved in with her grandmother, they had calmed down, but they'd been very simple affairs.

Mina got up to pour herself more coffee. She glanced at her phone on the table as she sat down on the sofa again. Maybe she ought at least to text Vincent a Christmas greeting? The only question was what he'd read into it … Then again, it was surely pretty difficult to interpret 'Merry Christmas' as anything but that? Merry Christmas was Merry Christmas: the imparting of the desire for a good Christmas, shared between friends.

She reached for her phone and began to tap away. Then she deleted. Then she wrote more. Then she deleted. Yet more text.

She added a smiley after *Merry Christmas*, but then changed her mind right away. Vincent was not a man you sent smileys to. She removed the happy face but left *Merry Christmas* in place. Then she hit send.

She was already regretting her text message by the time Niklas Strömstedt brought his song to a close.

5

It had been snowing for more than a week. The garden and trees surrounding Vincent's house in Tyresö were covered in what looked like a thick layer of cotton wool. When he had been little, he had loved snow, but his enthusiasm had dissipated with age. Perhaps that was something to do with the snow shovel currently in his hands. Snow wasn't as much fun when it was up to you to deal with it.

What was more, he was still aching all over after travelling overnight aboard the nightliner – as they referred to the tour bus with berths on board – from Karlstad. He hadn't fallen asleep until the bus had arrived in Stockholm at four o'clock in the morning and come to a halt by the Barnhusbron bridge, alongside the other tour buses that had also arrived in the city during the night. Vincent had managed to get three hours' sleep while the bus was stationary before he'd taken a taxi home, still drowsy.

Vincent glanced towards the kitchen window, through which he could see his family eating breakfast. He'd promised to clear the path before Aston and Rebecka left for school. He thrust the shovel into the snow, lifted as much of it as he could, and threw it onto the lawn hidden somewhere beneath the whiteness. A small, snowless rectangle opened up before him, the gravel path peeking through. It was a start, at least. But it also served to highlight just how far he had to go.

He stood up straight and put his hands to his back. His breath showed white in the air in front of him. The cold really had arrived. Snow didn't usually come until January, when it came at all. This far south, it was usually no more than slush. But this time around they were forecasting the coldest, snowiest winter for years. His garden was already under seven or eight inches of snow, and they'd only just entered the second half of December. As he stood there, fresh snow began to powder his neat rectangle.

Sisyphus.

He was Sisyphus.

With a sigh, he returned to the front door and propped the shovel against the wall of the house. The kids would just have to trudge through it to the road when it was time to go to school. Before he had time to open the door, Aston came tumbling out of it, clad in his snowsuit.

'More snow!' he yelled. 'I love snow!'

Aston threw himself onto his back and began to make snow angels, seemingly completely unaffected by the cold.

'Dad, can we build a snow fort this afternoon? Or an igloo? Please?!'

In his mind's eye, Vincent pictured the snow forts he had played in as a young boy. Well, the ones he had played beside, given that most of these 'forts' had been no more than a narrow passage through a shovelled pile of snow in the yard. He shivered. He'd never been able to bring himself to crawl through those passages, although he understood the temptation. There was something exciting about building your own world like that. Admittedly, everyone built their own world to some extent – at least mentally – since everyone's realities were different, but …

'Dad?' said Aston, who was now standing in front of him. 'Have you got snow in your brain or something?'

Vincent blinked. He opened his mouth to say something or other about a fort needing a lot more snow just as Maria appeared in the doorway.

'We'll have no snow forts here,' she said firmly, folding her arms. 'They can cave in. They're absolute deathtraps. And why on earth are you shovelling snow in leather gloves and a Hugo Boss coat? Why can't you wear practical winter gear like a normal person?'

Of course she was right. Both about the clothing and the fort. Then again, he didn't own a down jacket nor one of those knitted hats with a bobble on top that everyone else seemed to wear, and there were ways to build snow forts that ensured they didn't collapse. You just had to think hexagonally, like Buckminster Fuller, or work with blocks in an arc that distributed the weight evenly. If only there were more snow … Then he spotted Maria's look and cleared his throat.

'Your mother's right,' he said. 'And if we were going to build an igloo we'd need ice.'

'Great!' Aston said, lying back down in the snow. 'We can make that in the freezer!'

'Well, the freezer's capacity is two hundred and seventy-eight litres,' Vincent said. 'Across seven shelves. The exterior dimensions of an igloo need to …'

Vincent heard his wife clear her throat loudly behind him.

'The freezer isn't big enough,' he said. 'By the by, where's your backpack?'

Maria sighed and went back inside to retrieve the missing bag. Aston sat up and tried to shape a snowball. Vincent knew who it was meant for.

'Right, I suppose I'd better pop inside to get the car keys so that we can get going,' he said, turning around quickly.

The wallop of snow struck him before he'd even made it across the threshold. Behind him, Aston was howling with laughter.

Maria was standing in the hallway putting a change of clothes into Aston's bag.

'By the way,' Vincent said, 'I've been trying to reach your sister to sync arrangements for the kids ahead of Christmas, but her phone seems to be off. In fact, it seems to have been off for days. Do you know if she's away or something?'

Maria forced a pair of long johns into the backpack with brusque movements.

'I haven't spoken to Ulrika in ages,' she said acidly. 'You'll just have to keep tabs on your ex-wife by yourself.'

'That's what I'm trying to do,' Vincent said. 'It's just not like her.'

As he went into the kitchen to retrieve his car keys he pulled out his phone to call Ulrika again.

It was the same as before – no connection.

He texted her instead, asking her to get in touch as soon as she could. After all, there were only a few days left until Christmas.

He also saw that Mina had texted him a brief *Merry Christmas*. He wasn't quite sure how to respond to that. The message was like a challenge – as if she were asking him to define their relationship. They were currently at a tipping point in respect of each other, and it could go either way. If his response was just as succinct then he would be confirming that as of now they had no more than a superficial, cordial relationship. If he countered with something more personal then he would be making it clear once and for all that he wanted to be more than just colleagues. And that would open a Pandora's box of questions about *what* he wanted them to be.

Merry Christmas.

Damn it.

After giving the matter further consideration, he slipped the phone into his pocket instead. He would have to reply later when he had had more time to think.

'Dad! Are you coming or what?' Aston shouted from outside. 'I'll be late!'

'Coming!' he called out.

For half a second, he wondered whether to call Ulrika's work and ask if she was ill or otherwise indisposed. But Maria would probably have something to say about his thoughtfulness towards her sister. Ulrika would call when she could.

He swept the car keys off the side and before heading back outside he double-checked that his study door was locked. He had taken to locking it a month or so ago, out of concern for his family. If any of them happened to see what he had in there then it would not only lead to questions that he couldn't answer, but it would probably also leave them frightened. Almost as frightened as he was.

6

'And they're sure the bones are human?'

Mina forced herself to breathe, taking calm, deep inhalations. There were few places she wouldn't have preferred to be than the one she found herself in: the dark, dirty tunnels that made up Stockholm's metro system. Besides, it was icy cold. She normally liked the cold, but even she had her limits. Their breath turned into white smoke and she hugged herself to try and warm up a little.

'Yes, forensics were absolutely certain. One of them is an osteologist,' Adam said, stifling a yawn. 'A bone scientist. She knows her stuff. I doubt we'd be down here at the crack of dawn like this otherwise. Normally I'm barely even awake at this hour.'

She could tell from his voice that he too was not a fan of claustrophobic tunnels.

'And we're sure they've stopped the trains on this stretch of the line?' she said, carefully placing one foot in front of the other in the beam of light cast by her torch.

Something streaked past her feet. She didn't manage to see what it was and was unable to suppress a shriek.

She gritted her teeth and forced herself to carry on, even though her heart was pounding so hard in her ribs that it felt as if it might leap out of her body altogether. Some distance away, she saw more light and the movement of people. This helped her to shut out the horrors lurking in the darkness and made her focus on the task ahead of her.

'Good morning Mina. And Adam too,' said the head of forensics, nodding curtly to them. 'Not that this is a particularly good morning.'

He pointed towards what she realized had previously been a heap of gravel. The officers had now brushed away most of it, leaving behind a neat stack of bones.

'They're definitely human bones. Based on a quick visual inspection, they seem to be from the same body, but we won't be able to confirm that until the forensic anthropologist has laid them out on the table to check.'

Mina contemplated the bones while rubbing her cold arms. The heap almost looked like an altar. The bones were neatly arranged, symmetrically positioned with the skull atop them all. It felt somehow ritualistic, but she took care not to become too attached to that impression. It was dangerous to start making assumptions this early on in the investigation. Quite honestly, she was somewhat surprised that this one had landed in the team's in-tray. Old bones weren't usually their department, but she assumed that the circumstances in which they had been found elevated this into something out of the ordinary.

'Any identification?' she asked, taking a small step to one side so that Adam could get through.

They took care not to step too close to or otherwise contaminate the crime scene. Even though she knew better, she couldn't resist the impulse to look around. The lighting rigs illuminated much of the space. She felt the panic rising again. There was rubbish all over the place, and in the shadows she could make out things moving. Rats, she assumed, and she shuddered.

This wasn't her first time down here: as a new recruit, she'd come down into the tunnels on several occasions in pursuit of suspects. She knew there were people who lived down here too, in a shadowy existence separated from the world and hidden from reality. She couldn't even begin to imagine what that was like.

The forensic officer had begun talking again and she forced herself to focus on him and ignore the things moving in the dark corners that the floodlights did not reach.

'We haven't found any form of identification. No clothing. No ID. There might be DNA on some of the rubbish that we can tie to a possible killer. We'll collect everything there is in a wide radius around the remains and send it for analysis. However, I think if we find anything it'll be from the "artist" who called it in. Anyway, the teeth are still inside the skull, so that should help in identifying the body. And there's a severe fracture to one of the femurs. It's broken in several places and then healed again.'

'Broken femur ...' Mina said thoughtfully. 'How long did you say you think they've been down here?'

'Hard to say. It's up to Milda to tell us, but I suppose at least a few months? The bones don't look fresh. But that's me shooting from the hip. Like I said, it's Milda's call,' the officer said.

Mina looked at Adam to see whether he would make the same connection as she had. He furrowed his brow as he gazed at the bones, then his gaze lightened and he turned towards her.

'You think it's ...'

'Yes, I do,' Mina said. 'I'll call Julia right away.'

They contemplated the heap of bones in silence. If these remains belonged to the person they thought, then it was about to unleash a media storm. And it would raise all sorts of new questions.

7

Ruben woke up in a cold sweat. He'd been dreaming and he'd seen Peder's face. That happened a lot these days. Peder's skin had been grey and most of the back of his head had been missing – but that hadn't been the awful part about the dream. The awful thing had been the gaze – the eyes staring meaningfully at Ruben, eyes that had seen straight inside him. That was what had woken him up. Peder didn't have to say anything because Ruben already knew what the message was.

It could all be over at any moment.

That was Peder's lesson for him. There were two paths in life, and both were horrendous. On the one hand, it might end before Ruben was ready for it. On the other, if it didn't end he would grow old. Older with each passing day. He took a deep breath and ran his hands across his face. Fuck getting old – it was almost worse than the alternative.

Someone moved in the dark and the bedding next to him rustled. Bloody hell. She was still there. That was the problem with bringing home someone young. At least the ones over thirty realized it was better for both of them to wake up in their respective homes, alone, and never see each other again. The young ones hadn't been around the block as many times and still thought it was a nice idea to stay and cuddle in the morning. They had romantic notions of eating breakfast together and other crap like that. The truth was that it was never a good idea to see each other in the light of day *afterwards*.

Especially not when that light revealed how old he was.

He looked at the clock on his phone and swore silently. He had somehow managed to switch off the alarm last night. He would be late for work. What was more, Julia had been trying to reach him – something about a discovery the night before. At the same time as Ruben had been reeling in his catch outside the nightclub, something had apparently happened in a metro tunnel. Oh well. The others could man the fort without him.

His left calf suddenly spasmed and he had to bite his lip not to scream with pain. He pulled his leg towards him to massage it, taking care not to wake the sleeping woman by his side. He kneaded the muscle. It was rock hard. The cramps had started a while back. If he drank too little water the night before he would have cramps in the morning due to lack of fluid. But if he drank plenty of water then he had to get up to take a slash at least two or three times during the night, like some old codger.

Old, old, old.

His daughter Astrid probably wouldn't have a dad alive by the time she reached her teens.

He sighed deeply. He was pathetic. He knew it. Not only because he didn't want to age, but because he'd also resumed his past predatory behaviour in relation to the opposite sex. His psychologist, Amanda, had looked like she wanted to give him a slap when he'd told her. But what was he supposed to do? Amanda was still young – she didn't understand.

He reached towards the bedside table and grabbed the two capsules lying there. They were so-called dietary supplements he'd found online that were meant to aid both his virility and his testosterone production. It was probably all bullshit, but he'd paid for a year's subscription anyway just to be sure. Six hundred kronor a month. He swallowed the capsules and then lifted the covers to look at the person next to him. She was lying on her side with her bare hip just an inch or two away from him. He'd bumped into her outside his old watering hole on Stureplan, which he'd started frequenting again. He'd been on his way home after an unsuccessful night, when he'd seen her smoking outside. He'd gone up to her and asked her whether she liked uniforms, and unlike inside the bar it had worked, no matter how stupidly corny it was.

He placed his hand on her smooth hip and felt the vibrant

warmth of her skin. He was fairly certain her name was Emmy. Or was it Emily? Definitely something with a Y.

He carried on stroking her hip and she moved drowsily towards him. Julia could wait, and Amanda could say what she liked. Life was too short. And as Peder had so clearly shown him night after night: you never knew when it might be over.

8

Vincent was in his study. With the passing of the years the bookcase behind him had come to serve less as storage for books and more as a display case. Ever since it had become common knowledge that the Master Mentalist had helped to solve the mystery involving Jane two and a half years earlier, enthusiastic admirers had been sending him puzzles, rebuses and riddles to solve. They seemed to assume that unravelling mysterious enigmas were his favourite occupation. Of course, it was not widely known how close he had come to death on that occasion.

And they weren't entirely barking up the wrong tree … He *did* like them. When he had time. Many of them were simple. A common variant was to send a fan letter cut up into several parts, though others were more ambitious in their efforts. There was one anonymous sender who liked to send the most obscure puzzles and riddles that Vincent had ever encountered. They weren't home-made – in fact, they appeared to come from all corners of the world. His correspondent clearly knew their onions. Vincent knew they were from the same person thanks to the handwritten messages that were always enclosed, which often featured a riddle.

At present, however, it was a different kind of puzzle that was occupying his concentration. Specifically, the one that he had pinned to the wall above his desk. It was the same kind of mind map that Mina had set up at home in her apartment when they had worked together that first time. A collage of clues that might, with a little luck, explain a connection or show a pattern that had been hitherto hidden. Vincent's wall, however, did not consist of pictures and notes. Instead, it was covered in physical objects ordered chronologically with a note on a Post-it beneath each one.

This was the reason why no one in the family was allowed into his study. It would be bad if they came to believe he'd lost his mind, and even worse if the penny dropped what the timeline meant. For Vincent, the conclusion to be drawn from the wall was clear: someone wanted to cause him harm.

He didn't want to think of that person as his enemy. His nemesis? No, that sounded even worse. His shadow, perhaps? Well, why not? Each time he had received something new in the post, the shadow within had come to life. It was as if it no longer dwelled within him but had instead manifested itself in the real world and was now terrorizing him.

What was more, shadows took the same form as the person casting them, albeit a distorted one. And whoever had sent him the objects on the wall seemed to know exactly how he ticked. It was as if they were being sent by a nightmarish version of himself. He nodded. The Shadow was an apt name.

At the far left-hand end of the timeline was the old, laminated newspaper cutting from *Hallandsposten* – the one showing Vincent as a boy with the magic box in which his mother had died in the background.

MAGIC ENDS IN TRAGEDY!

He had lost count of how many times he'd read that headline. Two and a half years ago, someone had sent the article to Ruben, making Vincent the prime suspect in the investigation into the murders of Tuva, Agnes and Bobby – crimes that it had transpired his missing sister was responsible for. At first, he had thought Jane had sent the article, since part of her plan had been to pin the blame for the murders on Vincent. But it hadn't been her. The article had, however, forced Vincent's past back to the surface. It was a past that he had spent a great deal of time not daring to think about. The police had, with the utmost difficulty, managed to keep it out of the public domain.

Underneath the article were the Tetris-style pieces of puzzle taped together that he had started to receive shortly after his sister's death. These puzzles consisted of different anagrams of newspaper headlines and came together intricately to form the word GUILTY. He had thought they had been sent by Nova, in an attempt to distract from the goings on at Epicura. Nova –

who had based her teachings on the chronic pain that she suffered from and who had almost caused Nathalie's demise. But following a confrontation with Nova immediately prior to her own death, he had realized they must have been sent by the same person who had sent the clipping to Ruben.

His Shadow.

Next to the taped-together puzzle pieces was the Christmas card that had come with the final Tetris puzzle and which also contained an alarming inscription. In the four months since he had received it, he still hadn't managed to solve the riddle.

> It seems that you don't learn. I'm tired of waiting.
>
> And remember that there is no one to blame but you.
>
> You could have chosen a different path. But you didn't. So we have reached your omega. The beginning of your end.
>
> PS If you're wondering why you've received the puzzle now, it's because omega is, as you know, the 24th letter of the Greek alphabet. 24 divided by two – you and I – makes 12, which gives us 24/12. Christmas Eve. Wishing you an early Merry Christmas.

When Vincent had received the message about his omega – his implied end – he had immediately set about searching for what would be his alpha, his beginning. If he could find what had started it all then he might have a better understanding of what was going to end. Then he might be able to protect himself.

It hadn't been long before he had found it. It had once again been in the old newspaper article. In the photograph itself. His Shadow had followed the contours of the magic box with a pencil, with the lines forming an A. The sign for alpha.

What was going to end had begun there.

On the farm in Kvibille.

With his mother.

Back when he had stopped being Vincent Boman and become Vincent Walder.

Yet instead of the end threatened by the message, he had begun to receive gifts in the post. Christmas presents – even though it wasn't Christmas. The first had arrived in the summer, just after the end of the Epicura case. The parcel had contained a vinyl single titled 'Alpha Omega' by an unfamiliar rap group, Renegades.

The EP was on the wall to the right of the newspaper article, held up with adhesive pads at each corner. Underneath it was a note with the information he had found about the release, which wasn't much. The song had come out in 1987 on Coolaid Records and the EP had a red label. But the group only seemed to have made that one song, and the lyrics didn't mean anything to him either. So he had left it at that.

The following month in September, he had received another Christmas present – a new record. This time it had been a Led Zeppelin album called 'Alpha & Omega'. It turned out to be a rarity – a live bootleg recording of four LPs that was more or less impossible to get hold of these days. He had taken the records out of the sleeve and stuck the empty sleeve onto the wall.

In addition to the title, it had another thing in common with the previous record. It too had been released in 1987.

Vincent knew what the figures stood for. His sister had reminded him of that when she had led him to page 873 of a book. The eighth of July, three o'clock. Mum's last summer. When he had been seven years old and performed his magic show on the blanket in their garden.

87 was the eighth of July.

Mum's birthday.

On the farm in Kvibille.

Again.

To the right of the records was the Christmas present for October. On that occasion the parcel had contained a toy car – a replica of a German Opel Omega military police car. No Alpha this time. But the Opel Omega had first gone into production in 1987. Not to mention that the toy was in 1:87 scale.

Mum.

The magic box.

The illusion.

GUILTY.

By November, his gift giver had dropped the alpha–omega connection almost entirely in favour of a fairly over-explicit present. He'd been given a magic set. More specifically, a *Great Houdini Magic Starter Set* in good but used condition. Vincent hadn't even needed to Google that – the item had provided enough information.

Harry Houdini was the handcuff king and famous for being able to escape from a water-filled tank – the same kind of tank that Vincent and Mina had almost met their ends in at Jane and Kenneth's mink farm. The Houdini reference was also a blatant allusion to his mother and the box she had never been able to escape. Even before he had turned over the worn box to read the reverse, he'd guessed what the printed copy would say. It came as no surprise when he saw that the magic set with Houdini's name on it had been made in 1987.

Since then, Vincent hadn't received any more parcels, and he didn't want to receive any either. His Shadow had written some six months ago about the days that were now approaching.

Omega ... 24th letter of the Greek alphabet ... 24 divided by two – you and I – makes 12 ... 24/12 ... Christmas Eve ... Wishing you an early Merry Christmas.

You and I.

Christmas Eve.

Today was the eighteenth. That left only six days until Christmas Eve. Whatever this person was after, it would begin then. His omega. And he still didn't know what that meant.

Vincent gazed at the presents on the wall again.

Coolaid Records. The expert that he and Mina had visited to learn about cults had told them that the members of the Peoples Temple in Jonestown had committed mass suicide by drinking spiked Kool-Aid-branded grape juice. Not unlike Nova's followers at Östra Real upper secondary school.

A bootleg album that was practically impossible to obtain. So someone knew that he was a collector of vinyl, even if the genre wasn't a favourite of his.

The police car. He assumed it to be a reference to Mina.

A magic set for children. So the Shadow knew that he had loved magic as a child and that he had almost drowned in Houdini's water tank as an adult, alongside Mina.

The connection was clear. Whoever was behind all this, it wasn't just someone who was deeply familiar with Vincent's background, it was someone who also had detailed information about his work with the police.

He really did need to discuss this with Mina. He should have done so long ago, but something had held him back ever since he had received the ominous message and the Tetris puzzle six months ago. A small voice somewhere inside him was whispering that he might deserve what was coming to him. That the Shadow was right and he was somehow guilty.

The only question was: of what?

9

'How did you get on in the tunnels?'

The sympathetic tone adopted by Milda's assistant Loke bothered Mina at first, but then she shrugged. She simply had to accept that her … particular kind of behaviour was something people talked about.

'I can rise above the fear when I'm on duty,' she said briefly.

Loke seemed to understand where she was coming from.

'It's kind of like what we do when we're at work here,' he said. 'We take a step back – although not so far that we forget there's a human being on the table in front of us. But far enough that we can do what we've got to do without being overwhelmed by emotion.'

'Got it in one,' Mina said, smiling at him.

This was the longest conversation she had ever had with Milda's ordinarily taciturn assistant.

'She won't be long. I could hear that she was on the phone to her ex-husband,' Loke said apologetically, as he carefully laid out a number of tools on a sterilized steel tray.

'Don't worry. I can wait,' Mina said, observing Loke's long, slender fingers with fascination as they arranged the contents of the tray with military precision.

Silence echoed around the white room and she desperately searched for a way to break it.

'So what's the next step on the career path? Do you become a medical examiner?'

She swore silently. She sounded like a high school careers advisor faced with a sulky teenager. A smile flitted across Loke's face as he carefully set down a scalpel.

'I suppose that would be the usual way of things,' he said.

Mina noted with interest that he seemed to be placing

instrument after instrument on the tray without the slightest metallic sound whatsoever.

'But there's a big obstacle to my career ambitions. I'm satisfied.'

He shrugged. Mina gazed at him with greater interest than before. That was a word she rarely heard: satisfied.

'I'm happy with things the way they are, and so it would only upset a well-functioning equilibrium if something in the equation changed. I'm happy in my work, I don't need to strive for enhanced status or better finances ... well, I suppose you might have heard gossip about me being set up for life following an inheritance. A wealthy medical examiner's assistant. A rare beast, I suppose. Hence the gossip. I've got what I want in life. Few people are blessed with that. Being satisfied. So I see it as a gift that I can appreciate that. Ambition would only upset those in my immediate circles.'

Mina didn't reply. She was busy taking in what Loke had said, not to mention the fact that he had uttered several sentences in a row to her using amusingly highfalutin language. It was also some of the best wisdom imparted to her in a long time. What he had said made her consider how satisfied she was. In life. With her existence.

'The bones are in astoundingly fine condition,' Loke said, surveying the skeleton in front of them.

Mina searched for a suitable reply but came up short. Loke carried on speaking as he pointed at the bones.

'Look at this. They're perfectly clean. There are no biological remains whatsoever. All the flesh is gone. That's extremely unusual. And another thing that's strange ...'

'Hello! Sorry I'm late! I just had ... an issue that needed sorting out. But I'm here now! And I heard a whisper that you've got a theory on who this might be? That's quick work.'

Milda entered and took Loke's place by the tray of implements. Loke discreetly slipped away. Mina pointed at the bones spread out on the metal surface in front of them.

'There. The fractured femur. We've got a high-profile individual who has been missing for four months. Jon Langseth. He took a fairly well-known tumble and broke his leg while climbing Mount Everest a couple of years back.'

'Oh yes, I remember that. Wasn't the whole thing mired in controversy since there was a sherpa who died in the efforts to bring him down off the mountain?'

'Yes, exactly. And all that came up again when there was coverage of his disappearance. So when I saw the broken leg down in the tunnel, I made the connection right away. I may be wrong. Plenty of people break their legs. But maybe it's worth starting from there?'

Milda nodded.

'I hear what you're saying. I'll start by getting in touch with the forensic odontologist and have them come and capture images of the teeth, and then we can see if they match his dental records. In the meantime, I'll examine the bones and see whether there's anything else I can find.'

'That sounds good. You know where to find me.'

'Otherwise I'll only have you back down here knocking on my door,' Milda said with a laugh that failed to reach her eyes.

She looked tired, and Mina was on the brink of asking her whether everything was all right when she stopped herself. Milda was always having trouble with her private life. Before closing the door behind her, she glimpsed Milda leaning heavily against the table for a few seconds. Then she shook herself and reached for a pair of disposable gloves.

10

Sara Temeric looked up from her computer. Her closest colleague in the National Operations Department, Teresa, was standing there. Sara had been Teresa's boss before she'd gone to the USA. Since then, they had taken on different responsibilities, but Teresa was still the person she trusted most in the department.

'What do you know about ammonium nitrate?' Teresa said, without bothering to offer a greeting first.

Sara blinked in amazement.

'Er, it's a kind of salt?' she said, stretching her arms above her head. She was stiff from spending too long at her computer. 'It's used in fertilizer because it's got so much nitrogen in it. Interestingly enough, it turns into laughing gas when heated. The nitrate is usually diluted when making fertilizer since it's rather explosive in its concentrated form …'

Sara fell silent. She understood exactly what Teresa was getting at. She should have been thinking along the same lines too.

'Sorry,' she said with a sigh. 'I was thinking about how Zachary and Leah really need to visit a Swedish farm this summer while they're still around. The farms, that is. Hence the association. But we're not interested in fertilizer at NOA.'

She closed her laptop, propped her elbows on the desk and rested her chin on her hands. Her American ex-husband liked to refer to it as her engaging pose. He had words for everything – except why he'd chosen to stay behind in the USA.

'Ammonium nitrate is also one of the most common ingredients in home-made bombs,' she said. 'If it's mixed with flammable materials then it dramatically increases the likelihood of an explosion and causes much more damage. It's also an oxidizing agent, which means that even if it doesn't explode it adds extra oxygen to fires and makes them bigger and harder to extinguish. Both ANPP – that's technical ammonium nitrate – and the straight fertilizer known as N34 work as explosives. Am I right?'

'Have a gold star,' Teresa said with a smile. 'Now I remember why you were my boss.'

'But why do you ask?'

Teresa closed the door to Sara's office before continuing.

'We've received reports from several companies who sell products for use in agriculture down south in Skåne,' she said in a low voice. 'So you weren't a million miles off with your fertilizer talk. Ammonium nitrate has gone missing. Stolen. There are ten tonnes of it missing. That's more than enough to make us prick up our ears here at NOA. Do you remember the huge accidental explosion in Tianjin in China back in 2015? That was caused by ammonium nitrate.'

Sara remembered it well. The footage of the incident had continued to circulate in the news media for a surprisingly long time afterwards, and online for even longer than that.

'But wasn't that something like eight hundred tonnes that exploded?' she said. 'And we're looking for ten?'

'Sure. But that nitrate hadn't been primed for use as an explosive. And they could still see the blast from space.'

Sara whistled.

'About a thousand people were injured or died, even though it happened in a deserted corner of the port,' Teresa added. 'I hope I never find out what ten tonnes of primed ammonium nitrate can do to a built-up area. A city, for example. But my guess is there wouldn't be much of it left.'

'Couldn't there be another reason for someone to have stolen ten tonnes of ammonium nitrate?' Sara said. 'Does it have to be for a bomb?'

'Can you think of another reason? I'm having a hard time imagining that it's just a farmer trying to cut their fertilizer costs.'

Teresa was right, of course. Sara furrowed her brow and stared into space. Bomb threats were nothing new. All the major cities in Sweden – towns too – were the subject of regular bomb threats. Most were no more than empty attempts to cause fear.

This was different. Precisely because there had been no threat. If Teresa's suspicion was correct then a party or parties unknown were building a very big bomb very quietly. That was much worse, because it probably meant they were serious.

'Not quite the Christmas present I was hoping for this year,' said Sara. 'But I'll take what I can get. So how are we going to find this bomb?'

11

As had become the case, it felt strange when they all gathered in the conference room. Everyone had the feeling that something was missing. That *someone* was missing. No one had yet taken Peder's seat. It was left empty – a constant reminder of what and who they had lost.

Julia watched them closely as they entered the room one by one. She looked at everyone except for Adam. She had made the whole team, including herself, see crisis support counsellors following Peder's death in the summer, but she wasn't sure how much it had helped. Judging by her own progress, it hadn't made a damn bit of difference. The grief was still like a heavy mass in the pit of her stomach and had grown neither heavier nor lighter since then.

And the responsibility was ultimately and inescapably borne by her as the team leader. The hierarchy and division of responsibilities in the police force was clear. She had spent many sleepless nights going over what had happened step by step to see what she might have done differently; what she could have done to change the inevitable. But no matter how much she twisted and turned it, she kept concluding that there was nothing she could have done differently – not without having the answers ahead of time. And the police internal investigation had drawn the same conclusion as she had, but that did nothing to alleviate the grief. She stood up straight and cleared her throat to get everyone's attention.

'Right, that's everyone here. Good,' she said, going over to the whiteboard. 'I want to start by pointing out that we don't yet know exactly what we're investigating. We're almost certainly looking at offences involving desecration of a grave, but whether we're also looking at manslaughter or murder remains unclear for now. Let's maintain an open mind for the time being, OK?'

Bosse padded up to her and settled down at her feet. The dog looked up at her with pleading eyes and she gave him a small smile before producing a dog treat from her pocket and giving it to him. She and this dog had an agreement. Once he had consumed his treat, she pointed at Christer's feet and Bosse obeyed immediately. Then Julia once again became serious and pointed at the board, where she had put up a photograph and written a name underneath.

'Jon Langseth,' she said. 'Disappeared without trace on August tenth. That's four months and eight days ago. Forty-one years old, CEO and co-owner of the investment company Confido. He has a wife and three children. The media splashed the disappearance and took the angle that Jon had probably fled the country, given the current investigation into Confido's supposed illegal activities.'

'Bloody bankers,' Christer muttered, scratching Bosse behind the ears. 'Conning honest folks out of their pensions.'

'Please keep your personal views to yourself, Christer,' Julia said sternly, crossing her arms.

She still hadn't looked at Adam. She was convinced that it would be visible in her gaze that just a couple of hours earlier, his naked body had been on top of hers. Had been inside her. It always felt as if both the attraction and the guilt were writ large across her face afterwards. But Adam always reassured her that she looked just as cold and strict as ever. Perhaps he was right. Just as long as they didn't end up in the same room as Vincent Walder and his uncanny ability to read people, they'd be able to keep their secret just that.

'But Jon Langseth never left the country,' she said. 'It's been confirmed that the bones from the metro tunnel are his. Nice work, Mina. The fractures to the femur are an exact match to the X-rays taken after his mishap on Mount Everest. Milda has also confirmed that there is a match to his dental records.'

'Milda's assistant Loke made an interesting observation when I was down there,' Mina said. 'Something about the bones being unusually clean. The question is whether that has anything to do with where they were found? Could the rats have gnawed them clean?'

'Surely there would be teeth marks left on the bones?' said Julia. 'And I haven't heard anything to suggest that's the case.'

'So Mina, how did you manage to go down into those dirty tunnels?' Ruben said with a chuckle.

Mina glanced at him angrily, but he carried on.

'Did you see any rats, by the way? I've heard they're this big between the eyes,' he said, holding his fingers around two inches apart and looking at her meaningfully.

'Sorry, I thought you were showing us how big your dick is,' Mina said levelly.

Christer snorted so hard that coffee spurted out of his nose.

'Ouch!' he cried.

Julia sighed.

'Come on people, let's focus,' she said, fixing her gaze on Ruben and Mina. 'You two can handle the interview with Langseth's wife. Christer, can you check the files and see if there's anything that casts light on this? Adam, have a word with the lead detective on the Confido investigation. Peder …'

She fell silent. Good grief, what had she said? Tears welled up in her eyes and she quickly turned her back on the team so that they wouldn't see, although she knew it was already too late. The silence in the room thundered between the walls. She swallowed, turned back around and tried not to look at Peder's vacant seat.

'Get on with it,' she said hoarsely.

When the others had left the room, Julia slowly approached Peder's chair and placed a hand on the back of it. She pictured him, half-asleep with exhaustion after the triplets had been born. And yet such a constantly happy and thoughtful man. He'd left a void that would be impossible to fill. But they had to carry on without him. The work didn't stop.

She sighed and made for her office. She needed to prepare for an imminent press conference. The media would devour the news about Jon Langseth when it became public. She would at least have to try and control it. Thoughts of Peder would have to be pushed aside.

12

They were running through the tunnels. It was pitch black, but they knew every inch of those tunnels inside out. They knew when the trains were coming and how quickly they had to press themselves against the wall, get onto a platform or slip into one of the many nooks and crannies. They knew where to turn right and where to turn left, and they always knew how to find their way back home. This was their home. Their kingdom.

The footsteps behind him were approaching quickly and he picked up the pace as much as he could. His feet were pounding hard and fast against the uneven ground, but soon he felt someone else's breath on the back of his neck.

He stopped. He longed for what he knew was coming. Longed for the embrace, for those safe arms to hold him from behind, for the stubble to rasp against his smooth cheeks.

'Ha! Got you!'

Dad wrapped his arms around him just as he'd wanted him to and pressed him so tightly to his chest that he felt the soft leather of Dad's big jacket. Dad smelled of damp, tobacco and that sweetness that was always lingering around their camp like a light mist. He smelled of Dad.

'Time to stop playing and start looking for food,' Dad said, letting go of him. 'My tummy's rumbling.'

He nodded reluctantly.

He didn't like having to go topside. It was so bright and so noisy and so in-your-face with all its sounds and impressions and all the people staring at them.

He wanted to remain in the soft belly of the subterranean world, where he was safe and loved.

Where he was among his own.

But he knew they had to get food.

The bins up above were usually most bountiful with leftovers and scraps immediately after lunch. The watch he'd been given for his last birthday showed it was nearly two o'clock. They would have to hurry.

He took Dad by the hand. It wasn't that scary up there – as long as they were together.

13

'You know I was just kidding about the rats, right?'

Ruben held the handle above the car door tightly as Mina sped around a corner. She hadn't said a word since they had got into the car. He kept his sigh to himself, determined not to rile her up any further. Some people clearly had no sense of humour, and he never did seem to get it into his skull that she was one of them.

'There's a spot.'

He pointed to an empty parking space and Mina pulled in abruptly and turned off the engine. They were making for Narvavägen. Of course they were, Ruben thought sourly. Finance bros with something to hide always lived in Östermalm, didn't they?

'Are you going to keep sulking, or can we get on with the job?' he said as they got out of the police car.

He knew it always paid to appeal to Mina's sense of duty. The job seemed to be the only thing she cared about. He still wondered whether she and Vincent had got it on, but he had a hard time picturing it. Any attempt to visualize the combination of Mina and sex always resulted in images of plastic coveralls from head to foot. And rubber gloves.

'I'm not sulking,' she said. 'I just didn't want to talk. But of course we're going to get on with the job.'

She found the name Langseth on the intercom and pressed the button. After a few seconds, the door buzzed and they entered. A sign on the left-hand side of the grand foyer told them that the Langseths lived on the top floor. Obviously.

'Fuck me, imagine living like this,' Ruben said, struggling however to conceal a certain degree of envy that had washed over him in the foyer. It was an orgy of marble and gold.

'It's not really my cup of tea,' Mina said drily, getting into the lift.

Ruben pulled the black gate shut and pressed the button. They rose slowly and against a backdrop of worrying creaking noises, heading towards the sixth floor. The door to the apartment was ajar when they arrived. A blonde woman with a ponytail was waiting for them with an anxious expression. Ruben automatically wondered whether she would be tough to get into bed. He pulled open the gate on the lift.

'Is this about Jon?' she said, stepping aside to admit them.

The hallway within was striking – it was huge, with an expanse of polished parquet disappearing into the other rooms. Hanging from the ceiling was a crystal chandelier that appeared to take up more space than Ruben's entire living room.

'You called and said you wanted to come round, but you didn't say what it was about … Have you found Jon? Where is he?'

The anxious expression was giving way to one of anger. The woman led them into a living room that was so large it could easily have been converted into a sports hall.

'I knew he took the coward's way out,' she said. 'Ditching me and the kids. He's probably got some bimbo with him too. Three girls – *three* – have rung up since he did his bunk to tell me that he had affairs with them. And if three of them have called, you can imagine how many more there must be out there.'

She ushered them towards a large white sofa. Ruben sat down and felt himself sink several more inches than he had expected – it was like landing in a cloud.

'It's Josephine, isn't it?' Mina said, also sitting down.

'Oh, yes. I'm sorry. Josephine Langseth. That's me.'

She continued to talk at speed without asking them for their names and without leaving them any opportunity to interject with their own introductions. Ruben couldn't help but think that Josephine Langseth looked like she'd come straight from a Ralph Lauren advertisement. Glossy blonde hair in a perfect ponytail. Expensive-looking white shirt tucked into a pair of jeans he assumed cost a fortune. And Simone Pérèle lingerie underneath it all. Surely. He could see himself now, holding onto that ponytail tightly while doing her from behind. Then he pictured a furiously indignant Amanda and he swallowed hard. He needed to focus.

'So where is Jon?' Josephine said, sitting down on the sofa opposite them. 'The Caymans? The Bahamas? Dubai? Christ on a bike – I don't even know which countries *don't* have extradition treaties with Sweden. But he likes Dubai. We often went there on holiday and stayed at One&Only. You know, by the Palm Island. Is that where he is now?'

Mina exchanged a glance with Ruben. Then she began to speak.

'It's true that we have located Jon. But he isn't in Dubai. We've found his … remains. I'm afraid we're here to inform you that your husband is dead.'

The huge apartment fell completely silent. The only sound was a faint hum that suggested someone might be using a vacuum cleaner in a distant room. Josephine slumped backwards into the sofa and stared vacantly out of the window. Ruben followed her gaze. Beyond the snow-covered trees lining the avenue there was a glimpse of the Oscarskyrkan church. For some reason, he remembered the odd detail that it was home to one of the biggest organs in Sweden. It was strange what stuck in the mind.

'I've been so … so bloody angry at him,' Josephine said, her tone different from before. 'He's dropped me right in the shit. Three kids to look after, bailiffs and prosecutors at my door, the press writing piece after piece that hang him and his mates out to dry for being the worst kind of con artists. Everyone in the neighbourhood staring at me. The other parents at school won't even speak to me. And the girls who've been calling … I thought … I thought he'd legged it. And I was so fucked off. But I still love him …'

Josephine began to cry quietly.

Ruben shifted his weight uncomfortably on the fluffy sofa. All coital thoughts were vanquished. Women crying had always made him want to crawl out of his own skin.

'Did Jon have any enemies?' Mina said, pulling a tissue from a pack in her jacket pocket.

'He's at the centre of a scheme with billions of kronor missing,'

Josephine said, taking the tissue. 'So I'm sure he does. But I don't know a thing. Regardless of what the Prosecution Authority may think. He went to work; I looked after the house and kids. We had a clear division of tasks. If I asked him how work had been, he always said "good" and that was the end of that. I'd talk to his cronies if I were in your shoes.'

She blew her nose loudly into the tissue and then put it down on the coffee table.

'There's no one else you're aware of who might have wanted to harm him?' Ruben said carefully. 'No … scorned women?'

Josephine Langseth snorted.

'The girls who called were barely twenty and it didn't exactly sound like Jon had been interested in their brains. I know my husband well enough that I don't believe he would have let any of them get close – they were just casual flings. But what are you getting at? How did he die?'

'That's just it,' Ruben said. 'We don't know. But we can't rule out that he was killed.'

Josephine gasped and then began to cry again.

'We realize this will come as a shock to you,' Mina said, producing another tissue. 'But anything you can tell us is of great help. Is there anything else that springs to mind?'

Ruben noticed that Mina could barely take her wide eyes off the crumpled tissue on the table as she handed a new one to Josephine.

'I don't know,' Josephine said, blowing her nose again. 'A few weeks before he went missing, he started acting strangely. I don't know how to describe it, but he seemed to turn paranoid … He was constantly standing behind the curtains and peering out of the window down into the street. He was often up at night and it sounded like he was wandering around the whole flat. When we were out, he'd constantly be looking over his shoulder. But …' She paused, then shrugged. 'That could all have been tied up with the looming charges. That's what I assumed, anyway. Gustaf said they were all under a lot of pressure. I assumed he was just trying to stay out of the media eye.'

'Gustaf?' Ruben said.

'Gustaf Brons. That's Jon's colleague. One of the co-owners.

We're close friends. He used to tell me stuff that Jon held back when we … Well, that doesn't matter.'

'How did it make you feel when Jon changed like that?' Mina said.

Josephine looked down at the floor.

'It wasn't nice. The weekend before he went missing, I actually went to a resort for some me-time. The Ellery Beach House. You won't be surprised to hear that's weighing on my conscience now.'

She placed the second tissue next to the first on the table, and Ruben saw Mina hastily avert her eyes.

'What happens now?' Josephine said, her gaze shifting between them.

Ruben cleared his throat.

'We'll be keeping … Jon … for a while longer until the medical examiner has reviewed everything. Then you'll receive the body and be able to make the necessary arrangements.'

'Where was he found?'

'Inside a metro tunnel,' Mina said.

Josephine stared at her in bafflement.

'*In* the metro? What was he doing there? He's never taken a metro in his life.'

Good God, Ruben thought. What were people like?

'We don't know much yet,' Mina said. 'What little we do know we can't reveal without risking a compromised investigation. But there's likely to be significant media interest when they find out Jon has been found. We can't tell you what to do, but we'd urge you to say as little as possible.'

'Believe me, the media has been after us for months. The last thing I want to do is talk to them,' Josephine said grimly.

She escorted them back to the front door and proffered a surprisingly firm handshake in parting.

While the cramped lift stuttered and squealed its way back down six storeys, Mina applied hand sanitizer to her hands and Ruben tried to recall the shape of Josephine Langseth's rear end. But all he could see in his mind's eye was Jon's grinning skull.

14

'You've got to persuade the Security Service to increase your security,' Tor said, folding his arms. 'Just look at what happened to Anna Lindh. Or Ing-Marie Wieselgren. Or what happened to you at the end of the summer for that matter. It was a very close call. And the public is oblivious of all the other potential attacks we've averted. We live in uncertain times, and you – Niklas Stockenberg – are an obvious target. We would all sleep easier if you got them to increase your security. Maybe you would too. Those are some serious bags under your eyes.'

'Fine, fine. I hear what you say, Tor,' Niklas said, running a hand through his hair in frustration. 'It's just that I don't agree. The level of security you think appropriate makes it impossible to have a life.'

Tor was right that he had slept poorly. He reached for a report lying on his desk that was far too many pages long, and pretended to read it, hoping that his press secretary would take the hint and make himself scarce. But Tor rarely interpreted anything subtle, nor did he this time. Instead he stayed rooted to the spot.

'I'm begging you to reconsider,' Tor said with his brow furrowed. 'If not for your own sake then for Nathalie's.'

'Yes, of course. I'm sure my teenage daughter wants to be followed everywhere she goes by even more not particularly discreet bodyguards. It'll do wonders for her social life. What little of it she's managed to keep going.'

'Better that and that she stays alive,' Tor muttered, picking an invisible speck of dust off his lapel.

They never mixed privately, but Niklas could clearly imagine what his press secretary's wardrobe must be like. A row of identical suits. Next to a row of white shirts. Identical ties too. Apart from the one with the miniature Swedish flags on it that he always wore on the National Day. On the shelf below, he imagined there to be a row of identical Italian loafers made from patent leather. Tor was not a man of variety. He was, however, a faithful and able press secretary who had been by Niklas's side since he'd taken office. The only problem was that Tor didn't always know when to stop.

'I'll be the one to take responsibility for my daughter,' Niklas said. 'I appreciate your concern, but this is on the verge of nagging. I'm happy with the security detail as it is. The events of last summer aren't the kind of thing that happens every day. I just want to have as ordinary a life as possible.'

That wasn't entirely true. He wasn't happy at all. He wanted ten men with laser sights behind him at every moment – at least for the next two weeks. But that most probably wouldn't make any difference. The clock would keep counting down, no matter how many bodyguards he had.

'Well, you're the boss, but you know what I think,' Tor muttered before striding out of the room.

Niklas turned his gaze towards the report on his desk. It was more than a thousand pages long. He couldn't focus. His pulse was racing. When Mina had gone home after dinner the evening before, he had stayed up nursing a glass of rum into the small hours. On several occasions he'd been obliged to reassure Nathalie that nothing was the matter, but the truth was that he hadn't dared go to bed because he feared what he might dream about. He needn't have worried. He hadn't slept a wink after he'd finally settled down in bed.

The first thing he had done this morning was to call the number again. The message was the same. Except now it was saying that there were thirteen days instead of fourteen.

Tor had passed comment on the bags under Niklas's eyes, but it was worse than that. He didn't even know whether he had it in him to stand up. The feeling of powerlessness had him in a stranglehold. He pushed aside the thick stack of papers, shoved his chair – made from aged hardwood and upholstered in leather – away from the desk, and put his long legs up.

The business card was burning a hole in his jacket pocket. It was absurd. The whole thing was absurd. It felt as if he was in a bad action movie, or a third-rate thriller. Things like this didn't happen. Not in real life. But he still had to be on his guard. He should have known better.

It had been his choice. His choice to continue his life but on new terms. And he'd accepted the benefits that had come with that. Benefits that had brought him into the very heart of government.

He pulled out the business card and examined the symbol. Then he put the card face down on the desk. His predecessors were staring sternly at him from the surrounding walls. Had they sometimes chosen paths not knowing where they would lead? Paths that might not have been morally justifiable? And had they had to pay a price for that? Probably, one way or another.

The only thing that Niklas Stockenberg knew was that he couldn't sit there waiting. He had to do something. Anything. He had to feel like he was in control. And he might as well start with the most pressing issue.

He pulled out his phone, but his pulse was still racing; he had to force himself to take several deep breaths and wait until he was sure that his breathing was back to normal. There was no point in scaring people unnecessarily. Then he dialled his ex-wife.

15

Vincent had been grocery shopping. When he returned home and opened the front door, he heard his own voice coming from the living room. He stamped the snow off his shoes before stepping inside and removing them, hanging up his coat and then taking the shopping bags into the kitchen. The voice continued. When he entered the living room, he saw why. Benjamin and Rebecka were on the sofa, while on the TV Vincent was onstage. He had just pulled a blonde woman out of the audience to help him with his next number.

'I'd like you to think of a number that's personally significant,' TV-Vincent said to the woman, handing her a notepad and pen. 'Write it down, but keep the notepad close so that no one else can see what you've written. Especially not me.'

Vincent grimaced. Ever since his association with the police had been made public, they had been putting his performances onto the Viaplay streaming platform. Benjamin and Rebecka were watching his first ever production.

'Why are you watching that?' he said. 'And aren't you supposed to be at school, young lady?'

'To wind you up,' Rebecka said, without taking her eyes off the screen. 'Why do you always bring women up onstage? It seems very sexist. And it's the start of my Christmas holidays today. Aston's start in two days' time. Just so you know.'

'I don't always do that,' he said, defending himself. 'Bring women up onstage, I mean. But some numbers are better with women and others are better with men. When they're to do with emotions, women are usually better onstage. They're prepared to show more clearly what they're feeling compared to many men.'

'Dad! Come on!'

Rebecka looked shocked.

He shrugged. Maybe it wasn't the most modern view to hold, but onstage he tended to find it still held true most of the time.

TV-Vincent scrutinized the woman for what must have been a minute. Then he pulled out a slate and quickly wrote sixteen numbers on it, divided into four numbers across four rows.

Aha. It was *that* show. He'd completely forgotten about this number.

'This doesn't look all that emotional,' Rebecka said. 'I can't believe you actually made a piece of maths homework your closing number.'

'It's a magic square,' Vincent said. 'It's an old mathematical problem originating from China in 190 BC. Back then, of course, they did it with three times three numbers. The one I'm doing in the show is much more complex. I think it was another eight hundred years before mankind came up with that version. That was in India.'

'And now we're getting a history lesson too,' Rebecka said with a sigh. 'I don't know whether you heard, but my school's packed up for Christmas.'

'But you've actually seen a magic square before,' Vincent said, thinking of something. 'Give me a second and I'll get the photo album from Barcelona!'

He knew Rebecka had a point, but she had loved Barcelona when they had all gone as a family a few years earlier. At least she would be able to appreciate this. Vincent searched through his albums on the shelf. He preferred to have printed photo albums from their trips rather than just keeping the pictures on the computer. This was partly because it was more pleasant to leaf through a book, and partly because he could never find what he was looking for among the fifty thousand pictures on his computer.

'Here we are!' he said, pulling the right album down.

He sat down on the sofa between Rebecka and Benjamin, and flipped through it until he reached the photos of Gaudí's remarkable Sagrada Família. Out of the corner of his eye, he saw that the kids were both glancing over with interest. He knew it.

'Here,' he said, pointing to a photograph. 'This was made by the sculptor Subirachs, who made a lot of decorations for the façade. This is what they call the Passion Façade.'

The picture was a close-up of the detailing. Sixteen numbers were engraved into the wall inside a four-by-four grid.

'If you add up each row, you'll see that they all add up to thirty-three,' he said. 'And if you add them up in their columns instead, they also add up to thirty-three. It's the same if you add the four figures running diagonally across. Or if you add the four numbers in the corners. In fact, there are three hundred and ten combinations where these figures add up to thirty-three. Which was, of course, how old Jesus was when he died. At least according to a lot of Christians.'

Benjamin traced his finger over the picture. He appeared to be counting silently.

'That's actually pretty cool,' he said with a nod.

Vincent nodded in satisfaction. It *was* cool. And it was an incredible mathematical feat to construct. He put his own finger on the photograph.

'And if that wasn't enough, this particular grid of numbers also contains a hidden message,' he said. 'Almost all the numbers only appear once, but take a look at which ones are repeated. Ten and fourteen are featured twice. They add up to forty-eight. In the old Latin alphabet that's also the sum of the positions of the letters INRI.'

Rebecka stared at him unappreciatively.

'INRI is the abbreviation of *Iesus Nazarenus Rex Iudaeorum*. Or "Jesus, King of the Jews", which Pontius Pilate had carved onto his cross.'

Vincent waggled his eyebrows meaningfully.

'Oh God,' Rebecka said, burying her face in her hands. 'There are mentalists everywhere!'

On the TV, Vincent had just demonstrated how the sixteen figures he had written in his own grid added up to fifteen no matter which way they were added together.

'These numbers came to me through your presence alone,' TV-Vincent said to the woman standing next to him onstage. 'And no matter what I do, they keep leading me back to fifteen. Strange. I've no idea why it's fifteen in particular. Does that mean anything to you?'

The woman was close to tears.

'That's how long I've been married to my life partner,' she said in shock. 'It's our anniversary today.'

She turned over the pad of paper. The number fifteen was inscribed on it in large red handwriting. She'd also drawn a small heart next to it.

Rebecka laughed.

'OK, I've got no idea how you did that,' she said. 'But it doesn't help. It's still maths homework. You must be the nerdiest dad on earth. Anyway, weren't you supposed to be putting away the shopping?'

'Benjamin, a little help, please!' Vincent said, pointing first to the album and then to himself on the TV. '*Really* cool, right?'

'Sorry Dad,' Benjamin said. 'Rebecka's right.'

'Unrepentant,' Vincent said with a sigh, before standing up to return the album to the shelf.

But he knew that Benjamin at least was only pretending to think it was stupid. His eldest son had not only inherited Vincent's ability to see patterns and flesh out complex structures, but had in some cases surpassed it.

The words of the woman on the TV lingered in his head as he went back to the kitchen to deal with the groceries. *My life partner.* He hated terms like that. *Soulmate* was another one that was just as bad. Those kinds of ideas placed completely unreasonable demands on relationships. Words like that represented no degree of reality whatsoever. But if they happened to be true, if there really was something like a soulmate, then that only made matters worse. Because that meant his soulmate was Mina. And that made his life even more complicated. He still didn't know what to say to her in reply to her text.

16

Christer stretched his legs out underneath the desk, which caused Bosse to sit up in disapproval. Feeling guilty, his master thought better of it and drew his feet back to where they had been, so that Bosse could lie across them again. Christer logged on to the DurTvå database and entered Jon Langseth's name to see what he could find on the disappearance. It had been clever of Mina to make such a swift connection to the case. It usually took a long time to identify victims like this, but since Mina had been able to supply them with a possible name immediately, Milda had simply requested copies of Langseth's dental X-rays from his dentist and they'd had a match within twenty-four hours. Now the toughest part remained – working out whether, and if so why, the financier had been killed. And by whom.

Christer squinted as he read the screen. Lasse was always telling him that he needed glasses, but so far he had dug his heels in. It wasn't vanity – he'd let go of that long ago, since he'd accepted that nature hadn't given him an Adonis-like appearance even in the beginning. No, it was really that anything that was evidence of the rapid passing of time was also a painful reminder that everything was leading to an end. And for the first time in his life, Christer Bengtsson feared death, because for the first time in his life he was happy. It was an unfamiliar emotion – frightening even, although the most frightening thing was the thought that he now had something big that he could lose. It had taken every last ounce of courage for him to bet on a future with Lasse, because it meant he had to show who he really was. The stakes had been and remained sky-high.

So, no glasses.

He glowered towards the rear corner of the open-plan office. Some idiot had selected a Christmas playlist, which was now blaring from a speaker. Normally, music was not allowed to be played so loudly in the shared office, but it seemed as if everyone at police headquarters had capitulated in anticipation of Christmas. There was Christmas cheer in every direction he turned. But he was never going to be *so* happy that he started liking Christmas music. He couldn't bloody stand it. The worst thing was when people started playing it in October.

With Bosse serving as a heated, weighted blanket across his feet, he tried to focus on the screen and blank out the Christmas music hellscape. He squinted even more, trying to make the letters as clear as possible, and slowly read what they had on Jon Langseth's disappearance. He also went to his browser and googled for articles in the press. There were a lot of them. The media interest had been significant and the speculation boundless. But most people had made the assumption that Jon had disappeared of his own volition and that he was probably on some hot island somewhere with access to a fortune stashed in offshore accounts. It wasn't too far-fetched a guess given the circumstances, but it was one that had turned out to be completely wrong.

Before Jon's disappearance, the Confido scandal had been in the headlines. A bunch of city slickers had cunningly and deliberately cheated senior citizens out of their savings: of course it deeply upset people. The founders were living the high life with mansions on Lidingö, swish apartments in Östermalm, champagne, fast cars, expensive suits and wristwatches, and trips to St Moritz, Ibiza, Dubai and the Maldives. All at the expense of those with fewer means. It had all come to an abrupt end upon the filing of criminal charges and a trial in the court of public opinion. Christer had been following the coverage closely prior to Jon's disappearance, since there wasn't much that gave him the same degree of satisfaction as seeing arseholes like that get what was coming to them.

Jon had been reported missing by his wife on the morning of August the tenth. When asked why she hadn't reported his absence the night before, she said that Jon was often out entertaining and would come home after she had gone to bed. On the other hand, he was usually there in the morning. When she had discovered that he wasn't at home then, she called his secretary, who said that he hadn't been to the office the day before, and she realized that something must have happened.

And then the circus had rolled into town as the police had begun to search for him. There was a file containing interviews with Jon's wife, colleagues and anyone else who might conceivably have any idea where he'd gone. But the only thing they'd turned up was that after he had walked out of the door in the morning on his way to the office, no one had clapped eyes on him. Efforts had been made – no aspersions could be cast on the police's work. However, Christer reflected, perhaps no one had gone the extra mile, because everyone had been convinced that Jon had left the country and was living the good life in the best of health.

The Christmas playlist on the speaker moved on to 'Feliz Navidad'. Disgusting. Utterly vile.

His mother had been nuts about Christmas, so he'd had an excess of yuletide joy during his childhood. It didn't take a shrink to realize that was why his skin began to crawl whenever the festive season was on the horizon. But regrettably, he had admitted a Christmas fanatic into his home. Lasse had wanted to start putting up decorations in the middle of November, which had led to a compromise. Christmas music was permitted in the evening and at weekends, but not until December fifteenth. Now he was putting up with this misery at home and at work.

A few hours and countless Christmas hits later, Christer stretched on his uncomfortable office chair. He had read everything about Jon Langseth there was to read in the files, and he had read everything he could find about the case online, and he was none the wiser than when he had started. Nothing stood out – there was no thread to untangle. It really did seem as if Jon had left his apartment before disappearing into thin air. That was, until his bones had been found in the metro tunnel some four months later.

Christer frowned. There were so many different angles of attack when searching. Age, occupation, social circles, geography, sex, friends, family. Thousands of potential connections where just one tiny detail that showed a correlation might be hidden in the wealth of information stored in the database. Finding details in the monster archive at his fingertips was his strength. Page after page scrolled by on the screen in front of him.

There was a lot about Jon Langseth that made him a very different kind of victim when it came to his disappearance. Well, now there was his presumed killing, too. He didn't have a long criminal record – no connection to drugs or gangs or human trafficking or burglary. Or anything else that usually popped up when they found someone dead. The vast majority of people who were killed had a clear connection to risky activities – the kind of things that had probably caused their deaths, or so one might conclude without stretching the imagination. Not that they only had themselves to blame – that wasn't what Christer thought. It was just that when looked at through the eyes of a police detective, it was often not all that difficult to understand why someone had ended up in that situation.

Admittedly, Jon Langseth had been under criminal investigation. But financial crime rarely led to deadly violence, and certainly not in this stratum of society. These were not usually people who engaged in violence. These were people accustomed to robbing people from behind the anonymity and safety of their computer screens. They robbed people while wearing tailored suits and Italian leather shoes. These weren't even people who had access to guns. Their brain was their gun; they didn't need a Magnum or a Luger.

Unless Jon Langseth had been bumped off by a pissed-off pensioner he'd rinsed for cash. Christer chuckled. Murder, of course, was no laughing matter. But that would be some form of poetic justice.

'Our Christmas ham has escaped' floated across the open-plan office and Christer began to giggle to himself. Werner & Werner, otherwise known as Sven Melander and Åke Cato. That was some proper bloody humour. And not that falling-on-your-arse kind of humour that the kids were laughing at on their phones these days. Christer was a man who considered humour to be an indication of humankind's intelligence, but his observation was that nowadays it seemed to be a lost cause.

He sighed and stretched again. Somewhere in that database was something that would help them to advance. There always was. All it called for was patience – and he had an abundance of that.

17

Mina locked the car without really being aware of what she was doing. Her thoughts were fully occupied by the phone call she had just finished. She still found it hard to believe it had actually taken place. Niklas had called her. At work. While she had admittedly seen more and more of her daughter and ex-husband lately at their place, that was exactly the point. It had been at their place. And now Niklas had asked whether Nathalie could stay with her for a while.

Mina had been completely unprepared for that and her instinct had been to say a flat out no, but Niklas hadn't just asked, he'd *beseeched* her. He never did that. Despite the resumption of contact, Niklas had to-date made it clear that he remained Nathalie's primary parent and that her home was with him. But things changed – that was something Mina had learned of late. Her entire life had changed. And she simply hadn't been able to say no, so now Nathalie was going to be staying with her. Apparently she'd be turning up in two hours' time. Mina had hurried home.

She went up to her apartment and unlocked the door. She needed time to clean first. It wasn't actually necessary; rationally, she knew the apartment was just as antiseptic as it had been when she had left it that morning. However her emotions told her otherwise. And while the apartment might be ready for a visitor, the same could not be said for her.

She took off her shoes, left them on the doormat and began to wander around the apartment. She knew she was stirring up more dust by doing this compared with sitting down, but she couldn't help it. Her body was unable to find peace. Her apartment was her fortress, her safe place, and it had been hers alone until Vincent had visited. And now her daughter was going to *live* there. The drawbridge across the moat had apparently been lowered without her quite understanding how.

The question was where Nathalie would be sleeping. The only reasonable option was the study, but it was – as ever – full of cleaning products, multipacks of cheap knickers and vests, disposable gloves and boxes of hand sanitizer. If she let Nathalie in there, she wasn't sure whether her daughter would ever dare to return. Mina had to find somewhere else to put her stash, but there wasn't time for that now.

She put on gloves, filled a bucket with warm water and cleaning fluid, grabbed a microfibre cloth and began to dust every surface in the apartment, including the walls. When she was done, she got out the vacuum cleaner and gave the apartment a once over with that too. Then she wiped down the surfaces again – just in case the vacuum cleaner had kicked up any more dust.

One hour left until Nathalie arrived.

The cleaning had left Mina slightly sweaty, which meant she had no choice but to take a shower. She took care to use a freshly opened tub of exfoliating cream across her entire body. The hot water was probably washing away all the dust that had got on her, but sweat and dead skin were almost more disgusting. The cream promised to remove all skin cells no longer in use.

She knew that the human body shed between thirty and forty thousand dead skin cells every hour. That was around 0.09 grammes. *Per hour.* Over the course of a day, she released around two grammes of skin. Every day. All year round. The mere thought of it made her want to throw up. She rubbed the cream harder against her leg. The small grains in the product abraded her skin so nicely.

Before she could stop the thought, she pictured her whole home covered in invisible flakes of skin, being constantly replenished, no matter how much she cleaned. How long would it take until there was enough for a full-size copy of her in the living room, made of nothing but skin flakes? She began to count in her head. In a year she released … Good God. Almost eight hundred grammes. A little less than a kilogram. Of nothing but dead skin.

She began to sob and sank onto all fours in the shower, leaning over the clean, shiny drain.

Fortunately, it went no further. She didn't have time for this. Nathalie was due to arrive imminently. If Mina hurried, she'd have time to apply another layer of exfoliating cream to her whole body.

18

Peter Kronlund had been in Kronoberg Remand Prison for almost two weeks, which meant he was right next door to police headquarters. Julia ran through her mental checklist to ensure that she had done everything necessary in order to enter the prison. She had an approved visitor's permit, she had called ahead, and she had brought identification. Everything was in order.

She saw Adam approaching in the distance. Julia had come straight from the office and had only put on a cardigan for the brief walk outside, but he was heavily wrapped up in a Canada Goose coat, hat and gloves. It was far too many degrees below zero outside. She regretted not bringing a coat – the cold had already penetrated through her clothes in the few moments she had been outdoors. But soon they would be back inside in the warmth.

'Hi – I hope you didn't have to wait,' he said breathlessly as he embraced her.

She responded to this awkwardly, feeling his hand against her backside and his breath against her ear. She pulled out of the embrace and avoided his gaze. Life was far too complicated, and the approach of Christmas only made it many times worse. It wasn't supposed to be like this. But a late gathering at the office with a little too much cheap white wine from a box was all it had taken for her to succumb to her attraction to him. She felt Adam's piercing gaze on her back as she led the way through the entrance.

'For once, I'm glad the justice system takes its sweet time,' she said. 'If Peter Kronlund had been remanded immediately he'd already have been released and he'd be out of our reach by now.'

The prison entrance was sterile and forbidding. The security checks were rigorous. The facility wasn't run by the police; instead it was under the charge of the Prison and Probation Service, and the woman who received them wore a prison officer's uniform.

'Identification?'

Both Adam and Julia handed over their police IDs and were scrupulously checked in.

'Peter Kronlund?'

Julia nodded.

'Yes, we called ahead to book.'

The woman didn't reply, instead proffering a blue plastic box and pointing at their shoes by way of a request. Both Julia and Adam had been inside the remand prison many times before and knew the drill. One at a time, they placed their shoes into the box to be X-rayed, after they had stamped as much snow off them as possible. They also had to put all their personal possessions into a separate box. Julia wasn't sure whether she needed to take off her wedding ring, but just to be on the safe side she slipped it off her finger and put it in the box. She didn't dare look at Adam as she took it off.

Then they went through the metal detector.

After that, it was time for the final step. A large German Shepherd had been waiting patiently, her tongue lolling as she gently panted, and now she responded swiftly to a command.

'Lissy, search.'

The dog immediately ran eagerly towards her and Adam to sniff them out, but she didn't signal that there were any drugs. They could come in.

They were shown into a visiting room with colourful walls.

'All the others are full, so you're in the family room,' the prison guard said, nodding towards the painted animals on one of the walls. 'The loo's through there. Would you like coffee?'

They both nodded and sat down to wait for Peter. He'd been there for thirteen days, which meant there was one day left before the prosecutor had to decide whether to order an extension to his remand.

When Peter Kronlund, the majority shareholder and chairman of Confido, entered the room, they both stood up. He looked haggard and worn out – not at all the same person they'd seen in photos in the newspapers, clutching a champagne flute at some event or wearing flashy summer attire at a party in Ibiza or Marbella. His hair was greasy and unwashed, his skin was faded and sallow, and he smelled faintly of sweat. Julia knew that all people on remand had access to showers and toiletries, but it wasn't uncommon for the shock of being in a cell to make the prisoner lose all interest in personal hygiene.

'I've nothing more to say. You'll have to talk to my lawyer. I'll be out of here tomorrow,' Peter said, reaching greedily for the cup of coffee that had just arrived.

'We're not here to talk about your case,' Adam said drily. 'We'd like to talk about Jon Langseth.'

'Jon …'

Peter shook his head and sipped the coffee, but grimaced when he found it too hot to drink. Julia gently blew on hers.

'Well,' he said bitterly, 'Jon was the smartest of us all. I dare say he's got a G&T in one hand and a blonde in the other, somewhere far, far away. While I'm stuck here.'

Peter ran his hand through his greasy hair. Julia exchanged a quick glance with Adam. They didn't know whether the news about Jon had reached Peter, but they had been hoping he would still be unaware of it. There was a lot of value to be derived from the first, spontaneous reaction.

Julia made a quick decision. She didn't want Peter to know that they had found the remains of his colleague – not quite yet. She shot Adam a warning look and he seemed to understand exactly what she was thinking.

'What makes you think Jon has fled the country?' she said.

Peter shrugged.

'Why wouldn't he? Surely it's the logical thing to do. Right? Look at where I am. In fucking jail.'

He held his hands out dramatically.

'But you're innocent, aren't you?' said Adam.

Julia could hear that he was unable to prevent a tart note from creeping into his voice. Peter curled his upper lip.

'Yes. I'm innocent. But in this damn country I doubt anyone will care about that. It's considered vulgar to make money in Sweden. Everyone has to be a nine-to-fiver. Everyone has to be equally poor. When I was growing up in Södertälje, no one cared what I did. That was when I was the same as everyone else. But now it's different. Now that I've got dosh and I'm successful … Out come the hyenas. Fuck the Welfare Staters and their dreams of mediocrity. No one's allowed to stand out. That's what I'm being forced to pay for now. And that's what Jon was smart enough to figure out, so he got out of here.'

'Do you know for sure that's what happened?' Adam said. 'Did he say anything before he disappeared? About heading abroad?'

'No, I suppose not,' Peter said, once again trying to sip his coffee. 'But he was up to something.'

'Why do you say that?'

Adam leaned forward with interest. It made his pectoral muscles stand out clearly underneath his white T-shirt. Julia tried not to look at them or to think about what they felt like under her hands.

'Oh, just little things. It's hard to say.'

'Try,' Julia said. 'Describe them to us as best you can.'

'Well, he was behaving pretty weirdly for the last month. Super jumpy. Constantly looking over his shoulder.'

'Tell us more,' Julia said.

'It's sort of hard to describe,' Peter said, furrowing his brow. 'But he started acting as if he was being followed. Kept taking different routes to and from the office. Boosted security in reception. If we went out for a bite to eat, we could only book places with two exits. Bollocks like that. It just started all of a sudden. But it was around the same time that bloody hack from *Dagens Industri* started snooping around our affairs, so I assumed he was just reacting badly to that. Everyone handles stress differently, and Jon was being driven up the wall. So to be perfectly honest I wasn't at all surprised when he did a bunk.'

'But it was out of the ordinary for him?'

Julia tried the coffee and grimaced. It was no longer too hot, but it was truly vile.

'Fuck no. Jon was the most cool-headed human being I've ever met. Nothing made him lose control. There was no one who could keep a poker face in meetings quite like Jon. You know, he's the kind of guy who doesn't even sweat when he's doing his workout. Every strand of hair in its rightful place, suit neatly pressed. I know he once said that he'd gone through a really tough time years ago, but I have a hard time believing it. Jon was Mr Perfect.'

'Until suddenly he wasn't.'

'Yes, exactly.'

Silence descended.

Julia gazed at the painted wall. The theme appeared to be happy animals in the jungle. There was a monkey hanging off a branch. A couple of elephants spraying water. A zebra that mostly looked like it was high. Harry would have loved it. On the other hand, it didn't take much to make him happy. He was an extremely cheerful baby and it took no more than a doorknob to make him burst into laughter.

She pushed away thoughts of her son – thoughts about Harry were intimately intertwined with thoughts about Torkel. And the fact that she had a family. At least for the time being.

'Do you know whether he has any enemies?' Adam said, his gaze fixed on Julia.

She realized that her expression must have given her away, and she forced herself to silence the tumult awoken within her by the children's mural. She leaned forward.

'Nothing so dramatic,' Peter said, shaking his head. 'Of course, there are always people in our world whose toes we'll have stepped on. It comes with the territory. But I don't think anyone would want to hurt him. So no, I still think he's alive and well and working on his suntan.'

'Jon's dead,' Julia said abruptly.

Peter started. His pale face became even whiter. He stared at her, his mouth opening and closing like a fish's. Julia waited. The initial reaction was valuable. Everything about Peter's behaviour suggested to her that he'd been completely unaware that Jon wasn't alive.

'Dead? How? What? Who?'

The questions tumbled out of him in quick succession, and he grasped the edge of the table so tightly his knuckles went white.

'We can't reveal any details of our investigation. But the

fact that he's dead suggests that his behaviour prior to his disappearance may be related to why he was killed.'

'Did you say *killed*?'

'That's our current hypothesis. So thinking it over again, is there anything about what he did that particularly stands out? Anything he said? Anything you saw?'

Julia leaned back on her chair, intently scrutinizing Peter's face to see whether he was hiding anything, but it was frank and open as he shook his head.

'No. No, it never crossed my mind that it might be connected to anything except our … affairs.'

'OK, I think we're done here,' she said, standing up.

She needed to get out of there before the animals on the walls began talking to her – that was how palpable their presence felt to her. And what they represented.

'I'll be out tomorrow,' Peter said feebly as he clutched his cup of coffee.

'Good luck,' Adam said with a nod.

The irony was clearly layered into his voice.

As they left the visiting room, they passed the guard who had come to fetch Peter. Behind her, Julia could feel the elephants' on her back.

19

When Nathalie got out of the lift at the Ministry of Justice, Tor was already waiting for her in reception. He cracked a big smile when he saw her.

'Nathalie! It's been a long time,' he said loudly. 'I barely recognize you.'

She was about to ask him whether he'd forgotten about all the meetings they'd had six months earlier about whether she would have to testify in court against Epicura, but she suspected that Tor's remark was mostly for the guy sitting behind the reception desk. Her involvement in the kerfuffle around the cult had been kept as secret as possible and apparently they were going to keep pretending.

They'd told her that although she was obliged to give evidence since she was sixteen years old, there was also the need to consider her safety as the daughter of the Minister for Justice. In the end it had been enough for that tall policeman to testify – the one who had been there when Epicura's members tried to kill themselves and each other. Adam, or whatever his name was. Anyway, Nathalie had been with Nova when it had all kicked off. And Nova was dead.

'Hi Tor,' she said. 'My goodness, how you've grown.'

She was tempted to pinch his cheek, but perhaps that would have been taking it too far.

He beckoned to her to follow him and they walked along the familiar corridor in silence. Tor said nothing until they reached the door to her dad's office, when he pursed his lips.

'I don't know what's up with him today, but if you find anything out, then please do tell. He doesn't seem to be talking to me any longer.'

Then he left.

Nathalie stifled a giggle, knocked on the door and entered. Her father was sitting behind his desk reading the thickest binder she had ever seen. The desk itself was cluttered with papers. This was definitely not like him: she had never seen more than two pages at once on the desk in his study at home. He'd been acting strangely since dinner the night before. A knot formed in her stomach.

'Hi Natti,' he said, looking up. 'Look, there's something I've been discussing with your mother. I think it would be a good idea if you stayed with her for a while.'

'Er … really?' she said, stopping mid-step. 'That's … unexpected. What do you mean? Like every other week or something when the spring term starts? I don't really know if I want to. I like things the way they are.'

'I mean that you should move in with her full-time for a while. Right away. As soon as possible. Why wait, if it's a good idea?'

He attempted a smile but failed completely.

'You need some one-on-one time,' he said, leaning back in his chair. 'Wouldn't it be nice to spend Christmas with her? Maybe New Year too?'

Nathalie stared at her dad. His shirt was crumpled. It never usually was. And now that she thought about it, his hair appeared to be uncombed.

'Dad, what's happened?' she said.

'Happened? Nothing. Nothing at all. I'm just a little overworked.'

He was clearly lying, but she wasn't going to push him. After all, maybe he had a point. She had slowly started getting to know Mina in recent months and had realized that she probably liked her mother. Of course, Mina was batshit crazy, but rather that than someone deadly boring. The idea of *living* with her still made Nathalie's stomach flip – it was a very big step. But then, like Dad said, perhaps it wouldn't be a bad idea to spend some time alone with Mina.

With Mum.

Maybe.

'I suppose,' she said uncertainly.

'Splendid. Perhaps you could go round there now to discuss it? I've already called her to say you're on your way.' He glanced at his watch. 'She's actually expecting you right now. I'll give you the address.'

'Well, thanks very much for including me in the decision,' she said resentfully.

Part of her wanted to rebel against Dad. She wanted to protest that he was always controlling her life without checking what she actually wanted. It had always been that way – he had always decided what was best for her without consulting her. But she was also a little curious about Mina's living situation. She would just have to pick her battles.

'Well, fine. I haven't got anything better to do right now,' she said.

She found a piece of paper on the desk, jotted down the address her father told her and then slipped it into her pocket.

'I've just got one question before I go home and pack my bags. What was so important about this that I had to come here? You've already decided everything. You could have just texted me.'

Her father looked at her for a while without answering. Then he blinked a few times and rubbed his hand across his eyes.

'I wanted to see you,' he said. 'Who knows how many more opportunities I'll have to do that? You're getting big now.'

She wanted to make a quip about hearing a sentimental film score in the background, but her father's behaviour was actually worrying her. She knew what he was like when he was overworked, but this was something else. It was something she didn't know how to handle. It would be good to spend some time apart.

'Be nice to Tor while I'm gone,' she said, opening the door to leave. 'I think he needs a new chew toy or something.'

20

Rebecka was in the kitchen looking at the calendar that Vincent had put up on the wall above the coffee maker. There were deep furrows in her forehead. Vincent had found a calendar where each month's illustration was a mathematical problem rather than cute kittens or amusing words of wisdom.

He peered over her shoulder at December's problem. Fermat's Last Theorem. It was rather mean of the calendar maker to include it, since it had taken almost 360 years for the mathematical geniuses of the world to solve it. When Pierre Fermat had set out his proposition in 1637, he had postulated the existence of a solution, but had conveniently forgotten to write it down. However, when the solution was published in 1995 it relied upon mathematics that had been undiscovered in the seventeenth century. Vincent smiled to himself. He strongly suspected that Pierre Fermat had simply played the greatest prank of all time on the mathematical world. That was humour.

'Are you trying to solve Fermat's riddle?' he said to his daughter. 'It's quite a task. I think the solution when written down is about as thick as a brick.'

'Huh? No, that's lame,' she said. 'What kind of person has maths problems on the wall? I get enough of that at school. I was just wondering why you've circled 21st, 24th and 28th December. Are you going away then? That's right over Christmas. And you promised to drive me to the station on the twenty-second. Don't you dare try and wriggle out of that.'

'Of course I'll drive you to your train,' Vincent said, nodding. 'Is Denis joining you on this skiing trip? You are off to the French Alps, aren't you?'

'I'm going with Edith and Sigrid,' Rebecka said firmly. 'Denis can go to hell.'

Vincent had failed to keep up with developments – Rebecka's French boyfriend was clearly out in the cold.

'So *you* don't have to be at home for Christmas, but *I* do?' he said, winking at her.

Rebecka gave him a look that could have destroyed any father on earth. She had honed it during the months he had spent at home on crutches.

'Anyway,' he said, 'I wasn't the one who circled those dates. It must have been Maria.'

'Sure, whatever,' Rebecka said with a shrug. 'As long as you can drive me to the station.'

His daughter went to her room and closed the door behind her. Vincent realized that he hadn't set foot inside her bedroom in a long time. He wondered what he would find in there when she eventually moved out. Probably landmines. With his name on them.

His gaze was drawn back to the calendar. Twenty-one, twenty-four and twenty-eight were indeed circled. He automatically added them up before he could stop himself. Seventy-three. The twenty-first prime number. The numbers twenty-one, seven and three also had another strange relationship: seven times three was twenty-one. And seven, three, twenty-one and seventy-three written in binary form were all palindromes, meaning that they read the same forwards and backwards: 111, 11, 10101 and 1001001. The same was true in relation to seventy-three's mathematical function as a prime number. It was one of those prime numbers that was still a prime number if you reversed it and read it as thirty-seven. He smiled to himself as he recalled the geeky fact that this was known as an 'emirp' – the word 'prime' backwards. Sometimes they had a sense of humour, those mathematicians. Just look at Fermat.

Vincent put a hand to his head. It had begun to ache at the back. That was the thing about overheating his brain.

He couldn't help but glance at the circled numbers one last time.

There was something about them that bothered him.

Twenty-one. Twenty-four. Twenty-eight.

He couldn't put his finger on it; they just looked ... unnerving.

Vincent frowned. There were three days left until the first date. He made a mental note to ask Maria what she was going to do then.

21

Mina was just getting dressed after showering when the doorbell rang. She realized she was quivering with nerves. Her daughter. At her home. Now there was no going back. Should she offer her coffee? Should she have bought biscuits? If so, what kind? She had no idea what to do in this kind of situation.

She took a deep breath and opened the door. Nathalie was standing on the threshold smiling at her uncertainly. In one hand she had a wheelie suitcase and in the other she had a scrap of paper on which Mina's address appeared to have been scrawled.

'Oh … gosh,' Nathalie said, her smile disappearing. 'Have you just done a workout or something? You're completely red.'

'No, I was …' Mina said, before stopping.

Nathalie was unaware of her issues, and Mina preferred it to stay that way for a while longer. She would notice soon enough, but right now Mina was fighting to be accepted as a normal mother. The abnormal – like the fact that she'd just gone through an entire tub of exfoliating cream so her body and face were still stinging, or that the study was bursting with sufficient stocks of antiseptic products to see a small country through several years – would have to come later.

'Come in! So this is where I live! Well, where *we* live now!' she said, horrified by her cheery tone.

Mina tried not to stare at Nathalie's feet as her daughter came into the apartment, walked straight past the rug and kicked her trainers off into a corner. Mina noted with alarm the trail of gravel left on the hall floor. She swallowed. She wanted nothing more than to deal with it at once before it spread further into the apartment, but she forced herself to refrain.

'Well, this is nice isn't it?' Nathalie said as she looked around. 'It's very clean and tidy. Do all cops live like this?'

Mina thought about Peder and Anette and the triplets. Peder's home had been an explosion of toys, leftover food and laughing children. She smiled and shook her head.

'No,' she said. 'Not all of them. Do you fancy a coffee? Tea? Juice?'

This time it was Nathalie's turn to smile.

'There's no need to be so polite, Mum,' she said, trundling the bag into the corner where her shoes had been deposited. 'This is weird for me too, but it's actually been six months since I found out you existed. I should have come here ages ago.'

They went into the living room and sat down next to each other on the sofa. Nathalie was sitting so close that she could have touched her. Mina made sure to keep her hands to herself, clasping them on her lap. She didn't know how to cope with the emotions that were suddenly overwhelming her. She had come so close to losing Nathalie. First when she had left her family, and then in the summer when her own mother Ines and the cult leader Nova had got their claws into her. Never again. She would do anything to heal the wound between them, if only Nathalie would let her. Living together was a step forward. It was just that it had happened so … fast.

'I was probably just as surprised as you when your father called me,' she said. 'If not more so. And I don't like Niklas thinking he can make these kinds of decisions without talking to us first. After all, he's not the one who's coming to live here. But maybe it isn't such a bad idea. What do you think?'

'I agree. It's pretty much typical Dad,' Nathalie said, fidgeting with the scrap of paper with Mina's address on it. 'By the way, he's been super weird ever since dinner last night. He seems to be really nervous, but he says there's nothing wrong when I ask.'

'I think Ministers of Justice probably know things that would make more or less anyone nervous,' Mina said. 'It might not be anything more than that.'

'That's what he said too. That it was work. But he's weird. So … how are we going to do this? You and me, I mean.'

'I was going to ask you the same thing,' said Mina. 'I completely understand if you want to be left alone. You can have your own shelf in the fridge for your food, I thought you could have the study once I've had time to tidy up in there, and that door has a lock, so you can—'

'Mum,' Nathalie interrupted. 'I'm your daughter. Not a lodger. I think the idea is that we're supposed to live *together*.'

'I just didn't want to make any assumptions.'

Silence descended. Nathalie put the slip of paper on the table.

'I suppose I wouldn't mind a coffee,' she said. 'With plenty of milk.'

22

TWELVE DAYS TO GO

Vincent was in the kitchen in his dressing gown, going through the post that he'd brought in from the mailbox the night before. The path leading to the road and the mailbox had finally been cleared, but he was expecting it to be blanketed in snow again by the evening if the weather kept up its efforts of the last few days.

It was mostly junk mail, but he wanted to be sure he didn't miss anything before it went into the recycling. And he was quite right to do so. Tucked between a flyer of the latest supermarket promotions and a begging letter from Save The Children there was a letter addressed to him. He could have sworn he hadn't seen it when he went through the heap of post the night before. Not only did he have a constant headache, but he was also becoming inattentive – or so it seemed.

Benjamin wandered into the kitchen and yawned.

'Want a coffee?' he asked as he began to rummage through the capsules.

Vincent pointed to his newly filled mug in response.

'I don't get how we're supposed to wake up while it's still dark outside,' Benjamin muttered as he inserted a capsule into the machine. 'It's the same thing every winter. Do you think we'll ever get used to it?'

'Do I think we'll get used to the dark?' said Vincent. 'That's a very existential question for this hour of the morning.'

Aston came out of his bedroom rubbing his eyes. He set a straight course for the living room and Vincent heard him throw himself onto the sofa.

'Breakfast first, then TV,' Vincent shouted.

Aston muttered something in response. Just a few days earlier he had stumbled across the TV show 'Sweden's Worst Driver' and he was now bingeing every episode of it that he could find. He was even getting through half an episode before it was time to leave for school.

'Well then, I want toast,' Aston said, coming into the kitchen and going to the fridge where he took out a squeezy bottle of strawberry jam. 'With lots of jam.'

'Well, get on it then!' Vincent said, beginning to open the envelope addressed to him. 'Well, not on the toast itself. Then you'd have Aston on toast. Has either of you seen your sister?'

'She was at a party yesterday,' Aston said as he slipped two slices of bread into the toaster. 'So she's asleep. I'll wake her up soon.'

'You'd better put on a bullet-proof vest then,' Benjamin said, laughing. 'And a helmet. Rebecka the morning after the night before is not to be trifled with.'

Vincent wasn't sure whether Rebecka was even old enough to be having a morning after the night before, but he'd delegated that part of her upbringing to Maria. Lately, his wife had shown an unusually keen understanding of the teenage phase her stepdaughter was going through.

As if he had conjured her with his thoughts alone, Maria came out of the bedroom, tugged at the sash on her dressing gown, and began to rummage around in the pantry.

'Has anyone seen my chia seeds?' she said.

Since Maria had started her own business, it had become difficult to keep track of time in the household. Vincent tried not to be annoyed by it, but he always had breakfast on the table for the family at half past seven, whether or not it was needed. There was a reason for the existence of routines.

He peered down and realized he was holding a letter.

There was post for him. Oh yes, that was what he'd been doing.

He finished opening the envelope while Maria changed her mind and joined Aston for toast with jam instead. He understood why. Who felt like eating healthily when it was dark and cold outside?

Inside the envelope was a Christmas card. It wasn't the first of the year – both Umberto at ShowLife Productions and Julia's team at the police had sent him cards already. Sometimes he also received cards from theatres he'd performed at. But the Christmas cards he received were always work-related. What he was holding in his hand was personal. There was a handwritten message. He never usually got those.

When he read it, he suddenly found he had difficulty swallowing.

The shadow that had been inside him since the age of seven when his mother died rose within him with a roar.

'I need to check something,' he said much too loudly, and rushed into his study before the kids could see how violently he was trembling.

He slammed the door shut.

In the study, he added the new Christmas card to the right-hand end of the timeline. If this was serious then it was lucky he hadn't got the police involved. He wanted to talk to Mina about this – now more than ever. But the new message made that impossible. He read it again even though he didn't want to.

Are you ready for the end, Vincent?

I'm going to take your family.

Then you.

And you won't be able to do anything about it. It'll still happen even if you go to the police – just a lot faster. You and I, divided by two.

Merry Christmas.

He listened for Benjamin's breakfast chatter. For Aston and Maria's voices from the living room as they bickered about whether Aston would be allowed to finish this episode of 'Sweden's Worst Driver' before he had to leave for the Christmas assembly at school. Anything to suggest that his family were still there. But it was suddenly completely silent.

23

Mina was at her desk in police headquarters, staring at the colourful image on her computer for what was surely the umpteenth time. The temperature in her office was a degree or two colder than it was in her colleagues' rooms. She preferred the cold; indeed she invited it in. Unlike the others, she was far happier in the winter than she was in the summer. But despite the cool room, beads of sweat threatened to break out on her brow. And it was all the picture's fault.

See you at the police Christmas do!

She'd received the email weeks ago, but had suppressed the thought of it. The invitation showed a photograph of a Baltic Sea ferry, onto which a creative colleague had photoshopped a Santa hat. Not to mention writing 'POLICE' along the hull of the ship, so that it looked like a police car. But on water. And giant. Great.

Usually, each department organized its own Christmas festivities, but Julia's team was so small that it got invited to join a few other groups that had merged their own parties. The picture was enough to make Mina hyperventilate. The ferries plying the Baltic waters to Finland might be spick and span these days, but in her head boats like that were an orgy of sticky carpets marinated in decades of beer spillages, with air that was reused by thousands of people on each sailing, and claustrophobic cabins with beds that had been used by far too many people and that would be best sanitized using a sandblaster.

In short, they were teeming with bacteria. So many that she could practically see them with the naked eye in the picture. She was tempted to apply some hand sanitizer to the monitor.

She also knew that several departments had gone on a similar cruise a few years ago. Luckily, Mina hadn't been invited since she hadn't worked for the same department back then, but the stories of that outing lived on at police headquarters. Ruben could barely mention it without getting a greedy look in his eyes. Julia, meanwhile, always fidgeted awkwardly.

Mina really didn't want to know – and she really didn't want to go.

She checked the date. 'See you on December 19th!' was emblazoned across the picture in festive, snow-capped red lettering. Today was the 19th. She was due to check in in three hours' time. She still hadn't thought of an acceptable reason to decline, especially not since Julia had emphasized how important it was to their cohesion that the whole team went along.

But she just couldn't.

Surely there was something in the Jon Langseth case she needed to prioritize? Something that Julia would accept as a good reason for not going? Mina could hardly use Nathalie as an excuse – her daughter was sixteen and quite capable of looking after herself.

Mina minimized the email and its abominable boat and instead opened the report on Jon. She read it carefully. She had two hours and forty-five minutes to find something.

When she reached Adam's notes from the interview with Peter Kronlund, the CEO of Confido, she started. Peter had said that Jon underwent a personality change shortly before his disappearance. She recalled Jon's wife Josephine saying the same thing. Just like Josephine, Peter had taken this to be the media storm taking its toll. It was a reasonable interpretation. No one could keep their spirits up when they had investigative journalists on their heels day and night, regardless of whether they were innocent or not.

But Josephine hadn't said anything about Jon talking a lot about the press coverage at home. If the press was wearing him down like that, then surely he would have mentioned it to his nearest and dearest? What if it was something else entirely?

It wasn't beyond the realms of doubt. Jon's personality transformation might be for a completely different reason. For example, he might already have known that something was going to happen to him. Maybe that was why he had been on his guard and nervous. But if that were the case, then why hadn't he said anything to anyone? Or called the police? He must have feared for his life.

What had Jon known?

That question was exactly the pretext she needed.

She glanced back at the invitation. Check-in at 3 p.m. She pulled out her phone and composed a text message to Vincent. Finally they had the perfect reason to meet up. It was about work. She needed to talk to him about Jon's change of behaviour – in around two and a half hours' time.

24

He held Dad's hand as tightly as he could, but each time they reached a promising looking bin, he had to let go and help to go through its contents, carefully hunting for hidden treasures. People threw a surprising amount of stuff away. He didn't understand why anyone would buy a hamburger and only eat half. Or why a tasty cheese and ham sandwich would be tossed away after just a couple of bites. Topside people were weird.

Sometimes faint memories of their own life topside would intrude – usually when he was in that borderland between sleep and wakefulness. The memories were fuzzy and hard to capture. Not that he wanted to. They just hurt. Especially the ones in which he could smell Mum's scent. That floral scent that had been hers, and which was intimately linked to the feeling of being enveloped in her embrace, with the soft fabric of her blouse against his cheek.

But he'd been so little then. He didn't know whether they were real memories or just fantasies concocted afterwards, after hearing all of Dad's stories about her. What he did remember clearly, however, was when he and Dad came home and she was gone. He and Dad had been gone for a few days. Dad had gone on one of his 'outings', as Mum called them, and had taken him along.

When they'd left, Mum had been alive. Angry, but alive. She didn't like Dad's outings, and she liked it even less when Dad took him along. He loved it when he got to go. They would usually stay in the forest. And while he was afraid of the dark, he wasn't even scared at night in the forest since Dad was there with him.

He shook himself so he would stop thinking about things he didn't want to think about.

Dad had crossed the street to a bin in the middle of the big square at Odenplan. It was Dad's favourite place topside, since the bins there were often filled with goodies.

Dad waved to him impatiently and he looked around before scurrying across the street. When he reached him, Dad offered him something. His favourite chocolate. One square left. A rare find. Chocolate wrappers were usually empty. Then Dad triumphantly held up the carrier bag to show him its contents. Lots of food. Mostly pieces of sandwiches. That would be enough to last a couple of days. A couple of days when they wouldn't have to come back up here again.

He took Dad's hand as they walked back towards the metro. He saw all the looks they got from the people hurrying past them, but it didn't matter. They didn't understand. They didn't know. His dad was a king. He proudly held Dad's hand even more tightly. Soon they would be back in his kingdom.

25

'How did you find this place?' Vincent said, looking around.

Mina did the same. The joint was coldly lit and there wasn't a Christmas decoration in sight. Perfect.

'I googled it,' she said. 'My search for "restaurant without Christmas Stockholm" turned up a few thousand hits. Apparently I'm not the only one who's allergic to tinsel.'

The small restaurant in the Vasastan district was indeed full. Admittedly there was some sort of Christmas special being offered on their lunch menu, but it was couched in terms such as crossover, alternative and Asian, so Mina was confident it wouldn't contain any greasy sausages or spongy meatballs. Vincent looked a little crestfallen.

'I mean, I like Christmas,' he said. 'The clichéd version with too much of everything. And thanks for getting in touch. I'd been meaning to contact you so many times, but …'

A stressed waiter appeared with a bundle of menus tucked under his arm.

'Do you have a booking?' he said. 'Otherwise I'm sorry but we're full up.'

'Don't be,' Vincent said, smiling warmly. 'Be *happy* that it's going so well for you.'

This garnered an uncertain smile in response.

The waiter was clearly more accustomed to patrons being upset when they were informed there was no room at the inn. Mina noticed the way Vincent gently touched the man's upper arm when he said 'happy'.

'Like that,' Vincent said, touching the man's arm again. 'You'd do anything for that happy feeling, wouldn't you?'

The waiter was now smiling broadly and nodding.

'Notice how *good* that feels,' Vincent said. 'A *good* table for two?'

'Good … I'm sure we can arrange that,' the waiter said, his eyes somewhat unfocused. 'I've got a couple in the corner who are about to leave. I'll see if I can hurry them. Follow me.'

The waiter led them through the restaurant, retrieving a credit card machine which he took to the corner table to process the payment of the couple there.

The pair got up and glanced suspiciously at Mina and Vincent as they pushed past them with their coats over their arms. The waiter placed two menus on the table before discreetly absenting himself.

'You're outrageous,' Mina said in a low voice as she watched the waiter moving away.

'Why? We got a table, and he's happy,' Vincent said innocently.

Mina smiled and sat down on the chair with its back to the wall. Vincent took the seat opposite and moved it to the side of the table before sitting down.

'I don't like it when people sit opposite each other,' he said in response to her questioning look. 'It feels so confrontational. So formal. And with a physical barrier in the shape of the table removing half the visible body language it makes it so unnecessarily difficult to communicate. Sitting like this, perpendicular to each other, makes for much better conversation. Do you feel the difference?'

He was right. Mina could definitely feel the difference. Above all, she could feel how close he was and how she could no longer hide anything. She thought about whether to explain the major advantage of physical barriers – well, all types of barriers, really – between people, but she wasn't sure she *wanted* him to move.

'By the way, thanks for the dramatic text,' he said, holding up his mobile where Mina's message glowed on the display.

[display text]*We need to talk. Can you meet right away?*[/display text]

'Maria seems to have taken it well,' Mina said, pointing to the small Post-it stuck onto the phone with a handwritten question on it that she assumed had been authored by Vincent's wife: *Have you got her pregnant?*

She had to stifle a laugh when she saw how embarrassed Vincent was.

'So, Christmas huh?' she said, clearing her throat. 'You like it then? Isn't it all a bit too chaotic for you?'

'Well, it *was*,' the mentalist said.

He frowned, removed the Post-it and scrunched it up before putting it and his phone away.

'I used not to like it. Because of what you say – it was chaos. I'd stress out like a madman ahead of the big day to get everything ready, and then I'd spend two days in the midst of anxiety-laden family anarchy and then it would all be over. It always gave me a stomach-ache and the feeling that I was somehow missing the point of the whole thing.'

Someone cleared their throat beside them.

'Two Christmas lunches, is it?' a waitress asked.

Vincent looked enquiringly at Mina and she nodded. The waitress disappeared just as quickly as she had arrived.

'Then what happened?' Mina said.

'Well, I started celebrating Christmas at the end of September instead,' Vincent said. 'Don't look like that – it's a completely rational decision. It gives me plenty of time to enjoy the Christmas spirit on my own terms, so that when things get properly started in early December it doesn't hit me the same way. I'm already way ahead. Christmas Eve for me is a lovely end to a longer period of time instead of the whole package being confined to a single day.'

He paused as a troubled look crossed his face.

'Of course, my family think I'm an idiot for wearing my Christmas socks in October,' he said. 'But what's new about that? Them thinking I'm an idiot, I mean.'

She stared at him. She bit her lip and tried to maintain eye contact to stop herself from ducking under the table to inspect Vincent's socks, but she couldn't help herself. A quick glance at Vincent's feet revealed bright shades of red and green at his ankles.

When she looked up again, he still looked concerned, but then he pulled himself together and went back to looking like his usual self.

'What's up?' she said. 'You don't seem quite yourself today.'

He shook his head. A little too fervently, she thought.

'No, I was just thinking about my family,' he said. 'And what a nuisance I must be to them.'

A worried wrinkle returned, then disappeared again. There was quite obviously something he wasn't telling her.

'But if you don't like Christmas …' he said hesitantly, putting his hand into the pocket of his coat, which was hanging over the back of his chair. 'I've brought you a Christmas present. Was that a stupid thing to do?'

He pulled out a parcel wrapped in robust brown paper and thick, coarse black string tied into a bow. A warmth erupted in her breast and spread throughout her body.

'You can't open it until Christmas Eve,' he said, handing it over.

'Not a chance,' she said, grinning as she began to tug at the string. 'Then I won't be able to hold you personally accountable.'

Inside the parcel there was a box, and inside that there was a soft grey lump. Clay. Fortunately it was wrapped in cling film so she didn't have to touch it with her hands. She shivered. But she didn't understand. Why clay …? She looked at Vincent, who looked back at her with a smile.

'I'm giving you pottery classes,' he said innocently.

Pottery. Sticky clay, water everywhere, stains on her clothing. Surrounded by a bunch of artsy hippies.

'Do you even know me at all?' she said. 'Isn't your thing about reading people and their minds? You of all people ought to be able to get me the perfect gift. This is basically … the opposite.'

She weighed the cling-filmed lump in her hand, trying to determine whether it would do any serious damage if she threw it at Vincent's head. It was doubtful.

'Don't be like that,' he said. 'The clay in your hand is completely bacteria-free. And you like water. You told me that. As you so deftly put it, my whole schtick is reading people. And what I've read in you is that you need to push your limits. I think you'll be pleasantly surprised. Confront your demons!'

'I think you'll meet a demon unlike any you've seen before if you don't take back …'

A throat was cleared. Mina hadn't noticed the arrival of two plates at the table. The waitress was back.

'Would you like anything other than water to drink?' she said.

'Something with arsenic for him,' Mina said, without taking her eyes off Vincent.

'What if I go with you?' the mentalist said. 'I've already drunk poison for you once. Well, for your daughter. I'd much rather throw clay than do that again.'

The waitress seemed to realize she wouldn't get a better answer than that and made herself scarce.

'By the way, was there any particular reason you wanted to meet up?' Vincent said. 'Apart from getting your Christmas present?'

'We're not done talking about the clay,' Mina said. 'Just so you know. But yes. We've had a rather odd case come across our desks. Skeletal remains were found in a metro tunnel the day before yesterday. Human remains.'

'Gosh,' Vincent said, curiously prodding his food with two metal chopsticks before managing to pincer a dumpling. 'Although surely that's not so unusual? I mean people have been buried more or less all over this town over the centuries. You can barely put a shovel in the ground on Riddarholmen without hitting the bones of people buried there in the fourteenth century and onwards. Of course, it's been two hundred years since the cemetery disappeared, but the skeletons don't leave by themselves. Not to mention the channel between Riddarholmen and the old town, which is nothing less than a mass grave for all the mariners, criminals and pagans who weren't allowed to be laid to rest in consecrated ground.'

'These bones are much more recent,' Mina interrupted. 'And we know whose they are. A financier who went missing four months ago.'

Vincent frowned.

'And you found his skeleton?' he said. 'Is decomposition really that fast?'

Mina pulled out a shrink-wrapped straw from her jacket pocket and put it into the water glass. Despite the morbid topic of conversation, she could smell the heavenly aromas from her plate, none of which reminded her of Christmas. Perfection. She picked up her chopsticks, applied some sanitizer to a napkin and wiped them down before spearing a piece of broccoli tempura. It tasted delicious.

'No, that's a fair point,' she said, after swallowing. 'And this is not a case of standard decomposition. The bones were separated from the flesh and tissue with almost clinical precision. And then they were left in a neat pile.'

Vincent put his chopsticks down on the edge of his plate with a clatter.

'*Mos Teutonicus*?' he said.

'Moss what?'

'*Mos Teutonicus*. It was a form of VIP treatment for high-status individuals when they died far from home. Royalty, nobility, clergy.'

'Nobility?' she said.

It suddenly felt as if she was back in middle school.

Vincent nodded enthusiastically.

'We're talking the High Middle Ages. The 1200s and 1300s,' he said. 'Although the custom may have its roots as far back as the tenth century. If it was impractical to transport the whole body home – say a bigwig died abroad – then they used *Mos Teutonicus*. It loosely translates as "the German custom", and it involved boiling the body in water and wine or vinegar to remove the flesh from the skeleton. That allows them to transport the bones alone for burial on home turf. In the end the Pope put a stop to it. Christianity regards the body as sacred and it can't be destroyed. Apparently they thought it was better to let it rot in a warm carriage for a few weeks.'

Mina looked down at her plate. There were two pieces of sushi on one side. The raw fish on the bed of white rice was a little too reminiscent of raw flesh on bone. She pushed the plate aside.

'But do you think that's what might have happened here?' Vincent said. 'That the bones were part of some kind of VIP burial? You did say it was a prominent financier.'

'That sounds completely deranged,' she said. 'And about a thousand years too late, according to you.'

'Not quite a thousand years, but I know what you mean,' Vincent said, looking pensive. 'What about the logistical explanation? That someone needed to move the body post-mortem and wanted to make things easy for themselves? So they boiled it?'

She shook her head sceptically. The positioning of Jon Langseth's bones had been far too deliberate. Someone was supposed to find them. The only question was why. Before she had time to answer, her phone buzzed on the table. It was a text message from Julia sent to the whole team.

'Sorry, but I've got to check this,' she said, opening the message while Vincent made short work of the food on his plate.

> I know many of you have been looking forward to the Christmas cruise this afternoon but I'm afraid we have to prioritize the Langseth case. Adam and I will be holding a press conference at 14:00 to prevent the spread of any further rumours. After that we'll meet in the conference room. I promise we'll make up for the missed cruise. /Julia

Vincent was looking at her with an almost amused expression when she had finished reading.

'Have you won money on a scratch card or something?' he said.

She realized that she was grinning and that her shoulders had dropped at least a couple of inches.

'Pretty much.'

'Well, congratulations then – you know what the odds of that are, don't you? Your chances of winning ten thousand kronor are one in thirty-two thousand, and since it costs thirty kronor to buy a scratch card you might have to spend a cool one million kronor to win your ten thousand. But it seems that people don't get that, given that they sell in the region of one hundred and thirty million of the things each year in this country.'

'Vincent,' she said. 'Langseth. Bones. Boiled. Rewind.'

She snapped her fingers in front of the mentalist.

'You mentioned *Mos Teutonicus*,' she said. 'But why would someone treat a missing financier like a medieval king?'

For a moment, Vincent looked utterly bewildered. Then he regained his senses.

'Sorry. Er … OK. Perhaps he had a big ego?'

'That's exactly what I wanted to ask you about. That's why I texted. It's about his ego – well, his behaviour just before he disappeared. The people closest to him say he changed in those final weeks.'

'Hmm. It's easy to think you know the reason for a change in behaviour with the benefit of hindsight,' Vincent said thoughtfully. 'When you think you already know what happened. That knowledge changes the memory of what you saw. There's a well-known study from 1974 by Elizabeth Loftus and John Palmer in which people watched a film showing cars driving into each other, and then they were asked questions about what they had seen. But the questions contained different verbs. The subjects who had to say how fast the cars had been going when they *crashed* also recalled that there had been shards of glass on the ground afterwards. Meanwhile, the subjects who were asked to talk about the cars that had *struck* one another didn't see the broken glass. Different words used to describe the same incident affected the participants' tangible memories of it. For the record, there's no broken glass in the film.'

'What is it you're trying to say?'

'I would need to read exactly what the people around Jon experienced before I'd venture an opinion on what it might mean, and whether it's all just interpretations that have occurred since he went missing.'

Vincent made eye contact with the waiter at a table further away and signalled that he wanted to pay. Mina had long ago given up on any sense of equality in these matters. If he wanted to pay so badly each time they met then she would let him.

The waiter beamed when he saw Vincent and hurried over with the credit card machine. Vincent thanked him for the delicious food and gently touched the waiter's arm again – the man's smile became even wider, if that were possible.

'I was thinking about the bones,' Vincent said as he tapped his phone against the card reader. 'I assume they're still in Milda's custody. Do you think … Could I take a look?'

'I thought we'd make that our next stop. You can always tell Maria we're getting an ultrasound.'

26

Ruben was in the World of Toys in the Gallerian shopping mall and could feel the anxiety descending upon him. The plan had been to spend his lunch break buying Astrid Christmas presents. He'd been slow off the mark, leaving it until five days before Christmas Eve, but the crowds inside the toy shop revealed that he was not the only bad planner.

The other customers were moving among the shelves with almost remote-controlled purposefulness. He, on the other hand, had no idea how this worked. What did a ten-year-old girl want? Did she even play with toys any longer? Clothing was an even riskier option, so that was off the cards. Anyway, he'd already bought her a new martial arts suit.

Maybe she'd like new pencils to draw with. She liked painting. Or would she prefer brushes and oil paints like her mum used? Were colouring pencils childish?

He'd been seeing Astrid once a week for almost six months, but when faced with the shelves of board games, Lego and dolls, he felt as if he didn't know anything about her. He couldn't do this. The shelf of stuffed animals, however, gave him an idea. She liked the police dogs – that much he knew. She loved visiting them. But Ellinor would probably murder him if he gave their daughter a real-life Alsatian pup.

Bloody hell.

He mopped the sweat from his brow and fled the toy shop. He wasn't looking where he was going and bumped into a woman passing by in a thick quilted jacket.

'Sorry!' he said quickly.

'Oops,' she said with a laugh.

It was a familiar laugh.

'Sara?'

He hadn't seen Sara from NOA's analysis department since the summer when they'd worked together on the child abductions and she had told him that her husband had just left her and the kids. But he remembered having appreciated her company. And then she had disappeared. He assumed she'd changed jobs or moved back stateside. Instead, here she was, with snow in her dark hair and a twinkle in her eye.

'Hey Ruben,' she said, peering over his shoulder into the toy shop. 'Christmas present hunting for one of your hook-ups? I know they're young, but *that* young …?'

For one of his … He stared at her, gaping, unsure what to say. He ought to be angry. Surely his private life was none of her business? However, to his surprise he felt himself blushing instead.

'Christmas present hunting, yes. But not … It's for my daughter. But how …' He cleared his throat. 'Perhaps you can give me a few hints about what ten-year-old girls want?'

Sara smiled at him without saying a word. The twinkle was still there. He immediately felt uncertain. He didn't like being scrutinized like this. None of the young girls he took home ever looked at him like that – that was what was so good about them. They mostly saw his uniform and sometimes his handcuffs, if they were in the mood. No strings.

'I'm freezing,' she said. 'It's bloody freezing out here. Why don't you buy me a hot chocolate and I'll tell you about what ten-year-old girls like? Although only on the condition that it's got marshmallows in it.'

Although it was wrapped up in a thick coat, Ruben surveyed Sara's figure on reflex. The coat revealed nothing, but he seemed to recall Sara was a curvaceous woman. The ones he liked to bring home for the night were often stick thin and wouldn't even dare to be in the same room as a marshmallow lest they ruin their figure. He liked that Sara didn't seem bothered by that kind of thing.

'This way, young lady,' he said, gesturing with his arm.

He wanted marshmallows too, although he couldn't help but suck in his stomach as Sara walked past him.

They had to plough their way through a sea of panicked

shoppers until they found two empty seats in a café. Ruben bought two cinnamon and orange hot chocolates for them – it was Christmas, after all. With extra marshmallows.

'I haven't seen you for a while,' he said, once he'd set down the steaming mugs on the table and sat down opposite her.

She had taken off her coat and he couldn't stop his gaze from being drawn to her neckline. All the right shapes were undeniably in the right places.

'How are things?' he said, forcing himself to look her in the eye.

'There's a lot going on right now,' she said, blowing on her hot chocolate. 'The latest is that we've got a lead on what might be suspected terrorist activity. Some agricultural companies have reported the theft of ammonium nitrate.'

'Ammonium?'

'It's used to make fertilizer. But you can also blow it up – if you're really determined. We're looking into whether anyone else has lost similar chemicals that might be used as explosives precursors. At worst, someone is building a home-made bomb. It happens every now and then. They usually fail. Of course, the thefts might be pure coincidence. But we still have to look into it. We're also – well, I'm not really allowed to say this, but I know I can trust you …'

Sara looked around and leaned forward.

'Ted Hansson,' she whispered.

'The Sweden's Future party leader?' Ruben said in a low voice, and Sara nodded. 'What's up with him?'

'He's mixed up in some bad shit. Obviously we keep tabs on various politicians when we have to. For example, the Security Service has asked us to keep an eye on any threats to the minister of justice. But Ted Hansson seems to have plenty of his own skeletons in the closet. So far we're just keeping an eye on him, but like I said: it's a lot.'

Ruben nodded. He was silent for a few seconds. Then he plucked up his courage and asked the question that had been running through his head for the last few minutes.

'To change the subject completely – what do you know about my … extracurricular activities?'

In years gone by he would gladly have told anyone who would listen about his debauchery. Indeed, he would have told people who didn't want to listen, too. Then he'd started therapy with Amanda and realized that he didn't have to live like that any longer. But then Peder had died, and that had changed everything. When Ruben had started going out looking to pick up girls again, he'd been careful not to make a thing of it with his colleagues – both because he was ashamed and because Peder wouldn't have liked it. So how come Sara knew?

'My daughter has this young supply teacher,' she said with a wry smile. 'When she heard where I worked, she started telling me about the Silver Fox Cop, which is what she and her friends had christened this bloke they would encounter on nights out …'

Ruben buried his face in his hands.

'Well, they're all around twenty-five,' Sara said. 'I think.'

'The Silver Fox Cop,' Ruben groaned. 'I'm not that old.'

'Is that what it's about?' she said. 'That you feel old?'

He looked at her. Some things were best kept to oneself. Some things he didn't even discuss with Amanda. But Sara's gaze didn't allow him to say anything but the truth.

'I don't want to die,' he said quietly.

'Who does?' she said, leaning forward and patting his hand. 'Fortunately you've extended your line by another generation: your daughter. Why don't we talk about her Christmas presents now?'

Sara's hand was still on top of his. It was warm from the mug – warm and alive.

'She's into martial arts,' he said. 'So my backup plan was to buy her a Bruce Lee poster. But they don't seem to do those any longer. All I can find are posters of pop groups I've never heard of. I think one was called Blackpink, and there was another starting with B … I've no idea what she likes. What the hell is K-pop, come to that?'

Sara laughed. Then she sipped her hot chocolate. It left a thin stripe along her upper lip. A marshmallow tumbled onto the table.

'Bruce Lee? There's hope for you yet, Silver Fox Cop,' she said.

27

Julia was patiently waiting for everyone to fall silent. Her team could act like children sometimes, but they were a marvel of conscientiousness compared with the journalists and photographers she was currently facing. They had started shouting questions before the press conference had even begun.

Adam was standing next to her in case he was needed, and he was visibly annoyed. More than once, Julia had been obliged to put a hand on his arm to prevent him from telling off the assembled media. Of course, it was quite possible she had touched him more frequently than the situation merited, but she didn't think anyone had noticed.

As expected, the room was filled with the usual suspects from the broadsheets and tabloids, the news agencies, and TV and radio. Julia recognized correspondents from *Aftonbladet*, *Expressen*, *Dagens Nyheter* and *Svenska Dagbladet*, as well as TV4, SVT and TT. But given the palaver around Confido, Jon Langseth's name had also lured in reporters from newspapers such as *Dagens Industri* and *Resumé*. Julia saw no reason to exclude them. It was as well they heard what she had to say in person rather than through the rumour mill. Julia guessed that it was the *Resumé* correspondent who was standing by the coffee table at the far end of the room gesticulating wildly. Despite the distance, she could clearly hear him asking a security guard whether he could get him a latte. Julia shook her head.

'Order,' she said, waiting until everyone was looking at her and Adam. 'I'll keep this brief.'

The gesticulating reporter slipped discontentedly into the back row clutching a cup of filter coffee.

'Jon Langseth, whom you all know as one of Confido's founders, has been found dead,' Julia said. 'Given the circumstances in which he was found, we're unable to disclose any further details at this stage.'

There was a murmur from the journalists.

'Can we assume it was suicide?' shouted a hack from *Svenska Dagbladet*. 'Presumably he didn't die of natural causes, given the controversies around the company?'

'The circumstances around Jon Langseth's death are such that we're unable to determine whether his death was by natural causes or not,' said Julia. 'And I'm not being deliberately vague here. We really don't know yet. It could have been a heart attack. The autopsy is … complicated.'

The murmur developed into a louder buzz.

'We can't rule out foul play for precisely the reason you've given,' Adam said, turning towards the journalist from *Svenska Dagbladet*. 'But the manner in which he was found doesn't align with suicide, or acts of revenge carried out by organized crime that we've seen in the past. We'll naturally be investigating all applicable theories as to what may have happened.'

'What kind of circumstances are we talking about?' shouted the reporter from *Resumé*. 'Why exactly did you invite us here? You must be able to give us something else.'

Julia glanced at Adam and he nodded. They'd been given the go-ahead by Jon's wife to announce it. It might lead to something but would also guarantee front-page headlines. They had to be sure it was worth it, and in her view it was.

'We've found Jon Langseth's skeleton,' she said. 'That's all we've got. We know it's him. And we know that the skeleton has been cleaned thoroughly and professionally. But we have no cause of death and we don't have any motive for the cleaning of the skeletal remains. Obviously we realize this is catnip for you all – that's why we've invited you here. You'll probably hear rumours about where we found the skeleton. If you publish those rumours, members of the public will be drawn to the site out of curiosity. That in turn might lead to accidents. I would therefore ask that you refrain from publishing any such details. If any of you mention where Jon Langseth was allegedly found, you'll be charged with wilfully endangering the life of another. Is that understood?'

She fixed her gaze on the journalists, who all nodded gravely at her, but the man from *Resumé* was smiling wryly as he tapped away furiously on his phone. Julia sighed. She didn't even dare contemplate what the headlines would be in the morning.

28

Milda had laid out the skeleton on a table by the wall. The bones were positioned with her usual precision, and Mina once again admired Milda's mastery of her craft. Jon Langseth lay there in all his glory – apart from the fact that he didn't have any flesh or skin. But the bones had their own story to tell.

Mina and Vincent had gone straight to Milda's after lunch. As usual, Vincent gave the impression that the National Board of Forensic Medicine was not his favourite place on earth. But Mina thought there was something beautiful about the bare bones set against the sterile, gleaming metal around them. The objects lying on the table were – or had been – a human being. But all the gooey bits, the insalubrious and infectious bits of humans, were gone. Leaving behind just purity. Simplicity. Reflected perfectly in the metal the bones were lying on – without so much as a grease mark.

'All two hundred and six bones are there,' Milda said, nodding towards the skeleton. 'Whoever cleaned him up is a very careful and meticulous person. With anatomical knowledge to boot.'

Milda passed disposable gloves to Mina and Vincent, who donned them.

'I had a theory that he was boiled, but I don't know for sure that's what happened,' Vincent said, bending over the bones.

'What do you mean?' said Milda.

'I gather that museums use terrariums filled with beetles to remove the flesh remains from animal carcasses. They often have a purpose-built room or building for it – a dermestarium. Anyway. Apparently the beetles, or mostly the larvae, are incredibly thorough when it comes to cleansing bones, and much more gentle in the preservation of brittle bones than other processes. In fact, they're so good at it that they can pose problems when there are animals that the museums actually want to keep. That could be what's happened here.'

'What about a combination?' said a cautious voice behind them. 'To expedite the process.'

Mina hadn't even heard Loke enter the room. Milda's assistant was, as ever, practically invisible, even when he was there. But according to Milda he was the best she'd ever had. He was presumably also the only one she'd managed to get to sing along to her beloved Schlager music while they worked.

Loke smelled faintly of smoke. So that was why he hadn't been there from the very beginning – he'd been on a smoke break. Mina thought the smell sullied the purity she had just experienced, but it wasn't her place to comment on that. Working in this place probably required everyone to have their own emotional outlet of one kind or another. Milda had her music. Loke had his cigarettes.

'Boiled first, then maybe the beetles finished off the job?' Loke said. 'By the way, the museums don't use regular beetles, they use so-called skin beetles. *Dermestidae* in Latin.'

Vincent groaned and looked like he wanted to slap his own forehead.

'Hence dermestarium,' he said. 'Of course. Thank you!'

Loke smiled broadly and nodded.

'Speaking of processing the body after death,' Vincent said. 'I assume in your line of work that you've heard of human composting? Where you put the body in a container along with something like wood chips, straw and fungi, and leave nature to take its course so that the body is broken down into pure soil? You get just shy of a cubic metre of soil out of a human being, plus the composting material.'

Milda nodded.

'Yes, it's a smart approach,' she said. 'It's already been legalized here and in the UK. And it's springing up in various parts of the USA.'

'There's actually an American company who've taken it a step further,' Loke said enthusiastically. 'They plant a young tree chosen by the immediate family on top of the composting body. The tree absorbs the nutrients and molecules from the body and as it grows, it contains more and more of your dearly departed loved one. In the end, you can pretty much accurately say that the tree is your grandmother.'

'How poetic,' Vincent said.

Mina stared at him. Was he out of his mind?

'The only problem is the skeleton, which is left over,' Milda said. 'No one ever really mentions what happens to the bones afterwards.'

'Speaking of bones, perhaps we could redirect our attention back to the present and Jon Langseth,' Mina said drily. 'Have you been able to determine any cause of death?'

Milda shook her head.

'It's effectively impossible. Let's say that he really was murdered. A bullet might create a recognizable fracture to something like a rib. The same goes for scratches from a knife wound. I would have seen that. Here, for example.'

She pointed at the loose pieces of skeleton, indicating the ribs.

'At the same time, a bullet or a knife might have completely missed the skeleton but still caused fatal damage. Not to mention suffocation and other causes of death that only affect the soft tissue. Finally, he might have died of completely natural causes that I can't see either. Stroke. Heart attack. Cerebral haemorrhage. There's just no way of knowing.'

'He might have been boiled alive,' Loke muttered.

'Thank you very much for that picture,' Mina said.

For a brief moment, she had an image of Jon Langseth naked inside a large cauldron, as if it were some kind of racist cartoon about cannibals. There was nothing funny about that picture.

'The metro tunnel part of it is what surprises me,' Vincent said, inspecting the bones. 'All sorts of myths abound about which tunnels remain underneath this city. Some of the stories are true, although construction of the City Line and the new interchange at Slussen has destroyed some of them. But the old post office telephone cable tunnels are still to be found in plenty of places. Of course, it's much harder to go down into them now that the regular locks have been changed for keypads.'

'I'm not even going to ask how you know that they've changed the locks,' Mina said. 'What are you getting at?'

'Well, the metro is a pretty dangerous place to be. There are other tunnels that are much safer. If someone wanted to bury Langseth underground then why not do it in one of those safer tunnels?'

Mina nodded to Milda to indicate they were done and that the skeleton on the table could tell them nothing more. Milda left them and went over to the table in the centre of the room. Lying on it was yet another body whose cause of death was yet to be determined. This time, however, it was easy – even for Mina. It was a teenager in his late teens with several bullet wounds to the chest. She didn't need to see the tattoo to know that it was probably gang-related. She couldn't fathom how Milda coped.

'Unless, of course, the plan was for him to be found,' Loke said, tearing her away from her own thoughts.

'I was thinking the same thing,' she said, looking at him. 'Work crews regularly move around in the metro tunnels. Had he been in any other tunnel, it could have been years before he was found. Or he might have been gone for good. In this case, it was only a matter of time before someone found the bones. And we don't actually know whether he was killed. We only know how he was positioned post-mortem.'

Loke tapped the outside of his pocket and then disappeared through a door. Apparently he was off for another smoke break. Vincent, however, was still examining the bones.

'A VIP burial,' he said, stroking his chin thoughtfully. 'Underground.'

'So what does it mean?' she said.

Vincent paused before answering.

'It means there's more to this than we understand,' he said finally. 'Now I'm even more curious about this change of behaviour you mentioned.'

'I think it's time you met the team again. Julia's called a meeting for this afternoon.'

Vincent beamed like the sun.

'It's been too long,' he said.

'I'm not sure that everyone else agrees with you,' she said, laughing.

Mina nodded in parting farewell to Milda as they left. Loke still hadn't returned, but if his next job was to assist Milda with the boy on the table, she could understand why.

29

'Since when do you meddle in my work?'

Julia felt the anger rising within her in a way that was hardly healthy. Few people made her as angry as her father. In her more lucid moments, she was aware it was probably because she was made in his image. On the desk there was a gilded name plate with *Egil Hammarsten* on it in clear I-Mean-Business letters. She didn't think anyone used signs like that any longer. But her father was old school.

Julia hadn't taken Torkel's name when they had married. In retrospect, she realized this might have been a mistake, because if she had done then the connection between her and the Stockholm police commissioner would not have been as obvious. But if she had taken Torkel's name she would have been forced to add a name change to the list of all the other things that needed sorting out, if she did end up leaving him.

'Please don't see it as me meddling,' her father said. 'Policing is teamwork. A little bird told me that the National Operations Department are currently engaged in a survey of organized crime. Among others, they're looking at the Serbian mafia.'

'The Serbian mafia? You mean the ones led by that psycho Dragan Manojlovic?' Julia said. 'What's he got to do with this?'

'Perhaps nothing. Perhaps everything. And as I said, strictly speaking I haven't heard any of this. But it would be a breach of my duties not to point you in the right direction.'

'The right direction?' she snapped. 'Our investigation has only just begun and you think you can just barge in and tell us what the right direction is?'

Julia heard her own voice rising to a falsetto. She was bright enough to realize that her agitated emotions were not just linked to him, but also her feelings about family in general.

Both Torkel and her father made her feel as if she had her back against the wall.

'Julia, this is in no way a criticism of your conduct,' her father said calmly. 'I can honestly say that I have heard many good things about you, especially since last summer, and you did splendidly at the press conference. *Entre nous*, I wouldn't be surprised if you ended up sitting on this side of the desk one day. After I retire, of course.'

Involuntarily she was flattered and felt her cheeks beginning to cool down slightly.

'OK, I'm obviously happy to receive any information that may assist our investigation, formal and informal alike,' she said in a calmer voice. 'But I just think it's too early to ...'

'What do you know about Gustaf Brons?' her father interrupted.

'Er ... he's one of Confido's founders, along with Jon Langseth and Peter Kronlund. Nothing special about his background apart from the obvious: he's as much of a scumbag as the others. Why do you ask?'

'Because NOA's information – of which I am of course unaware – is that Gustaf has been receiving payments from Dragan Manojlovic. From the mob. And that we're talking about more than loose change.'

Julia stared at her father, who sighed.

'Even you have to agree that it's highly suspicious,' he said. 'One of Confido's co-owners goes missing and is found dead, while another has been in receipt of large sums of money from one of the foremost criminal gangs in Sweden.'

'I don't know,' she said, thinking. 'It doesn't have to be connected. Although obviously we have to leave no stone unturned.'

'Good. Then we agree that you'll bring in Gustaf Brons for questioning. My many years of policing tell me we've solved the case of Jon Langseth's death. This was a contract killing with Brons's name all over it. Don't forget that the simplest solutions are often the right ones.'

'Just a second, we're not ready to ...'

'Julia, there are times in life when you just have to do as you're told. This is one of those occasions.'

Julia opened her mouth. Then she closed it again. The heat in her cheeks returned and she knew there would be big, flame-red patches on her face and at her throat. Her father had an almost magical ability to make them flare up.

'Sure thing, boss,' she said through gritted teeth. 'Sure thing.'

'And don't forget we're expecting you at one o'clock on Christmas Eve,' her father called out cheerfully as she left his office.

She didn't reply.

30

Mina was struck by the change since she had introduced Vincent to the team for the first time almost three years earlier. On that occasion, everyone's faces had been pictures of suspicion and scepticism. Now there was nothing but happy smiles.

'Vincent – great to see you! It's been ages!'

Julia gave Vincent a lingering embrace, and to her surprise Mina felt a pang of jealousy. She grimly tugged her sleeves down and contemplated her hands, which were raw from being washed. Her trimmed-back fingernails and cuticles had been dried out by the hand sanitizer. Julia always looked effortlessly groomed, as if she got out of bed every morning looking perfect and beautiful and with not a hair out of place.

Mina sighed and sat down at the conference table. Only Vincent could make her think such stupid things, but she didn't understand why. She just had such tremendous respect for his sharp mind and his knowledge of areas that fascinated her. She felt oddly relieved when Julia let go of Vincent so that he could take his seat next to her after greeting everyone else around the table.

She had to get it together. She cleared her throat to get everyone's attention. As she looked around, she spotted that the board at the end of the room had accumulated further material since the last briefing and was now almost half-full with notes, images and press cuttings about Jon Langseth.

'You may be wondering why I've brought in Vincent,' she said, finding herself confronted by a broad grin from Ruben.

'To do card tricks. I guarantee it. Or he's promised to conjure us a pay rise and more resources,' Ruben said.

'The latter is a trick that I don't even think someone with genuine magical abilities would be able to pull off,' Vincent said, receiving wry smiles and nods in reply.

Mina cleared her throat again, seeking to regain people's attention.

'I took Vincent to see Milda because he has a theory about the bones. Vincent, would you please elaborate? I'm afraid I can't remember half the terms you used.'

'Not a problem. What I told Mina when she contacted me about Jon Langseth and the peculiar placement of the bones was that my first association was with *Mos Teutonicus*.'

'*Gesundheit*,' Ruben said, which made Christer chuckle.

'Ruben,' Julia said, her gaze stern.

He rolled his eyes but fell silent.

'As I told Mina,' Vincent said, '*Mos Teutonicus* is an old custom from the High Middle Ages. When high-ranking individuals died a long way from home, they had to find a way to transport them back for burial. But it's not very practical or pleasant to store and transport a rotting corpse, so they came up with a method based on boiling the body to remove all the flesh from the skeleton. That way it was easier to transport the remains for a fitting burial at home. *Mos Teutonicus*.'

'Ew!' Christer said emphatically, looking somewhat nauseous.

'What did Milda make of it?' Julia said curiously. 'Did she think it was interesting? As a theory, I mean. That there might have been some kind of ... ritual like this at play?'

'She thought it was definitely worth taking a closer look at,' Mina said, nodding. 'Milda's assistant Loke also had an intriguing suggestion about it possibly being a combination – the perpetrator might have boiled the bones and then used beetle larvae to polish them into the state we found them in.'

'It was me who ...' Vincent said, but then he fell silent.

'Larvae,' Christer whimpered, his face taking on an increasingly green hue.

'What kind of beetles?' Adam said, leaning forward with his elbows propped on the table. 'Can you use any old kind of beetle for this, or do you need a particular species?'

'Someone's been watching too much *CSI*,' Ruben muttered, which was rewarded with another warning glance from Julia.

'No, no, that's a very relevant question,' Vincent said. 'It's most probably a family of insects known as skin beetles. Or *dermestidae* in Latin, as Loke pointed out.'

'Wait a second,' Ruben said, holding up a hand. 'You're seriously considering a theory that we're dealing with a murderer who first boils a body and then has a bunch of disgusting little beetles cleanse any remaining flesh from the bones. Have I got the right end of the stick?'

'Most definitely,' Vincent said, apparently without noting the sarcasm in Ruben's voice.

'I'm sorry, but am I the only one who thinks this sounds completely fucking crazy?' Ruben said, beginning to laugh. 'This is Stockholm – our low-lifes mostly do what low-lifes do. This isn't some dumb action movie with Tom Hanks running around Paris. Well, except that *The Da Vinci Code* is actually based on real facts, unlike the delusional fantasies …'

'Well,' Vincent said hesitantly, 'that's not actually true. *The Da Vinci Code* in its entirety is based on a falsification which was first set out in a different book, *The Holy Blood, and the Holy Grail*. That book in turn got its ideas from a man by the name of Plantard. In 1956, he founded an order that he called the Prieuré de Sion, which he claimed would preserve the history of a lineage descended from the children of Jesus Christ and Mary Magdalene, which would then make them the true heirs to the French throne. Plantard claimed to be part of this dynasty and asserted that he was thus the true king of France. When Plantard found a new collaborator with a lively imagination by the name of Philippe de Chérisey, they began to falsify documents to support their claims. These false documents were planted—'

'Vincent,' Mina said in a low voice, giving him a meaningful look.

He cut himself off mid-sentence and swallowed in embarrassment.

'Sorry. That was quite the exegesis. Again.'

'Damn it,' Ruben said sarcastically. 'That's my favourite film ruined too.'

'You mean your favourite book?' Vincent said.

Ruben gazed at him while shaking his head.

'Good God, Vincent. Try to keep up. It's a movie. It's not a bloody book.'

Vincent appeared to be fighting an inner battle, but then he changed tack and continued.

'It's not easy to get bones as clean as Jon Langseth's are. It requires human involvement of some kind, which makes this the most plausible scenario.'

'That still leaves us with the issue of motive unresolved,' Julia said. 'I've just met with the commissioner. He's convinced that Gustaf Brons – the third co-owner of Confido – is behind this, and that he may have murdered Jon. Apparently Gustaf has received a total of one million kronor from Dragan Manojlovic. I don't have to tell you who he is. The assumption is that this is payment for something. If we can find out what, then we might also find the motive behind killing Jon.'

Mina heard everyone in the room collectively inhale when they heard the name.

'This just took a turn for the worse,' Christer said.

'We'll be bringing in Brons for questioning, but since his lawyer has to be present we can't talk to him any sooner than tomorrow,' Julia said. 'I can't say that the idea it was a contract killing is implausible, but it doesn't explain the subsequent cleaning of Jon's skeleton.'

'Are those skin beetles you mentioned unusual?' Adam said. 'Are they hard to get hold of?'

'I don't know as yet,' Vincent said. 'But I thought I'd ask someone who knows. I know a good entomologist – that's an insect expert – who I'm sure can help us.'

'Good idea,' Julia said, reaching for a clementine from the bowl in the centre of the table. 'See whether you can find out more about those beetles. We won't have much else to go on until Gustaf Brons has been questioned.'

Mina could feel the colour draining from her face as she thought about the beetles. After jumping into a container filled with dead minks in Norrtälje and then crawling through the sewage pipe at John Wennhagen's farm, creepy-crawlies were at the top of a very long list of things that she intended to avoid in future.

'Of course,' Vincent said, glancing at Mina.

She stared back at him in horror.

'And just to make sure I've understood,' he said, turning to Julia, 'I assume that by "you", you mean me and Loke. The guy who actually knew which beetles they might be.'

Mina let out a sigh of relief so loud everyone in the room heard it.

'Er, that wasn't actually what … Never mind, good idea,' said Julia. 'I'll call Milda and see if she can spare him for a few hours. As soon as possible.'

The tart scent of citrus filled the room as Julia began to peel her clementine. It was a smell Mina loved. Her cleaning supplies at home had that same fresh, zesty scent. Julia pulled a segment free and as she chewed on it her face contorted into a grimace. It was obviously very sour.

'You might be interested to know that the clementine was named after a French priest, Marie-Clément Rodier, who crossed the Mediterranean mandarin and the orange,' Vincent said cheerfully. 'He—'

'Vincent,' Mina said, her tone one of warning.

Abashed, he fell silent.

Julia abandoned the rest of her clementine and stood up. 'Christer, you keep digging through the archives. Ruben, you keep going with Confido's bullshit. Sometimes the simplest solution is the right one.'

'Yes, Occam's razor,' Vincent said cheerily. 'It's—'

Mina kicked him hard on the shin. He let out a yelp and grabbed his leg as Julia stifled a smile.

'Adam, can you talk to the personnel who work in the area around the metro tunnel where Jon's bones were found? You should probably have a chat with the street artist who found the bones as well. See whether he knows anything or saw anything. It doesn't seem to me as if just anyone can make their way into the tunnels unnoticed.'

'On it,' said Adam.

'Well, there we are. You've all got your orders.'

Before anyone had time to stand up, Christer cleared his throat.

'Uh, since we didn't manage to join the Christmas do on the ferry …' he said falteringly, 'Lasse was wondering whether we could host you at ours tonight for a spontaneous Christmas supper. You've all got the evening off thanks to the boat trip, and even cops have to eat. To quote Lasse.'

Everyone around the table looked surprised.

'What a lovely idea!' Julia said. 'We'd be delighted!'

Everyone nodded in agreement, but Christer looked anything but happy. Mina suspected that it had been Lasse's suggestion alone.

'Why don't you come as well, Vincent, if you don't have anything on tonight?' Christer said as they rose from the conference table.

Mina held her breath. Christmas dinner without Vincent and Christmas dinner with him were two entirely different things. She preferred the latter every day of the week.

'I'd love to! Thank you for the invitation,' Vincent said cheerfully as he put on his coat.

As they were leaving the room, Vincent turned to Ruben.

'Getting back to *The Da Vinci Code*. You know, the people that Dan Brown got his idea from, the authors of that book I mentioned, Michael Baigent, Richard Leigh and Henry Lincoln …? You can actually see references to them in the book. Well, the movie. For example, the character Sir Leigh Teabing is a reference to Leigh and Baigent. I suppose Leigh is obvious, but Teabing is an anagram of Baigent. Cool, huh?'

Mina giggled. Ruben looked very unhappy.

31

Niklas listened to the recorded message yet again. He'd naively hoped that the countdown might have stopped simply because he wanted it to. Obviously that hadn't happened. He had twelve days to go. The tangibility of his imminent death affected him in on a visceral level. We might all say that we are going to die, but no one except those facing an actual sentence of death tends to take it seriously. Quite simply because it is impossible for us to grasp what it means. It is an abstraction. But he understood now. His body understood it.

He stood on the chair to reach the clock on the wall, took it off the nail and removed the battery. He didn't need any more reminder than necessary about the constant movement of time. Then he wrote a brief text message and sent it.

[display text]*Can you come here?*[/display text]

Each time he summoned Tor like that, he felt more and more like the evil boss in some American movie from the seventies, summoning his underlings via the intercom to fire them or at the very least deliver a stern ticking-off. Sending a text was the modern equivalent of pressing a button on your desk.

On the other hand, Tor rarely left his side, so he wouldn't be far away. As expected, the door opened within a minute, only moments after Niklas had returned the chair to its regular position after re-hanging the now stopped clock.

'You're right,' Niklas said before Tor could say a word. 'About the need for increased security. I've changed my mind. How many days will it take to put it in place?'

Tor nodded eagerly, looking very pleased.

'I took the liberty of making preparations,' he said. 'I'm in dialogue with the Security Service – we have somewhat differing views on the level required, but I'm demanding top security.

They're working to redirect personnel and they're reviewing their capabilities in terms of call tracing. I'm also in contact with NOA.'

'The National Operations Department? Why?'

'So that they can flag if they see any unusual behaviour or patterns in criminal circles that we need to be vigilant about. We don't want to see a repeat of what happened last summer.'

Niklas gazed out of the window at the few people who were defying the falling snow. There was a man in the street walking bent double and head first into the wind. Even though Niklas was sitting inside in the safety and warmth, he felt like that man, defying powers greater than himself, and frozen to his very soul.

He wanted to explain to Tor that the threat probably wouldn't come from the direction he thought, and that they needed to look out for the unexpected. But he couldn't say that. Not if he didn't want to be asked questions that he couldn't allow himself to answer.

'Thank you,' he settled for instead. 'Let me know when it's all arranged.'

Tor nodded and left him again.

Niklas looked at his desk. It had once been a model of perfect order, but it had long ago crossed the line into chaos. However, there were more important things to think about – such as time. He had far too little time. He couldn't waste another second on hanging about the office.

He retrieved his thick winter coat from the hook on the wall, put it on and stuffed his hands into the pockets. Strange. He had thought the business card was in the coat pocket. No, that wasn't right. He'd removed it. He gazed at the messy desk. It was probably lying there somewhere – in one of those stacks of papers. Anyway, the card didn't matter that much – he'd saved the phone number on his mobile. But sometimes that piece of card was a useful reminder of the fact that this was for real and not just a nightmare.

On his way to the lift, he stuck his head into Tor's office.

'I'm going to walk home,' he said. 'It's not far.'

'In this weather?'

Niklas could tell that Tor didn't like it, but it wasn't his choice.

He could still make his own decisions for a while longer. It would be different once the enhanced security arrangements were in place. Then Niklas would be a prisoner, but at least he'd be alive.

When he and his bodyguards emerged into the street, the snow struck his face immediately. Tor needn't have worried. Not even the troublemakers went out in this weather. Niklas hunched over and began to walk on stiff legs – he didn't look over his shoulder in response to every unexpected sound, but he did for most of them.

When he got home, he nodded at the bodyguards to stay by the main door while he took the lift up to the empty flat. Mechanically, he removed his coat and left it lying on the carpet in the hallway. Then he took off his snow-covered shoes and dropped them onto the floor before making for the living room, where he flopped into an armchair. He leaned forward to turn on the floor lamp beside the armchair so that his security detail in the street would know which room he was in. Then he pulled out his phone and called the saved number again, hoping that the message would at some point change.

That he would be spared.

But the message was the same as before. He put down the phone and closed his eyes. When Nathalie and Mina hove into sight in his mind's eye, he could no longer hold it back. The tears began to run down his cheeks whether he wanted them to or not.

32

They had dutifully decorated their small house in Stureby for Christmas. In practice neither Julia nor Torkel was particularly fond of Christmas, but they both had a notion that when you had children you had to mark Christmas in the home. Granted, Harry was only a year old, but he loved tinsel, candles and glittery things with the intensity of a miniature diva. Julia had to admit that his gurgling laugh each time he saw everything shining and glistening made the hassle worth it.

On the other hand, the backdrop of artificial Christmas cheer was a painful reminder of how little goodwill there was to be found in their household. Following a desperate effort to find their way back to what they'd once had, they had now relapsed into dejected silence. They didn't even row any more, instead, moving past each other like two celestial bodies millions of miles apart.

'When will you be home tonight?'

Torkel was standing in the bedroom doorway with Harry in his arms. Their son was very much tied to his mother's apron-strings right now and reached towards her with a whimper, but she wanted to dress quickly, so she ignored him.

'I don't know. But I doubt it'll be that late. We've got a lot on our plates with the investigation.'

'I might pop out for a bit when you get back then, if it won't be that late.'

Julia stopped mid-movement. She'd just got one leg into her pair of tights and was preparing to insert the other. Torkel avoided her gaze.

'Thought I'd get a beer with a friend.'

'Who's that then?'

Torkel hesitated.

'Filip.'

'Ah, right.'

She resumed her efforts with the tights and jumped up and down on the spot as she adjusted them. Men had no idea how good they had it, not having to bother with such loathsome clothing. But, as her mother had always said: beauty is pain. And she wanted to be beautiful. Adam would be there tonight, and no matter how much it went against the grain for her, she wanted to be beautiful for him.

'I'll try to hurry,' she said, reaching for the skirt.

It was her favourite skirt. She had paired it with a black top that left one shoulder bare.

'You're looking very nice – didn't you say it was just a work dinner?' Torkel said, shifting Harry onto his other hip.

Julia shrugged nonchalantly and pulled on the top.

'I just thought it would be nice to dress up a bit. I've worn nothing but work clothes for too long.'

Torkel didn't look as if he believed her.

The suspicion that had crept in between them was new. In their many years together, they had never been jealous, but there was so much that was different now. It was as if all their longing for a baby, which had been satisfied with the arrival of Harry, had exposed gaping holes in their relationship.

They had attempted couples therapy, and the therapist had theorized that for many years they'd shared one common goal – becoming parents. During that dream, problems had been able to flourish without them noticing. Harry's birth and the end of their mutual struggle had left them with nothing but the problems.

It sounded reasonable. But understanding why it had ended up like that hadn't helped her or Torkel to find the solution to their problems. They'd quit therapy – they had given up by silent consensus. But neither of them had as yet said it aloud or taken the practical steps necessary. There were so many new, difficult issues that had to be dealt with.

And in the midst of it all was Harry, whom they both loved beyond all rhyme and reason. Julia reached out towards him and was rewarded with a big smile and chubby arms outstretched.

'He's a real mummy's boy, isn't he?' Torkel said with a smile, and she was pleased to see in his eyes a glimpse of the tenderness he had previously shown her, now being directed at their son.

'Oh yes you are, you're Mummy's little boy,' Julia quipped, tickling Harry's belly and making him gurgle with laughter. 'Mummy's got to go soon, but why don't we go and have a look at the Christmas tree first? Let's look at all those beautiful red baubles.'

She carried him into the living room, where the big tree was adorned with decorations. He waved his arms and legs in excitement – the Christmas tree was the great love of his life. It filled his heart with joy of epic proportions. Julia buried her face in his neck and inhaled his heavenly scent. Her mobile phone buzzed. Her taxi had arrived. She hugged and kissed Harry again before handing him to Torkel.

As she was about to close the front door, she saw Torkel still standing by the Christmas tree. It was just a tree, she told herself. She zipped her coat up tightly as she walked towards the taxi. She really did hope Adam would appreciate her top.

33

Vincent was standing in the bedroom wondering which suit and shirt to select for dinner, when the doorbell rang.

'Can someone get that?' he called out into the hallway.

No reply. Vincent sighed and went to open it himself. The FedEx courier raised her eyebrows slightly when he opened the door in nothing but boxer shorts. But her reaction was only momentary. She'd presumably seen far worse.

'Package for Vincent Walder,' she said. 'I assume that's you?'

'You assume correctly,' Vincent said.

She handed over a parcel the size of a shoe box.

'Looks like an early Christmas present,' she said, smiling. 'Merry Christmas.'

'Merry Christmas,' Vincent said, closing the door.

The package was unexpectedly heavy given its size. He went into the kitchen to find a knife. Then he placed the box on the kitchen table and carefully opened the packaging. Inside there was a black wooden box.

'What's that you've got?' Rebecka said, entering the kitchen. 'And why aren't you wearing any clothes?'

'Hush, dear daughter,' he said. 'This is far more interesting than clothes. Come and look.'

The box had been polished to a high shine, and it looked exclusive. There was a silver plaque on the lid, and when he examined it closely he saw it was engraved with the words *To Vincent Walder*.

He lifted the lid. Inside there was a wooden frame containing four hourglasses in a row.

'Wow, I haven't seen one of these in a long time,' he said, removing the frame from the box. 'Isn't it magnificent?'

'What are they?' Rebecka asked.

'Hourglasses. It's an old way of measuring time,' he said. 'The four different hourglasses contain different quantities of sand. When the whole frame is used, the first one might run out of sand after fifteen minutes, the next after thirty, the third after forty-five and the final one after sixty. They used to have these in churches so the priest could see how long his sermon had lasted for. I think they've still got one on show at St Ragnhild's in Södertälje.'

Vincent turned the frame over. The sand immediately began to flow downwards in all four hourglasses.

'The Romans reportedly used hourglasses to keep people to time when giving speeches in the senate,' he said. 'Rumour has it that the hourglasses got smaller and smaller as a reflection of the deteriorating quality of the speeches. However, the first documented use of hourglasses is from the fourteenth century. Isn't it a fascinating object?'

He turned the frame over again, making the sand fall in reverse before holding it up to the light.

'OK, let's pretend some of what you just said is interesting,' Rebecka said. 'But I don't get why someone has sent one of these things to you?'

'I'm not sure either,' he said, looking inside the box again.

There was a note lying in the bottom. It must have been under the hourglass frame. The paper was covered in neat handwritten words in blue ink. He set down the hourglasses, picked up the note and read it aloud.

'Find the fourth one before time runs out.'

He was more than familiar with the handwriting. He had seen it countless times over the last eighteen months. And it had always been in conjunction with an intriguing and well-constructed puzzle.

'Ever since that business with my sister ...' he said, suddenly unsure whether he had ever told Rebecka that he and Mina had almost drowned in a tank. Surely he must have? 'Ever since then, people have been sending me home-made mysteries, riddles and puzzles that they want me to solve. This is from one of the smarter ones. I've no idea who he or she is, but I recognize the handwriting. They're very knowledgeable.'

The hourglasses really were incredibly beautiful. He turned them over again.

'So what's this all about then?' said Rebecka. 'What is "the fourth one"?'

She actually seemed to be reluctantly interested.

'I don't know,' he said. 'It might be symbolic, something to do with what the hourglass represents. It could be that time is irretrievably running out, or the reverse, Schuon's eternal polarity shift on a micro- and macro-cosmic—'

'Of course, it might be about the actual amount of time it takes for the sand to pass through,' Benjamin said, interrupting them. Vincent hadn't noticed him entering the kitchen. 'There might be a secret in the fourth hourglass that you find when the sand has all run through. And how come you aren't wearing any clothes?'

'What a lot of fuss there is about clothes,' Vincent said. 'Good ideas, my boy, but I don't think it's quite that simple. Would you mind helping me to time the hourglasses?'

'Dad,' Rebecka said. 'Clothes. Now. Before someone sees you. And weren't you supposed to be going out to a dinner?'

Vincent sighed. He would be well advised to obey. He looked one last time at the hourglasses. There was something different about this. There wasn't an obvious task to solve. There was no tricky challenge, with pieces to be put together. It was almost as if the hourglasses were a message in themselves.

The unwavering movement of the sand into the glass reminded him that everything came to an end sooner or later.

He too would have an ending.

We have reached your omega.

Before he left the kitchen, he turned the hourglasses over one more time.

34

They always shared. That was how they lived. That was how they survived. Some of the others couldn't help, but that didn't matter. There was no judgement.

'We should be grateful that we've been given the opportunity to help. It's a gift.'

Sometimes he thought that was a rather odd statement. After all, Dad always said that everyone had to help. But then again, it wasn't so easy for some of Dad's friends to go topside. The guy with the yellow hat was always high, as if floating on his own cloud, while the woman who collected straws thought she was on holiday in Greece with her two daughters. They never went up. But they worked together to take care of them too. Dad always said that was the most beautiful word in the Swedish language: 'together'.

Before he got ill, Dad had been a Swedish teacher. That meant he knew a lot of nice words, which came in handy now that he was king. But Dad was only king when he was happy. When the laughter fell silent and Dad disappeared into the darkness, he was no longer king. He said so himself: when the darkness came, he abdicated. That was another one of the excellent words that Dad knew: 'abdicate'. But each time he returned they crowned him anew.

The others took care of him when Dad was away. And he took care of them. They were a family.

Now they had all gathered around the fire. It was a steel barrel full of combustible rubbish, filling the tunnel with smoke and making them cough. But it was also a source of warmth and light. They held their hands to the fire and felt its warmth on their faces as they shared the proceeds of his and Dad's treasure hunt. He didn't know whether the feeling in his chest was pride, but he thought it was.

The old man with the kind eyes gave him a piece of ham sandwich. He devoured almost all of it – he hadn't realized how hungry he was until now. That was often how it was. Hunger had become such a commonplace companion that he barely noticed it any longer. Not until food touched his lips did his body awaken and realize that hunger was raging within. 'Look around,' Dad said, sweeping his arm around the fire.

'Look around. How favoured are we? We are protected from the world above, protected from a world that is about to end. We are protected. We are together. We are fed. We are warm.'

The man in the yellow hat hummed quietly to himself. He tried to catch the melody, but it wasn't one he recognized. It wasn't any of the songs that Mum had sung to him when he'd been little.

He still had a piece of sandwich in his hand. The hunger was still there, but it had been tamed and was under control. He left the piece for the new woman. She was always so skinny. Always so cold. She had already been given half a burger by Dad from the big bag, but she was still shaking violently, so she got his piece of sandwich too. They took care of each other. They were a family. That was what Dad always said. And there was nothing he wanted more than to be like Dad.

35

Vincent felt the Christmas spirit burst into life as he pulled onto the driveway of the house at the address Mina had given to him. Colourful lights were flashing at him and he remained in the car for a while, taking it all in. The whole garden was full of illuminated figures: Santas, reindeer, snowmen.

Thoughts about the message from the Shadow that he had read that morning had returned to him and made him feel uneasy. If he couldn't contain the worry it would ruin the whole evening. Taking slow, deep breaths, he closed his eyes and visualized the house in front of him, adorned for Christmas. He absorbed the feeling of Christmas, the joy in every light that had been put up. He let that Christmas feeling seep through his whole body. Then he opened his eyes. Instead of worry, he now felt like having a Holly Jolly Christmas. Much better.

The garden was filled with strings of fairy lights, and there was a string of red lights suspended between the figurines closest to the car. Vincent counted how many bulbs there were, but then the string moved in a gust of wind. In the end he concluded that there were twenty-three.

Damn it. Not good. That was the kind of thing to bring the anxiety back. He carefully got out of the car, watching where he placed his feet. It was treacherously slippery and he had already almost gone down twice that day. A broken hip was the last thing he needed, now that his broken foot had finally healed. He walked slowly across the grass and began to unscrew one of the bulbs from the string of lights. Twenty-two would be better. He could live with that.

When he removed the bulb, the whole string went out.

'Hello there! Are the lights playing up?'

A handsome man in his sixties wearing a Santa hat was

standing in the doorway waving at him. That had to be Lasse. Vincent hid the bulb in his hand and made for the door. He could hear Christmas music coming from inside, and there was light flooding out of every window. Vincent realized that his perception of Christer didn't quite match up with this cosy Christmas dream. It was going to be an interesting evening.

'The others have already arrived. We're on the mulled wine. Do you want some? Of course you do. It's Christmas, and at Christmas you've got to drink mulled wine. Those are just the rules, aren't they?'

Lasse continued to chat away happily as he took Vincent's coat and showed him into a small living room with big views. The whole group was there already, each member clutching a mulled wine cup in their hand. Vincent noticed that Mina looked troubled. It was probably unbearable for her to visit someone else's home, given the bacteria. Additionally, the abundance of Christmas surrounding her was probably more than she could handle: porcelain Santas, straw goats, flashing strings of fairy lights, Christmas-themed musical boxes slowly revolving, curtains covered in gingerbread men, and tablecloths adorned with Christmas wreaths. He looked around. There was mistletoe hanging above every doorway. He loved it.

'Vincent!' Adam said. 'It's great that you could make it!'

Ruben's and Julia's cheeks had a warm glow that revealed they'd drunk their fair share of mulled wine already. Vincent asked for a non-alcoholic version, since he was driving.

Something brushed against his legs, and when he looked down he saw Bosse eagerly pressing himself against him, in the hope of being scratched between the ears. To mark the occasion, the dog was wearing a plastic headband with glittery reindeer antlers on it.

'A little too much maybe?' Christer said as he came over to stand by Vincent. 'If I'd known that Lasse was a Christmas fiend I'm not sure I would have let him move in.'

'I think it's amazing,' Vincent said, and he meant it.

'Well, it's definitely something,' Christer muttered.

Vincent scratched Bosse behind the ears and looked at the others. It was strange seeing them in a setting other than police headquarters, but it also provided him with an excellent opportunity to learn more about them. Mina was standing hesitantly to one side. Ruben was nearby, but had clearly given up any attempt to talk to her and now had his phone out and was scrolling on it. Adam and Julia were engaged in intense conversation, their heads close together. Interesting.

Vincent went over to Mina, checking that everyone else was distracted elsewhere. Then he slipped the red light bulb from the garden into her hand.

'Don't ask,' he said. 'Just put it in your pocket.'

Lasse appeared in the doorway to the dining room and cleared his throat.

'Food's up!'

Vincent offered Mina his arm and she hesitated before gently taking it.

'I've just had it dry-cleaned,' he whispered, winking at her.

'Lucky you offered me your arm rather than your hand, given where it's just been,' she said, nodding towards Bosse.

'I didn't realize you thought we should be holding hands,' he said with a wry smile.

'Ha ha,' she said, letting go of his arm and walking ahead of him into the dining room.

As he passed through the doorway he glanced up at the mistletoe, gazing at Mina's back. At that moment, she turned and smiled at him with her plump, naturally red lips. His gaze lingered on them for a moment too long.

She turned away again and headed towards the dining table. He also headed for the sumptuously laid table, where he pulled out Mina's chair for her and then sat down next to her. He watched Julia and Adam as they sat down next to each other too, but without Adam pulling out Julia's chair for her. It seemed gentlemanly manners were on the wane. Or perhaps Adam had some other reason for behaving distantly from Julia? Most interesting.

'What do you think we're having?' Mina said in a low voice. 'Should I have eaten before I came?'

He realized the question was not about Christer's or Lasse's culinary expertise, but about having to eat something she hadn't been in control of. He knew just how dearly this dinner was costing her.

'I wouldn't put money on Christer being much of a chef. We'll just have to pin our hopes on Lasse.'

'If you say so,' Mina said uncertainly. 'If I have to get my stomach pumped then I'm making you come with me.'

'Here are the starters!' Christer said suddenly from the kitchen door.

He and Lasse appeared with plates balanced on their hands and forearms and deftly placed them on the table. Vincent stared at the plate before him in amazement. Christer clapped his hands in satisfaction and called for their attention.

'For your starter, I've made a cocotte with porcini and truffle foam.'

'Fuck me, Christer,' Ruben said as his eyes shifted from his colleague to the elegant dish before him and back again. 'I had no idea you could cook! You usually burn the coffee at work. And that's using a machine!'

'Christer is incredible!' Lasse said, gazing adoringly at his beloved. 'I'm always telling him that he could get a job in our kitchen at Ulla Winbladh any day.'

'Oh, you know, it's just a hobby,' Christer said, blushing. 'Tuck in. I'll be back in a moment. I just have to do a few bits and pieces for the main course.'

They ate in astonished silence. 'Silent Night' was playing at a discreet volume in the background.

'Bloody hell,' Ruben kept saying over and over, shaking his head in disbelief. 'Bloody hell.'

'Has anything worthwhile come in since the press conference?' Mina said to Julia.

'That's a world record for bad dinner conversation, Mina,' Vincent said in a low voice.

Mina hadn't touched her starter, and Vincent discreetly swapped plates with her. It was not a difficult sacrifice. The starter had tickled his tastebuds in ways he didn't know were possible.

'Hush now, no work talk this evening,' Lasse said, waving his finger in admonishment. 'This evening, I want to get to know you as people, and I don't want to hear another word about death or misery. I get enough of that from Christer. Why don't we start with you, Mina? What's your story?'

Mina looked terrified. Being forced to be personal with strangers was not her favourite thing, but etiquette demanded an answer.

'Not much of a story here,' she said. 'I've been a police officer for nearly ten years. I've got a teenage daughter and an ex-husband. I live in Årsta. That's pretty much it.'

'Except that you've been the focus in two of our most complicated investigations to date,' Julia interjected. 'Mina is truly one of the rising stars at police headquarters. It's lucky for the rest of us that most of the building doesn't know about it – that way we get to keep her. But it's only going to be a matter of time.'

Mina stared at Julia in surprise as the baton was passed on. They had made it as far as Adam when Christer returned and announced that the main course was ready to be served.

The main was just as astounding as the starter: saddle of venison with hasselback potatoes and gravy made with Christer's own stock and the perfect amount of port. Conversation around the table flowed more and more easily as the contents of the wine bottles decreased. Out of the corner of his eye, Vincent saw that Julia and Adam had resumed conversation with their heads close together. Well then, it seemed he hadn't been mistaken.

Mina ate a little of the main course, but mostly moved the food around on her plate. When Vincent subtly liberated her potatoes and venison, she threw him a grateful look.

The dessert was pavlova bursting with cloudberries. Ruben had resigned himself to his astonishment and devoured everything on his plate.

'Jesus Christ, that was good,' he said, after polishing off his dessert and patting his belly.

'I don't think I could eat another bite,' Julia groaned.

'Can I go home with you?' Mina whispered, and Vincent nodded.

He wanted nothing more than to go home with her, but he knew that wasn't what she meant.

'We can nip off now if you like,' he whispered in reply.

The panic had been clearly writ across her face for the last half hour. Vincent stood up and cleared his throat.

'Lasse and Christer, this has been just wonderful. Thank you so much for inviting me. I'm afraid I have to be the dull one here by being the first to leave. My wife is away and I have to get back for the babysitter. I'm so sorry to miss the coffee, but I'm certain it would have been the best coffee I'd ever tasted. Mina, I'm sorry if I'm ruining your evening by leaving so early – I know I promised you a lift. Regrettably your ride is departing now. I really am sorry if that puts you out.'

He saw the joy in Mina's gaze, but she did her best to contain this and feign disappointment so as not to upset her hosts. She too offered her thanks and said her farewells.

As they emerged from the house, the winter chill nipped at their cheeks. Mina let out a long sigh, and Vincent could feel the relief flooding through her.

'Thank you,' she said. 'I could only have managed another few seconds.'

They went to his car.

'Do you still have that light bulb I gave you?' he asked.

She pulled it from her pocket and handed it back to him.

Then she spotted the string of dead lights.

'Come on,' she said. 'How old are you?'

He screwed the bulb back in and the lights came back to life. All twenty-three of them. Vincent quickly averted his gaze and opened the boot. He pulled out a roll of wrapping paper. Then he opened the passenger-side door.

'I'm afraid I don't have any cling film for your seat,' he said, waving the roll around. 'But I do have Christmas wrapping paper. If you can cope with sitting on a few Santas. Who knows? They might suffocate. Two birds with one stone for an avowed Grinch.'

Mina punched his arm.

'Are you implying I'm heavy? Be careful or I might sit on you instead.'

Then she blushed.

'Er … I didn't mean …'

Vincent also felt his face flush and then he began to roar with laughter. He got into the car and waited for her. It was another few seconds before she got in.

'Stop smiling,' she said.

Vincent started the car and reversed off the driveway.

'Apropos of nothing,' he said. 'How long have Julia and Adam been sleeping with each other?'

Mina gaped at him.

36

Ruben had got back from Christer and Lasse's an hour ago. He had spent most of the time since then staring at the rolls of Christmas wrapping paper that he'd laid out on the kitchen table, unsure which one to choose, while simultaneously trying to sober up. The cartoon Santas on the shiny paper looked stupid. Astrid would probably think that was too childish.

The second option was just matte red paper. That was it. Perhaps that was too grown-up – or maybe she'd like it. He had no idea. He was not good at this.

It hardly helped matters that he had to cling onto the edge of the table to remain upright. Christer's mulled wine had been incredible, while the regular wine had been flowing generously all evening. As such, Ruben's motor skills were not quite what they should have been. The red wrapping paper would do. He pulled out a metre of it and began to wrap the present. Around and around. He had no idea how much paper was needed, but five times around seemed about right. Then the wrapping became far too thick and it was impossible to fold the ends, which forced him to hold it all together while he searched for tape.

The bloody dispenser had ended up on the floor. Of course it had. He reached for it without letting go of the package in his other hand. It was just out of reach. He tried to reach it with his toes instead, but all he managed to do was kick it further away. What the actual fuck? How on earth did people manage to do this?

His phone buzzed on the table as a text message arrived. Any interruptions were welcome at this juncture. He clumsily took hold of his phone with his left hand since he needed his right to hold the paper in place.

The message was from the girl whose name ended in -y.

The one who had stayed over the night before last. Ruben had no idea how she had got hold of his number – he must have been indiscreet. She was asking whether she could pop by to 'give him a Christmas present'. In the accompanying picture she was smiling at the camera while wearing a Santa hat. She was wearing nothing else. Just in case the message was at all unclear. Good God, she really was very naked.

Ruben looked up at the ceiling and sighed.

'You think this is very funny, don't you Peder?' he said aloud.

It took him a while to write a reply using his left thumb only. Truth be told, he wanted nothing more than for her to come round, but priorities were priorities. He said he was unfortunately busy with something important this evening. Which was true, in a way. He would wrap Astrid's present if it was the last thing he did.

37

ELEVEN DAYS TO GO

There was something about Peter Kronlund that bothered Ruben. Adam and Julia hadn't turned up much that was new after their interview with him in the remand prison. But there was something about Peter's face on Ruben's screen that seemed familiar. And Ruben never forgot a face.

He went online and clicked around a few articles about the Confido scandal. Peter Kronlund was pictured in most of the articles. Always impeccably dressed. Usually in a blue suit, pale pink shirt and matching striped or checked tie. And an expensive wristwatch, naturally. Ruben squinted and then zoomed in on one of the pictures and saw that it wasn't a Rolex but instead something of a connoisseur's choice, for a change. The watch of the discreetly wealthy. The watch of the well-informed. It was a Patek Philippe.

Out of curiosity, Ruben opened another tab and googled his way to a website showing expensive watches. Then he let out a low whistle. A watch like the one Peter Kronlund was nonchalantly wearing around his wrist cost a cool one million kronor. On his right wrist rather than his left, so that the chicks would get a better look at it when they were getting a lift in his expensive car. Ruben smiled. He'd pulled that trick before. But never with anything close to that expensive, of course. A watch like that was dangerous, no matter which wrist it was on. Watch thefts had become increasingly common, especially in Östermalm. Wandering around with something like that on your arm was asking to be robbed.

He frowned. Damn it, this Peter guy really did look familiar.

There was something about those thick dark eyebrows and thin lips that was ringing so many bells it sounded like a performance of 'Jingle Bells'. Ruben forced himself to concentrate, digging into his memory. It contained every face he had ever seen. For better and for worse. There were a few of those hook-ups he would have liked to erase from the memory banks.

Peter ... Peter ... There was something rustling on the fringes of his memory, and he tried to relax. Trying too hard rarely helped. Instead, the memory had to be left to do its thing. He allowed each thought and impression to wash over him, along with all the associations they gave rise to as he saw the name and picture on the screen.

Peter ... Peter ... Peter Manojlovic! That was it! The man known in the media as Peter Kronlund had originally been called Peter Manojlovic. That was a surname that he'd heard quite a few times of late, including during their last team meeting. Surely that was what had finally pointed his mind in the right direction?

He quickly did a Google image search for the name. Peter had been diligent in removing any pictures of him published with his old name. Reuben guessed that he'd been helped. It was evident that Kronlund wanted to scrub out all family ties, but information online rarely disappeared completely. Finally, in the end, Ruben found what he was looking for in an article in *Aftonbladet*. The black and white photograph was slightly out of focus, but there was no doubt that one of the men in the picture was Peter Kronlund. The caption read: *Victor, Milan and Peter Manojlovic, sons of the notorious Dragan Manojlovic.*

Satisfaction washed over him in waves. Ruben began frantically to search the police database, unable to prevent a big smile from spreading across his face as the information began to flood into his computer. The surname Manojlovic was a veritable fount of information in the police computer systems. The earliest hits were against Peter's father, Dragan Manojlovic, but with the passing of years the sons' criminal enterprises had also started to appear: Victor, Milan – and Peter Manojlovic. Peter's name had suddenly vanished some fifteen years earlier. A quick google revealed that Kronlund was Peter's wife's maiden name, and that he had taken her name when they married. Peter had obviously done his utmost to hide his past. He'd changed his name, address and social circles. There was nothing tying him to his past life.

Ruben frowned. It was one thing for it to say nothing about Peter's background in the police files on Confido. The accusations were all to do with financial crimes and the detectives had quite reasonably focused on what had happened in the company. They'd had no reason to look at the families of the accused. But the tabloids should have picked up on it. After all, they made their living from digging up every last skeleton they could find when someone was in trouble. It seemed unlikely they would have missed something this tantalizing. Yet Ruben hadn't found a single published word about it.

There was only one sensible explanation. The papers *had* discovered that Peter hailed from Sweden's most notorious crime family with its roots in Serbia, but they hadn't dared to publish the information. Or they had been pressured into not doing so. The Manojlovic family was behind countless businesses involved in drug distribution, human trafficking and prostitution. There was a long list.

Peter seemed to have absconded from the family business to be reborn as a successful financier. But Ruben knew better. No one left a family like the Manojlovics behind.

38

Niklas was standing by the door leading into the SVT studio, staring at the breakfast spread. He was usually very particular about what he consumed in the morning. Freshly squeezed orange juice. Natural quark with fresh blueberries. Coffee. One egg. But all of a sudden, life was too short for such qualms. He might not be able to settle the unease in his stomach, but he could at least stop it from rumbling. It wouldn't be a good thing for it to start making noises on live television.

'What a pleasure to have you with us this morning, minister,' a familiar voice said.

It was Micke Niedermann Möller, the ever-pleasant floor manager, who was at his side with a microphone in his hand.

'I thought I'd mike you up now,' he said, 'and then you'll be on in about five minutes. There's plenty of time for you to have a bite now if you'd like something.'

'Thank you,' Niklas said, holding out the lapel of his jacket so that Micke could complete his task.

Once the floor manager was satisfied with the position of the microphone, Niklas helped himself to toast and spread it liberally with butter and jam. He didn't need to look at Tor, who was leaning against the wall not far from him, to know that his press secretary's eyebrows had probably just hit the ceiling. Tor himself usually ate no more than half a grapefruit for breakfast. He referred to it as the Fredrik Reinfeldt diet, in honour of the former prime minister. It took Niklas less than a minute to devour the toast.

Perhaps he shouldn't have accepted the invitation to appear on the breakfast show, but it was part of his job. And his press secretary had double-checked all the questions with the production team in advance to ensure that the interview would go in the right direction. He had to consider what image of Niklas Stockenberg he would bequeath to the world.

'Shall we?' Micke said, suddenly at his side again. 'I can bring that in for you if you like.'

The floor manager pointed to the mug of coffee in Niklas's hand, which was a sombre black without any logos on it. That was public service broadcasting through and through. Niklas nodded gratefully and handed it to him.

'Let's go.'

Niklas watched Tor detach himself from the wall and issue a brief command into his lapel microphone. Niklas hadn't seen the new security detail, but that didn't mean they weren't there. They were probably following his every move, and not just his either, but those of everyone else. The camera operators, the sound crew, the technicians. All of them would be under close real-time scrutiny.

Niklas followed Micke into the studio where the presenters, Karin Magnusson and Alexander Letic, were in the process of introducing a video montage. Micke indicated that Niklas should wait behind the camera, and then vanished. A red clock was counting down the seconds left until the pre-recorded segment began. As it started rolling, the live cameras were turned off. Niklas didn't need to see the montage to know what it was about. He'd been there when it had happened.

The floor manager returned and showed him to a chair at the high table where Karin and Alexander were sitting. The mug of coffee was already in place. Niklas couldn't help but admire the efficiency of the well-oiled machinery that underpinned SVT's live breakfast show.

He proffered his hand across the table and there was just time for him to greet the two presenters briefly before the segment ended and they were live again.

'Those were the scenes we were confronted with on the island of Öland in the late summer,' Karin Magnusson said to camera. 'Joining us now is the minister of justice, Niklas Stockenberg, who was the target of this attack. Welcome to the show.'

'Thank you,' Niklas said, deploying his best, most reassuring ministerial smile.

'Mr Stockenberg, you were attacked in the street in broad daylight with a knife. Your attacker was clearly looking to harm or kill you specifically. How do you feel about that now? How are you doing?'

'Compared with how I would be if he had succeeded, I'm obviously feeling fantastic,' Niklas said with a wry smile before turning serious. 'But it goes without saying that this kind of thing leaves a mark. I would once again like to thank everyone who is involved in ensuring my safety and security, and who saw what was happening long before I noticed myself.'

'There are theories out there saying this wasn't an attack by a lone madman, but that there was actually a far more organized effort behind it. What do you have to say about that?'

Niklas hesitated. He had his own suspicions that weren't a million miles from the conspiracy theories circulating on Twitter, but he also knew that it was sometimes necessary to protect the public from things they didn't want to know about.

'I believe the prosecutor did a splendid job during the trial of Albin Johannesson, and clearly showed all the facts of the case. Mr Johannesson is now where he should be, and I'd certainly welcome the opportunity to discuss the correlation between crime rates and the so-called reforms to mental healthcare in the 1990s.'

He glanced towards Tor, who was in the shadows behind the cameras. Tor nodded briefly. Whether it had been a lone wolf or not, the truth was that Tor had saved his life. If it hadn't been for his trained eye and lightning reflexes, Niklas would not have been there talking about the incident now.

'You opted not to take any time out and went straight back to work,' Alexander Letic said. 'Has the attack had any impact on the way you regard your role as minister of justice?'

Niklas took a sip of coffee to make it look like he was pausing for thought. The truth was that he had already been asked that question countless times.

'Not really,' he said. 'We're working to establish a society in which law and order prevail, and my views on what that entails haven't changed. Would more police patrolling the streets have meant that we could have avoided the incident in Öland? Maybe.

Yet having more officers is merely putting a bandage on an already bleeding wound. Bandages are important, but we need to deal with the cause of the wound itself so that we can ensure it doesn't occur again. It's in that respect that we face such a major task in society today.'

'What do you say to those people who may feel afraid?' Karin Magnusson said, reading her notes.

It was a question his press officer had insisted on including. Niklas was somewhat surprised they had agreed to this.

'Fear is an emotion, and those can be hard to switch off,' he said. 'But it's important to remember that Sweden is one of the safest countries on earth. Just look at Iran. Russia. China. Egypt. Turkey. Afghanistan. Qatar. These are all countries in which you have cause to be afraid. But here? We live in an incredibly safe country with the protection of the law on our side. Unless you are involved in criminal activity, the risk of anything dangerous happening to you is in reality vanishingly small.'

The presenters nodded earnestly.

'Even on the beautiful island of Öland,' he added, attempting to lighten the mood.

He picked up the mug to take another sip and noticed something rough under his thumb. He had felt it the last time he had picked up the mug as well, but he hadn't given it any thought then. He glanced down and saw a piece of green tape on the top of the mug handle – the kind that he knew technicians and studio crews used. It seemed someone had written his name on the tape, presumably to avoid muddling his mug up with someone else's.

'But to focus on the personal here,' Alexander Letic said, 'how long does it take you to stop looking over your shoulder after an event like that?'

Niklas blinked. That question hadn't been in the approved running order. He didn't like talking about himself, and there was always the risk that he would be criticized for mixing the personal with politics after the fact. The ministerial press officer would have to raise that with the SVT production team later. But he smiled and studied the presenter, trying to ascertain whether the question had been asked out of curiosity or whether there was a tricky follow-up lurking in the wings. Then he looked down at the mug again and moved his thumb. He had been right. There was something written on the tape. But it wasn't his name.

It was the number eight.

With the bottom half coloured in.

It was the same symbol as on the business card.

And after it was the number eleven.

Eleven days to go.

Someone in the studio had managed to apply it despite Tor's careful supervision. Despite the bodyguards.

Panic welled up inside him, filling him from head to toe. There were pins and needles in his arms and legs. He simply wanted to rush off, but he had to stay sitting there. After all, he was on live television. He looked at his mug until he had calmed down, and only then did he raise his gaze again.

Nonetheless, Tor appeared to have spotted his expression. Niklas saw him whispering into the feature producer's ear and she then signalled to the presenters that they needed to stop.

'Is it difficult to think about?' said Letic, who hadn't seen the producer's flailing arms and had apparently interpreted Niklas's reaction as being to the question.

'Sometimes,' Niklas said, clearing his throat. 'But to answer your question about how long it takes before you stop looking over your shoulder: you never stop.'

There was febrile activity in the shadows of the studio as the security detail took up their positions by all the exits, but Niklas knew there was no point. Whoever was after him was no longer in the studio. It wasn't time yet.

The message was quite clear – it didn't matter what he did or how many bodyguards he had. Once Niklas's time was up, there was no security detail in the world that would be able to help. He wasn't going to get away.

39

Christer was doing a better job than usual of ignoring the Christmas music blaring across the open-plan office. What little of it was there in the periphery was giving way to the case that was occupying more and more of his waking hours. He had moved onto looking for other missing persons cases to see whether he could identify any similarities to the Jon Langseth case – or what little they knew about it. But he had gone through every recorded disappearance over and over, without turning anything up. Page after page of people who appeared to have been erased from the face of the earth.

Some cases had rather more obvious explanations than others. Demented Olga, who had plodded off from her old folks' home, never to be found. Jorge with his lengthy rap sheet and obvious gang affiliation, who had vanished after telling his girlfriend he was going to 'meet some guys'. Or nineteen-year-old Elva who, following her release from her third spell in the psych ward following repeated suicide attempts, had never been seen again. There were probable explanations in all those cases as to what might have happened.

Sometimes he felt disheartened when he had spent too long perusing strangers' fates on his screen, but the lists he was reviewing now were at least for people who had been reported missing. Someone had noticed they were gone.

The worst thing for him were the cases where no one noticed that someone was missing. Where someone had been dead in their flat for months, only to be found because they hadn't paid the rent. In his own case, his colleagues had been all that stood between him and a similar fate. No one apart from his colleagues would have missed him. Before.

Now it was different. Now he had Lasse. And he was terrified of blowing this chance he'd been given. The chance of a new life. And not only that. The truth was that he was happy.

Perhaps that was why he couldn't work out what that stubborn little thing gnawing away at the back of his mind was. He knew it was in there somewhere. Perhaps he was too happy to be able to do his job properly? Or perhaps it was just the beginnings of dementia?

Christer continued scrolling. Face after face. Fate after fate. Somewhere in here there would be something connected to Jon Langseth, he knew it.

'How are you getting on?' said Mina.

Christer jumped – her voice seemed to have come from nowhere. He hadn't heard any footsteps approaching, but then again most sounds in the office were still being drowned out by the music.

'All right. Well, no, not really. It's not going well at all. I know there's something here I should remember. Something I've seen. But I cannot for the life of me figure out what.'

'You heard that Ruben realized Peter Kronlund is Dragan Manojlovic's son, didn't you?'

Christer nodded.

'Yes, Ruben's memory is clearly far better than mine. Bloody interesting connection, isn't it? I heard Julia got all fired up. But it doesn't help me one damn bit with my failing memory. It must be old age – these days my brain is like a sieve.'

Christer scratched his head and pushed his chair away from the desk in frustration.

'You haven't considered asking Vincent for help, have you?' Mina asked cautiously.

'Vincent?' Christer let out a low chuckle. 'How could he help me? With some kind of hocus pocus? Conjure up my memory?'

'He helped me to remember something important by hypnotizing me. Without that, we wouldn't have found the bunker at Wennhagen's farm.'

Mina glanced at the chair beside Christer's and appeared to consider whether to sit down, but she remained on her feet. He understood why. That upholstery had seen better days.

'Hell will freeze over before I let someone hypnotize me.

Firstly, it's nothing but quackery. Everyone knows none of that stuff works for real. Secondly, he'd probably take the chance to get up to some mischief while he was in there. Make me hop on one leg and quack like a duck. Or something.'

'So you're saying it doesn't work but he'd get you to quack like a duck?'

Mina raised an eyebrow in amusement. Christer glowered at her. Then he rolled his chair back to his desk and faced the screen to indicate that the conversation was at an end.

'Nonsense,' he muttered, with his back towards her. 'I haven't got time for nonsense.'

'Either way, he'll be here soon,' Mina said. 'Give it some thought.'

He didn't hear Mina's footsteps as she left, but he took it for granted that she was gone. He had a job to do.

40

Vincent was late. He knew that Mina was waiting for him in the foyer at police headquarters. He could picture her impatient expression in his mind's eye. He had stopped to buy a coffee en route and parked the car, but while he was in the café the snowfall had intensified into a storm that no sensible person would have ventured out into.

He had waited for a while in the café, but the snow showed no signs of abating so eventually he hunched his shoulders and covered the lower half of his face with his scarf.

By the time he reached the police headquarters he felt like a frozen snowman, even though he had only walked one block. He went through the door and was met by Mina, who was indeed waiting for him with her arms folded. She had invited him there, but hadn't given a reason.

He couldn't help wondering whether Mina might be in danger because of him. He couldn't let that happen, but he also had no idea how to prevent it if the Shadow decided to involve her.

'I bought coffee on the way,' he said apologetically. 'But it turned into iced coffee before I got here.'

He abandoned the sagging paper cup beside a bin.

'Vincent, why aren't you wearing a hat?' Mina said with a sigh. 'Your hair is completely white.'

He shook his head, making snowflakes swirl around him.

'Because I'm a grown-up and don't want to?'

'You mean that you're vain. By the way, our coffee isn't as bad as you remember.'

Vincent took off his scarf and opened his coat before shaking that too, which made more snow fall onto the floor.

'There's a risk we'll end up snowed in here,' he said. 'It's lucky there are a few days left until Christmas so that we have time to dig our way out.'

'We won't be having that much fun,' Mina said, swiping her card to let them through the barrier.

'I'm going to make you appreciate Christmas if it's the last thing I do,' he said.

They strolled along the now familiar corridor towards the interview rooms. Vincent noticed that her hair was almost back to the same length it had been when they first met. It was also back in a tight ponytail that accentuated all her facial features. Good God – had it already been almost three years? To him it still felt like yesterday.

'We can start with some Christmas movies,' he said. 'How about a marathon featuring *Home Alone*, *Krampus* and *A Christmas Story*?'

Mina stopped and stared at him.

'First of all, you're here to work,' she said. 'Focus on that. Secondly, are those your *cosiest* Christmas movies?'

'Well, I thought *Gremlins* might be a bit much,' he said, smiling wryly.

'Like I said, you're here to work …'

'OK, OK,' he said. 'No more Christmas. For now. So why am I here today?'

They started walking again.

'You're here because we're about to question Gustaf Brons for the first time,' she said. 'The commissioner is convinced he's Jon Langseth's killer.'

Vincent glanced at Mina at the very moment that the winter sun illuminated her face through the window. When he saw her from certain angles, he had difficulty breathing. He was embarrassed by that superficial thought, but the truth was he could have looked at her for any amount of time. Or listened to her. Mina's voice had a roughness and full-bodied quality that fascinated him. He'd never heard a voice like it before, or perhaps he'd just never listened to anyone so closely before …

'Isn't it good … that he was able to come in so quickly?' he said, trying to get back to the conversation before she noticed the way he was looking at her. 'Especially if he is the killer.'

'Yes, for a potential murderer, he's surprisingly cooperative,' she said. 'I'm afraid I can't say the same for his lawyer.'

'When you said "we're" going to question Brons, did "we" mean you and I?' he asked.

Mina nodded grimly. Mina was clearly no fan of Gustaf Brons.

Vincent suddenly shivered. He had been freezing outside, and it was almost absurdly cold inside police headquarters. He imagined he could see his own breath. Mina didn't seem bothered. She was wearing a polo neck, but it was short-sleeved. She hadn't been kidding when she'd said she liked the cold.

'Why do I get the impression that Julia's father's view isn't one you share?' he said.

Mina sighed.

'Jon's colleague is a prize arsehole,' she said. 'He might very well get someone bumped off. He was also terrified that Jon would, in his own words, "wuss out" and go to the media when things began to kick off around their company. But Brons is more of a con-pensioners-out-of-their-savings kind of arsehole. He's not really a boil-the-body-afterwards kind of arsehole. If you get my drift. Of course, the bit about cleansing the skeleton doesn't have to have been his idea. But I have a hard time believing that a hired killer would go to that much trouble unless they were being paid to do it. And why are you smiling like that?'

Vincent bit his lip. Mina had just said arsehole three times. He'd never heard her come close to using words like that before. Whoever this Gustaf Brons was, Vincent didn't fancy being in his shoes.

'So what do you want me to do?' he said. 'I assume this Brons chap will claim he's innocent, and it sounds like you think the same thing?'

Mina let out a short and mirthless laugh. They stopped outside a door marked with the number 3 and Mina put a hand on the door handle.

'Gustaf Brons is definitely guilty of a lot of things,' she said, looking him in the eye. 'Murder might still be one of those things, regardless of the circumstances around the discovery. As I said, the commissioner is convinced of it. But Brons has

Europe's priciest lawyer and I don't want to waste any more time on him than is absolutely necessary.'

'So I'm your shortcut.'

'You're my shortcut. You're going to help me to interpret him.'

They entered the room.

Two men in impeccable attire were awaiting them inside the small space. Vincent suddenly felt like a slob by comparison in his Oscar Jacobson suit. He dumped his snow-sodden outer wear on a chair by the door. The two men appeared to be in competition to see who was best groomed. Vincent had expected to see dark bags under the eyes of one of them to provide a hint that he was Brons, but it seemed that expensive creams could work miracles.

'Who's this?' one of the men said to Mina. 'We've been obliging enough to attend, but we most certainly haven't agreed to an audience.'

So that was the lawyer. He didn't even look at Vincent. Mina had said that Brons had avoided remand, unlike Peter Kronlund. And now Vincent understood why. This brief would probably be capable of getting Olof Palme's killer out of prison even following a full confession. This wasn't going to be easy.

'This is Vincent – he works with us,' Mina said curtly.

'It's OK,' Brons said, gesturing in a measured fashion. 'I know who this guy is. Nothing more than a kids' magician. Anything that slows the police down is fine by me.'

Vincent glanced at Mina. He wasn't so sure that he was a shortcut here – he might be more of an obstacle.

Brons allowed his gaze to wander up and down Mina's body, an appreciative smile playing across his lips. Mina seemed completely unfazed and sat down opposite him at the table.

Vincent also sat down, on a chair away from them by the wall, so that he had a proper view of Brons and his lawyer.

'Thank you for coming,' Mina said, turning to Brons. 'I don't want to waste your time, so why don't we get down to it? What was Jon Langseth's role at Confido?'

'Jon?' Brons said, clearly surprised that the question wasn't about him. 'Well … He was our front man. He sold the product. But surely you already know that?'

Mina nodded.

'Yes, I know,' she said. 'What I mean is – how familiar was he with your … business affairs?'

The lawyer cleared his throat loudly and slapped his hand against the table.

'You are asking my client about trade secrets and he is under no obligation to answer.'

Mina propped her elbows on the table and leaned her chin on her hands without taking her gaze off Brons.

'Not even if it gets your client off a murder charge?' she said.

The financier started. The corners of his mouth twitched downwards for a moment.

Mina nodded at him to continue.

The lawyer looked as if he was about to interrupt again, but Brons waved him away.

'Look, Confido was our joint idea,' he said, leaning back and allowing his legs to relax into a blatant manspread.

Brons was clearly pleased to be talking about himself.

'Everyone had equal shares in the company. But Jon was always the timorous one. He didn't want to take risks. So Peter and I kept him in the dark about certain decisions. There were things we knew he would be too nervous to handle well.'

'Or were you afraid that Jon would blab about what was going on?' Mina said, apparently not reacting to his display of machismo.

'We were afraid that he might divulge information that could harm the company,' Brons said. 'For instance, to the press.'

'I see,' Mina said. 'So what did you think when he disappeared?'

Brons unconsciously raised his eyebrows in a way that gave them a slight slope. It was a subtle but clear expression of sadness. He was clearly moved by the subject, even if he was trying to pretend that the opposite was the case. Mina suddenly smiled at him warmly and Brons smiled back at her automatically. He leaned in a few inches towards her to signal familiarity.

Vincent put his hand to his mouth to avoid showing that he too had started to smile. Men like Brons thought they were God's gift to women. They couldn't conceive of the idea that they were being manipulated. When Mina didn't respond to

Brons's primitive display of his crotch, which he was presumably unaccustomed to, she had subconsciously made the man start to seek her validation. So when Mina then smiled at him, he immediately took the bait and began to change his behaviour to try to hold her attention. Vincent was impressed. But then again, Mina was the smartest person he knew.

'Business-wise, it was obviously a tremendous relief when Jon was out of the picture,' Brons said in a softer tone than before. 'But it wasn't easy for Josephine. That's Jon's wife. By the way, is he just going to sit over there?'

Brons nodded towards Vincent. The lawyer once again cleared his throat.

'What my client means by his statement,' he said, emphasizing each word, 'is that he was naturally deeply concerned for his friend on a personal level, but that as far as the company was concerned it streamlined their communications.'

'So you didn't have anything to do with Jon's disappearance?' Mina said, leaning even closer to Brons.

'Of course not. I'm a businessman – not a crook.'

'How come you've received large payments from Dragan Manojlovic?'

Mina let the question sink in during the silence that followed.

'Now you've lost me,' Brons said.

The gaze that met Mina's was suddenly ice cold.

'Where are you trying to go with this?' the lawyer said, also glaring at Mina.

But for a brief moment he looked unsure.

'It's not something you should waste a moment of your time or energy denying,' Mina said. 'We're across every single deposit. Every last penny. You've received money from Dragan Manojlovic and I don't require any explanation of who he is. Besides the fact that he's Peter Kronlund's father, that is. So what I'm wondering is what his involvement in Confido was? Or was it personal?'

Brons blinked. Finally a reaction. Mina had already launched her attack and Vincent thought she might as well finish it and see what else it gave.

'Did you and Peter kill Jon together?' she said. 'Peter out

of family solidarity, while you were paid hard cash? Almost a million kronor. Don't look so surprised. We know that's the sum you received from Dragan. Not bad value for a contract kill.'

She didn't shy away from Brons's gaze, but whatever had thrown him off balance before, he seemed to have regained his stability. The lawyer leaned forward to whisper into his client's ear.

Brons nodded.

'Coffeehousing,' he said to the lawyer with a shrug.

His lawyer didn't answer, but straightened up, picked up his briefcase and nodded at Brons.

'We came here to confirm my client's innocence and demonstrate our goodwill,' the lawyer said, standing up brusquely. 'Not to be faced with accusations. We're done here. And we will be filing a complaint on grounds of defamation.'

'Just a moment,' Brons said, a crooked smile playing across his face. 'I'm in no rush. Before we go, I'm curious to know what the magician has to say about all of this.'

He turned to Vincent.

'I assume you're here to analyse me. What do you say? Am I guilty? Of whatever she said … hiring a contract killer?'

Vincent looked at him for a moment. Then he stood up and approached him slowly.

'At this stage, I think there's only one thing I can say,' Vincent said.

He bent forward and whispered into Brons's ear – his voice quiet enough that no one else could hear him. When he stood up again, he saw that the financier had turned visibly pale and his eyes had glazed over, as if he were doing his best not to cry.

Gustaf Brons stood up abruptly, nodded curtly at Mina and then exited the room without even a glance at Vincent or his lawyer, who, taken aback, hurried after his client.

'So?' Mina said, once the door had closed behind them. 'What do you say?'

Vincent leaned against the edge of the table and thought. There was much to dissect about Brons's behaviour, but it wasn't easy to tell what were triggered defence mechanisms and what was simply his natural conduct.

'Brons *might* have had something to do with Jon's disappearance,' he said at last. 'His face showed visible sadness when we were talking about Jon.'

'Sadness?'

'Yes, but the expression for guilt looks just the same. And the strategy of initially trying to get both you and I off balance by insulting me and objectifying you and then trying to own the situation and your relationship to each other feels like over-compensation. That makes me lean heavily towards guilt. There's something there. The only question is what he's guilty of. He did a good job of seeming unmoved when you brought up the payments from Dragan. But he blinked particularly slowly, as if he was trying to shut you and the question out, which demonstrated that you'd hit on a sore spot. I think you spotted that too. Speaking of body language, nicely done getting him to open up to you like that. Making yourself unavailable and then mirroring his body language was a great move.'

Mina laughed. It was a rough, deep laugh that warmed the cockles of Vincent's heart.

'After a few years working with you, I'm apparently just as damaged as you are,' she said. 'But you're saying you agree with the commissioner? Should we be detaining Gustaf Brons? I'd like to ask some more questions about Dragan, Confido and those payments. But right now, I don't think I'm going to make any more progress if it's dependent on Gustaf's goodwill.'

Vincent shook his head.

'I can't tell. He's mixed up in it somehow, but that's not the same as having killed Jon – or even ordering his death. As for *Mos Teutonicus* ... Someone else could have done that. It could have been someone who just stumbled across the body. We don't have a clue. It could be that you're actually looking for multiple people. By the way, did you notice how Brons cut himself short when he started talking about Josephine Langseth? I think I'd have another chat with her if I were you. She might have some insight into whatever it is he's feeling guilty about.'

Mina nodded thoughtfully. Her ponytail swayed gently as her head moved, and Vincent felt a strong compulsion to touch her hair. He sat on his hands just to be safe.

'OK,' she said. 'That's good to know. We'll go over that with the others. I just need to know one thing. What did you whisper to him at the end? He looked like he was about to burst into tears.'

'It was a gamble,' Vincent said. 'But you don't end up like him by chance. Unless, that is, you're a psychopath. But he didn't come across like one. So I just told him that it's over. I said he's not alone in having been bullied at school, but that he got his revenge over the bullies long ago. And they probably got what they deserved.'

Mina stared at him with an expression that he was for once unable to interpret.

'Are you in a hurry?' she said. 'If you've got time, I thought you might be able to help Christer with something.'

A hurry? To leave? If only she knew. He was always in a hurry to *get there*. But never to *leave*. He was never in a hurry to leave her.

'I'd be happy to help Christer,' he said. 'But surely Brons and his lawyer won't be able to leave the building by themselves? Don't you have to let them through the barriers?'

'Oh yes. And I'm sure they'll realize that very soon. But we can wait here until they come back.'

Vincent laughed. He would get to wait there with Mina.

41

Christer drummed his fingers nervously against his thigh. He had booked one of the smaller meeting rooms for some privacy, but it felt more like he was at a psychologist's office. Hypnosis? What utter guff. He didn't like it. Anyway, it probably wouldn't work on him – not like it had on Mina.

He looked up at the ceiling and saw that one of the fluorescent tubes was broken. The room was pretty uninspiring, with its tacky beige curtains. Someone ought to tell the interior designers at police headquarters that there was nothing wrong with a bit of colour. He smiled to himself. That was a thought he probably wouldn't have had six months ago. But then he'd met Lasse.

Christer's thoughts were interrupted by the door opening. Vincent entered, followed by Mina.

'So Christer, there's something you want to remember?' the mentalist said, taking a seat opposite him.

Mina was still standing up.

'Do you mind if I stay?' she asked.

Christer shrugged.

'Do whatever you like,' he said. 'This isn't going to work anyway. I'm not like you, Mina. I'm not so … receptive.'

'Receptive to what?' Vincent said, leaning forward.

'I don't know,' Christer said, crossing his arms.

The chair scraped against the floor as he shifted backwards a little.

'Hypnosis?' he said. 'Isn't that what you're going to do? Hypnotize me?'

'Not if you don't want me to,' Vincent said. 'Why don't we just start by talking?'

Christer nodded. As long as Vincent didn't hypnotize him …

'In order to remember something, it's good to engage the

power of imagination,' Vincent said. 'And I know you have a good one at that. But why don't we do a little exercise? I want you to put your right hand on your thigh and imagine that your hand is actually part of your leg. It's as if it's glued to your thigh, or cast from concrete. As if it's melted into the bone itself. Allow yourself to experience what that feels like.'

Christer furrowed his brow but did as the mentalist said. It was a strange exercise. But why not try it? To his surprise, he noticed that he was indeed able to imagine what it felt like to glue his hand to his leg.

'Now I'm wondering,' Vincent said, 'whether it's your palm or fingers that are most stuck?'

Christer checked. His palm felt strangely heavy against his leg, as if it wouldn't come away, but he could still move his fingers.

'My palm,' he said. 'But why ...'

'Excellent. Please start focusing on your fingers and take note of how many seconds it is until they're as stuck down as your palm. That'll start to happen ... now. Let me know when they're stuck too.'

Christer noticed to his astonishment that the more he thought about it, the more tightly his fingers were attached. He had no idea what was going on, but it felt quite pleasant. He nodded slowly.

'I think ... I think my hand is actually stuck,' he said. 'But I don't understand ...'

'That doesn't matter,' Vincent said. 'Do you feel hypnotized?'

Christer shook his head. Of course he wasn't. He was still fully aware of everything going on around him. He could clearly feel the chair beneath him and the curtains were just as tacky as ever. What was more, Vincent had barely been in the room for five minutes and he knew it took much longer than that to hypnotize someone. He'd seen it on television.

'Is this what you two did?' he said, glancing at Mina.

'Not exactly,' she said, smiling slightly.

'What happens if you try to lift your hand?' Vincent said. 'Can you do it?'

Christer tried to do as Vincent said. What on earth ...? He

frowned again. His hand really was stuck. No matter how hard he tried to lift it.

'What the …?'

'It's quite all right,' Vincent said, leaning forward and placing his fingertips on Christer's hand. 'That just shows us that you're going to be very good at remembering. Nothing more. That heaviness you feel in your hand – I want you to discover how it moves up through your arm, your throat, your head. And when it reaches your thoughts, simply close your eyes and relax even more.'

Christer not only felt heavy, he suddenly felt very tired. He sighed deeply and noticed that it had got dark. Somewhere along the way he must have closed his eyes, but at least he wasn't hypnotized. Just as long as that remained the case, it would all be fine.

'In front of you there are three doors leading to three different rooms,' Vincent said. 'Inside the first is the Stockholm metro. The tunnels disappear off, winding away. They're hiding something. A secret. In the next room you have Jon Langseth's skeleton. But it's been picked clean. It's lying there in a pile of bones. It might even be under a heap of gravel.'

Christer could indeed see three doors before him. Yet at the same time, he couldn't really see them at all. Part of his brain pointed out that none of this was real, but there the doors were anyway.

'In the third room there's something else and only you know what it is, but right now it's unknown to you,' Vincent said. 'The rooms are connected. Go into the first two rooms in whichever order you prefer and for as long as you want, until that leads you into the third room. While you do that, tell us what you can see.'

In his imagination, Christer reached out and opened the second door leading into Jon's room. He looked around. Jon was there. As were his bones. Christer realized something right away. What he was looking for didn't have anything to do with Jon Langseth the man, but it might have something to do with Jon's bones. The bones seemed … somehow more important.

He picked up a femur from the heap of skeletal remains and saw gravel tumble onto his feet even though he knew he was really sitting on a chair in a meeting room at police headquarters. He left that room and went into the first one with the tunnels in it.

'I'm inside the metro now,' he said. 'And I've brought one of Jon's bones with me. But the tunnels don't feel right.'

'How do you mean?' Mina's voice said, somewhere in the distance.

'I can't explain it,' he said. 'But the bone I'm holding … I know what I'm looking for in here. It's a place. But it's not supposed to be this close to the trains.'

He walked along the tracks, trying to go further in.

'Where should it be then?' said Vincent.

'Somewhere safer,' he said. 'Somewhere you can be safely out of sight.'

He kept walking until the tunnels changed, yet at the same time he hadn't moved from the chair. It was a strange experience. Then the tracks disappeared and he entered a different tunnel system. It looked like the tunnels for district heating and sewage systems. Faint lights were suspended from the ceiling and he could see tatty mattresses and scraps of cardboard on the floor. Christer nodded to himself. This felt more right.

'I've found the place,' he said. 'It's here.'

Suddenly, someone tugged at the bone he was carrying.

'That's mine,' said a man behind him.

Christer turned around. The man was filthy and had a matted beard and long, equally matted hair. On his head he wore a hat that had probably once been red, but like the thick layers of tattered clothes he wore, it was now as grey as the tunnel walls. Christer knew him. Well, *knew* was the wrong word, but he knew who he was. The man flashed a toothless grin at him as he snatched the bone and ran away.

Christer realized what was in the third room. The solution to the mystery.

He opened the third door and was met by a howling guitar solo. A young man was on a big stage receiving the acclaim of the audience against a backdrop of exploding pyrotechnics. Christer drew breath.

'Mark Eric,' he said, opening his eyes.

He immediately felt dazed.

'Take it easy,' Vincent said. 'Close your eyes and take a few deep breaths before you continue.'

Christer did as Vincent told him to and closed his eyes again, but he'd seen Mina's reaction.

Vincent counted to five and said something that Christer didn't quite catch – something about how he should feel strong and rested. When Vincent reached five, Christer automatically opened his eyes. He felt more alert than he had in a long time.

'Mark Eric,' he exclaimed enthusiastically. 'That musician who went missing – what, two years ago? They found a deranged homeless man wearing Mark's jacket months later. And in one of his plastic bags he also had some of Mark's remains. Well, his bones. The assumption was that the man had killed Mark and then eaten him. However sick that sounded. But the man was in a very bad way and it was impossible to get any sense out of him. He was kept in isolation, but died not long after.'

'You must have read about it,' Mina said, turning to Vincent. 'The story about the "cannibal" who ate a rock star was in all the papers.'

Vincent shook his head.

'If it was after Jane and Kenneth tried to kill us … I think I was trying to avoid the news for a while then, especially anything to do with the police.'

The mentalist appeared to be blushing.

'Anyway,' said Christer. 'What if we were wrong? What if that lunatic didn't murder and eat Mark Eric? After all, the only evidence was the jacket and the bones he was carrying around. But maybe he just found the bones somewhere. What if the same person who killed Jon also murdered the rock star?'

Mina stared at him.

'Christer, when you get home you should ask Lasse for a smacking great kiss,' she said. 'That's brilliant work. We need to talk to Mark Eric's next of kin.'

42

Ruben was sweating profusely. It had taken him a ridiculous length of time to wrap Astrid's Christmas present the evening before. Nevertheless, he thought his parcel looked like an accident tied up with string when he compared it with the perfect examples laid out beside Ellinor's tree.

'I'm glad you could come,' Ellinor said. 'Astrid was so keen to celebrate Christmas with you before we head north to the cabin.'

She was curled up on the large sofa with a mug of tea, and clad in a loose-fitting woolly jumper that still managed to suit her. Astrid had lit lots of candles and their glow lent an almost unreal golden light to the room. Ruben's eyes suddenly began to fill with tears. It was probably the smoke from the candles …

'I'm just sorry about the pitiful tree,' Ellinor said with a laugh. 'We were beaten to it – this shrub was all that was left.'

It was by no means a big tree – Ruben wasn't even sure it was a spruce. There were so many baubles hanging from it that the branches were almost touching the floor, and it was garlanded in so much tinsel that Ruben couldn't guess what colour the branches had been to start with.

He thought it was absolutely perfect.

'Is there any more tea?' he said, his voice unsteady.

Ellinor nodded, got up from the sofa and went into the kitchen.

Astrid was sitting on the floor eating her way through a box of marshmallow Santas at an impressive pace.

'Dad, can I open the present from you now?' she said as she bit the head off another Santa.

'Of course,' Ruben said. 'It's our Christmas Eve today. On the condition you give me a marshmallow Santa before they're all gone.'

Astrid hooted with joy and put the box of sweets on the sofa next to Ruben. Then she began to tug at the string on his unevenly wrapped parcel. She managed to undo the paper just as Ellinor returned. Ellinor placed a cup of something hot and steaming into Ruben's hands, but he was fully occupied watching his daughter.

Inside the parcel there were two more packages – that was why it had taken so long to wrap it all.

'Oh wow!' Ellinor said, clapping her hands. 'A double present!'

Ruben realized he was probably smiling sheepishly. Inside one parcel was a book, which had been Sara's idea. They had gone into a bookshop and Sara had asked an assistant what thirteen-year-olds were reading at the moment. Ruben had tried to protest that Astrid was only ten years old, but Sara had argued that that was precisely the point. He had never heard of the book recommended to them, but the jacket was signalling forbidden teenage love from a distance. He had been sceptical to put it mildly, but based on Astrid's reaction he needn't have worried.

'Oh woooow!' she exclaimed. 'Thank you! Everyone's talking about how good this is!'

Her eyes were practically sparkling as she examined the cover. Ruben didn't even dare look at Ellinor.

Inside the second parcel there were two black wooden sticks joined together at one end by a chain. A nunchaku. That had been his own idea. Astrid frowned at first because she didn't understand what it was, but then she beamed.

'Like Bruce Lee!' she said. 'Haaaai!'

'Who?' Ellinor said in confusion.

'It's not for you, Mum,' Astrid said. 'Nor is this book.'

She hid the book underneath the shredded wrapping paper.

Ellinor nudged Ruben in the side and shared a smile with him. He exhaled. It hadn't been a complete disaster after all.

'I've got a present for you too, Dad,' Astrid said proudly, standing up. 'Wait here.'

Ruben looked at Ellinor in amazement.

'I take no responsibility,' she said. 'She chose it all by herself.'

Astrid returned with a big, round package. The paper rustled in Ruben's hands when he took it.

'Open it now, Dad!' she said eagerly, sitting down on the floor opposite him.

Ruben carefully loosened the pieces of tape – he didn't want to ruin the paper. After all, his own daughter had wrapped this parcel. But in the end he had to tear it anyway. Inside was the biggest hat he'd ever laid eyes on. It was brown and shaggy and had huge ear flaps. It was the kind of hat you can knot underneath your chin.

'Astrid chose it,' Ellinor said, starting to laugh. 'But I was more than happy to pay for it.'

Ruben solemnly donned the hat and carefully tied the ear flap strings together under his chin.

'I think it's perfect,' he said, and he meant it.

'You can wear it when you're working in the winter,' said Astrid. 'So you don't get cold.'

Ruben looked at his daughter, and for the first time in all these months Peder's ghost wasn't there.

43

Vincent was walking with Mina through Rålambshovsparken close to police headquarters. The park had started to feel like it was theirs. The first time they had walked there together it had been the end of winter and he remembered how the soggy snow had stuck to their boots. Today however, the snow was like a thick, frozen blanket covering the whole park. It reflected the glow of the streetlights lining the paths, but the world was otherwise immersed in darkness. The sky above them was overcast, meaning there weren't even any stars to be seen. They had reached the very darkest days of the year.

He would happily have been excused from strolling through the park with the mercury that low, but Mina seemed to appreciate the cold. And he wanted to do what she wanted to do. What was more, her investigation gave him something to think about other than the threat posed by the Shadow. If he thought about that too much he was worried that his brain might stop working, and he needed full access to his intellectual faculties now more than ever.

'I can't stop thinking about Gustaf Brons and those payments,' Mina said. 'Why would he take money from Dragan Manojlovic?'

'As I said before, you ought to talk to Jon's wife. There was something about Gustaf's demeanour during the interview that implied a personal relationship there. What kind, I don't know. My magical mind-reading powers only go so far. You common muggles have to do the rest.'

'You're a right muggle too,' Mina muttered. 'So, about this cannibal, to change the subject completely – what do you make of that?'

'At first glance, it's got nothing to do with Jon Langseth,' Vincent replied, thinking back to what Christer had said. 'Except that it involved skeletal remains and someone who might have been holed up in the tunnels. And you don't seem to have much else to go on at the moment. Unless it turns out that the commissioner was right about Gustaf Brons, that is. I'm sorry I don't have a better answer for you, but I feel as if I don't have anything to add.'

'You mean that there's no complicated puzzle to solve?'

He smiled while keeping his head down. They walked through the dark park in silence for a while.

'By the way, I've got a new present for you,' Vincent said, stopping and pulling out the small glass jar he had been carrying in his pocket. It was a rather awkward manoeuvre given the thick gloves he was wearing. 'Instead of the lump of clay you got.'

He handed the jar to her. He had deliberately not wrapped it, choosing instead to fasten a bow to the lid so that she could see the rust-brown contents.

'What is this?' she said sceptically, twisting and turning the jar.

'It's umber – one of the most common pigments used by humankind to paint over the course of modern history. It's actually a type of soil that has high levels of manganese oxide, hence the particular colour. The most famous umber comes from Cyprus, but there's plenty more to be found in Lebanon, Syria and Turkey as well. They've found paintings that use umber pigments from as far back as 200 BC. The word umber means "shadow" in Latin, or perhaps even "the darkest shadow", the core shadow, since it's often been used to paint just that. Shadows.'

'So my present is a history lesson?' Mina said.

'No, no. You're getting a painting course instead of a pottery class. Not as messy.'

Mina looked at him. Then she shook her head and stuffed the jar in her pocket. He wasn't quite sure, but he thought she was a little happier with it than she had been with the clay.

They moved on.

Puzzles ... He knew there was something he'd forgotten to mention.

'Speaking of puzzles,' he said. 'You might say that's what I've received – from a stranger. A fan, I dare say. I recognize the handwriting. He or she has sent me ingenious problems before that I've enjoyed solving. I've still got several of them on my bookshelf. But this is different. It consists of four hourglasses in a frame. Each one measuring a different amount of time. The problem is, I don't know what I'm supposed to solve. There are just the hourglasses and a clue that says something about finding "the fourth one". I've got no idea where to start. That sort of thing was never a problem before. I'm obviously not as bright as I once was. I'm almost starting to worry about myself.'

He didn't want to mention that the hourglass and message had made him anxious.

Mina only seemed to have been half-listening to him. She looked at him in bewilderment.

'Hourglasses? What do they have to do with anything?'

He shrugged and they walked on in silence again.

'Speaking of hourglasses, Frithjof Schuon wrote about the symbolism of hourglasses. Back in 1966 I think it was,' he said. 'The sand obviously reminds us that time is finite and that it only flows in one direction, whether we like it or not. The sand is sterile and merciless and when it has run out all movement ceases. Just like in death. That means that an hourglass has two "spheres" which can represent the divine and the terrestrial, high and low, heaven and earth. Yin and Yang. Or the visible world and the invisible world. Two opposite poles, where the only one available to us and towards which all movement is directed is the lower half. Of course, a more positive interpretation would be the cosmological one, which says that the movement of sand can be compared with all the possibilities that exist and not until they are completely exhausted does the sand stop moving. As I said, I've been sent four. But I don't know why.'

He fell silent again. He knew he was talking too much, even if Mina hadn't said that. So he deliberately avoided talking about the very paradox of an hourglass – the painful passage between the two spheres, which according to Jünger, was the place where human enlightenment was created. Or the more than obvious erotic connection outlined by Yukio Mishima.

He glanced at Mina, who shook her head.

'I'm going to paint an umber hourglass for you in my class,' she said with a smile, before slipping her gloved hand under his arm.

44

TEN DAYS TO GO

'It's a lot emptier in here than it's going to be in January,' Sara said in amusement, making Ruben start.

He was doing leg presses in the police headquarters gym. He immediately hoped that Sara wasn't checking how much weight – well, how little – he was pressing on the machine. When Ruben had got home after the previous evening's Christmas festivities with Astrid and Ellinor, Peder's ghost had hit him like an express train. Full of anxiety, he'd headed off to Spy Bar where he'd lingered until closing time. That meant that he was not feeling at all strong today.

'It just seems to be the two of us,' he said, mopping sweat from his brow with his towel. 'How's your Christmas shaping up then?'

He sat down to conceal the weights behind him.

'I've got the kids,' Sara said, a smile appearing on her face.

'Do you take them every other week?' he said, realizing just how much he wanted to get to know his NOA colleague.

'No, thank God. Their dad is still in the USA and after going a thousand rounds in court I finally got sole custody, but with certain stipulations about when he gets to have them. Once every three Christmases, every other summer, and … Well, there's a pretty complicated schedule of half terms. But it works. But now he's met someone new and they're having a baby in March, so it's all calmed down a bit. But Christmas alone sucks, so I'm really glad it's one of my years this year …'

She sat down on the abdominal machine. Ruben tried not to stare at her low neckline. Her bust was rather prominent in her tight vest top, emblazoned with the word *Stronger* across the bosom.

'Astrid, Ellinor and I did early Christmas yesterday,' he said. 'It was great. Thanks for your help with the present – she was thrilled with the book. I'm so grateful that I get to be involved. And Astrid seemed pleased that I was there.'

'Of course she was!' Sara said, smiling at him.

Her smile lit up the drab gym. Ruben felt awkward. He didn't want to be dazzled by a smile. Tits and arses – those were his things. *Not* a smile with dimples. Even if it did make him melt in a place that had been frozen for many years. Perhaps ever since Ellinor.

'How are things going with the possible bomb?' he said, trying to master his own emotions. 'Was it the real thing, or what?'

Sara looked around before answering, even though the gym was empty.

'We don't know yet, but what's worrying is how much ammonium nitrate is missing,' she said in a low voice. 'Do you remember the explosion in the port of Beirut in Lebanon in 2020? More than five thousand people were injured and around two hundred died. Seventy thousand homes were left in ruins, affecting three hundred thousand people. If the same thing happened here, a lot of the city would sustain serious damage.'

'I remember that,' Ruben said. 'Hadn't customs been storing seized ammonium nitrate without any safety measures for years, and then one day it got so hot that the whole thing blew up?'

'Exactly. Ammonium nitrate doesn't necessarily explode by itself, but if it's warm enough it does. Beirut was one of the ten worst civilian explosions in history.'

'But wasn't that a few thousand tonnes that detonated? Are you missing that much?'

'No, luckily we aren't. Right now we're only missing about ten tonnes in Sweden. But believe me, that will go a long way in the wrong hands.'

Ruben stared at her.

'How big a hole are we talking?'

'You don't want to know. But I dare say that the perpetrator is going to mix it with other materials to increase the explosive effect. If a charge like that were to explode somewhere like Stockholm city centre then … well, let me put it like this, there wouldn't be much city left. Thousands dead. And the national healthcare system would collapse from having to tend to the wounded.'

Ruben stared at her.

'Oh shit,' he said. 'I really hope it's a false alarm then.'

'How's your investigation going?'

'Good. Bad. I don't know.' He sighed. 'It's progressing, though it still seems very strange and messy. But we picked up a good lead. One of the people we questioned – the owner of Confido – is called Peter Kronlund. But the thing is, he wasn't always Peter Kronlund. He used to be Peter Manojlovic. That makes him the son of—'

'Dragan Manojlovic,' Sara interjected, sitting bolt upright on the bench. 'The leader of the Serbian mafia in Sweden. I know. So what else do you have?'

'Not much more than that. I think it's probably the best lead we've got so far. I mean, what are the odds of us finding a dead body with a direct connection to the Manojlovic family without them being involved in the death somehow? I'd lay money on the Serbs being involved. But what do you mean you know? Did you know that Peter was Dragan's son? Why didn't you say anything?'

Ruben wiped more sweat away with his towel. The sweat didn't seem to be stopping, and it smelled faintly of booze. He sincerely hoped that Sara wouldn't notice.

There was a clatter as the door opened and one of their colleagues entered. He headed straight for the dumb-bells after exchanging brief nods with Sara and Ruben. The officer had the body shape seen in many of the older guard. Big arms and a big belly. 'Good arms' was a quip among that generation of police, who quite seriously seemed to think that muscular arms offset a huge keg built on burgers and chips.

Sara leaned in closer towards Ruben and lowered her voice. He instinctively wanted to move backwards so that she wouldn't catch a whiff of the tequila shots escaping through his pores, but he couldn't go any further back than he was already.

'Sorry,' she said quietly. 'You know what the politics are like in this place. NOA is currently carrying out a survey of organized crime in Sweden. The Manojlovics are naturally high on that list. But it's all very sensitive, so it was deemed best that we didn't share any of what we know, to avoid jeopardizing our own investigation. There was one hell of a fuss at NOA when we realized you'd received a tip about Gustaf Brons.'

'Cops working against each other,' Ruben said with a shake of the head. 'So it's better for us to do twice the work in parallel?'

'Yes, well, according to some anyway, but I don't agree. If you raise it with Julia and I take it to my superiors then maybe they might approve an exchange of information between us. I think we would probably both benefit from it.'

'We bloody would,' Ruben said eagerly. 'I assume you'd like me to hold off visiting Peter until this has been signed off?'

'I think that would be best. Anyway, I'm not sure you've realized how dangerous these people are. The stuff in the public domain is bad enough. But we've got information to suggest … well. Be careful.'

For a moment, his heart skipped a beat at the thought that Sara actually cared about him, but it was probably just collegiality. She would have said that to any police officer.

He got up. The smell of booze was becoming too intrusive and he wanted to take a couple of steps away from Sara. In a perfect world he would also be able to move the pin on the leg press machine before she saw what weight it was set to.

Sara got up at the same time. They stood facing each other in silence for far too long. Their colleague by the weights was bellowing like a rutting roebuck as he struggled to make his biceps bulge even more. In the end, it was Sara who broke the silence.

'Look … maybe this is crazy. We don't really know each other. But … it seems a pity for you to spend Christmas Eve all alone. Do you want to come round to ours? We don't make a big deal out of it. We eat something tasty that isn't Christmassy and watch a movie. And no need for any gifts. Well, something small for the kids if you want. There are already far too many parcels under the tree for them. The life of an over-compensating single parent …'

She casually held out her hands and Ruben tried to look nonchalant as he shrugged.

'Sure,' he said, tossing his head. 'I guess that would work. What time?'

'Five o'clock?'

'Sure thing.'

Ruben waited until she had gone over to the rowing machines. Then he spun around, tugged the pin out from the 80 kilos mark on the leg press machine and shoved it into the 200 kilos mark. All of a sudden, he wanted to be in the best shape he could be ahead of Christmas Eve. He had another hour until he was due to meet Christer.

45

Mina watched in amusement as Ruben sauntered into the office, his hair damp and a gym bag slung over his shoulder.

'Good workout?' she asked.

'Hell yes,' he said, putting his bag down. 'Why are you smirking like that?'

A distinct blush began to spread across his cheeks, but before she had time to ask the reason for his rosy countenance, he sat down and the smile disappeared from her face.

'I heard on the grapevine that charges against Dragan Manojlovic are being prepared,' he said.

'Oh right – what else did Sara say then? I saw her leaving the gym.'

The blush spread to Ruben's throat.

'Oh, shut up. But yes, she was the one who told me. I also heard that Gustaf Brons played the lawyer card when he was here. Isn't it time we bring him in more officially?'

'We need more to go on first. The key is what the money was meant for. And why Brons needed it. His annual income in recent years hasn't exactly been modest. Why did he need to take cash under the table from the Serbian mob? A million kronor might be a lot to most people, but for Gustaf Brons, I bet that's what he burns through in a week on the Riviera.'

'Dope, chicks or gambling,' said Ruben. 'In my experience, that's always what it goes on. Possibly a combination of the above.'

'Dope, chicks or gambling …'

Something shifted ever so slightly in Mina's memory. It was something that Gustaf Brons had said, but she couldn't quite recall what. It brought about an association with coffee, but for the life of her she couldn't fathom what her brain was getting at.

'Could Dragan have been using Confido to launder money?' she said, thinking aloud.

'So you're ditching the theory that the money was to pay for Jon's murder?' said Ruben.

He took a towel from his bag and mopped his brow.

'I'm not ditching anything. I'm just trying to cover every angle.'

Ruben stood up and put the towel away again.

'So what's on your agenda for today?' Mina said, staring glumly into her mug of coffee.

A shimmering film reminiscent of petrol had formed on the cold surface.

'I'm about to meet Christer. We're going to see Marcus's mother.'

Mina gazed at him blankly.

'Mark Eric …' he clarified.

'Oh yes. Of course.'

Mina was absent-minded. Her brain was fully occupied by pondering what it was from the interview with Gustaf Brons that had caught her attention. She stood up to get a refill of petrol coffee. Sometimes it helped to stop thinking about it.

46

Vincent was awakened by someone shaking his shoulder. It could not possibly be morning already. It felt as if he had only just fallen asleep, but the shaking continued.

'Dad,' said an impatient voice that was very close by. 'Dad!'

Vincent forced himself to open his eyes and tried to focus. Aston was standing by his bedside tugging at the covers.

'What is it?' Vincent mumbled. 'Has something happened?'

He squinted at the practically antique alarm clock on the nightstand. The hands showed it was five minutes to six in the morning. Aston tugged at the covers again and Vincent tugged back.

'Get your own duvet,' he muttered. 'Why have you woken me up? And why are you already awake?'

'Because today's the first day of the Christmas holidays!' Aston cried cheerfully. 'And there's loads of snow outside! Come on, Dad! If you dig, I'll build!'

Vincent pulled the duvet over his head and groaned.

'Go and play video games like a normal child,' he said. 'And don't wake your mother.'

'But she's not asleep.'

Vincent pulled the duvet off his head and looked towards the other side of the bed. Aston was right. Maria wasn't there. Her side of the bed was not only empty, it had also been made. He knew only one person in the whole world who bothered to make half a bed. While Maria might have a 'follow the winds' and 'listen to the will of the cosmos' vibe on the outside, to use her words, it was a toss-up which of them had the greatest need for control. She must have been awake for a while.

'I'm coming,' he said, waving his hand at Aston. 'Just give me some room for … takeoff.'

Aston hooted with joy so loudly that it could probably be heard in the next county, and then vacated the bedroom. Vincent sighed, pulled off the covers, sat up and put on his dressing gown. He searched for a while before he found his slippers. The floor in the house was very cold and he never went anywhere without a snuggly protective layer around his feet.

When he went into the kitchen, he was surprised to see that Maria wasn't there. Nor was she in the living room. Or the bathroom. And it was far too early for her to have gone off to do anything related to her business. All of a sudden Vincent was shivering, even though he had wrapped the dressing gown tightly around his body. The words in the Shadow's message resonated inside his head.

I'm going to take your family. Then you. And there's nothing you can do about it.

'Maria!' he called out. 'Are you here? Maria!'

He couldn't panic. There was guaranteed to be a natural explanation for why his wife wasn't there.

On his way back to the kitchen, he heard a crash that made him jump. It had come from Rebecka's room, and it sounded like a bookcase being overturned. Then her door opened and Rebecka popped her head out, her hair standing on end.

'What the hell are you doing?' she snapped. 'It's the middle of the bloody night.'

'Have you seen Maria?' Vincent said quickly. 'I can't find her anywhere. And what was that noise?'

'I fell out of bed when you shouted.'

'Sorry,' Vincent said with a grimace. 'But have you seen her?'

'Middle. Of. The. Night,' his daughter said, fixing her gaze on him. 'No, I haven't seen her and I'm going to pretend I haven't seen you either.'

She glared at him for a few seconds before closing her door again. At that moment, the front door opened. Maria came inside clutching the newspaper. She was only wearing thin pyjamas underneath her quilted jacket, and her teeth were chattering hard.

'*Brr*, it's freezing out there,' she said.

'How come you're up so early?' Vincent said, feeling himself exhale.

'I couldn't sleep,' Maria said, taking off her coat. 'And it's not that early. It's gone six. I'm expecting a package today. The Christmas shoppers have run riot in my online shop and I'm almost out of angels, especially the bronze ones with the big wings, so I'm hoping some more of them will arrive. I need to get them off today if they're going to make it before Christmas Eve.'

'You mean the ones depicting Metatron, the voice of God, that some people say stopped Abraham when he was about to kill his son Isaac? *That* angel?'

Maria shrugged.

'It's a good seller at Christmas. I suppose people like to put it up in their windows.'

'For Christmas? But Metatron isn't really Christian. He's Jewish …'

He fell silent. It didn't matter. The important thing was that she was there. Safe. The only question was how safe anyone in his family was while they continued to share a house with him.

I'm going to take your family. Then you.

'Why don't I sort us some breakfast?' Maria said, making for the kitchen. 'Since you're up.'

Vincent followed. He realized he had to get them out of here.

'Didn't your parents invite us for Christmas this year?' he said as casually as he could. 'I think it would be a great idea if we weren't here this year.'

Maria had just opened the kitchen cupboard where they kept the mugs and she turned to him, eyebrows raised.

'Have you had a bump on the head?' she said. 'You know my parents invite us and Ulrika every year, but you never want to go.'

'I've changed my mind,' he said, reaching for a red Christmas mug. 'It's the twenty-first today. There are only three days to go until Christmas Eve. How about you head over to theirs tomorrow? Take Aston too. I know it's been a long time since you saw your parents. Rebecka's leaving for France tomorrow, and Benjamin and I will come on to your parents later.'

Maria took down a mug emblazoned with the words *My balls are bigger than yours*.

'So you *have* hit your head,' she said with a smile. 'But sure, that sounds nice.'

'Unless you were doing something else today?' he said, nodding towards the calendar where his wife had circled the date.

'Huh? No, it wasn't me who did that. But do you know what? It's a fantastic idea,' she said, gently placing her hand on his arm. 'If you promise that you'll actually come and not change your mind at the last minute. It would be good for my parents to see that I'm not making you up.'

Maria added water to the filter coffee machine. Like Vincent, she had gone back to using it after growing tired of the capsule coffee maker.

'Have you got hold of Ulrika yet?' she asked as she measured out ground coffee.

'No, not yet.'

Maria laughed in delight.

'Can you picture her face when we all show up? And without getting a divorce. I'll be living on that for years to come.'

Maria stopped moving the scoop in mid-air. Then she put it down on the side and turned towards Vincent. Her laughter had been replaced by a look of suspicion.

'Why can't you two come with us right away? Aston's finished school, Rebecka can look after herself, Benjamin's doing uni remotely, and you haven't got any performances. Is all this put on, to get you a few days' alone time with Mina? Perhaps even in our bed? Is that your plan?'

Vincent sighed. They had almost got past the familiar jealousy. Almost.

'Mum!' Aston shouted as he ran in and interrupted them. 'Dad has to get dressed now. We're going outside to build snowmen!'

Aston grabbed his snow coveralls which had been drying on the radiator and began to pull them on.

'You'd better save your energies for Mina – you're not twenty-five any more,' Maria said, pursing her lips and grumpily turning back to continue setting up the coffee maker.

Vincent tousled his son's hair and re-knotted his dressing gown sash which had begun to loosen.

'Aston, let's at least have breakfast first,' he said. 'You need to eat if you're going to do lots of digging.'

'Eat snow!' his son shouted before rushing out of the door. 'I'm going to!'

Vincent's mobile buzzed. It was a reminder that he had a meeting with Umberto later that day. Vincent sighed. His manager wasn't going to be happy when he heard what Vincent had to tell him.

He went into the living room to feed the fish. When he picked up the fish food, the headache suddenly slammed into him, as if he'd been hit by a train. He gasped and had to support himself against the aquarium. He needed to take another tablet. He tried to focus on the wall behind the aquarium, but that only made matters worse. He had the curious feeling that there was something written on the wall, though he could clearly see that the only things there were framed photographs of his family. But the feeling was overwhelming. His field of vision began to flicker.

He remembered when he had been with his mates at school and they had tried to 'magic' away objects by placing them in their blind spot. You had to look dead ahead and have the object at the very edge of your field of vision to make it work. He was experiencing that precise feeling now – as if he could see something while at the same time he couldn't.

He closed his eyes and concentrated on his breathing.

Before long, his headache began to dissipate. But it didn't go entirely. It never did these days. It was always there in the background, constantly gnawing away at him like a disturbing sound that you didn't notice until it was gone. He looked out of the open front door at the cold snow. He might like Christmas, but he hated winter.

47

'Do you mind if we come in?' said Christer.

The face peering out at them over a door chain bridging the narrow open crack was thin and wrinkled. The woman was silent for a moment.

'I presume you're not selling raffle tickets,' she said in a brittle voice.

'That's correct,' he said. 'We'd like to talk to you about Marcus, if we may.'

The woman looked at them again. Then the door closed and they heard the sound of the chain rattling. The door was opened fully and the light in the hallway slanted towards them in welcome. Christer crossed the threshold ahead of Ruben. He stamped the snow from his shoes onto the doormat, which had Santa Claus in a sled on it.

Mark Eric's mother bore her seventy or so years with dignity and was the exact opposite to how Mark looked in the pictures from his career.

A Salvation Army uniform was hanging neatly on a hanger in the hallway. Marcus Eriksson hadn't had children of his own, or any siblings, so following the early death of his father his mother had been his only relative. Christmas music was playing at a low volume, and there was the aroma of mulled wine and cinnamon.

'Come in and warm up,' the dainty little woman said, leading them into the kitchen.

'As you know, we're here to … to talk about collecting Mark,' Christer said hesitantly, unsure whether he'd opted for the right term as he took a seat on one of the kitchen chairs.

A crossword puzzle was lying on the table, half-complete, with a pair of reading glasses beside it.

'Oh please, call him Marcus,' the woman said, pouring mulled wine from a saucepan into three small cups. 'And I'm Gudrun. Although I go by Gun.'

She set down the steaming cups in front of them.

'Marcus wasn't … Mark Eric. Not to me, anyway. It was all an act – it was a role he played. To me he was always my Marcus.'

'What was he like?'

Christer sipped his mulled wine, but the heat made him grimace and he put it down again. Gun perked up.

'Oh, he was such a lovely boy. It was always just the two of us, but we were the best of friends. Ever since he was born. God knows he had his demons, but he found his path through life. I don't know how things would have worked out if he hadn't.'

'I've already read the police report, but would you mind telling us in your own words about his disappearance?'

'Well …'

She fidgeted with the newspaper containing the crossword, seeming to become lost in her own thoughts.

'My Granny Astrid does these too,' Ruben said, pointing to the crossword. 'The ones with picture clues. I guess the first two are Leif GW Persson and Viktor Frisk, but who are the other two?'

Gun smiled and looked at the men depicted as clues in the crossword.

'I suppose one of them is some celebrity chef,' she said. 'The other … I think he must be a singer. You find him everywhere these days.'

Then she placed her hands over the crossword and looked at them.

'Marcus had started having problems again. It had been so many years. I never thought he'd wind up there again.'

'Do you mean drugs?' Christer said carefully.

He sipped the mulled wine, which was by now drinkable.

'It was all so long ago,' Gun said, without directly answering his question.

She brushed her hand over the crossword.

'Benjamin Ingrosso!' Ruben said suddenly.

Christer jumped and then stared at him, but Gun smiled, picked up her pencil and diligently inserted the correct letters.

'That's it,' she said, putting down the pencil again. 'That fits exactly. Anyway, Marcus went through a tough time many years ago. Drugs were involved, but that wasn't the whole picture. He was mulling things over. Searching. He thought he'd found what he was looking for in drugs. But he was fundamentally always a sensible boy. He went through a very dark spell for a while. He'd be gone at night and I would have no idea whether he was coming home or not. Have you ever had nightmares about your child jumping in front of a train or off a bridge?'

Christer shook his head. The topic was one that he was more unfamiliar with than he wanted to let on.

'Take solace in that,' Gun said. 'Anyway, he eventually got out of this hole. Around the same time, his music started to pick up. He never touched drugs again. Not even alcohol. The whole … bad boy thing, or whatever the papers called it … It was all just a façade. His record label cooked it up. Marcus lived the quiet life when he wasn't on tour. We spent a lot of time together. He never did have his own family, so … Well, he had me.'

'That sounds lovely,' said Ruben. 'Given how close you were, did he ever say anything to you that might explain his disappearance?'

Christer saw that he was glancing longingly at the crossword. He had clearly solved a few of them with his grandmother.

'No, not in so many words,' Gun said, frowning. 'But a couple of weeks before he disappeared, he started to behave differently. I've often thought about that since then.'

'How so?' Christer said, leaning forward.

'I don't know how long it was going on for, because I didn't see him every day. But he was scared. Always checking his phone. He'd park his car at the back and keep an eye on it all the time while he was here. I assumed it was linked to drugs again. I actually asked him about that, but he denied it.'

Gun stood up and began to heat up more mulled wine with her back turned to them.

'What's going to happen to him now?' she said, a slight tremor in her voice.

Christer wasn't really sure what to say in response. They were talking about the remains of her only child.

'Per Morberg!' Ruben said loudly.

Christer jumped yet again and spilled some of his mulled wine.

'Per Morberg,' Ruben said in a lower voice, pointing to the crossword. 'The chef.'

'The bones are going to be looked at one more time by our medical examiner,' Christer said, glaring at his colleague. 'We believe there may be more to his disappearance and death than we previously thought. There are ... similarities to another case.'

Gun nodded and sat down after refilling their cups. Then she picked up the pencil and dutifully entered Per Morberg's name in the empty squares running down from his picture.

'Do what you must,' she said as the faint sound of Christmas music continued in the background. 'You have my blessing. Do what you must.'

'Yes, well. Merry Christmas for the time being,' Christer murmured. 'Or something.'

As they left, Gun remained at the kitchen table hunched over the crossword with a deep line of concentration running across her forehead as she continued to scrawl letters into empty boxes.

'I'm going to pay Granny a visit just as soon as I can,' Ruben said as they left the flat. 'Time's a real bastard. All of a sudden, it runs out.'

48

That moment between dreaming and reality was when she was closest. In the dreams, she was hard to capture and when he was awake, he struggled to see her features clearly. But in those seconds after the dream and before reality hit, he always saw her clearly. Dad had called her 'our sun'. As always, Dad was right. There was light shining around her as if she had her own sun that followed her and illuminated her and everyone in proximity to her.

That was why it was always so cold when the sun went out. That was why Dad had chosen to bring him with him into the darkness when the sun had gone out for good. It was better to live completely without what had once been. Without Mum dancing in their kitchen with the kitchen table covered in the checked wax cloth and the chairs that all looked different and that Mum had salvaged.

It wasn't something that Dad had said; he had worked it out all by himself. Down here in the dark, his chest hurt a lot less than it did topside. Down here, it was safe. For them at least. Down here, they were loved and cared for, and they could take care of others. They could give and take. Dad said that was important.

A rat wandered across the cardboard he was lying on – it was so close he could count the whiskers. That was Buster. He recognized him by the scar on his nose. Sometimes he would share a few crumbs with Buster. It amused him to see the rat holding the crumbs between his tiny paws with his eager nose held aloft.

Give and take.

One of the newcomers had wanted to kill Buster but Dad had stopped him. He had explained the conditions of being part of the family down here. Life was to be respected. Life was sacred. Taking a life was not a human right – that was what Dad always said. So Buster got to keep toddling around.

The guy in the yellow hat was calling out anxiously in his sleep, but he stopped when he turned over. The sound of the trains was soporific and calming.

He turned over too and tugged the blanket closer. When he closed his eyes, he felt the dream taking hold of him again. He was at home. He was safe.

49

'Why don't we head over to see if there's anyone we can talk to about Crazy-Tom?' Christer said, glancing towards Ruben. 'We might be able to get to the bottom of just how Mark's remains came to be found.'

'Yes, I had the same thought,' Ruben said, setting a course for Huddinge.

The Helix secure psychiatric facility was not far from Huddinge hospital, and they had no difficulty finding their way. It wasn't somewhere they often went. All the patients were receiving psychiatric care rather than serving prison sentences, having been assessed as too mentally ill to be incarcerated in the regular prison system.

Christer felt depressed each time he went there. But he also felt happy each time he left – simply because he could. The people receiving visitors had to stay. He sighed deeply.

It took them a while to reach the ugly brown building since there were still idiots with summer tyres out on the roads.

'Bloody Stockholmers,' Christer muttered. 'They never learn that winter comes round every year.'

'Aren't you a Stockholmer?' Ruben said.

'Yeah, but still.'

They parked and headed towards the entrance. The security was very obvious. There was not only a big wall but also an electric fence surrounding the building.

'Do you think there's anyone left working here from Crazy-Tom's time? After all, it's been almost two years since he died and I'd guess personnel turnover is high,' Christer said grimly as they entered.

Ruben shrugged.

'I suppose we'll find out.'

A dreary looking plastic Christmas tree with a few baubles and meagre tinsel on it was the only indication of the festive season in the foyer. A woman in large spectacles and even bigger earrings looked at them quizzically as they approached the hatch at reception.

'I don't think we called you, did we?' she said.

'No, no,' Ruben said, waving his hands dismissively. 'We've got a case relating to one of your former patients. Now deceased. We'd like to speak to anyone working here who took care of him. Crazy-Tom – the guy they called the Cannibal.'

'I know who Crazy-Tom was,' the woman said shortly. 'And I know that Arnold was the one who dealt with him the most. He's on duty now. I'll call him.'

They sat down on uncomfortable chairs while they waited.

The clock on the wall was ticking slowly. Christer thought the hands were moving with unnatural torpor. It was like being in a different, isolated world. He wondered what it was like to work here. He and his colleagues met their fair share of disturbed people in the line of duty, but here it was a constant in all the work they did. Not to mention that some of the people in here were not to be trifled with.

'Arnold's going to pop out and see you. He said he needed a smoke anyway.'

The woman with the big earrings hung up the phone and went back to her paperwork. Christer continued to watch the second hand and its slow orbit of the clock as they waited. However, it only took a few minutes before a rotund man with a big grey beard appeared and came over to them. He was like a Santa Claus for the institutionalized. He breathed heavily as he moved, and the pack of Marlboros in his hand didn't seem like a very good idea.

'Let's go outside,' he said, huffing and puffing his way ahead of them through the door.

Once outside, he lit a cigarette with trembling fingers and took a long drag from it before he turned towards them with an expression of relief.

'Fuck me, I needed that.'

'We're Ruben Höök and Christer Bengtsson. We're investigating the death of Marcus Eriksson.'

'Marcus Eriksson?'

Arnold's brow creased as he took another long drag.

'Mark Eric,' Christer clarified.

The cold was penetrating through his thick police uniform coat. He had never liked the winter. When he was a child his mother had often forced him out into the snow for hours on end, but Christer had never wanted to play in the snow. He had usually curled up under some nearby tree and waited for his mother to call him back inside.

'Oh yes, Mark. So this is about Crazy-Tom. You know he's dead, right? Hanged himself in his room. No one could have predicted it. There hadn't been any indications that he was suicidal. But that's how it is with some of them. Suddenly they're done with life.'

'How familiar are you with the case?'

'I'm familiar,' Arnold said, puffing out a smoke ring that slowly rose into the grey sky. 'And not for one moment did I ever believe that Crazy-Tom killed and ate that guy. Tom – well, Tomas was his real name – was one of the kindest souls I've ever met. I know it's a cliché, but he wouldn't have hurt a fly.'

'But Marcus's bones were found in his bags along with his belongings.'

Arnold shrugged, making his grey beard wag.

'That means nothing. He was convicted on far too flimsy grounds. There wasn't any evidence that Tom had murdered him or eaten him. He was convicted because of who he was – a mad bloke who looked dangerous. He always claimed he'd found the bones. He was even proud of the fact that it was, as he put it, an almost complete collection. Tom collected everything.'

'A complete collection?' Ruben said.

'The human body has – what do they say? – two hundred and six bones in it, right? Crazy-Tom had found two hundred of them.'

'I note you're also saying he found them. If so, where?'

'Not far from where he lived. He said all the bones were in a heap just by the Bagarmossen metro station. Inside the tunnel.'

'Bagarmossen,' Christer said thoughtfully. 'Do you know what he was doing down there?'

Another drag on the cigarette delayed the reply.

'He lived there. In the tunnels. Of course, you're not really supposed to. So they keep out of the way. But especially when the winter is like this, it's way warmer down there than it is on the streets. And at least you have a roof over your head.'

Ruben let out a low whistle.

'Do you think anyone who knew him down there will still be around?' he said.

'I'd guess at least a few of Crazy-Tom's old mates are still alive and kicking,' Arnold said, stubbing out his cigarette. 'Or someone who knows who they were, anyway. There are more homeless in Stockholm than ever.'

Christer looked at Ruben to see whether he was thinking the same thing he was. There were other people in the tunnels. Other people who might have seen something. Who might have seen Marcus's and Jon's murderer. The only question was how they would find these people, who clearly wanted to stay hidden.

50

The name Marcus Eriksson was inscribed into the headstone. Adam thought it a surprisingly commonplace name for such an exceedingly flamboyant person.

'I assume there's a good reason why you're prioritizing being here for an exhumation?' he said, glancing at Julia.

'I know all his songs by heart,' she said with an embarrassed smile. 'The man was a musical genius. A pretty messy genius at that – but aren't most brilliant people?'

'Well, I think I'm pretty orderly …'

'Oh shut up.'

Julia nudged him with her elbow.

Adam looked away. He knew his eyes would give away what he was so desperately trying to hide: how helplessly, totally and unfathomably in love with her he was.

But he didn't want to put any pressure on her. She had a family. He of all people understood the value of that, especially now that he was alone after the passing of his mother Miriam. With the best will in the world, he couldn't force someone to break up their family. So he settled for the crumbs he got, even though he intensely yearned for more. It wasn't about the sex, although that was obviously amazing. No, what he longed for most of all was to share the everyday with her. To tug back the duvet she was hogging. To bicker about whose turn it was to take out the bins. To get stomach flu together. Perhaps it sounded like the dream of a madman, but it was only once you had thrown up together that you knew you really did share everything.

'They're bringing up the coffin,' Julia said quietly, bowing her head slightly.

He did the same.

There was something about a cemetery that summoned a

spirituality that wasn't to be found in daily life. He always found it to be particularly present in the Skogskyrkogården cemetery. A couple of years ago, he had briefly lived in a small flat in nearby Enskede and he had often taken his runs to and around the cemetery. It was not only beautiful but also large and took a fair time to get around. He had, however, always avoided the section with children's graves.

In front of them, a white coffin was slowly being lifted out of the ground.

'What do you make of the connection to the Serbs?' he said as his eyes tracked the coffin.

Julia sighed in frustration.

'It seems a strong lead to me, but I've got two problems with that approach to the investigation. Partly that currently we can only link it to Jon and not Marcus. And partly that the top brass have got nervous and are delaying all attempts I'm making to proceed down that path. They're worried it will clash with a major investigation that's currently taking place into organized crime.'

'Got it,' Adam said tersely.

Then he took a deep breath and asked the question that had been on the tip of his tongue for days.

'How are things at home?'

The silence seemed to echo in the wake of his question. It was the forbidden question. They had agreed not to discuss what Julia referred to as 'reality'. Their affair could only exist in a parallel world alongside their normal one. He knew that. He understood that. He respected that. Yet the question had now passed over his lips and was hovering in the air, as fateful as the coffin suspended halfway between the grave and the ground. White smoke rose from their mouths, eddying upwards and merging in the space between them.

'I think I want a divorce.'

Julia's words rushed towards him, onto him, at the very moment that Marcus Eriksson's coffin landed on the snow-covered ground with a thud.

Adam didn't dare look at her. He stood completely still, but inside him the blood was racing through his body, pumped by a heart suddenly working at double-time.

They walked towards the coffin.

The silence between them echoed.

51

Vincent leaned back in the designer armchair. It still smelled new. Things were clearly going well for ShowLife Productions given the furniture upgrades. And it wasn't just the furniture either, he thought as he looked around. Everything in the office was new. Even the walls now had a darker, more exclusive tone.

'I like what you've done to the place,' he said.

Vincent's agent, Umberto, smiled like a proud child.

'It is nice, isn't it?' he said, holding out his hands. 'I'm not quite sure about *that*, but I'm not the boss.'

Umberto pointed to a spot above Vincent's head.

On the wall behind him there was a huge self-portrait by the photo artist Lisa Love, in which she was dressed in queenly attire made entirely from playing cards. Vincent immediately liked it. It reminded him of Alice in Wonderland. But he could also understand Umberto's concerns. Given that the Red Queen's favourite line was 'off with their heads!', it was easy to see the picture as a veiled threat about what might happen if Umberto didn't do his job.

'Your tour receipts have obviously contributed towards this,' Umberto said. 'And it also means better eats with your coffee from here on out.'

On the new marble-topped table between them stood two double espressos made from freshly ground coffee beans that Umberto had probably had specially imported. There was also a platter of spectacularly beautiful pastries.

'I had them sent over from Magnus Johansson's,' Umberto said with satisfaction. 'It may be on the other side of town, but it's worth it.'

'Have I ever complained about the factory-made biscuits?' Vincent said, inspecting the pastries.

He had to concede that the pastries did look completely symmetrical. That baker knew his stuff.

'Biscuits,' Umberto said, laughing. 'Don't let Magnus Johansson hear you use that word.'

'But on the topic of it going well for you,' Vincent said, knocking back half his espresso in one go, 'I've made my mind up about something. I'm going to take a break from touring.'

Umberto's hand stopped above one of the pastries. His face paled a shade, but he said nothing. He did, however, look at Vincent with that familiar what-mischief-have-you-cooked-up-now look.

'Various things have cropped up on the home front that I need to deal with,' Vincent said.

He had no desire to go into any further details about the threats he had received.

'And to be honest, I'm not feeling too well,' he added. 'I have a headache after almost every performance and it seems to be getting worse.'

'You're probably just exhausted,' Umberto said with a stiff smile. '*Amico mio*, you're really straining your brain onstage. It's no wonder you're so spent afterwards. But it's nothing a bag of sweets after your show won't solve. I can add that to your rider if you like.'

'Well, the bit about lots of energy being used to think isn't quite true,' Vincent said. 'There was a study that found that the extra energy required by an "overworked" brain equated to less than the sugar in one tenth of a Tic Tac. But there's some fascinating new research from Antonius Wiehler in Paris that shows that glutamate residues build up in the frontal lobes – where we do our rational thinking – when we put a lot of strain on the brain. In the end, the cognitive functions are forced to shift down a gear so that the brain can clear all this glutamate that shouldn't be there. That's why we find it easier to make decisions that require minimal effort when we've been working hard. We're no longer capable of activating the more advanced cognitive functions. Ergo pizza and Netflix after a long day at work. And I wonder whether that might be the source of my headaches. I've never had the chance to clear my glutamate.'

Umberto stared at him.

'Glutamate on the brain,' he said slowly. 'That's your reason? You know that we're currently paying four lighting professionals, two drivers, a tour manager and a project manager for your show alone? What exactly am I supposed to tell them?'

Vincent shrugged.

'That I'm taking a break,' he said.

'A break,' Umberto repeated, as if the word was not to his liking. 'You're unlikely to get many Christmas presents from them this year. Or me, for that matter. How long are you going to be taking a break for?'

'I think … until further notice.'

Umberto slumped in his armchair. There was no pastry in his hand. He was even paler now.

'Are you doing this to punish me?' he said. 'I can always pop round the corner to the supermarket to buy you your cheap biscuits if that's what—'

'It's nothing to do with you. Or the biscuits. I'm sure they're great. It's just that I need to take a break from … everything.'

'Your fans won't be happy,' Umberto said. 'They're still sending post here, you know.'

He stood up to retrieve something from his desk and then handed over two postcards addressed to Vincent.

'These were in reception last week. The day after you and I met, actually. I've no idea how the person who dropped them off got in without us noticing.'

When Vincent turned them over, he saw that they were actually just two halves of one big postcard. The address was given as *Vincent Walder / ShowLife Productions*. No stamp. Someone must have hand delivered them before leaving … without anyone seeing them. The messages on the postcards were odd to say the least.

The steady dripping of rain and the nagging of a wife are one and the same, it said on one of them.

Don't fall into the trap of making promises to God before you think, it said on the other.

No signature.

'Some old Swedish proverbs?' Umberto said. 'What do they mean?'

'Not that I know of,' Vincent said, tucking the cards into his jacket pocket. 'And I've no idea. But thank you.'

'So … a break,' Umberto said with displeasure. 'If you say so.'

He glanced up at the picture of the Queen of Wonderland, and let out a deep sigh.

52

'I've been thinking about what you said, about being satisfied.'

Loke stopped mid-step and gazed at her in astonishment. Then he continued to push the trolley with a body on it in front of him.

It was an elderly man, exposed in his nakedness. The Y-incision had been neatly stitched back together and, apart from that, he looked as if he was asleep. Loke carefully returned him to one of the chilled storage cabinets.

'Mercy killing,' he said, by way of explanation for the man on the trolley. 'He had terminal cancer. Only had a few months left. He was in a lot of pain, but he refused to go to hospital so his wife killed him. With his approval. Well, at his behest, actually. Now she's likely to see out her final years in prison.'

'The law's quite clear,' Mina said, furrowing her brow. 'You can't kill another human being regardless of the circumstances. What kind of society would we live in if that weren't the case?'

Loke didn't reply. He removed his disposable gloves and then reached for a new pair. Then he turned to her.

'Has it made any difference?'

'Huh? What?' said Mina, whose thoughts were still focused on the man in the cabinet.

Milda was late again. This was most unusual. And it meant Mina had to engage in far too many wooden conversations with the medical examiner's assistant.

'Has it made any difference? Thinking about what I said about being satisfied?'

'Oh that,' Mina said, averting her gaze from the cabinet. 'I don't know whether it's made any difference. But it's given me a lot to think about. It's made me take stock of my life, I guess. What's good? What's bad? What can I change? What can't I change?'

'Give us the serenity to accept what cannot be changed, the courage to change what can be changed, and the wisdom to know the one from the other.'

'The Serenity Prayer. Twelve-step? You too?'

Loke hesitated for a moment. He picked up a cloth and began to polish a tabletop that already looked more than sterile. Then he stopped and looked at Mina.

'Not me. Someone who was … close to me. In a past life.'

She nodded. After many years in the twelve-step programme, she knew better than to ask anything more.

'Sorry, sorry, sorry!' Milda said as she rushed in, her face bright red and catching her breath. 'I don't seem to be able to keep it together right now.'

Then she beckoned to Mina to follow her over to a table with a skeleton laid out on it. Coming here to see a skeleton brought about a sense of déjà vu, and the repetition concerned Mina. It reminded her clearly that someone out there might have killed more than the two people they were aware of. And the killer might not be done yet. How many times would she have to come here to look at bones laid out anatomically on a metal table without knowing the reason why?

'What I can say is that the last few days have been excellent practice for us in the placement of bones in the human body,' Milda said drily.

She waved to Loke and he put down the cloth, removed his gloves and donned a new pair. Mina loved it. Each new pair of gloves made everything feel clean, renewed and sterile. If it were socially acceptable, she would have worn disposable gloves around the clock.

'Loke, can you elaborate? You have some sensible observations.'

Milda stepped aside, allowing Loke to step up to the bones on the table. He gazed down at them almost lovingly.

'We're being shown samples of peerless work here,' he said. 'I can barely contain my fascination with this – just like Jon Langseth, these bones have been cleaned with uncanny precision.'

'How were they cleaned? The same way as Jon's?'

Mina leaned forward to look more closely at the bones. Loke was right. They were a model of cleanliness. There were no remnants of flesh, tendons, skin or any other soft tissue on the bones.

'It's impossible to know; I can only guess,' Loke said cautiously as he gently touched the bones. 'But yes, I think my guess is right. The bones were boiled first, then beetles were used.'

'So it's not possible to get the bones this clean just by boiling them?' Mina asked.

'I don't think so. Probably not.'

Loke looked thoughtful for a few moments then became more animated.

'I could test it. We could do a boiling experiment.'

'With … human bones?' Mina asked.

'Human bones? No, no,' Loke said, shaking his head gravely. 'That's not allowed. I obviously meant an animal. A cow. Or maybe a pig.'

'I think that sounds like a great idea,' Milda said, putting a hand on Loke's shoulder. 'It might give us a lot of valuable information.'

'Is there anything else the bones can tell us? Cause of death?' Mina asked the medical examiner.

'I'll take one more look at them, but I'm not holding out much hope. I can't see anything that indicates a cause of death, and Mark's, well … Marcus Eriksson's bones are completely clean. All I can find are residual materials from the coffin and the soil that penetrated it. That's pretty much it.'

'OK,' Mina said in disappointment. 'Let me know once you've boiled up your … pig. Hopefully that'll give us something.'

'I'll call you right away!' Loke said enthusiastically. Mina didn't doubt it for one second.

53

Christer scrolled through the document on his computer. He had come back to the list of people who had gone missing in the last two years, but this time he knew what he was looking for. The connection between Jon Langseth and Mark Eric hadn't been instantly obvious. And perhaps it was wishful thinking on his part, but he thought he had finally found at least a small piece of the puzzle.

The fact was that both Jon and Mark had been men who had made an impression. Mark had been in the public eye with his brilliant music career. While Jon would never have been as well known as he was at the end were it not for the Confido scandal, he was nevertheless a rock star in the world of finance.

And if there were two rock stars then there might be others. That meant the first step was to find people who stood out. People whose careers had taken them to the top and who were considered guiding lights in their fields. And who had then disappeared.

After an hour's reading, he had managed to find three such people in addition to Jon and Mark. There was an internationally renowned lecturer, a fashion designer and an architect. Christer pulled up the files for each missing person report. The architect had gone to Brazil and not come back. Her siblings had contacted the Swedish embassy and the Brazilian authorities without any success in finding her.

However naive it might be, Christer hoped that she had simply grown tired of being an architect and was now living it up on the Copacabana and didn't want to be found. Regardless of what had happened to her, she was probably not the victim of the phantom prowling through Stockholm's metro tunnels.

The fashion designer was a different story altogether. One day, he had walked out of his second home in Österlen and never come back. It was feared that he had drowned and that his body had been swept away by the currents. Given that he had disappeared after a party at which the booze had been freely flowing and there had been a storm that day, it was a reasonable assumption.

The lecturer was an interesting prospect. She went by the name of Erika Sävelden. The name sounded vaguely familiar. Hadn't she been the speaker at one of those supposedly inspirational away days that the top brass had wanted them to attend a few years back? Yes, that was it. The flyer had boasted that the speakers would include Henrik Schyffert, some bloke from Apple – and Erika Sävelden. He was sure of it now. It paid to mix in elevated circles.

In the report, it said that Erika didn't have a family of her own, so it hadn't been until she had failed to show up for a speaking engagement that anyone had realized something was amiss. It had been her sister, Diana Sävelden, who had contacted the police. She had gone to her sister's flat and found it empty. No one had heard anything from Erika since. That had been more than a year ago.

Christer picked up the phone and dialled the sister's number. She picked up almost immediately.

'Diana speaking. Hello?'

'Hello there. My name is Christer Bengtsson and I'm calling from the police. Am I interrupting?'

A few seconds' silence followed. Christer could hear the sound of traffic down the line.

'No, I was just on my way back from lunch,' Diana said eventually. 'But I can talk. Is it about Erika?'

Christer could hear the trepidation in her voice despite the background noise. Diana had been left in limbo for a whole year. He couldn't imagine what that did to a person, but he suspected that the fear of one day receiving the wrong kind of news might be paralysing. What he said next might turn her world upside down.

'I want to start by saying that I'm afraid I have no news about Erika,' he said. 'I wish I did. But I've just been reading the report on her disappearance and I was wondering about something that it doesn't really cover. What was … *is* Erika like as a person? Not just now. What was she like when you were growing up?'

The quality of sound on the phone changed. It sounded as if

Diana had walked through a door; the rumble of the street had disappeared.

'I know the meeting's started,' she said, now further from the phone than she had been. 'But I've got to take this. Sorry about that, now we can talk,' she said, closer to the receiver again. 'Why do you want to know about Erika's childhood?'

'I'm just trying to understand who she was – to increase the chances of finding her.'

Christer avoided explaining what state he thought they might find her in if the worst-case scenario came to fruition.

'What can I say?' Diana said. 'I was the big sister. Erika was the little sister. So everything was a competition between us. At least she saw it that way. She always had to be the best at everything. Especially if it was something that I did. Since I was a tennis player, she decided when she was a little girl that she was going to be the best tennis player in Sweden.'

While Diana talked, Christer pulled up photos of Erika's flat. There was a glass cabinet filled with various trophies clearly visible in the living room.

'And did she do it?' he said. 'Was she the best in Sweden?'

'She got good,' Diana said. 'Much better than me. But certainly not the best. She kept going for a long time, but she never made it all the way. In fact, it drove her into a depression around … gosh, it's been a long time. Say around twenty years ago. She refused to touch a tennis racket and just lay in bed for months, barely eating. Erika has always been fragile, even if she pretends she isn't, but that was an unusually dark time for her. I was genuinely worried she might jump off a bridge or something. She talked about doing it in her darkest moments.'

None of this had been in the report. Christer could understand why – a twenty-year-old bad patch wasn't particularly relevant when looking at a disappearance in the present day. But faint alarm bells had begun to ring in his head and they were slowly intensifying. There was something about what the sister had just said.

'So what happened?' he asked.

'I'm not quite sure. She turned it around on her own. When she was at rock bottom, she seemed to decide she wanted to be Sweden's best motivational speaker instead, by talking about her experiences. I've no idea where the drive to do that came from. But that's what she's been doing ever since. And she's done far better at it than she did at tennis.'

'Would you say she was the best in Sweden at that?'

Diana was silent again.

'I'm sorry, but I've got to go soon,' she said. 'My boss is waving at me like mad. I've got to go into a meeting. Erika was a bit of a funny one. I don't think she ever realized how well things were going for her. She was always terrified that the jobs would dry up. That was despite the fact that she was commuting between Stockholm and London, Dubai, LA ... She was constantly annoyed that things seemed to be going so well for others while she had to toil for her own success. You know, for some people the glass isn't even half empty.'

Christer knew very well. He had been one of them, but then Lasse had come along and filled the glass. Erika didn't seem to have been so lucky. She had been alone, prioritizing work. A stance that was all too familiar to his own

'Was she like that until she disappeared?' he said. 'Do you think she just burned out?'

Yet more silence.

'Now that you mention it, something did happen,' Diana said. 'Just before she ... disappeared. Like two weeks earlier. She'd gone from being someone who created stressful five-year plans to suddenly living in the moment. She started calling more often. Stopped looking for new gigs. Always wanted to go out for coffees. It was as if she'd finally managed to calm down, in a way. We all wondered whether some kind of penny had dropped, but before we found out, she was gone. All the fuss around that made me completely forget how calm she was in the weeks before. If it didn't sound so macabre, I would say she'd found ... peace.'

The alarm bells in Christer's head were now almost deafening. Erika Sävelden had undergone a personality change just two weeks before she disappeared. And she was a rock star in her field. He thanked Diana for her time and promised to get back to her if anything else came up, then he ended the call.

He rubbed his face with his hands and looked again at the headshot of Erika on his computer screen. They were going to have to search for more skeletal remains in the metro tunnels.

54

'I can feel some positive energy in the room today,' Julia said, her gaze resting on each of them in turn.

She turned her back to them and looked at the whiteboard, which was covered with content that had begun to spread onto the walls. She tapped her finger on a photo of a professionally made-up and styled woman with the broad smile of a preacher.

'Christer – I'll let you brief us on what you've found.'

Julia stepped aside and leaned against the wall. She folded her arms and looked at Christer encouragingly. Mina couldn't help but notice that Adam's gaze was drawn to her cleavage.

Vincent had been right, and once you had seen it, it was obvious. Julia and Adam were in a relationship.

She could feel Vincent's gaze on her back. She had arrived just moments earlier from the National Board of Forensic Medicine, and they had only managed to exchange a few words before the meeting had begun.

Bosse sat up as Christer cleared his throat and pushed his chair away from the table. He put down a saffron bun and brushed beads of pearl sugar from his hands.

'Erika …'

The word sounded muffled as he said it – he'd just taken a big bite of bun and he made them wait as he swallowed.

'Erika Sävelden,' he said, now speaking far more clearly as he pointed to the photo. 'She went missing around a year ago – just as inexplicably as Jon Langseth and Mark Eric. She was a motivational speaker. Well, I'm sure you all recognize her. Like our other two, she had a successful career and was a leader in her field. That was the first similarity I identified, but there's more to it than that.'

He paused and looked around.

'Drama queen,' Ruben snorted, rolling his eyes.

Christer ignored him.

'There were also similarities in their behaviour before their disappearances. I followed up with Erika's sister, and just like Jon and Mark, she exhibited signs of behavioural change – although it was the other way round with her. Jon and Mark both turned paranoid and acted as if someone was after them. Erika went from being very stressed and irascible, if we're to believe her sister, to being calm and happy. Satisfied. The sister said Erika slowed down and started living in the moment.'

'Erika might have known what was coming for her, just like Jon and Marcus,' said Vincent. 'The knowledge of an inevitable and imminent death allows some people to find a peace they didn't have before.'

'That's right. That's why so many suicides are such a surprise to the people around them,' Christer said with a grim nod. 'They have a friend or relative who has been in a bad way for a long time but suddenly seems to be doing well and is happy and positive. Everyone breathes a sigh of relief and thinks the danger is over – instead of realizing that the positivity is the biggest warning sign of all.'

'So they all knew that something was going to happen?' Ruben said, letting out a low whistle.

Out of the corner of her eye, Mina could see Bosse sneaking nearer and nearer to the bun that Christer had left a little too close to the edge of the table.

'I believe that Erika met with the same fate as the others,' Christer said, moving the bun, to Bosse's evident disappointment.

'Good work, Christer,' Julia said. 'You all know what that means. We need to carry out a thorough search of the tunnels to see whether we can locate Erika's bones. With a little luck, we might be able to do it tomorrow. We also need to locate any of Crazy-Tom's friends who may still be holed up down there, but that'll have to be another time. One thing at a time.'

Mina swallowed. She could almost hear the faint rustling of rats and smell the stench of urine and festering rubbish. At the same time, she was just as eager as the others to make progress. If Christer was right that Erika Sävelden was a victim, and that her bones were in the metro tunnels somewhere, then their discovery might represent a breakthrough in the case. Murderers were only human. They made mistakes. Erika's bones might provide the team with the boost they needed.

'Mina, I know you'd like to keep exploring the Gustaf Brons angle, and the top brass agree with you,' Julia said. 'See if you can find a connection between him and the other victims.'

She turned to the rest of the team.

'However, I want you all to exercise extreme caution around anything to do with Dragan Manojlovic. I'm still awaiting orders from on high as to how we can best deal with this issue so that we don't clash with other interests. NOA's investigation is at a very sensitive stage just now. So if you're at all unsure how to proceed in anything, please come to me and I'll try to find a solution.'

Julia turned to Mina again.

'You've been over to the National Board of Forensic Medicine – we haven't had time to talk about that yet. Has it led to anything? It's always a significant violation of a person's privacy and dignity to exhume their remains, so I don't want this to have been for nothing.'

'Yes and no,' said Mina. 'I don't really have anything new to report except that Marcus Eriksson's bones are in exactly the same condition as Jon Langseth's. Very, very clean. And Loke, Milda's assistant, is completely sold on Vincent's idea that the method used was boiling followed by some type of beetle.'

'Bloody hell,' Adam said. He looked as if he wanted to claw his own skin off.

Mina had previously noticed that he had an aversion to creepy-crawlies. All it took was a small spider to send Adam to the far end of the room. On that point, she agreed with him wholeheartedly. The very word beetle made her shudder.

'It makes sense,' Vincent said behind her.

She turned towards him.

'It's a very plausible theory,' he said. 'I'd like to see it tested.'

'Loke has already suggested that,' said Mina. 'He's going to test it out with pig remains and see whether he gets the same outcome as the bones found in the tunnels.'

'Where's he going to get the beetles from?' Ruben said, which made Adam's face turn a shade of green.

He was now vigorously scratching his arms. Mina resisted an impulse to do the same. Her devastated skin couldn't handle being scratched by nails.

'I … didn't actually ask that,' she said, swallowing hard.

'I'm seeing Loke after we're done here,' said Vincent. 'We're going to see the entomologist to find out what we can about the beetles.'

'Yes, Loke was like a child about to open his Christmas presents when I called Milda to ask,' Julia said.

She rubbed her hands on her jacket. Even she didn't seem to be completely unfazed by the subject matter.

'I think that's enough to be getting on with for now,' she said. 'There's just one more thing.' She cleared her throat. 'On the subject of children opening their Christmas presents, I've wrapped up some gifts for the triplets.' She looked towards Peder's empty chair. 'And a Christmas hamper for Anette. Anyone who would like to is welcome to join me this evening when I go round to give it all to them.'

The silence afterwards was broken only by the distant sound of 'All I Want For Christmas' being played down the corridor.

After a few more moments, they all nodded and then trooped out of the conference room.

Mina stopped Vincent as they left.

'I know you're off to see that bug expert, but have you got a minute?'

'Of course,' he said. 'I've got as much time as you need. What can I do for you?'

They stepped aside.

'It's about the interview with Gustaf Brons,' she said. 'I spoke to Ruben about why Brons might have needed cash from Dragan, and Ruben's reply was that it's always for "dope, chicks or gambling". Something about that pressed a button somewhere, but I can't put my finger on what. All that came to mind was a cup of coffee. Do you know where I got that from?'

Mina could hear just how mad this sounded, but Vincent beamed at her.

'Oh, was that it?' he said. 'I can almost guarantee that Gustaf's vice is gambling.'

'Gambling?' said Mina.

'Yep. When you were questioning him, Brons used a poker term, but it wasn't one of the common ones. It takes a serious poker player to recognize it. Or someone who takes an interest in more or less everything to do with cards – an old card trickster like me, for example.'

'What did he say?' Mina said in confusion. 'I don't remember any poker jargon. And what's it got to do with coffee?'

'He said *coffeehousing* to his lawyer when he wanted to leave. He said that was what you were up to,' Vincent said.

'I've never even heard of the expression.'

'Precisely my point. Most people have probably heard of words like bluff, call, fold and so on, if they've ever played a round of poker. But *coffeehousing* is much more unusual.'

'So what does it mean?' said Mina. 'If that was what I was doing?'

She was preparing for an exposition. Asking Vincent about the significance of things was always a risk, but she had to know.

'It's the term used to describe talking about your hand while the game is in play, often with the intention of deceiving your opponent. I think he thought you were doing that when you asked whether he'd been paid to kill Jon. In poker circles, *coffeehousing* is considered to be an underhand tactic, and there are actually casinos that have rules against it.'

'So there's a high likelihood that Brons is a gambler?' she said. 'Gambling addiction has burned through bigger fortunes than his.'

'Yes, it's a strong probability,' Vincent said.

Mina exhaled in relief. She had found out what it was from the interview that had been bothering her. Moreover, Vincent had managed to keep his lecture to the point.

'Did you know there are three rather different theories about the origins of poker?' he said as she was making for the door. He sounded eager now. 'The first says that the game was invented in China in the tenth century – a kind of evolution of the domino games that were around back then. The second says that it is derived from the classic Persian game of *as-nas*, which was first invented during the seventeenth century. And the third says that French emigrants took the French game *pocque* with them to New Orleans, where the game gradually became what we now know as poker. I would say this is the most likely of the three possible origins, given the many similarities between poker and *pocque*. On the other hand, early decks of cards only contained twenty cards instead of the fifty-two we have today, and the colours or suits were the same that we find in decks of tarot cards. Coins, wands, cups and swords. And tarot cards are very interesting in that respect …'

Mina heard Vincent pause for breath, but before he could continue she had left the room.

55

Vincent went straight down to the car park in the basement to retrieve his car after speaking to Mina. *Coffeehousing*. And Mina had been thinking about a cup of coffee without knowing why. Vincent smiled to himself from behind the wheel as he set a course for Djursholm. Mina was obviously starting to think like him.

Once he reached Djursholm, he pulled onto Strandvägen. It went without saying that the most fashionable street in the most luxurious of Stockholm's suburbs bore the same name as the priciest street in the city centre. Milda had told him Loke was flush with cash, but he was still impressed by the address. On one side of the road the houses towered above him. Some of them were more like small palaces. On the other side of the road was the water, and the fancy yachts belonging to the homeowners, of course.

His satnav told him he had reached the address, but he still had to double-check. In front of him there was a large, automated gate at least three metres high. On the other side of the gate the road continued between an avenue of trees to a large brick building just visible beyond.

He saw Loke walking towards him on the other side of the gate, a cigarette in the corner of his mouth. When he caught sight of Vincent in the car, he smiled and stubbed his cigarette out. He emerged via a side gate and jogged towards the car, rubbing his hands together.

'Hi Vincent,' he said, getting into the passenger seat. 'It's bloody cold out there. Shall we get going?'

Vincent started the car. He had been crossing paths with Loke on and off for almost three years, and had always felt that the man was basically apologizing for his own existence as soon as he entered a room. More than once, he'd contemplated giving

Loke a self-help book to improve his self-esteem. But the young man sitting beside him now was full of energy and practically jumping with excitement.

'So we're off to see one of the leading entomologists in Sweden?' Loke said, more loudly than Vincent had ever heard him speak before.

'That's right,' Vincent said, leaving Djursholm behind them and making for the E4 motorway to head south. 'He's an expert on beetles. I thought you might find it interesting. And I think you can interpret what we find out today from a perspective that I don't have. After all, you're the one who works with dead bodies day in, day out.'

Vincent paused and glanced over at Loke. It was Vincent's job to read people and see how they actually felt so that he could respond to them in the best way, but Loke was a mystery. He wasn't giving off any of the signals that Vincent usually picked up on. It was like staring at a blank sheet of paper. Of course, that wasn't Loke's fault, but Vincent wasn't entirely at ease with the situation.

'I have to ask you something,' he said. 'Please don't take this the wrong way. I saw how you live. Why do you work at the National Board of Forensic Medicine? You can't possibly need the money.'

Loke looked at him in surprise.

'I'm a qualified osteologist,' he said. 'I'm an expert in bones and skeletons. It's my passion. You of all people must realize what a pleasure it is to work on your greatest interest? Anyway, Milda is a genius. I'd work there even if I had to pay them.'

Vincent nodded. Yes, he did know what that was like. And it oughtn't to have surprised him that bones were someone's passion, given his own interests.

'You might actually know the entomologist we're off to meet, given that you seem to know a fair bit about insects,' he said. 'His name's Sebastian Bugh with a silent H, and he lives near Häringe.'

'Yes, that's definitely another passion of mine. But I don't know him. Anyway, surely he's not really called Bugh? Given he works with bugs?'

Loke made a hacking sound that Vincent assumed was a blend of laughter and coughing.

'You've heard of nominative determinism, right?' Vincent said. 'The theory that your last name governs your career choice.'

'You mean the whole thing about there being lots of bakers by the name of Baker, and Sigmund Freud when being into sexuality literally means joy? Wasn't it Jung who wrote about it?'

Vincent nodded in satisfaction. Loke knew his onions.

'And now we're off to meet Sebastian Bugh,' Loke said with a wry smile. '*Nomen est omen*.'

'The name is a sign? So says someone who shares a name with the god Loki himself.'

'I know at least a few people who would say you're onto something,' Loke said, making the same hacking sound as before.

Shortly before they reached Häringe Palace, Vincent pulled off the main road. As they were approaching the address entered into his satnav, a grand white house – more of a manor really – appeared before them. Set in the winter landscape, it looked like a huge snow sculpture.

'Blow me down,' Loke said quietly. 'I had no idea entomologists made that kind of money. Milda should change jobs.'

'But think of the glamour,' Vincent said. 'I dare say entomologists have far fewer groupies than osteologists.'

Loke croaked again.

Vincent parked next to a Hyundai on the gravel in front of the house. Loke lit a cigarette as soon as he got out of the car. A slender, white-haired man in his seventies wearing a big white fur coat appeared at the front door.

'Come in, come in,' he said. 'You'll catch your deaths out here.'

Loke took a few hasty drags on his cigarette before throwing it into the snow and stamping on it. After glancing towards Sebastian Bugh, he picked up the butt and pocketed it.

Sebastian nodded briefly and greeted them, then showed them into the hallway and invited them to take off their coats.

'This is my family's old steading – luckily for me, it's been handed down through the generations, which means it costs me more or less nothing to live here. Entomology is my passion, but it doesn't exactly pay the bills.'

Vincent glanced at Loke to see whether he was thinking the same thing. They had clearly been wrong about Sebastian's financial situation. Not that Sebastian seemed to show it. His wavy white hair was perfectly trimmed and he wore an impeccable white safari suit – like an adventurer from the past.

Vincent looked around. He had been expecting an eccentric house filled with taxidermied animals and scientific books piled up to the ceiling. Instead, the house was just as neat as Sebastian himself. Admittedly the walls were adorned with frames containing many different insect species, but the frames were positioned at precise and equal intervals.

Sebastian showed them into the living room where they settled down on huge leather armchairs, which were incredibly comfortable even though they appeared to be as old as the rest of the house. Vincent could almost picture generations of Bughs sitting in these armchairs. For decades they had sat in here in their adventurer's attire, reading important books.

'Given the cold, I fear tea may not be enough,' Sebastian said, going over to a drinks cabinet. 'I'd be happy to offer you something stronger.'

'I don't drink,' Loke said in a low voice.

He was back to his taciturn, withdrawn self.

'And I'm driving,' Vincent said. 'But I appreciate the offer.'

Sebastian shrugged and filled a glass with amber liquid for himself. Then he took a pipette, sucked up water from another glass, and dripped four drops into his own before sitting down.

'So you two want to know about skin beetles?' he said. 'Dermestidae. Funny little creepy-crawlies. Did you know there are eight hundred and fifty different species of skin beetles? Regrettably there are just thirty-six of them to be found in Sweden. Truly nature's little cleaners.'

'And why do these particular insects do that?' said Vincent.

His armchair creaked as he shifted position.

'Being coleoptera, skin beetles naturally develop holometabolously,' Sebastian said, sipping his drink.

'Naturally,' Loke said.

Vincent couldn't tell whether he was being ironic or whether he was familiar with the subject matter. Presumably the latter.

'They go through the four stages of egg, larva, pupa and imago. The last of those is when they are a fully formed adult beetle. Once fully developed, they subsist on pollen and nectar like all other insects. But during the larval stage, they feed primarily on animal-based substances.'

'Do they eat all types of animals?' Vincent said.

'As long as they're dead,' Sebastian said, nodding. 'Skin beetles are scavengers. They clean up dead animals in nature.'

'They're necrophages,' Loke said quietly.

'Exactly!' Sebastian said cheerfully. 'And in that respect, they've come to specialize in slightly different areas. *Attagenus pellio*, better known as the fur beetle, prefers to eat fur – as the common name has it. And since wool is taken from sheep's fleeces and is thus a type of fur, they really go for any woolly jumpers you have in the house. Not to mention any other textiles they can find. *Dermestes lardarius*, the larder beetle, has a name that is literally translated and is another species you almost only find indoors in Sweden. It enjoys nibbling away on hair and skin flakes, among other things.'

Vincent grimaced. Mina had no idea how fortunate an escape she'd had. She wouldn't have slept for a week if she had heard what Sebastian was telling them.

'Of course, you'll want to see for yourselves,' the entomologist said. 'Just a moment.'

Sebastian disappeared and returned quickly with a frame like the ones on the walls. He handed it to Vincent. Inside the frame there were a large number of tiny beetles, all with tiny slips of paper underneath them describing which species they were.

'We haven't encountered many *Anthrenus* in Sweden since most of them can't survive here,' Sebastian said, sitting down again. 'There are only four species that do. Take a look at the one in the bottom left-hand corner.'

Vincent saw an inconspicuous looking insect in shades of brown and black with white markings.

'That's *Anthrenus museorum*,' Sebastian said, sipping his drink. 'The museum beetle. A hungry little critter. The larvae like to set up house in birds' and wasps' nests, but they're also found in spiders' egg sacs, where they eat any spider eggs that don't hatch. Unless they get lucky and happen upon some dead flies or something like that.'

Vincent made a mental note never to tell Mina about this.

'Why are they known as museum beetles?' he said. 'Fur beetles and larder beetles I can understand, but museum beetles?'

'Because if they get into a museum they gobble up all the stuffed animals. They eat fur, wool, carpets, silk, feathers, skin. An infestation of them is the worst nightmare of any natural history museum out there.'

Vincent nodded thoughtfully. What Sebastian had said sounded familiar.

'We're looking for someone who may have a large collection of, say, these museum beetles,' he said. 'How would we go about finding such a person? Is there any forum we can get in touch with, or perhaps even an association? I assume it's not all that common to have collections of live beetles.'

Sebastian drained the rest of his drink before answering.

'*Anthrenus museorum* is the most common species of *Anthrenus* we have in this country,' he said. 'It's found more or less everywhere. Even, as I said, in places where you definitely don't want it to be.'

Sebastian glanced towards the armchair that Vincent was sitting in. The previous image of many generations of Bughs sharing the seat suddenly no longer seemed quite as appealing. All the skin and hair that had fallen into the cracks over the decades would be a feast for skin beetles. Vincent had to make an effort not to stand up immediately. He suddenly knew how Mina felt.

'But it's a little trickier than that,' Sebastian continued. 'It's actually a different type of skin beetle that is most commonly used to clean bones. Abroad they use *Dermestes maculatus*. We'd call them hide beetles. In Sweden, we prefer to use *Dermestes haemorrhoidalis*.'

He looked out of the window.

'In this weather, you'd need a temperature-controlled terrarium to keep the larvae alive. Anyway, the beetles reach full development over the course of six weeks, so any that were larvae in the autumn will by now be beetles. You need to know what you're looking for if you want to find them. May I say something in confidence?'

Sebastian turned towards Vincent and dug his hands into his pockets, raising his eyebrows. Vincent showed the palms of his hands.

'Anything that might help,' he said.

'I really do hope you've got more than this to go on,' Sebastian said. 'Please don't quote me on this, but I have to tell you that insect people are a bit weird.'

56

'So you're going to play Santa Claus?'

Mina nodded at the sack that Christer was making ready.

'Yeah. I've got the best belly for it, as Ruben says,' Christer said.

He avoided Mina's gaze. Anything related to Peder was still a sore spot and source of grief for all of them.

'You're coming too, aren't you?' he said.

Mina shook her head fiercely.

'I know I'm useless,' she said, 'but I just can't do it. Not yet. I've got to get there at my own pace …'

She could hear how hollow it sounded, how weak she was for avoiding Anette and the triplets. They couldn't escape their grief – they were stuck living in the middle of it, every minute and every second.

'Don't worry about it,' Christer said, awkwardly patting her shoulder and then hastily withdrawing his hand. 'Sorry, I didn't think.'

'It's OK,' Mina said, and she actually meant it.

Christer smiled but said nothing. He continued to pack his Santa Claus kit, neatly folding a stiff Santa mask with a large white beard attached into the sack.

'Anyway, there's one thing I'd like you to take a look at before you leave,' Mina said, clicking her mouse. 'If you have a moment?'

'Sure thing,' Christer said, closing the drawstring on the sack and testing its weight tentatively. 'What is it?'

'Gambling. I can't figure out why Gustaf Brons would need money from the Serbs given the income he's been making on his own in recent years, unless it was to pay something off. One explanation would be a gambling addiction. Can you follow the money? Use those contacts I know you've got at the gambling companies, and see whether there's anything to show that Brons has frittered away large sums gambling?'

'That'll require me to get them to disclose data about their customers,' Christer said thoughtfully. 'I take it you don't have permission to do that from the prosecutor?'

Mina shook her head.

'Not yet. So do what you can without breaking the law. I know you've got good contacts in place and I thought you might be able to … chew the fat with them. And perhaps check what can be deduced from the publicly available information about Brons's finances for the last … say, five years?'

'No problem,' Christer said, pulling on his coat.

He heaved the sack over his shoulder.

'Don't suppose you've changed your mind, have you?'

'No. I need more time. But give Anette a hug from me.'

'Santa promises to deliver one hug. Ho ho ho!' Christer patted his round belly.

Mina smiled and watched him leave. She could still feel the warmth of his hand on her shoulder.

57

Julia knew the presents weren't enough, but at least they were something. It was an attempt to help Anette and the triplets have a normal life. This was the first Christmas for the triplets without their father and for Anette without her husband. It was the first Christmas of all the Christmases for the rest of their lives. There was no present on earth that could compensate for that.

Nevertheless, Christer in his Santa suit was hauling a bulging sack. It was all they could do – that, and being there. Almost the full team was gathered outside the small terraced house, spending a moment collecting their thoughts. No one said anything. Ruben was concentrating on scraping the snow off his boots. Julia tried to catch Adam's eye, but he was staring down at the ground like the rest of them. She took a deep breath and rang the doorbell. Through the door, she could hear the pattering footsteps of the triplets and then:

'Mum! The doorbell's ringing!'

'Mum! Who is it?'

It took another few seconds before Anette was able to open the door and the triplets tumbled into the snow at her ankles. Molly beamed when she caught sight of Christer.

'Jister!' she said, hurling herself at Christer's legs and almost toppling him over, sack and all. 'Santa Jister!'

Then her smile was replaced by a furrowed brow.

'But ... where's Uncle Asse?'

Julia looked at Christer, her eyebrows raised. She hadn't known that Christer and Lasse were regular visitors.

'What?' he said, while trying to regain his balance. 'It's not like I know who you spend your free time with.'

Of course, he was right about that. And the smile twitching at the corners of Adam's mouth reminded her that it was for the best that Christer didn't know anything about that.

'Won't you come in?' Anette said, beckoning them all into the hall where they took off their shoes and coats.

Julia handed over the hamper of goodies and hugged Anette.

'I've brought you some saffron lussekatt buns,' Adam said, proffering a bag.

'And I've brought mulled wine,' said Ruben. 'Just add the spices.'

'I hope it's strong,' Anette said, glancing across the living room at the triplets, who were now dragging Christer in their wake. He had barely managed to take off his shoes.

The rest of them followed and sat down in the living room while Ruben clattered about in the kitchen with Anette. After a little while, they brought out a spread of Christmas snacks. Anette sank onto the sofa with a loud sigh. For the time being, the triplets seemed to have forgotten that Christer was in fact Santa bearing gifts, and had instead transformed him into a human climbing frame. He was lying on the floor, completely overpowered.

'I think this is my first free second for about a month,' Anette said, leaning back with her eyes closed.

'How are you guys getting on?' Julia asked gently.

Anette opened her eyes again and shrugged.

'I try to find a moment every day when we're happy and just allow ourselves to be that way,' she says. 'Because it's hard. It's easy to feel guilty about being happy occasionally.'

A shadow crossed Anette's face and she glanced away. Julia looked at her. Then she looked at the triplets clambering all over her colleague and laying siege to the living room with their toys. If you didn't look too closely, Anette and the kids looked like any regular family, but the grief was ever-present. Anette's smile rarely reached her eyes. Her family had been torn apart by a maniac brandishing a gun. It could never be repaired.

Julia wasn't brandishing a gun, but she might as well have been, given what she was doing to her own family. To Torkel and Harry. Unlike Anette, she had a choice. She didn't have to smash her family apart. Assuming she had one left.

She and Adam needed to talk, and soon.

58

When Vincent returned home, he found Benjamin and Rebecka already in the kitchen eating dinner. Well, instant noodle pots. Vincent wasn't sure whether that qualified as food at all, on nutritional grounds.

'Whose turn is it to make dinner?' he said from the hall as he took off his shoes.

Benjamin shrugged.

'I think it's your turn, but we sorted ourselves out. The fridge is looking a bit bare.'

Vincent sighed. He had forgotten to shop – one of the many things he seemed to be forgetting these days. Like clockwork, his headache returned as he was hanging up his coat.

'By the way Dad,' Benjamin said, waving a piece of paper, 'what's this?'

Vincent went into the kitchen and took it from his son's hand. It was one of the postcards Umberto had passed on to him. The ones left anonymously in reception at ShowLife Productions. Vincent shrugged and retrieved the other postcard before laying them both out on the table in front of Benjamin.

'Pre Instagram, we had to write our platitudes – I'm sorry, I mean words of wisdom – on postcards,' he said. 'These ones are from an unknown admirer. Please appreciate your father's greatness.'

Rebecka slurped on her noodles as she picked up one of the cards.

'"*The steady dripping of rain and the nagging of a wife are one and the same*",' she read. 'Hello century-old values. Nice, Dad. What kind of fans do you have?'

'"*Don't fall into the trap of making promises to God before you think*",' Benjamin read off the other one. 'I've got to agree, they're kind of weird. But I was thinking about the wording itself. They don't seem quite natural, I mean. It's as if they were translated. Or, like you said Rebecka, old.'

Vincent almost burst out laughing. Of course Rebecka had jumped straight to analysing who had sent the cards – that was just the way she was. She related everything to social contexts. And Benjamin had zoomed in on the language itself. His son's analytical brain had probably already got to work finding patterns among the letters. It was as if Vincent had outsourced two of his own personality traits.

The front door flew open and Aston marched in wearing his winter coveralls, hat and gloves. He was covered in snow from head to foot.

'I gotta pooooooooo!' he yelled, before heading to the toilet without taking his boots off first.

Vincent sighed and went to the cleaning cupboard to get a cloth for the hall floor. If Benjamin and Rebecka were two aspects of him, then which part of him was Aston? He wasn't sure he wanted to know.

'I hope you've eaten plenty of snow,' he shouted towards the closed bathroom door. 'Because I've forgotten to buy anything for dinner.'

He would just have to take Aston out in the car to have hamburgers at the shopping mall in Tyresö. The rest of them could come too, in the unlikely event they wanted to.

He was surprised that Maria wasn't home yet, but on the other hand he couldn't remember what she was supposed to have been doing for the day. It could all have been easily resolved with a telephone call, but he couldn't bring himself to speak to her because she would only ask about Mina and then he would have to give her an answer.

Suddenly he saw something out of the corner of his eye and turned towards the living room. There was nothing there. He must have been mistaken – but for a moment, he'd thought he could see something on the wall. It had looked like letters. Or a word? He frowned as the familiar headache resumed its dull throb.

59

NINE DAYS TO GO

Mina was better prepared for the tunnels this time. The afternoon before, she had acquired a pair of sturdy boots that were going straight in the bin once the search was over. She was wearing gloves since it was icy cold inside the tunnels, but over her leather ones she was also wearing XL-sized disposable gloves. She had another five pairs in her pocket. Of course, she was wearing a mask too.

Ruben, who was at her side, had no protection whatsoever. That was, unless you counted the almost obscenely large hat with ear flaps that he was wearing. It was apparently an early Christmas present from his daughter. He looked ridiculous.

'Jesus Christ, it's freezing down here,' he said, hugging himself as they stepped down off the platform at Odenplan station and entered the tunnel. 'I thought it would be warmer.'

'Hmm, this isn't exactly how I imagined spending the run-up to Christmas either,' Mina said, sparing a thought for Nathalie, who had moved in with her but whom she had barely seen.

This provoked a smile from the representative from the council-owned metro operator, who was escorting them for safety reasons.

'But isn't all the history down here fascinating?' she said. 'What was your name again? Ruben? I'm sorry, but you have to wear a safety helmet down here.'

The very first thing Mina had done was to disinfect her own. Ruben was still clutching his.

'Astrid's hat is all I need,' he said, scowling at the metro woman.

The woman was partly right about the history thing. What she had told them had been interesting – at least for the first two stations they had visited. The charms of yet another set of points had begun to wane after a while.

The theory was that since Jon Langseth's bones had been found fairly close to a station, as had Marcus Eriksson's if Crazy-Tom was to be believed, then the murderer wanted them to be found. So if there were more bones in the tunnels, these too would be found in proximity to a station. Which was lucky for them, because searching the whole tunnel network would be an impossible job.

'There are one hundred stations on the Stockholm metro,' Mina muttered. 'Forty-seven of them are underground. We're on our way to our third. I think Adam and Julia have done four. If the other two teams have got through as many as we have in a day, then I think we'd better prepare to celebrate Christmas underground. We may be here a while.'

They switched on their torches and went further into the tunnel. The light from the station behind them grew fainter. Soon they had gone far enough. There was no pile of gravel in this tunnel either. Mina was almost disappointed that they hadn't found anything. While a new find would obviously be tragic, it would also get things moving. All of a sudden, the phone in her pocket began to ring. She pulled it out and checked the display. Julia.

'Yes?' she said.

'Hi,' Julia said, slightly out of breath. 'We're at Karlaplan. And we've found a new heap. One with bones in it. Adam's called forensics and they're not here yet, but I'd put money on Christer being right about it being that missing lecturer, Erika Sävelden.'

The light from Mina's torch bounced off something ahead of them. Ruben gasped and she stopped in her tracks.

'But if you've got Erika there,' Mina said slowly, 'then who have we got here?'

The beam of light was playing across a heap of gravel in front of them. A heap just big enough to hide a human skeleton. A heap from which there was something white protruding.

60

'But shouldn't I drive you to your train?' Vincent said. 'You've got a long journey ahead of you before you get to your parents.'

Maria and Aston were in the hallway putting on their coats. Maria had packed a large suitcase and Aston was grappling with a backpack that was definitely designed for children. It was almost comical how much more luggage was needed in winter.

'We'll be fine,' Maria said ungraciously. 'We might as well take the bus to the station. You know how much Aston loves taking the bus. And it would be silly for you to be wasting time on us. You might suddenly be needed for that ... police investigation.'

Vincent knew exactly what his wife was getting at. Or rather, who. But he couldn't bring himself to put up a defence – not again. Anyway, he had to admit that Maria's constant accusations had begun to assume a veneer of truth. Mina occupied most of his thoughts. He knew it could never be more than that, but he also knew that he would be completely lost without her. Unfortunately, he couldn't say the same thing about his wife. It might have been true once upon a time, but if so, that had been a long time ago. It was just as well Mina harboured no romantic feelings towards him, because if she had done it really would have made things difficult.

'We're going on the bus and then the train!' Aston shouted, finally managing to put on his backpack. 'I'm going to sit at the very front of the bus.'

'Unless someone elderly who needs the seat more than you gets on,' Maria said sententiously. 'If they do, you'll have to move.'

'If some old person gets on they can sit on my knee and tell me stories.'

Vincent smiled at his son and then turned to look at his wife. He realized how little he knew about her, still, after all these years. In the beginning, it had all been down to passion. Pure carnal lust. By the time that 'they no longer needed it', to quote Maria, they were already living together as a couple. All without really knowing each other. Maria had made valiant attempts to understand him – he knew that much. But he was very unsure about the outcome.

Was it really possible to know anything about another person beyond one's own projections and unconfirmed assumptions? Probably not. He would of course miss Maria if they were no longer married. But how much? Did he even dare ask himself that question?

Maria, who had been in the middle of finding dry mittens for Aston, stopped and gave Vincent a strange look. It was as if she could read his mind.

'You've been very quiet lately,' she said. 'Is everything OK?'

Vincent shook his head. Everything was most definitely not OK.

'I've got such a bad headache, constantly,' he said. 'And a kind of uneasy feeling that seems to be creeping up on me more and more with each passing day.'

'I don't think it did you much good being at home so much in the autumn,' she said. 'When the dark winter arrives it makes the melancholy even worse.'

She gave Aston his mittens. Then she stood on tiptoe to kiss Vincent on the cheek. She placed her hand on the spot where she had just kissed him and looked him in the eyes.

'Do you promise to follow me?' she said.

'I promise,' he said, taking her hand in his. 'But I can't promise I'll eat your father's pigs' trotters.'

'Grandad has pigs' trotters?' Aston said in horrified fascination. 'I've never seen them!'

'Then ask him to show you,' Vincent said, escorting them to the front door. 'They're big and hairy!'

As they left, he was suddenly overcome by the overwhelming feeling that he might never see them again. It came close to knocking him over. He wanted to run out into the snow in his socks, grab them in his arms and tell them how much he loved them. Tell them that they shouldn't go. Instead, he took a deep breath and closed the door.

61

Mina crossed the threshold into her apartment. Julia had given her a dispensation to go home and shower after her stint in the tunnels. The thick winter gear, gloves and mask had done their job, but she could still feel the dirt making its way into her pores. She had left her boots outside the front door for the time being. She undressed as quickly as possible while still standing in the hall. She jumped out of her trousers, tugged her top over her head, and then spotted the shoes.

It took her a split second to remember who they belonged to. Nathalie. Mina had completely forgotten that her daughter now had her own key. She quickly pulled the top back on over her head and picked up her trousers from the floor, but then she stopped mid-movement before she had time to put them on again.

The study door was open.

The door that she was always so careful to keep locked. There were stacks of cardboard boxes on the living-room floor outside. She knew perfectly well what they contained. Her disposable knickers and vests. Hand sanitizer and alcohol gel. Various cleaning supplies and equipment, which had been taking up the rest of the space, were in another pile. And, as if that weren't bad enough, she could hear Nathalie rummaging around inside.

'Mum?' Nathalie said, popping her head out of the door. 'Hi! I'm just having a tidy up. I don't know why you've got so many boxes and stuff in here. The place looks more like a stockroom than a study! Anyway I thought I'd try and move in here. It didn't feel right, you giving me your bedroom while you sleep on the sofa. This room will be great if we just sort it out a bit. Hang on – why aren't you wearing any trousers?'

Mina could only stare. She had no idea what to say. She walked stiffly into the living room and placed her trousers on top of the stack of boxes.

There it was. For her, it had long been a perfectly reasonable way, the *only* way, to live. A deep-seated source of shame that she hid from everyone to avoid being seen as completely abnormal. And now her secret was just lying there, scattered across the floor. And her daughter was standing in the middle of it.

'You weren't allowed …' Mina said. 'I haven't …'

She cleared her throat and tried again. How was she supposed to explain?

'I think there's something … I have to explain.'

'That you're kinda crazy?' Nathalie said, laughing. 'I knew that. I've never known anyone who needed two hundred pairs of knickers before.'

'This is my …' Mina began in a low voice. She was about to say 'my life', but stopped herself at the very last moment. 'You have no right to do this. There are some things that are private. You can't just come in here and …'

'Muummm,' Nathalie said. 'It's just cleaning stuff. And knickers. Well, it's an absurd quantity of knickers. But it's not like I've found some basement where you whip kids or something. It's just stuff. If we do a bit of reorganizing then most of it should fit into your bedroom.'

Her daughter squinted at her before continuing.

'I really hope you've got something more private than this for me to find next time you're out. Taking the piss out of you for having some vests and hand sanitizer just isn't all that.'

Mina looked at her daughter, trying to detect mockery in her gaze. Disapproval at the corners of her mouth. Or horror at being presented with a parent who was off their head. But she saw none of that. Nathalie just seemed to be … happy.

'Come and help me clean up,' Nathalie said, grinning at her as she handed her a pair of rubber gloves, although she wasn't wearing any herself.

Mina swallowed. The fort had not only been occupied and the drawbridge lowered, but the castle ghosts had also been drawn out into the light. She was definitely not ready for this – but she guessed she might never be. And she'd experienced worse. She'd been into the Stockholm metro tunnels, and *survived*. She would just have to shower later. She swallowed again. Then she smiled back.

'Did you say clean up?' she said, pulling on the rubber gloves. 'Let me show you how the professionals do it.'

62

Niklas was standing by the window in his office, as he often did nowadays. The people in the street below were wrapped up warm in winter coats, carrying bags filled with Christmas presents and looking happy. But one of them might be out to get him. With each passing day, the likelihood that his fate was awaiting him in the street below increased.

'We've spoken to everyone who was working at the TV studio two days ago,' Tor said from behind him. 'The Security Service have also run additional background checks on them. They've looked into their social media networks and their political views.'

'Political views?' Niklas said, turning around. 'Are we even allowed to do that?'

Tor shrugged.

'Well, we did. You can pretend you didn't hear about that bit of it, if you like.'

Niklas slumped into his chair and ran a hand over his face.

'And?' he said. 'What did you find?'

Tor swallowed before answering. His Adam's apple was bobbing up and down. There would have been something comical about the discomfort this compact man was feeling, except the subject matter was deeply unfunny.

'Nothing,' Tor said, his voice faltering. 'Nothing on anyone. Apart from one of them having an affair, but I doubt that matters much. The editorial team is beside itself, and the SVT management have unofficially sent their apologies, and—'

'Unofficially?' Niklas said, raising his eyebrows.

Tor cleared his throat.

'We'd like to keep the whole thing a secret so that the perpetrator doesn't have any confirmation. And SVT can't issue an official apology if nothing has happened. The presenters, the floor managers and the camera operators who were working are devastated that this happened right before their very eyes.'

'So the perpetrator came and went without anyone seeing them?'

'That's impossible,' Tor said. 'The security detail would have noticed right away if there were any unauthorized persons in the studio.'

Niklas spun on his chair so that he could look out of the window again. There was a man walking along the street with his head bowed against the snow.

'So that means it was one of the people who works there?' he said.

'I'm afraid that's not likely either. We had already run background checks on everyone who was there. Everyone who was in the studio had been given the all-clear by the Security Service.'

Niklas had seen the man in the street before.

'Take a look down there,' he said, pointing out of the window. 'That man down there. I've seen him several times before – always outside here. What's he doing here? I swear he's watching me. I assume you've got security people on the street – ask them to bring him in!'

Tor peered out of the window and sighed.

'That's our caretaker,' he said. 'He always goes home about this time.'

Obviously. Now Niklas recognized him. Of course he was becoming paranoid. He looked again at the man trudging through the snow. The caretaker would keep going home each and every day – perhaps to his family in Södermalm who were missing him, or perhaps to a bachelor pad in Upplands Väsby. Niklas had no idea. The point was that the caretaker would still be doing the same thing next week. And the week after that. But by then, Niklas would no longer exist.

He closed his eyes and visualized the symbol in his mind.

An eight with the bottom half coloured in.

'You can go now,' he said wearily to Tor, his eyes still closed.

Maybe, just maybe, it was time to accept the facts. And why not? The last twenty years had been amazing. But all good things had to come to an end sooner or later. In nine days it would all be over. He would no longer exist. He wondered whether Nathalie would understand. And he hoped it wouldn't hurt too much when his time came.

63

Mina was waiting for Vincent in Kronobergsparken on the hill above police headquarters. She needed a change of scene and to cool down after her cleaning session with Nathalie. She couldn't shower all the time now that her daughter was in the apartment. She'd had to make do with once.

Mina exhaled and stared in fascination at the condensation hovering in the air in front of her mouth. Perhaps it was her imagination, but she almost thought she could make out ice crystals forming on her own breath. Then they dissolved into the air.

She was no fan of winter storms, but she thought the cold was beautiful. Cold preserved, it disinfected. It stopped time and space. She knew that when others called her the ice queen, they weren't paying her a compliment.

A blond man in a black coat with a distinctive shape appeared at the far end of the park. Vincent. Despite all her thoughts about the cold, a surprisingly warm feeling spread through her body. Although describing it as warm was feeble. As he approached, her temperature rose until she felt like an oven. She had to undo her coat to cool off.

'Oh wow, is it that hot?' Vincent said when he reached her.

Mina didn't know what to say. She could feel herself beginning to blush. What was happening?

'Let's take a walk,' she said, setting off.

'So how are we doing?' he said.

This was delivered as if it were the most obvious question in the world. She had no idea how to respond.

'Er, I … we—' she said, but Vincent interrupted her.

'Well, the investigation I mean,' he said. 'I see you've brought the file with you.' She looked down at the file in her hand – she had completely forgotten about it.

'We … we've actually found another two heaps of bones,' she said, clearing her throat. 'So that makes four in total. The fourth one is something of a mystery since it doesn't match any of the people reported missing in recent years.'

Vincent had an air of concentration about him.

There was the sound of children laughing from somewhere ahead of them in the park. As Mina and Vincent got closer, they saw a small sledging hill crowded with children from a nursery.

'Come on!' Vincent said, a glint in his eye.

He grabbed her by the hand and began to head briskly for the top of the hill. She had no choice but to follow.

'There's going to be a fifth pile of bones – mentalist bones – if you do what I think you're going to do,' she said.

'Didn't you tell me once that it's important to do normal stuff when other people are watching?' he said, grabbing two empty sledges.

The children around them didn't seem to care one bit about the grown-up man in his dark coat – not even when he got onto a sledge that was much too small for him, with the words *Kronan Nursery* emblazoned on the side.

'Didn't I also once say something about you being insane?' Mina said, shaking her head.

He pointed to the sledge next to him and she reluctantly got on.

She had to fold her legs to fit, and as she struggled to maintain her balance while clutching the file, she realized that the snow must have stopped falling a while ago. The sun was making the snow on the hill sparkle.

Vincent leaned towards her and took hold of her sledge, laughing. Amidst the winter clothing, the merry cries of the children and the impossibility of it all, she could make out his scent. She inhaled deeply, well aware that scents were actually particles and therefore the last thing she wanted in her own nostrils. But they were his particles. His scent.

'If any nursery staff ask, I'm going to tell them I'm in the process of arresting you,' she said, then shrieked as Vincent pushed her sledge so hard that she flew down the slope.

She couldn't help but laugh. He arrived immediately behind

her and they landed in the midst of the pack of children at the bottom of the slope. They had to struggle back to their feet.

'Thanks for the loan,' Vincent said, handing the sledges to two wide-eyed boys wearing over-sized winter coveralls.

Then he strolled away as if nothing had happened.

'Weird,' Mina murmured to herself, but she couldn't help smiling as she followed him.

'Have you found out any more in the investigation?' Vincent said after a while.

Mina shook her head.

'Just a lengthy write-up from Loke about beetles that I'm never ever going to read.'

Vincent appeared to pause for thought.

'Occam's razor, as I always say,' he said. 'The victims' identities haven't led us any further. Nor has the curious treatment of their remains. Or even their actual remains. Or the connection to the metro tunnels, if there even is one. What does that leave us?'

He stopped suddenly.

'Do you have any pictures of the heaps of gravel themselves? I mean, how they looked before you removed the skeletons from them?'

Mina opened the file and took out the four reports. One for each victim, and one for the unidentified heap of bones.

'Forensics documented it all carefully before we touched anything. Of course, the first heap had already started to slide apart because of the graffiti artist who found it, but that doesn't matter much. They're just heaps of gravel.'

She opened the reports one after another and handed the pictures to Vincent. He looked at them, leafing between them and comparing them. Mina reflected that she could probably have set fire to his coat right now and he wouldn't have noticed, so deep was his concentration.

'Look at this,' he said at last. 'You're right about the heaps looking the same. They really are nothing more than heaps of gravel. But look at the ground around them.'

He pointed to one of the pictures. A darker band was visible in the gravel around the heap.

'Someone has drawn circles around the heaps – I'd guess

using a stick,' she said, nodding. Then she checked the time. 'Oh crap, I've got to be getting back. Ruben and I are off to see Josephine Langseth again – as per your suggestion.'

'They aren't circles,' Vincent said, handing the photos back to her. 'Take another look.'

He was right. On three of them, she could see the dark band crossing over itself behind the heaps of gravel and then disappearing into the dark.

'They're all taken from slightly different angles,' Vincent said, 'but it looks like the same pattern in most of them. It's impossible to guess why it's not there in the fourth location with the unidentified bones, but let's focus on the places where we know who the victims are.'

Mina looked at the pictures and tried to form a three-dimensional image in her head, adding details from the photographs.

'It's two circles on top of each other,' she said at last. 'Like a big eight, with the heap of gravel inside the lower half of the number.'

'Interesting that you see a number,' said Vincent. 'Because I see something else. I see an hourglass with all the sand in the lower half. An hourglass ...'

'... where time has run out,' Mina said.

She had no idea what it meant, but she grasped Vincent's arm tightly. The sun was gone again and the snow-laden clouds had returned to fill the sky. Her own words were echoing inside her head. She had heard someone say something like that just a few days ago. Something about it all coming to an end. Had the person in question been referring to ... this? To hourglasses and piles of bones? She was afraid that the murderer might not be done – and that the next victim might be someone she knew.

64

When he entered her room, he found Granny Astrid waiting for him in bed. She looked more fragile than usual. That was probably because of the harsh winter. The absence of sunlight led to vitamin D deficiency and depression for many in the population. Ten million Swedes became as pale as ghosts and spent four months with their shoulders hunched to stave off the cold. And it hit the elderly twice as hard, so it would be no surprise if she seemed a little out of sorts.

But when Astrid caught sight of Ruben, she beamed at him. The smile was just as visible in her eyes as it was at her mouth, and it was as warm as the sun in July.

He saw that she had dressed up for the Christmas season, wearing the cardigan that his grandad had knitted for her. Grandad had been a cloth cutter and it had been his habit to dress his wife in the most incredible creations made by his own hand. The neighbouring wives in Älvsjö had always been green with envy. Granny had hung onto many of her favourite items of clothing from back then.

'Excuse me, ma'am. Have you seen my grandmother?' Ruben said, feigning surprise. 'The elderly lady who used to have this room? Or should we just forget about her and I'll take you to the dance instead?'

Astrid giggled in delight.

'Well, you don't look too shabby yourself, what with that jacket,' she said. 'Quite the smart gentleman.'

Astrid slipped out of bed and peered into the corridor, then she closed the door.

'Might I offer you an almond cookie?' she said conspiratorially, producing a biscuit tin from her nightstand.

The staff had long ago given up trying to get Astrid to stop eating almond cookies. Of course it wasn't good for her health, but she was so old that their admonitions had become rather half-hearted. Astrid, however, took them quite seriously and made a point of hiding her cookies very carefully – though it was quite probable that everyone in the department knew about them.

'Yes please,' he said. 'And I've brought you a top-up.'

He pulled out another tin of almond cookies from his bag. There was a red ribbon tied around it.

'Oh my, what a lovely Christmas present!' Astrid chirped, deftly taking the tin from him. 'Now, sit. Tell me: how is my great-granddaughter with the beautiful name?'

Granny was still so proud she could burst at the fact that Ellinor had given Ruben's daughter the same name as his grandmother.

'Astrid's a smart girl,' he said. 'She loves to paint, just like her mum. She's still doing martial arts, although not quite as much any longer as she's also taken up ballet. She still wants to be a police officer when she grows up.'

Granny squinted at him and smiled.

'Then what's up?' she said, prodding him in the side. 'I can see it. You're acting like a schoolboy.'

Ruben fidgeted on his chair. Granny had always had the ability to see right through him. Ever since he had been little, it had been pointless keeping secrets from her. He could come up with an excuse, but she would see through it right away.

He just had no idea where to start.

'I mean, it's way too early to say really,' he said, squirming even more. 'But ... I might have met someone.'

'Well, well, well!' Astrid cried out, clapping her hands together. Cookie crumbs flew everywhere. 'Not a moment too soon either! Who is it?'

'Her name's Sara. We worked together briefly last summer and that was great. But I hadn't seen her all autumn until three days ago. We bumped into each other in town. And she's really ... Well, I don't think she even knows that I exist. Not like that, I mean. I'm definitely not her type. We barely know each other, but it's as if—'

'Ruben,' Granny interrupted him sharply. 'You're delirious as a seventeen-year-old. Now have a cookie and get some sugar into you before you pass out.'

He did as he was told and bit into a biscuit.

'I'd lost all hope in you,' she said. 'Since Ellinor, you haven't been a good boy. I've been so angry at you. I know you lied to me about how you were getting on, but I didn't say anything. After all, I am rather fond of you.'

'Sorry,' he said.

'Don't apologize. You straightened things out. You found out you had a daughter. And you're a great father. Even Ellinor seems to have stopped being angry with you. So I'm sure you can make this work too. Be careful and take it easy. Just put macho cop Ruben back in the box and I'm sure it'll be fine.'

'No risk of him being around. She's not impressed by that kind of stuff. We're going to be celebrating Christmas together.'

'I like her already,' Granny said, laboriously opening the new biscuit tin.

She stopped halfway through the process.

'I do hope she likes almond cookies?' she said suspiciously.

'Who doesn't?' Ruben said, laughing. 'She's not mad.'

Astrid nodded contentedly. She popped another cookie into her mouth and munched away. Granny might have seemed fragile when he'd arrived, but now she was back to her usual self.

'I expect to hear all about her the next time we meet,' she said. 'Or even better – bring her along! Yes, why don't we settle on that? It's a date.'

'One thing at a time, Granny,' Ruben laughed. 'One thing at a time.'

But he already knew he would do as his grandmother asked. She always got her way, somehow.

65

'Mina!' Christer yelled as he jogged lethargically down the corridor in pursuit of her.

Mina briefly wondered whether she would need to find the defibrillator she knew was somewhere on the premises. Christer's face was bright red and there was a wheezing sound each time he breathed.

'I've managed to get what you asked me for,' he panted, his hands on his knees. 'Jesus, you walk fast. And you don't hear people shouting your name either.'

'I'm not really here,' she said. 'I just went for a walk with Vincent in Kronobergsparken and only popped in to get Ruben so that we can go on to Josephine Langseth's. You haven't seen me.'

'So you don't want to know about Gustaf Brons?'

Mina came to a halt.

'Gustaf Brons?' she said. 'Let me guess. He's racked up gambling debts?'

'And then some,' Christer said. He was still squeaking and wheezing as he breathed. 'He's blown a fortune. There's not a penny left of the cash he pilfered through his Confido scheme. In fact, he's heavily in debt. And to all the wrong people, to top it off. That's what the money from Dragan Manojlovic was for. He's been borrowing all over the shop. The halcyon days are over for Mr Brons. No more luxury hotels, posh restaurants or fancy travel for him. Not to mention the expensive lawyer he's always got in tow. He'll be lucky if he's got enough change left over to buy crispbread.'

There was a degree of *Schadenfreude* in Christer's statement.

Mina's thoughts began to run in new directions. Gustaf Brons. Gambling debts. Some of the puzzle was becoming clearer, but there was still so much of it that was obscured. For instance, why were Jon, Mark and Erika dead?

'Thanks Christer,' she said, looking at him pityingly. 'That breathing doesn't sound too hot, does it? You know there's a gym in the basement. I can draw you a map if you're struggling to find it.'

'Very funny. I'm in excellent physical condition. Thank you for asking. I'm just going through a bit of a dip in form right now.'

'A dip? I suppose that's one way of putting it.'

Christer glared at her and then turned on his heel. As he headed for the far end of the corridor, she heard him muttering grumpily.

'You pitch in and do your job and what do you get? Shit. That's what you get.'

Mina smiled to herself and set off in the other direction. It was probably for the best if she did draw him that map. She hoped to keep teasing Christer for many years to come – and there was Lasse to consider too.

Then she came to an abrupt halt.

Something about what he'd said about luxury hotels had triggered an idea. A thought about Josephine Langseth. After a quick Google search, she had a phone number. As she was dialling, she hurried down the corridor to fetch Ruben.

66

The house in Stureby was no longer the safe refuge that it had once been. When Mina went home to take a shower, Julia did the same thing. After a day spent in the tunnels, her skin had assumed a steely grey hue from all the dust.

But nowadays, Julia always felt low-spirited whenever she stepped through her own front door – as if she were entering a stranger's home. In a way, that was true. Torkel had become a stranger to her. And she had become a stranger to herself. She had always known who she was. She had constantly been defined by her relationship to others. The daughter of the police commissioner. Top of her class at police college. Torkel's wife. Head of her own team of police detectives. Harry's mum.

Adam's mistress.

But somewhere along the way she had got lost. She had forgotten who she was when no one else was around, and she didn't know whether she was willing to find out.

Her words to Adam at the exhumation of Marcus Eriksson's remains had taken her by surprise – and horrified her too. She wasn't yet prepared to deal with the consequences of them. And she had covered herself with the word 'think'. If she were perfectly honest, she hadn't actually said she definitely wanted to get divorced.

At Anette's, she had felt like a real villain about to smash her family to pieces. But now she was at home, it didn't even feel as if they were a family. What was there to smash?

The noise from the bathroom revealed that Torkel was showering. Why was he doing that in the middle of the day? She assumed that Harry was asleep, and a peek into the bedroom confirmed her assumption. He was lying on his back with his arms outstretched above his head, his mouth half-open and his fringe a little sweaty. There was nothing more serene than watching him sleep. She suddenly felt very soft inside. Could she really change his world? Destroy it? She and Torkel – together, under the same roof – was all he knew.

There was a glow on the bedside table on Torkel's side. Out of sheer reflex, she looked. It was a notification on his phone.

Julia moved closer and tapped on the screen, which had now faded to black. The notification was still there. She squinted. She thought she was mistaken, or that it was some kind of advertising. But the notification told its own clear story. It announced that Torkel had several matches on Tinder. Well, not Torkel. SturebyDad81 had several matches.

Her hands trembling, she put in his PIN code. It was the same as hers. In another world, in another era, their trust in each other had been so great that they had agreed on the same PIN for both their phones. Now that code was the gateway to hell.

She slumped onto the edge of the bed while she opened the app and read on. It was a strange feeling to climb straight into Torkel's brain and see how he communicated with other women. Which jokes he told. What he told them about himself. The compliments he paid them. She dreaded the prospect of finding dick pics, or pictures of any female sexual organs for that matter, but thank goodness there were none. Although perhaps he'd taken that side of the conversation to text or email … Nausea began to well up within her.

She was sitting there as if paralysed, clutching the phone with the Tinder app open, when Torkel emerged from the shower with a towel wrapped around his waist.

'Would you like me to take a snap to send to hotmamainthecity95?' Julia asked stiffly, holding up his phone.

Torkel's face turned white.

'Why are you snooping on my phone?'

'Is that really the question to be asking right now? Wouldn't a more pressing question be why you're on Tinder?'

His gaze wavered and he began to stammer.

'Yes, well … I … you see … Tinder has a much better interface than the other apps. It's user-friendly and it's got a lower frequency of fake profiles than you find on platforms like Ashley Madison.'

Julia stared at him. Harry whimpered in his sleep and she lowered her voice to a hiss.

'Are you completely out of your fucking mind?! I didn't ask you why you'd picked Tinder in particular – I wanted to know why you're *on* Tinder, full stop!'

Torkel shifted his weight from foot to foot. A small puddle of water had formed on the floor beneath him.

'Er ... I ... well, you're never bloody around any more! I mean, how much attention do I get? It's no wonder I'm looking for some validation elsewhere! I don't *do* anything, I just talk to them. It's completely innocent!'

His indignant tone and exculpatory expression made her insides boil. She slowly stood up, threw his phone onto the bed and stepped close to him. The familiar smell of apple-scented shower gel hit her and for a moment she was about to relent. Then the rage rose once again. The safety on the metaphorical gun she was carrying around was definitely off.

'How dare you blame me for this? You're saying that it's *my* fault that you're Tindering a bunch of chicks? All because *you* don't get enough attention? When we have a one-year-old? And I've got a full-time job? You're fucking insane.'

She swept out of the bedroom, clenching her fists rhythmically as she made for the hallway. She was bloody relieved she was still called Hammarsten.

Fragments of memory flashed through her mind. Adam's body on top of hers. Her mouth against his. She knew she was applying double standards. She knew she had done something far worse than log onto Tinder. But that didn't make her any less angry.

As she slammed the front door, a large swathe of snow fell off the roof straight onto Torkel's car. She kept walking. That was Torkel's problem – not hers.

67

They weren't as impressed by the apartment this time around as they had been on the first occasion. Now they knew what to expect. And there was clearly no joy to be found in the expansive rooms. Josephine Langseth looked thin and haggard when she opened the front door.

There were moving boxes everywhere. The tabloids had gleefully trumpeted that Jon Langseth's large apartment on Narvavägen was to be sold to repay some of the money that had gone missing in the Confido affair.

'When are you moving?' Mina asked, unable to disguise her pity as she followed Josephine along the gigantic hallway.

Ruben was still stamping the snow off his shoes, but soon managed to remove them.

'This weekend. We've got until Sunday,' Josephine said in a low and trembling voice.

Mina knew she shouldn't feel pity. Josephine and Jon Langseth had lived lavishly for far too long at others' expense. It had been a life they didn't have the money for. But seeing the children's toys scattered between the moving boxes she had difficulty not feeling some degree of sympathy for this thin woman.

'Can we sit down?' Ruben said, pointing at the sofa that stood in lonely majesty in the middle of the living room, the sole remaining item of furniture.

'Of course. They've already taken the rest of the furniture away,' Josephine said, sitting carefully on the very edge of the sofa as they both sat down next to her. 'It's all being auctioned off next week.'

The snow had begun to fall again outside the big windows. Before long, the streets would be filled with snow ploughs. Narvavägen was probably a priority street that would be quickly cleared of all snow.

'We've got a question for you about your stay at the Ellery Beach House. You said you were there for some alone time just before Jon went missing?'

'Yes,' Josephine said, a flash of anxiety now visible in her eyes. 'Yes, I've got three children under the age of eight. Sometimes I need to get away and just be. And Jon's always been generous like that. He asked our nanny to stay in the apartment and take care of the children so that I could have a weekend to myself.'

'And were you? By yourself, I mean?' Mina said, scrutinizing Josephine.

Sometimes she hated this part of the job. She didn't want to know about people's dirty linen. She didn't want any insight into the less appealing aspects of people's lives. But all too often she had to. People's personal lives were often intimately connected to the crimes committed, and the police had to rule out that possibility.

'Yes ... I was there on my own. Why do you ask?'

Josephine's tone was alert, and she shifted even further out onto the edge of the sofa.

'You didn't bump into anyone you know at the hotel?' Ruben said.

'No ... no ... Well, what do you mean?'

Her gaze shifted between Ruben and Mina.

'We have reason to believe you were there with someone else.'

Mina held her breath. What Christer had said about Gustaf and expensive hotels had made her think about the fact that Josephine had mentioned the Ellery Beach House, the latest addition to the Stockholm hotel scene for those who could afford it. She could just about make out Ruben's quizzical look from the corner of her eye, but she glanced discreetly at him to encourage his continued silence while they awaited Josephine's reply. People had a natural desire to fill silence, and the silence that was lingering in the air following her statement was dense and uncomfortable.

It took a long time, but in the end Josephine appeared to make a decision. Her shoulders slumped and she surrendered.

'I was there with Gustaf.'

'How long have you ... been seeing each other?' Ruben asked.

He leaned back on the sofa and crossed one leg over the other. Mina spotted a big hole in the bottom of his sock.

'Not that long. About six months. It started at Peter Kronlund's midsummer party. He's the third owner. We had a few too many drinks, and Jon ended up in a room with a twenty-year-old influencer who was there with some board member as arm candy. And Gustaf … Gustaf *saw* me.'

She looked away and fiddled with an invisible thread on the arm of the sofa.

'Did Jon know?' Mina asked.

She was tracking the snowflakes outside the window as they slowly sailed towards the asphalt.

Josephine shook her head fiercely.

'No, no. I'm sure of that. He would never have accepted it. He didn't know anything.'

'Do you think it could have been a motive for Gustaf to get rid of Jon?' Ruben asked.

'God, no. Gustaf's not a killer. He would never hurt Jon … And I'm absolutely certain he'll sort this mess out too. The Confido business. I know how sleazy it looks, but it's more than just an affair between Gustaf and me. We've talked a lot since Jon's disappearance. He's been a huge support to me and I think we'll probably be throwing our lot in together for the future. He's just got to … sort things out at home first.'

'I see. Is that what he said?' Mina said, struggling to disguise her contempt. 'It's a good job that what you have is the real thing then, because I'm sure you realize he's going to need all the support you can offer him. Given the financial situation he's in now.'

'Financial situation?' Josephine said in confusion.

'I'm referring to the fact that Gustaf has gambled away his entire fortune,' Mina said as innocently as she could, 'and that he's still got huge debts. It's nice of you to give him a soft landing.'

The colour drained from Josephine's face. She said nothing – instead, she gasped for air like a fish dragged from the sea and thrown onto the shore.

'Thanks for speaking to us. We'll be back in contact if we have any more questions,' Mina said, standing up.

Josephine remained on the sofa amidst the sea of moving boxes while she and Ruben went into the hallway to put their shoes and coats back on.

The cramped lift with its ornate gate descended with agonizing torpor. Mina breathed through her nose as she examined her reflection in the lift's antique mirror. Annoyingly, a few strands of hair had come loose from her ponytail and were hanging down the sides of her face. Ruben met her gaze in the mirror and let out a low laugh.

'I think Gustaf's chances of making it last with Josephine just fell drastically,' he said. 'I didn't know you had that kind of sadistic streak in you. It was very entertaining.'

'I'll let you know next time so that you can bring popcorn,' Mina said.

'But I didn't buy any of her bullshit about Gustaf never hurting Jon,' Ruben said. 'I think we need to explore the possibility that the two of them might have worked together. Gustaf and Josephine.'

'I agree. We definitely need to take a closer look at them.'

68

The door chimed each time anyone entered or exited, and each time it did it made Adam think about the old movie *It's a Wonderful Life*. It had been his mother's favourite film and it had been their tradition that they watched it every year on Christmas Day. She knew all the lines by heart, and as soon as he heard the door chime he heard his mother's voice saying, 'Every time a bell rings, an angel gets his wings.'

It didn't feel as if any angels were going to get their wings tonight – not in the seedy Indian restaurant they had agreed to meet up in, anyway.

'You know it wouldn't be weird for us to be seen together. We work together. It's no stranger than Ruben and Christer going out for lunch together.'

'I know, I know, I'm just … being careful.'

Julia brusquely spooned more piping-hot tikka masala from the small copper pot.

'You could consider it … a good thing that Torkel's started to move on?' Adam said cautiously, well aware that he was venturing out into a minefield. At any moment, he might hear the click of a mental landmine being primed beneath his feet.

'A good thing? Good how? I think it's pretty disgusting that he's busy swiping right on Tinder.'

Adam said nothing. He tore a piece of naan bread in half and dipped it into the flavourful sauce.

Julia was an intelligent woman. It was one of the things he loved about her. She had to see the double standards in her thinking by herself. As if she had read his mind, she put down her cutlery and tapped her fingernails against the tabletop in irritation.

'I know, I know. It's the height of duplicity for me to claim the right to be upset. I'm the one having an affair. I'm the one sleeping with someone else.'

Adam still said nothing, but he couldn't help feeling slightly stung when she talked about their relationship like that. Affair. Sleeping with. It sounded cold and impersonal. It didn't sound at all like two people sharing something special, something that went beyond sex. He tore off another piece of bread and drowned it in sauce. Chewing bought him time because he honestly had no idea what to say.

'Taste good?'

The waiter came over and looked at them hopefully. They both smiled and nodded back. It was true. The decor and the food were a complete mismatch – the food was incredible.

'I don't know, Adam. I don't know what's right and wrong, which way's up and which way's down. I don't know anything any more.'

'But what do *you* want?'

Adam's voice was gentle, but inside him a thousand emotions were raging. He knew what he wanted Julia to say, but he didn't want to force anything. He wanted her to work it out for herself, for her to want the same thing he did.

'I know – but I don't know,' Julia said quietly. 'I know I can't carry on with Torkel. But I can't imagine tearing Harry's family apart. I want to be with you. But I can see a thousand problems ahead of us. I want Torkel to be happy. But I don't want him picking up chicks on Tinder. I know I'm applying double standards, but I can't help being upset and feeling betrayed – even though it's me doing the betraying. For Christ's sake, Adam. Why can't it be a little easier to live? Just a little? Sometimes?'

She used her thumb and forefinger to show just how little she meant. Adam took her hand and squeezed it. He could tell by her expression that she wanted to tear it from his grasp because she was afraid someone would see, but for once he ignored that.

'Julia, listen. There's no one in here who cares the slightest bit about us, and I'm not going to let go until you've heard what I have to say. Yes, it's definitely double standards. You don't really have any right to pass judgement on what Torkel does. But I still get it. I get that you feel betrayed, and I would probably have reacted the same way. It just needs time. It's that simple. I don't have kids, so I can't pretend I know how that feels. The only thing that matters to me is that you know I'm here.'

He let go of her hand. She didn't reply, but she smiled fleetingly.

The door chimed.

'Every time a bell rings, an angel gets his wings,' Adam said quietly.

'What did you say?' Julia looked at him in confusion.

He shrugged.

'Nothing. It was nothing. Now eat up before the food goes cold. It's too good not to.'

69

Milda watched in admiration as Loke carefully encased a piece of bone in bubble wrap and then applied tape to it. Reverence for the dead was the linchpin of her profession. It might sound simple, but it was easy to become jaded when coming into regular contact with dead bodies or parts thereof.

Loke was anything but jaded. He was treating the old skeletal remains with something akin to veneration, as if they were as important in death as they had been when the person had been alive, which was exactly how it should be, as far as Milda was concerned.

He placed the bundle containing the bone next to the others that had already been prepared.

'How long do you think it will take Gunilla to date them?' he said, starting to pack the bundles into a box.

'I wish I knew,' she said. 'Gunilla is the best forensic anthropologist we've got. I dare say she'll use methods we don't even know about. But given this is a priority case … two days. Maybe three. It depends how many people she can bribe to work with her over Christmas.'

Loke placed the wrapped skull on top of the pile of bundles in the box that Milda was going to take to Gunilla.

'But why don't we just give her part of the skeleton?' he said, with something bordering on anxiety in his gaze. 'Does she need all of it?'

'Well, I'd prefer not to split it up,' she said. 'It's better she gets all of it and then she can use it however she wants. No one else needs the bones more.'

Loke looked as if he wanted to object, but he said nothing. Instead, he closed the cardboard box and sealed it with tape.

'But then we'll get them back?' he said.

'Then we'll get them back.'

'Good. We owe it to these people to take care of them. *Someone* has to do it, until we know what happened.'

Milda looked at Loke in amusement. She didn't know whether to be troubled or moved by the depth of his concern.

'You know they're not going far,' she said. 'Gunilla is in the same building as us. With a little luck, dating these bones will make it easier for the police to identify them. Maybe it won't be too long before we know how it's all connected.'

'I hope you're right,' Loke said, his gaze wandering over to the skeletons of Jon, Erika and Marcus lying on their respective tables. 'I really hope so.'

70

Mina took a tin of coffee down from the kitchen cupboard. Inside there was an airtight bag that she carefully re-sealed once she had taken what she needed.

'There's something I've been thinking about,' Nathalie said from the living room. 'Do you have any idea why Dad suddenly decided it was so important for me to come and stay here? I mean, I really like it. But it was kinda fast, right?'

'I've been meaning to ask you the same thing,' Mina called out as she measured the ground coffee into the French press.

She switched on the kettle, took two pale grey Iittala mugs out of the cupboard and then went back into the living room.

'I told you already how he turned all weird after our Christmas dinner,' Nathalie said. 'It's as if he's ... constantly in a hurry. But I don't understand why. He's nervous. The slightest sound makes him jump. He wasn't even like that last summer when the attack happened. I don't think he can be feeling too well.'

When Mina put the mugs down on the table, a small piece of card that had been lying there slipped to the floor. It was the piece of card that Nathalie had written Mina's address on. Mina had forced herself not to throw it out so that Nathalie wouldn't realize how strange she was. That had been before her daughter had dragged her shameful secret into the light of day by tidying up the study. Then Mina had forgotten about it and the piece of card had remained where it was.

She picked it up from the floor and saw there was something printed on the back. It was obviously a business card. But instead of a name, there was just a phone number, and a large number eight that was half coloured in.

Vincent's voice resounded in her head. *Interesting that you see a number. Because I see something else. I see an hourglass with all the sand in the lower half. An hourglass ... where time has run out.*

She suddenly knew what it was that she had been trying to remember. Who it was who had said it would all be over soon.

Niklas.

It had been Niklas who had said it.

'What's this?' she said, her voice barely audible.

Nathalie shrugged. Then she frowned and looked more closely at the card.

'That ... Oh no, I didn't realize that was what I was writing on. He'll be livid if he realizes I've taken it. I've seen that card before. It was under Dad's chair after our Christmas dinner. I was going to throw it out, but he was furious when he saw me doing that. He said it was really important – which was weird because it was lying on the floor.'

Mina felt as if there was a cold hand wrapped around her throat. Niklas had been stressed and nervous ever since their dinner. A change in behaviour. And after dinner, Nathalie had found a business card she had never seen before, on which there was the same symbol they had found around the heaps of bones in the metro tunnels.

Something suddenly occurred to her. It wasn't necessarily that Niklas wanted Nathalie to live with her – he wanted Nathalie to no longer be living with him. He was trying to protect their daughter.

'Perhaps I ought to call this number,' Mina said, trying to sound as normal as she could.

She went to fetch her work phone and dialled the number on the card. It rang three times before it was connected.

'Hello Niklas Stockenberg,' said a soft female voice.

Mina was about to say that it wasn't Niklas calling when she realized it was a recording. It had the same clipped quality you sometimes found in self-service call centres where the messages were assembled from a database of pre-prepared phrases. The recording continued.

'We hope you have been satisfied with our services during this period which has now reached its end. You have ... nine days ... six hours ... and ... twenty ... three minutes ... left to live.'

The call ended. Mina stared at Nathalie, whose face had gone pale. Shit. She'd heard all of it. Mina quickly called the number again. There must have been some mistake.

'Hello Niklas Stockenberg,' said the now familiar female voice. 'We hope you have been satisfied with our services during this period which has now reached its end. You have … nine days … six hours … and … twenty … two minutes … left to live.'

'It's a joke, right?' Nathalie said faintly. 'It has to be. A joke.'

Mina was having trouble breathing. It felt as if someone had filled her throat with soil. But she didn't want Nathalie to see how scared she was.

'I don't think they're joking,' Mina said, quickly standing up. 'Come on. We've got to go and see Niklas.'

Nathalie sat there, stupefied. Her gaze was unfocused.

'That explains why he's been so weird,' she said, before standing up with a dogged expression.

Mine heaved a sigh of relief. She didn't have time to deal with someone in a state of shock – not right now. It was enough dealing with her own emotions.

As they headed out of the apartment, she barely noticed the customary sprinkling of gravel left by Nathalie's shoes in the hallway. All of a sudden, it no longer mattered.

71

Rebecka opened her suitcase on the living-room floor to check she had everything she needed. Vincent was standing in the doorway to the kitchen, watching her. He didn't like going into the living room. On the occasions when he had to, he avoided the wall by the aquarium. He knew full well how irrational his behaviour was, but the headaches sent their own clear message. Whether or not it was psychosomatic, it always got worse in the living room. Until he knew why that was, it was best not to tempt fate.

'Don't you have a checklist?' he said. 'Surely you need to take more than that?'

'Thermals, ski clothes, mobile, passport,' Rebecka said, pointing. 'A few changes' worth. Toothbrush. We'll rent our equipment there. What else do you think I need?'

Vincent shrugged. He was still unaccustomed to the fact that his daughter was perfectly capable of getting by on her own. Just a year ago, it would have been unthinkable to let her go on a week's trip abroad, but his children were growing more independent with each passing day. Soon they would no longer need him at all. He would be the one who needed them.

As Rebecka closed her bag, Vincent gazed out at the snowy garden and the woods beyond. The house was truly surrounded by winter. Everything was white. There were four black birds sitting in a row in the snow outside the window. There was a gap and a small trench in the snow between the first bird and the other three, as if there had been a fifth bird there that had flown away. He was hopeless at bird species, but he thought they might be ravens.

It felt as if they were looking back at him. The birds were completely still – unnaturally so, in fact. As if they were stuffed.

Vincent pinched the bridge of his nose between his thumb and forefinger and screwed his eyes shut. Who would leave stuffed birds on his lawn? It was an absolutely preposterous idea. He needed to be careful not to lose his grip on reality. Not now, with only two days left until Christmas Eve and the Shadow's threat about what would happen then.

Two days to go until he had to be ready for anything and everything.

'We should go,' Rebecka said, going into the hall. 'I just need to pop to the loo.'

Benjamin emerged from his room, his gaze fixed on something in his hand. He almost tripped over the suitcase.

'Dad, you know that cut-up postcard you got?' he said. 'That's a pretty good speed bump on the floor, by the way.'

Vincent blinked. It took him a moment to grasp what his son was referring to.

'The postcards with the odd turns of phrase on them?' he said.

'Exactly!' Benjamin said, waving them about. 'I've worked out where they're from. The sayings, I mean. They're from the Bible.'

'They don't seem very biblical,' Rebecka said, returning. 'Well, I suppose given their outlook on women they're about as antiquated as the Book of Genesis. You ready to go, Dad?'

'Anyway, they're from something called the Book of Proverbs,' Benjamin said. 'I jotted down the verse numbers here.'

He handed the postcards to Vincent. Benjamin had made neat annotations in black ink on the edge.

Vincent read the cards. On the first one, against '*A nagging wife is like the continual dripping of rain*,' Benjamin had written *Book of Proverbs 27:15*. On the second one, which said '*Do not make a sacred vow in haste or you may regret it*,' Benjamin had written *Book of Proverbs 20:25*.

'I found these versions in the Modern Swedish Bible,' Benjamin said. 'It's a new translation of the Bible that's supposed to be more reader-friendly while still being based on the original Hebrew, which is pretty unusual. And the Aramaic and Greek.'

Rebecka sighed.

'Stop distracting Dad,' she said. 'You know what he's like about this kind of stuff. If I don't catch my train, I'll hold you responsible. Crucifixion will be getting off lightly by comparison.'

Vincent was struggling to focus on what his children were saying. He had automatically added up the four figures in the verse references: 27:15 and 20:25. Twenty-seven plus fifteen plus twenty plus twenty-five made eighty-seven.

The eighth of the seventh.

Mum's birthday.

If he had been in any doubt about who the postcards were from, that was over. They had been sent by his Shadow. He'd sensed it all along. But this time they hadn't been sent to his home – instead, they'd been left at ShowLife's offices. The message was clear. The Shadow not only knew his routines, but he could also enter places where Vincent went, quite unnoticed.

And why he? It might just as well be a she.

'Dad? We've got to go!' Rebecka called from the hall.

She was wearing her coat but Vincent hadn't noticed her putting it on. He stood there as if petrified, his mouth dry, and swallowed hard. Did the postcards mean that the Shadow could enter his home too?

He couldn't handle this alone any more. He needed to talk to Mina and ask her for help.

But he'd also been warned against doing that.

It'll still happen even if you go to the police – just a lot faster.

At least Maria and Aston had already gone. Rebecka was about to leave. They would be safe. He had another day to get Benjamin out of the house somehow. By Christmas Eve he needed to be alone in the house and ready to face his tormentor. He cast one final glance through the window before going back into the hall. The four ravens were still sitting there staring at him.

72

'Don't worry,' her mother said.

'Why shouldn't I worry when you look like you're having a fully-fledged panic attack?'

Nathalie glared at her mother. Grown-ups and their lies drove her nuts. They didn't get that she wasn't a child any longer. That they shouldn't talk to her as if she was. It was bad enough when Dad did it. Mina didn't have to as well.

'I just have to find a parking spot.'

Mina looked around for somewhere to leave the car. The ministerial building loomed above them in all its magnificence.

'Parking spot? What does one parking ticket more or less matter right now? My God, I'll pick up the tab from my savings if a warden finds us.'

'That's quite enough of that attitude!'

Mina found a spot and parallel parked with practised elegance.

'Sorry,' Nathalie said reluctantly.

She didn't want to fall out with her mother. Fighting with Mina was still new and unpleasant. It was different with Dad. They'd been fighting for years – they knew where the line was drawn, they knew what the no-go zones were, and they knew what was allowed. It was all uncharted territory with Mina.

'Come on.'

Mina opened the door impatiently and almost slipped on a patch of black ice as she got out of the car.

'Maybe you need crampons,' Nathalie giggled, glad to have found an opportunity to lighten the mood.

'Ha ha, very funny. You'll be laughing on the other side of your face when I break my hip and you have to see to all my basic hygiene needs.'

'I'd just rub hand sanitizer all over your body.'

'Oh shut up.'

Mina smiled at her, and Nathalie felt warmth spreading through her chest. It alleviated a little of the anxiety that was gnawing away at her. She wasn't alone. She had her mother – who was a police detective. They were going to help each other find out what had happened to Dad. Together they would save him. Natti and Mina, the dynamic duo.

They entered through the heavy wooden doors, passed through security, and then Nathalie led the way to Niklas's office through a jumble of corridors.

Tor raised his eyebrows in surprise when he saw them approaching.

'Hello, hello! We've got the whole family! Where's Niklas? I've been having to cover for him all day.'

'Isn't he here?' said Nathalie.

Her heart sank. They had assumed he was at work – where he usually was. Sure, they had phoned and got no answer from Niklas or Tor, but that was not unusual. The day of a minister of justice was filled with important meetings and they couldn't always take personal calls from family members. Nathalie knew that. She had assumed he was at work and busy. Very busy.

'I thought he was with you,' Tor said with a note of concern, half standing up from his chair. 'He's not in the apartment. Has something happened? I can see it in your faces. What's happened?'

Nathalie slumped down onto one of the chairs in front of Tor's desk, Mina on the other. Nathalie looked at her mother and nodded. Mina pulled out the business card and handed it over to Tor, her hands trembling.

'Call the number on the card.'

'Call the number … What is this? Some kind of game? We don't have time for this – we've got to locate the minister. He's missed three meetings this morning and I've been calling him every two minutes. We've checked at home, but in the end I assumed he'd bunked off and was with you two. He hasn't been himself for a while, and I thought it might be to do with this … situation.'

He gestured towards Mina and Nathalie.

'I called!' Nathalie said. 'Loads of time! I called you! But you didn't pick up!'

'No, I've been calling you but *you* didn't pick up!' Tor said indignantly.

Nathalie opened her mouth to protest, then she realized.

'My phone's dead. I've been calling from Mum's phone,' she said apologetically.

Tor nodded.

'There have been several calls from an unknown number. I never answer if the number is unknown.'

'We haven't got time for this,' Mina said, fixing her gaze on Tor. 'Call the damn number on the card.'

Tor took a deep breath as if he needed to process the impertinence directed towards him before picking up his phone, putting on his reading glasses and then dialling the number on the card. As he listened, his face turned white.

'What is this?'

He put down his phone and took off his glasses again.

'It's a business card someone gave to Niklas,' Mina said.

'When the doorbell rang!' Nathalie said suddenly. She hadn't thought of it before. 'I mean during dinner. It must have been then! It was after that he got all weird.'

Her mother nodded at her and she felt a flash of pride. She had solved a mystery – like a real detective.

'My God,' said Tor. 'But what … what does this mean? Is it for real?'

He picked up the card, examined it and then put it down again.

'I don't know, but we think something's happened to Dad. He's not answering his phone and we've got no idea where he is. And you heard that awful message for yourself. Something's happened!'

Nathalie could hear how desperate she sounded, but she couldn't stop the fear from welling up.

'Nathalie's right,' Mina said, looking gravely at Tor. 'I also think something has happened.'

Tor sat in silence for a few moments as if he were considering various options. Then he picked up the phone without taking his eyes off Mina.

'I'm calling the director of the Security Service. I'm sure there's nothing to worry about.'

But there was nothing about his tone that reflected his soothing words.

73

'That sounded urgent?'

Vincent was trying to master the feeling of anxiety in the pit of his stomach. Somewhere at the back of his mind, there had probably always been a concern that Mina would get dragged into whatever was going on in his life. She was sitting in a dark corner at the very back of the almost empty restaurant in the old town.

Mina barely looked up at him when he sat down opposite her, and he felt his heart pounding in his chest. Had his Shadow finally made contact with her? It was a thought that made him want to leap to his feet and fight. It was unclear with whom.

Without saying anything, she pushed a business card towards him. He noticed that she didn't react to the fact that the table hadn't been wiped down, which showed how important the card must be.

'What's this?' he said, picking it up.

He held it between his fingers. It was made from thick, premium quality card. It was expensive.

'Call the number on it,' she said.

A gum-chewing waitress sauntered over to their table.

'Are you going to order anything?' she said, pointing towards the menu, which was on a wooden stand on the table.

'Black coffee,' Vincent said, glancing towards Mina.

She shook her head.

The waitress slunk off towards the kitchen.

Vincent pulled out his phone and dialled the number on the card. Mina suddenly turned and called out to the waitress, who reluctantly returned to the table.

'I've changed my mind,' Mina said. 'A glass of Chablis. A big one.'

Wine in the middle of the afternoon. This was a new side to Mina. Something was clearly not right.

A female voice answered and Vincent listened to the recorded message.

'Hello Niklas Stockenberg. We hope you have been satisfied with our services during this period which has now reached its end. You have … nine days … three hours … and … thirteen minutes … left to live.'

He slowly put his phone down on the table and handed the card back to Mina. She watched him intently.

The waitress returned with a mug of coffee in one hand and an enormous wine glass in the other.

'Where's it from?' Vincent said as he took his coffee, trying not to burn himself.

The coffee showed all the hallmarks of having been on the hotplate for far too long. It had a slightly oily surface and a smell reminiscent of burnt tar.

'Niklas received it by courier a few evenings ago,' said Mina. 'When Nathalie and I were having dinner with him.'

'And you don't have any idea who sent it? What did Niklas say?'

Mina picked up her glass and took a large slug of wine from it. Now he could tell she was really upset, given that the glass she was drinking from looked like it had barely been through the dishwasher; it was covered in fingerprints.

'Niklas made out like it was nothing important,' she said. 'But evidently he didn't tell anyone about it. Not the police or his own security people. And now he's missing. Vincent, what the hell is this?'

'I've no idea,' he said carefully. 'It could be a thousand things. A threat from some crank because of Niklas's job. A prank by a YouTuber. A "symbolic ritual" performed by some pretentious club that he's a member of. I could carry on – there are far too many possible explanations.'

'You're a lot of help,' she said. 'A prank by a YouTuber?! Is that what it sounded like to you? And why does the card have the same symbol that we saw in the gravel around the heaps of bones in the metro tunnels?'

'I don't know,' he said, trying to ignore the fact that she was unhappy with him. 'But it's not one hundred per cent certain that it's the same symbol. It might just be our brains looking for a correlation and interpreting it that way. I mean, all we saw were some circles on the ground.'

'Our brains … Do you think it's more plausible that there's *no* correlation? Do you really believe that?'

He gingerly tasted the coffee to avoid answering her. It tasted as vile as it looked.

'No,' he said. 'And I can't say how, but I think it's connected. That message also brings to mind a loose association with Faust.'

'Faust? How?' Mina said, taking another swig of her wine.

Vincent considered whether to point out the state of the wine glass, but decided it would be wisest not to.

'In a way, that story is also about someone making use of "services" and whose time then runs out. But as I said, it's just a loose association. I blame my malfunctioning synapses.'

'I'm only dimly aware of Faust. Isn't it something to do with the devil?'

'Well yes, the devil plays a big role. But Faust is really about time and what we do with our lives. Or at least that's my interpretation. It was originally a German folk tale about a young man named Faust who sells his soul to Mephistopheles – a demon. The adjective Faustian comes from the story about Faust, and is used to refer to someone ambitious who sacrifices their moral integrity in return for power and success in the short term.'

'Why does he sell his soul?' Mina said. 'What does he get in return?'

Vincent thought the worry line between her eyebrows was captivating.

'Well, the demon pitches up at a pivotal moment in Faust's life and promises to let him experience all that is good and wonderful in life in exchange for Faust's soul upon death.'

'So what does he do?'

'The demon?'

'No, Faust. What does he do with this opportunity offered to him by the demon?'

'Not much, I'm afraid,' Vincent said, considering whether to try the coffee again before pushing the mug away. 'Faust is in pursuit of power, love and the meaning of life. He is always looking for more – for something else – and he's consumed by his own anxiety. Along the way, he tramples over others, but strangely enough Goethe – who wrote the best-known work about Faust – never lets him really suffer the consequences for his actions. According to Goethe, Mephistopheles was a symbol of the French Revolution, but most literary scholars prefer to see Mephistopheles as Faust's alter ego – the bad side of himself that he doesn't want to accept.'

'Like in *Fight Club*?' Mina said, perking up.

'*Fight Club*? That's an interesting comparison. Do you know that the film is often considered one of the best examples of poor mental health being depicted in popular culture, given that the protagonist has dissociative identity disorder?'

'Dis-what?'

'You know – what used to be known as multiple personality disorder. When parts of your personality are split from one another. It's rare, but it does happen. People who suffer from it often struggle to understand who they are and feel they have no control over their own actions. What the film misses, however, is the fact that dissociative identity disorder is always rooted in profound childhood trauma. Kim Noble is a famous real-life case. She had a hundred different personalities as a result of the abuse she suffered as a child. Most of those personalities had no memory of the terrible things that had happened, which meant they gave her mental protection.'

Mina had drunk most of her wine while he had been talking.

'You seem to be very well informed about this,' she said.

Vincent shrugged.

'I just think it's interesting,' he said. 'The brain is both our greatest friend and our greatest enemy. The things it can do to protect us are … quite remarkable. As I said, Mephistopheles is perhaps just one side of Faust. To borrow from the psychologist Norman F. Dixon, sometimes we're our own worst enemies.'

Mina fidgeted with her wine glass.

'Was there any other reason you thought of Faust when you heard that message?'

'No, it was only the time-related aspect,' he said. 'A "service" that has been rendered and time that is running out.'

'So when time runs out, the devil gets Niklas's soul?' Mina said, and Vincent could clearly read the question behind her words.

The worry was writ across her face and Vincent knew better than to try to reassure her. For Mina, only the truth would do.

'Faust is just a story,' he said. 'And you've got several days to find him.'

That was also true.

'Speaking of time, I've got to get back to Nathalie,' Mina said, glancing at her phone. 'She went on ahead. I don't want her to be at home on her own for too long. If you think of anything that might help, please call me right away.'

She picked up the glass for another sip of wine, but stopped with it halfway to her lips.

'Oh my God, would you look at this! It's disgusting!'

She dropped the glass as if it were red hot. It landed on its side on the table and the wine that was still in it flowed towards Vincent. Mina didn't seem to care. She fixed her gaze on Vincent.

'Did you see that? Why didn't you say anything?' she said.

He squirmed uncomfortably. No matter what he did, he was wrong.

'I'll pick up the tab,' he said. 'It's not big after all. Get yourself home.'

Not taking her eyes off him, Mina wiped her mouth with a wet wipe she had taken from her jacket pocket.

Then she was gone. Vincent pulled out his phone and rang the number again to listen to the smooth female voice.

Behind the voice, he heard the laughter of Mephistopheles from the abyss.

74

EIGHT DAYS TO GO

For the first time, they were going to the National Board of Forensic Medicine but not to see Milda and Loke. Mina hesitated before grasping the door handle – long enough that Vincent beat her to it.

A slender blonde woman of indeterminate age was coming towards them. She had cheerful, lively eyes and radiated vibrancy in a way that was in marked contrast to the building they were visiting and what its walls housed.

'Gunilla Strömquist, forensic anthropologist,' she said by way of introduction. To Mina's great relief, she didn't offer to shake hands.

It was a custom she had difficulty understanding. It was completely unnecessary bodily contact, with all that it entailed in terms of the transfer of bacteria and uncomfortable proximity to a stranger. The Japanese had the right idea with their bowing at a respectful distance. Hygienic and much more dignified.

'Please come in. Do excuse the mess. I'm due to retire, so I'm busy packing up.'

Mina raised an eyebrow in surprise. She had guessed the woman might be fifty or so, rather than well over sixty.

'I'll just move some of this so you've got somewhere to sit.'

Gunilla picked up a random assortment of objects from two chairs positioned in front of a huge desk that was so cluttered the tabletop was no longer visible. The skull of an unknown animal species, a ceramic representation of a heart, a book about flies, and a T-shirt emblazoned with the slogan *Death rocks* were among the items removed.

'Goodness me, you really do accumulate all sorts over the years,' Gunilla said cheerfully, dropping the items without further consideration into open removal boxes on the floor. 'In my line of work, we often get presents with a dash of gallows humour to them. Well, you're police officers. You'll know what I mean. We tend to develop a certain sense of humour in our professions.'

'Did you know that the word humour originates from the Latin *humores*, which means liquids?' Vincent said. 'That in turn comes from the assumption in medical practices of old that there was a correlation between bodily fluids and a person's temperament. Having a sense of humour usually entails having not just a sense of what is funny, but also the ability to identify and accept with some degree of pleasure the imperfections of our existence. Which, it must be said, is very much what you're dealing with here. The imperfections of existence, I mean. Another conception of humour is that it is an emotional and cognitive process with a physiological basis. It's an experience that consists of the discovery and appreciation of absurd and funny ideas, events and situations. And let's not forget … The American DMS-5 diagnostic system describes humour as a defence mechanism that helps us to get to grips with emotional conflicts or stress factors by focusing on aspects of the cause of that stress that may be amusing or ironic. An excellent example is your T-shirt. *Death rocks*. Of course, we all know that death doesn't rock, which makes that kind of slogan—'

'Vincent, we get it.'

Mina held up a hand to stop him.

'Interesting. Most interesting,' Gunilla said, now that she had managed to remove enough items to allow them all to sit down.

She perched on a chair on the opposite side of the desk, but practically disappeared behind a couple of stacks of books that were so high they could only see the top of her blonde head.

'Oops, that didn't quite work out.'

She got to her feet, picked up the books and dumped them into another box before resuming her place.

'Right. Where were we? Oh, that's right, you're here about the bones Milda sent me. Looking at them is going to be more or less my final task here, and I must say it's a very exciting case. Skeletons in the tunnels. I've seen a lot, but this is a new one on me.'

'We've identified all the other bones we found, except the ones we sent to you,' said Mina. 'It would be extremely useful if you were able to help to determine their age.'

'Yes, I can definitely do that.'

Mina leaned back on her chair and felt something sharp jab her bottom. She felt it with her hand and found something hard and narrow. She pulled out the object and it took her a few seconds to realize what it was.

'There it is! Oscar's finger!'

Gunilla reached out to take the bone from Mina. Mina exchanged glances with Vincent, who was observing in amusement.

'Oscar?' Mina said, not sure she wanted to hear the answer.

'Our departmental skeleton. A charming addition to the staff, actually. Something of a mascot.' She put the bone to one side on a shelf. 'I'm not taking Oscar with me. The others would miss him.'

'Is he … real?' Mina asked, still unsure whether she wanted to know.

'Of course not. Or is he?'

Gunilla winked and then turned serious again.

'So – the bones. From the tunnel. Following a visual inspection of the abrasions to the pelvic bones, I surmised the man was between forty and fifty when he died. Then I used the carbon-14 method to determine a date of birth. As you may know, it's very accurate when it comes to determining age, especially with the bomb curve to help us.'

'The bomb curve?'

Mina had no idea what she was talking about.

Vincent cleared his throat.

'It's actually pretty interesting,' he said. 'Until 1955, the levels of carbon-14 in the world were stable. But after that, the atomic powers carried out more than two thousand nuclear weapons tests above ground. You know – all those photos and newsreels you've seen of big mushroom clouds and people cheerfully watching them through sunglasses while they're having a picnic.

A side effect of those detonations was that they substantially increased the carbon-14 levels in the atmosphere. We can now determine age using the carbon-14 method. Right?'

'Bravo!' said Gunilla, looking appreciatively at Vincent. 'Quite right. And it was only when they limited testing above ground in 1963 that carbon-14 levels began to decline again. Carbon-14 is a radioactive carbon isotope formed from cosmic radiation in the biosphere which is then absorbed by plants through photosynthesis. Humans eat the plants and the isotope ends up in our bodies. The carbon atoms, including the carbon-14, bind together when a cell divides, creating a sort of traceable "birth day" for our cells.'

Gunilla's explanation was directed wholly at Mina, who was trying to keep up. The forensic anthropologist probably reckoned that Vincent knew all this already.

'The variations in carbon-14 levels, in part thanks to the bomb curve, are what we use to determine when biological materials were created. There's a two-year margin of error.'

'Although isn't the bomb curve rather controversial, since it doesn't correlate with the Bern model?' Vincent said.

Gunilla dismissed him with a wave of her hand.

'It's good enough for our purposes,' she said.

'Do you test the bone itself?' Mina said.

Gunilla shook her head.

'No, in this case we've used the teeth. The carbon-14 content of the enamel, to be precise.'

'How does that relate to this … bomb curve?'

They both turned to face Mina. She would have preferred to cut to the chase, but she had crossed paths with enough boffins like Gunilla to know that it would never be a smooth experience. The whole process had to be dissected first.

'The bomb curve reached its peak in 1963. At that time, the volume of carbon-14 isotopes in the atmosphere was almost double the natural quantity that had always been found there. Since 1963, it's been decreasing year on year. That means we know the level for each year, and that level leaves a trace behind in parts of us such as our teeth. Higher values are found in teeth from 1955 onwards. But people born as much as thirteen years earlier – in 1942 – can also have increased carbon-14 levels in their wisdom teeth.'

'They're the ones that form last,' Mina said thoughtfully as the penny began to drop.

'Exactly.'

'So what year have you worked it out to be?'

'As I said, there's a margin of error either way. I would suggest the year of birth is around 1960. But remember, that could mean anything from 1958 to 1962. But you wanted to know when he died too, so I took a look at the ribs.'

'The ribs?' Mina said.

'Yes, you probably already know that the cells in your body are replaced at regular intervals. That's also true of your skeleton. It's constantly being reformed. Since the ribs are porous and soft in order to help us keep breathing, they have to reform more frequently. About once every ten years. Give or take. I could see the last time these ribs were reformed, our carbon was at 1998 levels, which would have made him about forty years old. That would mean the date of death was between 1998 and 2008.'

'How did you arrive at that?'

'As I said, the ribs are reformed every ten years. So I would have seen signs of them being reformed in 2008 if he'd been alive then. But I didn't. Of course, this is by no means an exact science, so take all dates with a pinch of salt. I do understand that you'd prefer to have a more precise date of death than a ten-year timespan. Luckily for us, there was a slight coating of moss on some of the bones, and I'd venture a guess that the moss was at least twenty years old.'

'So the bones have been in the tunnels for at least that long,' Vincent said. 'Which means he died closer to 1998 than 2008.'

'Exactly,' said Gunilla.

'Thank you so much,' said Mina. 'This is incredibly helpful.'

'Magnificent,' Vincent said with obvious admiration. Gunilla beamed.

The crow's feet around her eyes deepened and she laughed.

'Goodness me, I really will miss all of this. But I've got seven grandchildren to see to, so I don't think I'll be sitting on a bench feeding the pigeons.'

75

Tor took the phone away from his ear and silently counted to five in order to maintain his composure before he continued talking to the journalist.

'No, the minister still isn't back from his seminar,' he said. 'Yes, I know you had an interview scheduled for yesterday, but I'm afraid he was unavailable. And I regret to say that is the case today as well … Of course … Thank you. I know it's the day before Christmas Eve. But believe it or not, the efforts to build a nation of law and order don't stop, not even for Christmas … Yes … Thank you.'

He hung up and carefully put his phone down on the desk, adjusting it with his index fingers so that it was completely straight and in parallel with the edge of the table. Then he leaned back in the ergonomic office chair and screamed.

Egon, one of his security officers, hurtled into the room.

'Nothing to see here,' Tor said. 'I'm just a little … frustrated.'

Egon, who was shaven-headed and had an angular jawline, nodded curtly and vigorously. Sometimes Tor suspected that basic training at the Security Service included watching action movies to learn how their profession was perceived by popular culture and then ensure that they performed according to these roles, clichés and all.

'You had one job,' Tor sighed. 'One. You just had to make sure Niklas Stockenberg was always safe. Explain to me how on earth he can still be missing without trace after twenty-four hours.'

'I don't know,' Egon said. 'But if he's left the city we'll soon find out where he's gone. We're gathering all the video footage from speed cameras within a one-hundred-kilometre radius. You know – all the footage that's not supposed to exist. We've also got data on which registrations have left the city congestion charging zone, and we're reviewing that with the assistance of the police analysis team right now.'

Tor adjusted the phone's position again. He wasn't satisfied with how he had placed it. He carefully rotated it ninety degrees, taking care to touch it only with his fingertips.

'And if he's still in the city?' he said, furrowing his brow.

'Whoever has him, we'll find them,' Egon said, nodding with the same vigour as before. 'I promise.'

'Well do it quickly then,' said Tor, whose phone had begun to ring again. 'The hacks have already scented something is up. This is the fifteenth today.'

He counted to five again. Then he answered.

76

Vincent couldn't help but smile as Mina changed out of her usual winter boots into a pair of far sturdier ones. The new pair looked like they might see her through a week's hike in the middle of a nuclear winter.

'Why do you have a second pair of boots at work?' he said, perching on the edge of her desk. 'Is it in case you have to go mountaineering in the canteen?'

Mina had driven them to police headquarters after the meeting with the forensic anthropologist, and now he understood why. She was – for whatever reason – going to transform herself into a miner.

'Ha ha ha,' she said through gritted teeth as she struggled to lace up her boots. 'For your information, while you were off playing with the beetle expert, Julia ordered the rest of us to go back down into the tunnels. That includes me, as soon as we'd finished with Gunilla. The others are already waiting for me.'

The tunnels. The mere thought of it made him shudder.

'Weren't you just down there?' he said. 'Does she think there are more bones to be found?'

'Not bones. But that guy Crazy-Tom's mates might be down there. According to what Ruben and Christer were told by a member of staff at Helix, Crazy-Tom said he'd found the bones near to the metro station at Bagarmossen. But we have no idea whether that's true. Crazy-Tom is dead, but some of his friends are probably still alive and might be down there, or so Julia thinks. Someone might have seen something or know how Crazy-Tom got hold of Marcus Eriksson's remains. It's taken a while for Julia to make the arrangements for us to go down there – apparently there's a lot of red tape for arranging excursions into the tunnels. It makes the metro operator twitchy each time.'

'And you still haven't found any connection between the other victims and Gustaf Brons?'

'That's a complete minefield,' Mina said with a sigh. 'I tried to look into Brons's gambling debts as best I could without interfering in the charges I suspect they're currently building against Dragan Manojlovic. But I didn't find anything, and there's nothing to suggest that Brons and Josephine were in collusion either. On the contrary, they seem to have been preoccupied with seeing each other in Stockholm hotels in the run-up to Jon's disappearance. Frankly, I've no idea how they had the time to look after their kids, run a company or gamble away their fortunes, and especially not to murder someone, given the frequency of their hotel stays. But I'm still not ruling anything out. Ruben's going to have a chat with Peter Kronlund this afternoon and see what he has to say about his old man.'

'I see,' said Vincent. 'I'm afraid I haven't got anything much to add either.'

He realized he was sitting on a pair of thick gloves that were on the desk. He got up and handed them to her. Mina almost yanked them away from him.

'And not another word about the way I'm dressed,' she said. 'Pass me the disposable gloves in the drawer, please.'

He saw the box of disposable gloves by his side and handed them over. The truth was that while Mina was so thoroughly covered that the next step would be a full hazmat suit, she was still beautiful. Not only that, she was sexy. There was nothing layers of clothing or red, chapped hands could do to diminish that fact. Was he even allowed to think about her in those terms? Yes. He decided he was. Just as long as he kept those thoughts to himself.

'There are some more appropriate clothes for you too,' she said, pulling a thick jacket off a hook on the back of the door and handing it to him. 'So that you can come with me.'

'Into the tunnels?' he said, startled. 'Hmm, tunnels aren't exactly my thing. The last time we were in a tight tunnel I had to start counting prime numbers, if you recall. I think it's probably best if I stay here at the office and review all the documentation one more time. I'll make sure we haven't missed anything.'

'Wimp,' Mina said, hanging the jacket back up.

He could see she was smiling.

'Why don't you take a few rides in the lift while I'm gone – it'll be good therapy for you,' she said. 'Next time, if there is one, you won't have any choice. It'll be you and me down there in the dark. Deal?'

He stared at her.

'Deal,' he said hesitantly.

He made a mental note to obtain a guarantee from Julia that no one would have to go back down into the tunnels. He would never be able to do it.

'See you later,' said Mina. 'Have fun in the lift.'

Once she had gone, he stayed sitting on her desk. He was thinking about what she had said. *You and me down there in the dark.* If only she knew how right she was.

77

The metro operator had helped them to plan their search of the tunnels. It was a massive effort. When they had been down there searching for heaps of bones, Mina had thought it was not feasible to search the whole tunnel network, but somehow Julia had pulled it off. She was serious and determined, curtly assigning zones to the teams that the officers on the scene had been divided into.

'I'm seeing a lot of bozos here,' Ruben muttered with suspicion as he surveyed his colleagues.

'We should be grateful that we've been assigned this amount of manpower, given how close to Christmas we are,' Mina said smoothly. 'And that the metro operator agreed to let us do this again without a lot more fuss.'

She was actually inclined to agree with Ruben – she too could see a number of officers whose aptitude left a lot to be desired.

'Three of us will be searching our zone. Adam's with us,' she said.

'Merry fucking Christmas,' Ruben chuckled grimly. 'Thank God I've got a sense of humour.'

'You mean *humores*,' Mina said.

'Huh? Are you drunk?'

'Regrettably not. That might have improved the experience,' she said, pulling her disposable gloves a little further up her sleeves. 'But I'm glad you see the funny side of it all.'

She still wished Vincent had come along, but she understood.

'Time to get going,' Adam said as he passed them, heading for the tunnel they were going to enter. 'I've got the map. I know which zone we're covering.'

Mina and Ruben followed.

Even at the tunnel portal, she could feel her chest tightening. She found herself struggling to breathe.

'Just stick with me,' Adam said, keeping up a brisk pace.

There was rustling all around them – sounds that Mina didn't want to focus on. Instead, she concentrated on her breathing as they walked further and further into the darkness.

Ten minutes later they had reached their first assigned area, deep inside the metro system.

'This is stupid,' Ruben muttered. 'Firstly, most of the people who live down here are completely away with the fairies. Mentally ill or coked out of their minds. Secondly, they're not exactly fond of the police. So I don't know why they'd agree to talk to us, even if they do have some brain cells left.'

The darkness was eerily flighty. There were lights, but only a few were working, and several of those that were illuminated were flashing at irregular intervals.

'As ever, you're bang on, Ruben. I say we chuck this in and go for a pint instead,' Mina said sarcastically.

'There's no need to be sarky just because I offer logical input,' Ruben said morosely, as he continued to train his torch on different parts of the tunnel.

In front of them, something dark darted ahead of the beam of light, and they came to a halt.

'Hello?' Adam called out, his voice echoing between the walls. 'We'd like to talk to you.'

Ruben shouted just as loudly and was met with the same echo bouncing his words back to him.

'We're from the police,' Mina said loudly. 'And we have no quarrel with you. We're not here to arrest anyone or to take any interest in what you are or aren't doing down here. We just want to chat. About the bones we've found in the tunnels. And about Crazy-Tom.'

Silence. Nothing but silence. Mina hesitated. Was there even anyone there to hear what they were saying?

'Welcome to paradise!'

Mina jumped so high that it felt as if she might leap out of her clothes. An enormous giant of a man was suddenly standing in front of them, his arms outstretched. Mina saw Ruben slowly reaching for his service weapon. She placed a hand on his shoulder.

'Johnny! Come here! Don't scare them!'

A woman stepped into the light cast by their torches and held up her hands in a placatory gesture.

'He's not dangerous. He's just big. But not dangerous. That's my boy. He wouldn't hurt a fly.'

When Mina looked more closely, she saw that the man couldn't be more than about twenty-five years old, but his beard and bulk made him look twice that age.

'We'd like to talk to you, if we may,' Mina said softly, directing her words to the woman. 'About skeletal remains. Then we'll get out of your hair and leave you in peace. That's a promise.'

Silence. She felt the doubt radiating towards her. She wanted to say more, to persuade the woman, but she knew the best thing to do was to let the silence do the talking.

'Very well then. Follow me,' the woman said, before stepping out of the light.

Mina shone her torch in the direction she had gone and saw her back moving quickly down a tunnel to their left. The big man waved eagerly at them, indicating they should follow. Their route took them down several branches where the tunnels forked. Mina hoped fervently that they would be able to find their way back.

After a while, they saw a gentle glow. The tunnel opened up ahead of them into a larger space. As they drew closer, they could make out a small group of people gathered around a fire. They were sitting on the ground and didn't seem to be bothered by the smoke that hung heavily above them.

Ruben began coughing and she saw Adam holding his sleeve over his nose and mouth. That seemed a sensible thing to do, so she did likewise and immediately noticed it made breathing easier.

'You get used to it,' the woman said, beckoning them closer.

Big Johnny imitated her gesture, a happy grin extending from ear to ear.

'He's not quite right,' the woman said, caressing her son's cheek tenderly. 'Well, this is us. Ask away.'

She waved her arm at the motley assortment of people. There were five of them, including the woman and Johnny, all with expressions of suspicion. Mina hesitated for a moment. Then she stepped forward.

'My name is Mina. I'm going to come around you all and introduce myself, if that's all right?' No reply.

She took a deep breath and felt the smoke stinging her lungs. Then she took a couple of determined steps forward and proffered her hand to the man at the far left of the group.

'Mina.'

'Kjelle.'

She moved on to the next one – a woman.

'Mina.'

'Natasa.'

'Mina.'

The next man refused to take her hand and glared angrily at her.

'I'm not going to tell you my name. I'm wanted by the government for the murder of Olof Palme. I have to hide down here because they want to put me away for it. I have the same initials as Palme – that's all it took for them to decide it was me.'

'OP is quite … suspicious of people,' the woman who had led them there said, sounding apologetic. 'I'm Vivian.'

'No worries. You only have to introduce yourself if you want to,' Mina said.

By the time Mina had introduced herself to everyone except OP, part of her wanted to burst into tears and rush out of there, back home to her shower, home to her scalding water and more soap than could be bought in the whole country. She really *hated* shaking hands, but it had seemed like an important acknowledgement: they were human beings. They lived there. They had ended up there, for whatever reason. Perhaps they'd once had families, someone who loved them, another life.

In a way, their mere existence down here was the ultimate proof of humankind's deep-seated drive to survive at all costs, she thought, even when there didn't seem to be much left to live for.

'Do you mind if we sit down?' Mina said, which was met with looks of surprise and mild horror from Ruben and Adam.

Her entire being was protesting against sitting among the

rubble and dirt, but the police could hardly loom over the others if they wanted to talk to them sensibly.

'Please do,' the woman called Vivian said. 'Here.'

She generously nudged pieces of cardboard towards them. The three detectives accepted these as if they were precious gifts and carefully placed them underneath themselves.

'As I told you, we're here about the bones,' Mina said.

She pulled out her phone and started an audio recording before laying it down discreetly on the cardboard by her side. Adam and Ruben remained completely silent and passive. They had wisely read the situation and noted that Mina had managed to establish a rapport. The fact that she was a woman might also make her seem less threatening in this environment.

'We knew Crazy-Tom was innocent,' OP said, glaring at Mina. 'But once the state has made up its mind, it's impossible to get them to unmake it. It was the same with Palme.'

'How could you be so sure he was innocent?' Mina asked curiously.

She saw them exchanging glances.

'Don't look at me,' Natasa said in heavily accented Swedish. 'It was before my time. I never knew Crazy-Tom.'

'I knew him,' said Vivian.

She patted Johnny gently – he had begun to rock back and forth anxiously on the spot.

'Hungry,' he said dully. 'Johnny hungry.'

Vivian rummaged in her pockets and handed him half a cereal bar. He devoured it in one bite and it seemed to sate him, at least temporarily.

'Crazy-Tom was crazy, for sure,' she said. 'Hence the name. But he would never have hurt anyone. He was the kindest guy to ever walk this earth. But he should have known better than to take the bones from their resting place.'

'Resting place?' Mina said, pricking up her ears.

Something small scuttled across her hand, which was resting on the cardboard, and she quickly withdrew it. Oh God. She inhaled. In. Out. In. Out. The crackling sound of the fire helped her to maintain her composure.

'He had no business being in Bagarmossen,' Vivian said.

'It sounds like you're pretty familiar with the bones?'

Silence. More glances.

'We've seen it before. So when Crazy-Tom found them, we knew what it meant. It's a sign of respect to the person who's died. To death. It's an honour.'

'When would you say you saw it before?' Ruben said.

'A long time ago,' Vivian said, pursing her lips.

It was apparent that she didn't want to talk about it any more. OP was complaining loudly.

'The King knew they were trying to pin the Palme murder on me,' he said. 'He tried to take responsibility. He sacrificed himself. It was a stratagem. Worthy of a king. Still … They won't give in. He died in vain.'

Mina ignored him. His paranoia apparently extended beyond the government and the murder of Olof Palme to the royal family itself. At the risk of drawing ire from Vivian, she still had questions she wanted to ask.

'But you don't know who left the bones that Crazy-Tom found?' she said. 'How do you know it was a mark of respect?'

Vivian exchanged looks with OP and then she shrugged.

'Isn't it obvious from the way they were laid out? Like some kind of altar?'

'The king didn't want to die,' OP murmured. 'He didn't want to die, but the darkness took over. In the end, the darkness took over.'

'That doesn't mean much to me,' Mina said. 'But if you say so.' She picked up her phone and began to get to her feet, but she stopped mid-movement as if she had just thought of something.

'Actually, there was one more thing,' she said. 'We've found several heaps of bones in the last few days. In your tunnels.'

It was hard to make out the others' reactions in the flickering firelight, but she thought she saw Vivian, Natasa and OP exchange hasty glances. No one met her gaze. Johnny continued to stare straight at the ground. Whatever they knew – *if* they knew anything at all – wasn't something she'd find out now. She stood up and brushed down her trousers.

'Thank you for your time,' she said as kindly as she could. 'We might come back. I hope that's OK.'

'Bring buns if you do,' Johnny said with a giggle that made his bushy beard undulate.

'I'll show you the way out so that you don't get lost,' Vivian said, pointing to the tunnel they had come from.

Mina gave her a look of gratitude. She wanted nothing more than to escape from the darkness and dirt. She wanted to be at home in the shower.

78

Vincent had forgotten all about the reports he was reading. They were scattered across Mina's desk in front of him as he sat there in her office, but he'd been distracted by a text message. Benjamin's plan had been to stay the night with a friend who had just moved into their own place, which suited Vincent down to the ground. He was eager to be home alone – for everyone's safety.

But Benjamin had just texted that he'd prefer to wake up in his own home on Christmas Eve. Vincent knew he ought to be touched by the fact that his eldest son would prefer to spend the morning of Christmas Eve with his father instead of his friend, but this was not the Christmas Eve for that. Vincent had written back that he would be fine on his own; they could see each other later in the day, and Benjamin should prioritize hanging out with his friend.

His son still wanted to come home.

Vincent couldn't help feeling proud. It was presumably his own bed that was appealing to Benjamin, given that the alternative was sleeping on the floor at his friend's, but all the same … It would have been great any other time.

Vincent was clutching his phone, unsure what to say. After all, Benjamin was more or less grown-up. Surely Vincent would be able to protect *one* other member of the family … He would have to pick up some Saffron buns on his way home.

'My my, you're looking focused. Looking for porn, are we?'

Mina's voice made him jump. She was standing by the desk, leaning over to look at the display on his phone.

'Far from it,' he sighed. 'Family trouble.'

He detected the faint smell of cleaning fluids, which for some reason brought to mind white tiles and swimming baths. Then he saw that Mina's hair was damp and that she was wearing different clothes to when he'd seen her a few hours earlier.

'Have you been for a swim?'

Mina looked confused.

'Why would I have …?' she said, before sighing. 'Yes, Vincent. I've been for a swim. Spot on. In the middle of the working day. Have you found anything?'

Vincent cleared his throat and pushed aside the mental image of Mina in a swimming costume.

He furrowed his brow as if he were concentrating and began to rifle through the papers on the desk. He grabbed a sheet of paper.

'Well, I've been giving some more thought to the victims,' he said. 'Marcus Eriksson's mother said he had a tough spell years back. She said he was a seeker. It was after that when it all turned around for him. Erika Sävelden's sister said that Erika had what frankly sounds like depression some twenty years ago. After that, she went on to make a stellar career for herself. And Peter Kronlund told Adam and Julia that Jon Langseth had a "really tough time" a few years ago and that Jon was reluctant to talk about it. So all three of them were basically at rock bottom before life suddenly turned around. Of course, that could be down to good old-fashioned I'll-show-them impetus after some sort of revelatory insight. But anything that unites your victims is probably worth exploring further. If I were you, I would contact both Marcus's mother and Josephine Langseth and find out exactly when Marcus and Jon had their "tough times". It wouldn't surprise me if it was twenty years ago – right when Erika had hers.'

'You think they might have met back then? That their depression brought them all together somehow?'

'It's not impossible. And there's something else. Did Niklas ever have his own spell like that in the past?'

Mina's eyes widened.

'He never talks about the years before we met.'

'That's too bad. It would have been very good to know.'

79

The procedures for entering the remand prison were becoming routine. Ruben felt a degree of curiosity as he went into the visiting room to meet Peter Kronlund. Dragan Manojlovic was a legend in the criminal underworld, so inevitably Ruben wondered what his son was like – especially a son who had created a completely different life to his father's.

No one could deny that the murders were sophisticated, so it was hardly far-fetched to look more closely at a man with ties to a known criminal syndicate.

'Another visit,' the man in the visiting room said. 'I do seem to be popular with you lot.'

He stood up to greet Ruben.

'Peter Kronlund.'

The handshake was firm. Ruben could quite easily picture the man in front of him wearing a swish suit and pricey leather shoes, in a snazzy office. The grey prison tracksuit wasn't quite as flattering.

'I'll get straight to the point,' Ruben said. 'We've found a link between your father and Confido.'

There was dogged silence from Peter. Ruben kept waiting. Silence was the best weapon in a detective's arsenal. Finally, Peter clasped his hands on the table and leaned forward.

'So you know who I am,' he said, 'if you know who my dad is. Who my family are. I don't seem to be able to shake the fuckers off.'

'Yes, I know who you are, but I also know who you were,' Ruben said. 'To be honest, I'm surprised that more people don't know. You've done a good job hiding your background.'

'I had no other choice,' Peter said, sighing. 'It was the only way to have a real chance in life. But my old man, huh? I didn't think there was anything left that could surprise me. What kind of link are we talking about?'

'We've traced payments made by your father to Gustaf Brons. Big payments.'

Peter let out a low whistle.

'Well I'll be damned …'

He looked genuinely surprised, but Ruben asked anyway.

'You weren't aware of this?'

'No,' Peter said abruptly.

'Gustaf was borrowing money from your family to cover gambling debts. Did you know he was gambling?'

Peter looked up at the ceiling.

'What a fucking idiot,' he said. 'Yes, I knew he was gambling. That was his problem to solve. But borrowing money from my old man … He didn't mention that to me. And he should know better. Now I understand how you see it as a link to Confido. If my dad has a hold on Gustaf …'

'It gets better. Did you know that Gustaf and Josephine, Jon's wife, were having an affair?'

Peter chuckled loudly.

'Yes, I knew about *that*. I even walked in on them once when Gustaf had Josephine bent over his desk and was doing her from behind. Fuck me, the sight of his hairy pink arse isn't something I'll be forgetting any time soon.'

'As you can see, there are a lot of circumstances here, lots of reasons within your company to want to get Jon out of the way. Everything from infidelity to the fear that he would let the cat out of the bag about your business to save his own skin. Or – I'm just speculating here – perhaps there was a certain trepidation that he would reveal your true identity. So I'm going to put it to you straight. Were you or your father involved in the murder of Jon?'

Peter leaned forward.

'You're right that I've done everything to erase my last name,' he said in a low but clear voice. 'It was the only way out. Everything I have, I've earned by myself. The company, the Östermalm apartment, the Porsche Carrera, the second home in Sörmland. Everything that's mine has been earned by me. My old man had nothing to do with it. *Nothing*. And that's exactly how I want it.'

'Does your father accept that?'

Ruben mimicked Peter's body language, clasping his hands on the table in the same way. Vincent had once said that you could establish a rapport with people by imitating their body language and it seemed worth a try. Not everything that Vincent said was completely stupid.

'What the fuck do you think?' Peter said, seeming to relax a little. 'Of course he doesn't fucking accept it. I promise you that my old man will have forced Gustaf to spy on me for him.'

Peter laughed again and leaned back, his hands behind his head. Ruben wondered whether to mimic that movement too, but realized it might be a little too blatant.

'Could Jon have found out?' he said, sitting up a little straighter. 'That your father was using Gustaf? Could that be why he was killed?'

'Jesus Christ, what are you watching on TV? If anyone was going to kill anyone, it should have been Jon who murdered Gustaf for screwing his wife. But sure, *if* Dragan was using Gustaf to report insider information about Confido, and *if* Jon found out, then he could have been in trouble. At the same time, it would have brought down the whole company if one of the owners went missing, so it seems kind of unlikely my old man would have gone that far. Of course, the company ended up going down the pan anyway, but that was for other reasons.'

Ruben nodded. What Peter had said sounded reasonable. Then again …

'Do the names Mark Eric and Erika Sävelden mean anything to you?' he said.

If Dragan Manojlovic was involved in one of the murders then he had to be involved in all of them. Otherwise Ruben's hypothesis would crumble before it had even been fully formed.

'Of course,' said Peter. 'I think I've got all of Mark's albums. I assume you mean the singer? And we brought Erika in as a guest speaker at Confido on several occasions.'

'Do they have any connection to your father?'

'Not that I know of. As I said, I try to keep my family at a distance. But there aren't many corners of the events and entertainment industry where my dad doesn't have a finger in the pie, somehow or other. I challenge you to find a restaurant or stage in this town where he hasn't bullied his way in as a co-owner.'

'Funny – is that what protection's known as these days?' Ruben said acidly.

'Why are you asking about them?'

'I'm afraid I'm not at liberty to say.'

Ruben sighed in frustration. He wasn't getting anywhere with his questions. He had found out a lot and yet it was nothing at all. He didn't think Peter was involved, but Dragan Manojlovic was like a spectre lingering on the fringes of it all. Yet Ruben was unable to make any direct connection to the criminal mastermind. It was all just conjecture – as incomplete as it was insinuating.

He needed to find a way to prove Dragan's guilt – and fast.

80

'How often do you see your grandfather?' Mina asked Nathalie curiously as she pulled off towards Äppelviken.

Vincent's comment about Niklas's past had given her a brainwave. She couldn't ask her ex-husband, but she could ask his father, Walther Stockenberg. Niklas looked up to his father and harboured an incredible respect for him. They might not always have been close, but she thought Walther would know if Niklas had faced any problems in his youth.

It had been many, many years since she had last visited Walther. It had been in another era – in another life. She remembered the first summer when they had visited Niklas's parents. They'd had home-made strawberry cordial and freshly made raspberry cookies in the garden arbour. Back then, Nathalie's grandmother Beata had still been alive.

Walther had been a Supreme Court judge, a stern and faultless man who had always made Mina feel uncomfortable. And she hadn't been alone – Niklas had admitted that his father often made him uncomfortable too. She doubted much had changed.

'We see each other occasionally,' Nathalie said evasively.

Mina didn't pursue her line of enquiry. She hadn't really wanted to bring her daughter along, but Nathalie had refused to stay at home and Mina knew better than to waste time arguing. She could see too much of herself in the girl to bother.

'Park over to the side,' Nathalie said. 'Grandpa doesn't like it when people block the road so that he can't get his car out.'

'Of course,' Mina said, pulling onto the broad gravel driveway leading up to the house.

She had vague memories of having had that particular conversation before – with Niklas. She kept to the left and parked the car alongside a gleaming new Audi. The driveway had been carefully raked.

Mina checked her watch. They were just in time. Walther was not a man one paid a surprise visit to, and she had no desire to annoy him from the off. They needed his help. According to the recorded message, New Year's Eve was to be Niklas's final day alive and it was approaching much too quickly. With each passing hour, Mina had to struggle to keep the panic at bay.

After all these years apart, it was hard to know whether the fear stemmed from residual feelings for Niklas, or whether it was because of his importance to their daughter. It didn't really matter. It was the same outcome either way, and the clock was ticking on inexorably.

'Come in, come in before you freeze. But please do wipe your feet properly so that you don't bring in all the snow.'

Walther was standing in the doorway beckoning them up the steps.

The house was typical of the Äppelviken corner of Bromma. It was a large wooden gingerbread-style house from the turn of the nineteenth century. In the summer, it was surrounded by resplendent lilacs and roses. Although the plants were at present under a thick blanket of snow, Mina could still remember the smell of the lavender and the climbing roses that used to cover the front of the house. New Dawn – that had been the rose's name. The garden had been Beata's pride and joy, and no visitor ever escaped a thorough exposition on the names of all the plants.

Mina and Nathalie looked at each other. Thanks to the meticulously cleared driveway, there wasn't so much as a snowflake to be seen on their footwear. But they did as he had asked and wiped their feet on the mat outside the huge wooden front door. Walther stepped aside and admitted them into the hall, where they took off their shoes and coats. Then he embraced them awkwardly.

'Let's go into the drawing room. The girl who comes in to help me a couple of times a week has put out some of those dreadful biscuits from a shop.'

They followed Walther into a large, book-lined room. In the

centre was a huge suite of leather Chesterfield sofas. There was a silver tray with coffee and biscuits on the table.

'Do you know where Dad is?' Nathalie said, once she had sat down.

Mina could hear the worry in Nathalie's voice and wanted to place her hand on her daughter's, but she refrained. That sort of thing didn't yet come naturally to either of them.

'Don't you two know?' Walther said, his bushy grey eyebrows drawing together in a frown. 'You mean he's missing?'

He still had all his hair – it was a neatly combed, thick silver mane.

'We can't get hold of him, and no one knows where he is,' Nathalie said.

Her voice trembled and that made Mina's heart ache, but Walther looked entirely unconcerned. He waved a dismissive hand.

'I don't understand why you think I would know in that case,' he said with a shake of his head.

Walther poured them each a cup of coffee without pausing to ask Nathalie whether she drank coffee or not. There were some nut cookies on an ornate porcelain plate, each one adorned with a hazelnut. Walther pushed the plate towards Mina, but she shook her head as politely as she could. The thought of how many people with inadequate hygiene had handled those biscuits during their journey to the plate brought the bile into her throat. But Nathalie helped herself to one and began to munch away on it.

'Have you spoken to Tor?' Walther said. 'I'm sure he has the situation under control. It's probably just some misunderstanding. You must understand that Niklas is under a lot of stress, given his work. I dare say he just needed a break.'

'But it's not like him, especially not like this, just before Christmas,' Mina said. 'And why would he abandon Nathalie without saying anything?'

Nathalie gave her a warning look. But Walther fixed his gaze on her.

'Naturally it isn't easy to understand for someone who hasn't held a role of the same significance as we have in public life.

I suppose you might argue that you can't compare a minister of justice with a Supreme Court judge, but there are far more similarities than dissimilarities. The responsibility is enormous. There are few offices in the land – or even internationally – that come with the weight of responsibility that Niklas and I have borne.'

'Deal with,' Mina said, correcting him and glancing at Nathalie. 'I know you're retired, but Niklas is still the minister. Isn't there someone else in the Supreme Court in your place now? A woman, if I recall correctly.'

Walther blinked.

'Of course,' he said dismissively, sipping his coffee. Then he turned towards the kitchen.

'Beata!' he shouted. 'The coffee's much too strong, can you put on a new—'

He stopped himself and awkwardly looked at the floor. He slowly set down the cup, and for the first time Mina saw a real person behind the stern mask – an easily confused person.

'One forgets,' he said in a low voice. 'It's most odd. It's been five years since she left us, but … We were married for more than fifty years, and it often feels like she is still here.'

'I understand,' Mina said.

She pushed on in the hope that they might be able to have a real conversation instead of one where she asked questions that were met with critical answers from the ageing judge.

'I hope you understand why we're worried. After what happened last summer … And Nathalie and Niklas are so close to one another, partly because … because I disappeared.'

She had bared her throat as much as she could. She sincerely hoped that her former father-in-law would understand that and accept the outstretched hand.

There was a moment's silence. Then Walther's shoulders slumped.

'I don't mean to belittle your concerns,' he said more gently. 'All I'm saying is that it's entirely possible nothing has happened. Stress can do strange things to people. I'm sure he's fine and will be back home soon. Trust me.'

He patted Nathalie's hand.

'There are similarities between Niklas's disappearance and a number of other cases that we're looking at,' Mina said, aware that she was on very thin ice. 'The other people all have one thing in common. Twenty years ago, they all went through a difficult spell in their lives. Do you remember whether Niklas went through anything like that? He never mentioned anything like that to me.'

'I think there were some toffee cookies too,' Walther said, abruptly rising to his feet.

He went into the kitchen and Mina heard him opening cupboards and rummaging around. After a few minutes he returned with a transparent plastic box.

'Toffee cookies. I knew it! The girl had put them at the very back, behind the chopped tomatoes and rice. What's the logic behind that? Biscuits don't belong with chopped tomatoes and rice. One is food. The other is … well, biscuits. Take a look at what's in them. There's barely anything in this list of ingredients that one recognizes.'

Mina and Nathalie exchanged a look. Nathalie took a bite of another biscuit with a loud crunch. She didn't take her eyes off her grandfather as he twisted and turned the plastic container in frustration as he vainly tried to open it. Eventually he put it down on the table with a loud sigh.

'A difficult spell, you say? People are so obsessed with how they feel these days. It seems as if everyone wakes up in the morning and then stops to see how they're feeling. Well, of course, if you think about it then you'll always find some difficulty to latch onto. Back in my day, they didn't have any of those diagnoses that people like to wave about now. All the combinations of the alphabet. You might have said someone had a problem with their nerves, but then they went to the doctor and got some pills and that was that. Today people are signed off for everything imaginable. And in my line of work, we'd see people day after day trying to pin the blame on "mental troubles" so that they could escape the legal consequences of their actions.'

He snorted and stroked his chin.

'Granddad,' Nathalie said sharply.

Walther met his granddaughter's disapproving gaze, then he took a deep breath.

'Well, fine. Yes, as a matter of fact I do remember Niklas going through a difficult spell some … well, I suppose it was exactly twenty years ago, as it happens. Beata was very worried about him. She said he was depressed and that he didn't want to go on. Of course, I knew it was absolute tosh. He was just a little lost and didn't know where he was going in life, but it all worked out in the end. He went to see one of those headshrinkers that Beata found for him a couple of times, then he applied to university and the problem was gone. A bit of good, honest work or study is all it takes. That's what I've always said. People need to work themselves until they're tired. After a long day's work, you don't have the time to think about how you're feeling.'

'Do you happen to have the name of that psychologist?' Mina said in a low voice.

Her heart was thumping in her chest. Niklas fitted the pattern of the other victims. She had hoped all along that Niklas's disappearance wouldn't have any connection to the skeletons they had found. Now there was no longer any doubt. If they failed to find him, then he would die on New Year's Eve. And when he was found, it would be as a heap of bones in a metro tunnel with his skull on top.

'I dare say the name is in Beata's book,' Walther said, getting to his feet.

He opened a drawer in the ornate wooden desk by the window and took out a floral address book.

'Can we borrow it?' Nathalie asked eagerly.

Walther hesitated, but then nodded and handed it to her.

'But promise me you'll take care of it. It was Beata's.'

'I promise,' Nathalie said, tucking the book into her hoodie pocket.

'We have to go now,' Mina said, standing up.

The clock in her head was ticking so loudly it was thunderous. It took all the strength she could muster to remain calm in Nathalie's presence as her daughter sauntered along behind her into the hall.

As they were saying goodbye, Walther took her hand and

held it. Mina fought off the impulse to yank her hand back and drench it in hand sanitizer. The ticking of the clock helped, since it drowned out everything else.

'I'm glad you're back, so don't think otherwise,' Walther said. 'Nathalie needs a mother.'

'Thank you,' Mina said, surprised to find that her throat had constricted.

Surprisingly, Walther's words meant a lot to her, but she couldn't allow herself to reflect on that now. She needed to concentrate on finding Nathalie's father – before it was too late. And in the last half hour, she had begun to get the feeling that something else was amiss. It was connected – that much she knew. But there was something else. Something she had missed. Something important.

81

SEVEN DAYS TO GO

Vincent moaned. He was dog tired. Benjamin had come home from his friend's at midnight but Vincent hadn't been able to sleep properly. The night had consisted mainly of wandering around the house and ensuring that no one had got in. He had checked the lock on the front door umpteen times. He had shone a torch onto the snow both in front of and behind the house in case there were footprints to be found.

He had at intervals lain down and slept for no more than an hour before rising to do it all over again. He knew it was completely irrational, but the dark of night afforded little room for cold rationality.

He turned over and looked at the time. 07:30. There was no reason to drag it out any further. He rolled out of bed and managed to avoid tumbling onto the floor by the skin of his teeth as his feet became caught in the tangled sheets. He had evidently spent much of the brief final spell in bed tossing and turning.

'Merry Christmas to you,' he muttered.

Then he shook his head. This would not do. After all, it was Christmas Eve. He was going to start the day with mulled wine and a Saffron bun. He forewent the dressing gown in favour of a knitted Christmas jumper and a pair of green long johns covered in a pattern of printed red ribbons. As he made for the kitchen, he stopped by the record player. After searching for a while, he found the album 'A Midwinter Saga' by the electronic music pioneer Ralph Lundsten. It might not be traditional Christmas music, but it was perfect for when he needed perking up.

The romantic wintry tones of the music followed him into

the kitchen. He turned on the oven to heat up the bun wreath he had bought on his way home from police headquarters the day before. Lussekatt buns with their fragrant saffron always tasted best when they were warmed up. He waited briefly before sliding in the tray, and it wasn't long before the kitchen began to smell of Christmas baking. He pulled out the mulled wine, set up the coffee maker and was about to go and wake Benjamin when his phone rang. It was still lying in the bedroom.

He ran to it and answered breathlessly.

'Vincent speaking. Merry Christmas.'

'Hi, it's Loke,' the voice on the line said. 'I'm sorry to call this early, and on Christmas Eve, but I didn't really know who else to call.'

'Hi Loke. Has something happened?'

'Yeah, well … I just arrived at the lab and … we've had a break-in. Some equipment's been broken, but the main thing is that … well, the bones are gone. The old ones found by Odenplan station. We only just got them back from Gunilla late last night, but they're not here any more. I know because I put them on a table of their own and now it's empty. I've been looking everywhere.'

Vincent returned to the kitchen with the phone glued to his ear.

'Maybe Milda moved them?' he said, turning off the oven. Vincent opened the door with his free hand and touched the bun wreath. It was just the right, warm temperature.

'I don't think so. I arrived first. I think … I'm convinced they've been stolen,' Loke said. 'I just don't understand why.'

'And the best option was to call me?' He grabbed a potholder and pulled out the tray before closing the oven door with his foot.

'I was responsible for the bones,' Loke said dismally. 'I'm the one who lost them. They were stolen on my watch. I don't want to report it to the police officially. Not yet. I'll be out of this job the minute I do that. You know how much I love working here with Milda. And you're not a cop. So I thought you might … Maybe you'd think of something. Could we maybe keep this kind of … to ourselves …?'

Vincent sighed. There wasn't going to be any cosy Christmas breakfast for him and Benjamin.

'OK,' he said. 'I'm on my way. But I'm bringing Mina. She's usually better at this kind of thing than I am.'

'No, no, no,' Loke said, his voice filled with panic. 'No police. Not until we can figure out a way of ensuring I don't get fired.'

'Mina's off work today,' said Vincent. 'So she isn't a police officer at this moment. And she might be helpful – she knows the procedures better than me.'

Loke was silent for a while.

'If you're absolutely sure,' he said. 'I've just got to run and do something I promised Milda I would do, but I can meet you at the lab this afternoon. There's no rush, is there? The bones are already gone. And no one else will be coming in to access anything in the meantime. After all, it is Christmas Eve. I'll call later.'

Loke hung up. It wasn't quite how Vincent had envisaged his Christmas Eve morning, but he would at least have time to eat his breakfast, and hopefully he would get to see Mina. In fact, he couldn't have wished for a better Christmas Eve. If he were lucky, this would require him to stay in town for at least another day, which would be a good reason to delay his trip to join Maria at her parents'. He preferred to keep that particular family reunion as brief as possible. They would still have plenty of time to scold him anyway.

He switched on the coffee maker and went to knock on Benjamin's door.

'Good morning,' he said loudly. 'I know it's very early, but there's coffee and a lussekatt wreath out here. Soak up the Christmas cheer, my boy. Come and keep me company for a while and then you can go back to bed.'

There was silence from beyond the door.

'Just how hungover are you?' Vincent said, nudging the door ajar. 'You didn't get home that late last night.'

Benjamin's room was in perfect order – everything was exactly where it should be. It was a degree of order that ought to have been bordering on the impossible to achieve if one spent as much time in the room as Benjamin did. Even the bed was perfectly made. The bedspread was stretched over it and the pillows had been fluffed.

But Benjamin wasn't there.

A cold invisible hand grasped Vincent's throat. He told himself he was overreacting. Benjamin had probably just got up earlier than him and gone out.

But there was no reason at all for Benjamin to have gone out at seven o'clock in the morning on Christmas Eve … Vincent didn't want to give in to the feeling that was beginning to creep over him. That would not help at all.

He went back into the kitchen to call Benjamin, and stopped in the doorway. Lying on the kitchen table was a sheet of paper covered in handwriting. He must have been too tired to notice it before. He hurried over, picked it up and began to read in case it was a note from his son. The words he found instead made the kitchen spin around him. He grabbed the table to avoid losing his balance.

The coffee maker beeped in protest behind him. He had forgotten to return the jug after filling the reservoir and hot coffee was pouring onto the kitchen counter. There was going to be a flood any second now. There was a steady flow streaming towards the edge and very shortly it would be pouring onto the floor.

From the corner of his eye, he saw the disaster that was brewing, but he couldn't have cared less about it. He pulled out his phone and called Maria. She didn't pick up before it rang out. He tried Rebecka instead. Then Benjamin. And finally his ex-wife Ulrika. None of them answered.

The letter in his hand was from the Shadow. He read it again and tried calling everyone again, and all the time the cold hand tightened its grip around his throat.

82

'Grappa!' Harry yelled when Julia's father opened the front door.

Her son was almost vibrating with unbridled joy. He threw himself at his grandfather.

'Why, if it isn't Grandpa's little favourite come to visit,' Julia's father said fondly, tickling Harry's belly.

Harry howled with laughter.

Julia couldn't help smiling. At least one member of the family would have a good Christmas. Torkel was standing beside her looking as if he wanted to be somewhere else entirely – which was probably not far from the truth. Julia's parents had never been big fans of her husband. The relationship between her parents and Torkel had improved with the arrival of Harry, but there were still ice floes drifting past them.

'Come in, come in,' her father said, moving out of the way to admit them to the hall.

He glanced pointedly at the clock. They had been due at one o'clock. Julia knew they were late. Everything took longer at home now that she and Torkel had effectively stopped talking to each other. It was only ten past, but for the commissioner of police that was as much of a faux pas as arriving a week late.

'Dad, relax,' Julia said. 'It's not a staff meeting. It's Christmas Eve. Merry Christmas.'

'It starts small,' he said. 'But you're right. Come on Harry, let's show you our Christmas tree!'

The commissioner of police carried Harry into the living room and Julia heard another shriek of delight when Harry saw the tree.

'Isn't it pretty?' she heard her father say as she took off her coat. 'No, don't touch that, it's supposed to hang on the tree … and not that one … no, no, no, if you tug at the tinsel then the whole tree … No, oh, oh my! It doesn't matter. Don't worry. I don't think we needed that bauble anyway. And … well, not that one either.'

Julia laughed to herself. It was as if all the love he had forgotten to shower on his own daughter in her childhood had been pent up behind a dam that had now burst over his grandchild.

Torkel was still standing in the hall wearing his shoes.

'We're going to do this,' Julia said in a low voice to her husband. 'They'll be giving Harry sweets for at least an hour. Then we'll be off.'

Torkel nodded and took off his coat and shoes. Julia watched him walk past her. With each step that he took away from her, it felt easier to breathe. Soon. Soon this bloody Christmas would be over.

83

Mina had found the phone number for Niklas's psychologist the evening before, as soon as she had left Walther's grand Bromma home. It hadn't been difficult. Beata's address book had many entries, but it was faultlessly ordered. Mina had notified the team about Niklas's mental health issues and given them the phone number. She didn't think she had it in her to lead an interview about Niklas's past herself.

Then there had been nothing more she could do. And today it was Christmas Eve. Mina felt as if she was on enforced leave while the whole world was at a standstill, eating Christmas dinner and opening presents. And all the time the clock was ticking down to New Year's Eve. Niklas had seven days left. Wherever he was.

'It feels weird doing Christmas without Dad,' Nathalie said. 'We should be out there looking for him instead of just sitting here.'

'You sound like a cop,' Mina said, trying to smile. 'And I promise you that the police are doing all they can.'

Nathalie was curled up under a blanket on the sofa. She had been in that very spot all day without budging an inch.

'Have they talked to that psychologist yet?' she asked, for what was surely the thousandth time.

Mina forced herself to be patient – especially as she felt the same frustration as her daughter.

'Like I said, they're doing everything they can to try to reach him. But he's been retired for a number of years and seems to devote his time to adventures these days. Adam told me last night that he was in Rwanda, on some kind of expedition to see gorillas. If there's no signal in the jungle we won't be able to get hold of him.'

'OK,' said Nathalie, looking down at her phone again. 'I just want my dad back.'

Mina channel-hopped aimlessly but soon turned off the TV and got up.

'Look, I know it sucks. I know everything sucks right now while your dad's not here. But I think he'd want us to at least *try* and have a nice time. What do you say? Why don't we roll up our sleeves?'

Silence. A long silence. Then Nathalie looked at her uncertainly.

'So what are we going to do? How do we celebrate Christmas?' she asked in a low voice.

'I think that's completely up to us. What do you want to do?' Mina said, holding out her hands to show that there were no limits.

'What can you do?' Nathalie said, a wry smile on her lips.

Mina suddenly felt her pulse quicken. She didn't know what her daughter expected of her. What might Nathalie ask of her, of her limitations? It didn't matter. The maternal instinct was still there, coursing through her veins. It was more powerful than the instincts that she had long believed it was impossible to conquer.

'Everything,' she said, and she meant it. 'I can do everything.'

Nathalie looked at her searchingly. Then she got off the sofa and cast aside the blanket.

'Get dressed. Ica's open on Christmas Eve.'

'Ica?' Mina said, feeling another flutter of anxiety. 'Why do we need to go to the supermarket?'

'We need to buy a gingerbread house,' Nathalie said, putting on her coat. 'We've never made one together. Everyone else does that with their mums every Christmas. I've always been jealous of them. Dad tried once, but he's hopeless. He's basically all fingers and thumbs, and it ended up looking like it was fit for demolition. He can do food. But he can't do houses. Please can we do that? Can we build a gingerbread house together? With that melted sugar that we burn our fingers on and the icing that it's impossible to get out of the tube and loads of Smarties on the roof even though they're the most disgusting sweets ever …'

The words came out of Nathalie in a torrent and, without Mina even realizing what she was doing, she took a step forward. It was a small but huge step that bridged the gap between her and her daughter. She put her arms around Nathalie, and murmured barely audibly into her hair.

'Of course we can make a gingerbread house together. My darling, darling girl.'

They'd barely made it back from the supermarket and assembled the gingerbread house when the doorbell rang.

'Who could that be?' Nathalie said, licking icing from her fingers.

'No idea,' Mina said. 'I almost never have visitors – especially not on Christmas Eve.'

She stuffed a piece of broken gingerbread roof into her mouth before going to the door to open it. Standing outside was Vincent, his shoulders slumped. He was as white as a sheet.

'Oh God, what's happened?' she said in horror as she let him into the apartment.

There were times when polite small talk was appropriate, but there were also times when it got in the way – like now.

He seemed to struggle with her question. Whatever was going on inside Vincent, she had never seen anything like it before.

He alternated between looking at her and looking away. It was as if he was afraid of what he might say.

'I got this letter …' he began haltingly.

'Mum, do you know whether we bought any more Smarties?' Nathalie called from the kitchen. 'This bag has run out.'

Vincent glanced in the direction of Nathalie's voice. Then he looked straight at Mina. Whatever he had been about to say was gone.

'It's Loke,' he said. 'He wants us to come to the lab. Apparently someone broke in and stole the oldest bones.'

'Typical,' Mina said, reaching automatically for her coat. 'I assume it's urgent.'

'No, not at all. He called me first thing but said we should wait until he got back.'

'But he's reported it to the police, hasn't he?'

'Not yet. He's afraid he'll get the sack. And the damage is already done. He'll call us soon. I was waiting at home, but then I thought it might be best if we were in the same place when he did. They won't miss me at home.'

Mina hung her coat back up and shook her head.

'That might be the most tenuous reason I've ever heard for celebrating Christmas with someone,' she said. 'But seriously, you can't be scoring any brownie points running off on Christmas Eve? Maria must have gone through the roof.'

Vincent shrugged.

'They were … glad to be rid of me,' he said.

She thought he was talking a little too loudly, as if he needed to convince himself that what he was saying was true.

'Vincent, what's the matter?'

'I can't …' he began to say. 'I can't talk about it now. Oh yes, I brought a lussekatt bun wreath.'

He held up a bag.

'Although it might be a little dry,' he added, looking a little vexed as he peered inside the bag. 'There was no one at home who … .who …'

Vincent fell silent. He looked very strange again. He inhaled as if he was about to say something else, but instead he bent down, took off his shoes and put them next to Nathalie's on the recently purchased shoe rack.

'I see you've been doing the place up,' he said.

'If only you knew,' Mina said with a laugh. 'Nathalie has … well, come in and see for yourself.'

She led Vincent into the living room.

'Hi Vincent!' Nathalie said as she emerged from the kitchen. 'Merry Christmas! We've just built a gingerbread house. Now we're going to watch Donald Duck.'

'Take a seat,' Mina said. 'And take a ginger biscuit. But if you leave any crumbs on the sofa I'll kill you.'

The three of them sat down, Vincent between her and Nathalie. On the television, Petrina Solange was lighting a candle. The familiar voice of Bengt Feldreich began to speak.

'Donald Duck, eh?' Vincent said, nudging Nathalie in the side with his elbow. 'I haven't watched that since I was little. Aren't you too old for that?'

'How can you not have seen …? Don't you have kids?' said Nathalie. 'What *do* you watch on Christmas Eve?'

'Well, yes, of course I do,' Vincent said, squirming. 'But I'm always putting on my Santa costume then.'

Mina pictured the always impeccably dressed Vincent wriggling into a Santa suit while trying not to ruin his hair.

'Anyway, I'm not too old,' Nathalie said. 'I don't think you ever are. And just for that, I'm going to make you play Santa for us once Donald's done. Otherwise you won't get to try the gingerbread house.'

Vincent stared at Nathalie in horror.

Mina could no longer contain herself. She began to roar with laughter.

'Mulled wine, Vincent?' she said, wiping away a tear from her cheek.

'Yes please.'

Mina went into the kitchen to warm up the mulled wine on the hob. She poured two steaming cups – one for him and one for her.

'Thanks,' he said when she returned. 'It seems Loke is taking his time.'

She nodded and sipped her mulled wine. The warm alcohol was very soothing. Even Vincent seemed to relax a little.

'There's still some non-alcoholic mulled wine if you'd like some,' she said to Nathalie.

'Thanks, but I'll just have a Cola Zero. Apparently even I have a limit to how Christmassy I want it to be.'

They were sitting in a row on the sofa again with Vincent in the middle. Mina wanted so badly to ask him what was going on. But not here. Not in front of Nathalie.

On the television, wind-up toys were parading through Santa's workshop. Vincent and Nathalie were humming along to the music and swaying in time. Once again, Mina thought that Vincent's voice was a little too shrill, as if he was making a particular effort. And there was something about his eyes. His eyes were moist and unfocused, and filled with sadness.

Vincent continued to hum along with Nathalie, but his hand sought out Mina's and squeezed it – tightly. She sat still for a moment, unsure what to do. Then she squeezed back. They stayed like that, his hand in hers. He stopped singing, and in the glow of the television, she saw a tear slowly running down Vincent's cheek.

84

The doorbell rang and Sara wiped her hands on her apron. She quickly undid it, took it off and slung it over the back of a kitchen chair. Before opening the front door, she stopped in front of the hall mirror and adjusted her hair.

Then she snorted at herself. It was only Ruben. Ruben, whom she'd invited over as her good deed for Christmas, because she couldn't bear the thought of someone spending Christmas Eve alone.

'Mum, who is it?' Zachary called from the living room.

'It's Ruben, my mate from work,' she called back as she opened the door. 'I told you he was coming to celebrate Christmas with us!'

Ruben was standing outside, his arms full of Christmas presents and with a large bag over his shoulder. Snow was gently falling and she noticed for some reason that a snowflake had caught on his eyelashes.

'Hi,' he said awkwardly.

'Come in,' she said, stepping aside.

He dropped one of the packages balanced in his arms and she bent down to pick it up. Ruben bent down at exactly the same moment, causing them to bump heads softly, which made him drop the rest of his burden on the doormat.

'Ouch! How clumsy of me,' he said, laughing in embarrassment as she helped him to gather them up.

'I did say something small, didn't I?' she said, smiling wryly as they picked up the parcels. They were beautifully wrapped in dark red paper with shiny gold ribbons around them.

She wondered if he'd wrapped them himself. Her own presents always looked as though they'd been wrapped up by two squabbling cats.

'This is one hundred per cent your fault,' Ruben said. 'It was you who showed me how much fun it is to buy Christmas presents. And your kids are five and six, if I remember correctly? There's no such thing as too many presents at that age. I've even learned how to wrap things properly. It's been good practice.'

He took off his large scarf and thick coat and hung them on a hook.

'Come through. I'm just warming up some mulled wine,' Sara said, going to the kitchen.

It was strange seeing Ruben in her own home. She lived in a terraced house by Lake Sickla with big windows that allowed her to see the water from her home. She loved it. She had been raised by a lake and there was something about the presence of water that made her feel calm. Now the lake was frozen, which meant she and the kids had had many hours of fun ice skating in their free time. Leah had got really good even though she was so little – she'd even started trying to do pirouettes.

'Ooooh, more presents,' her daughter cried as she ran into the hallway, her cheeks glowing.

She stared at the pile in Ruben's arms.

'They're for you,' he said, winking. 'And maybe there's a little something for your mum too.'

'We weren't supposed to buy each other presents. I haven't got anything for you, you know.'

'But this is my Christmas present – getting to celebrate with you. All of you, I mean. And you will be feeding me … right?'

He suddenly looked anxious. Sara laughed.

'Don't worry,' she said.

She put a hand on his back and guided him into the kitchen.

'There's food. Far too much of it, in fact. But as I mentioned, I tend to give Christmas food a miss. We're all a bit sick of it, so we're having Italian.'

'Great. Where should I put the parcels? Does this house have a tree that stands guard over the presents?'

Leah nodded eagerly and pointed towards the large living room at the other end of the open-plan space that also contained the kitchen. In one corner there was a majestic spruce covered in silver and white baubles, as well as colourful home-made decorations, all hung up in no particular order.

'That's one of the things I find hardest when it comes to parenting,' Sara muttered. 'All the ugly decorations and other tat they drag home from nursery that you have to put up.'

'Ellinor let Astrid have her own tree in her bedroom,' Ruben said. 'She's been allowed to decorate it however she wants, and Ellinor did the one in the living room. It was a good idea, but I think Astrid saw it more as her having two trees. Or perhaps I'm misremembering Ellinor's style when it comes to Christmas tree decorations.'

'It's a genius idea though,' Sara said, impressed.

That was definitely a tactic she would adopt next year. Then it occurred to her that next Christmas was Michael's turn and the kids would be in the USA. She felt a sob catch in her throat, but she forced the thought out of her mind. They were here now, and she had to live in the moment.

'What happened about that bomb in the end?' Ruben said, lowering his voice. 'I know it's not the most Christmassy subject, but I was kind of worried.'

'About little old me?' Sara said, fluttering her eyelashes.

Ruben turned as red as a lobster.

'Well, things are moving forward,' Sara said. 'We received a tip-off from a disgruntled former employee at one of the companies. It turns out they've still got the ammonium nitrate they reported stolen. The employee was involved in transferring it to another location, but then he felt he wasn't being paid enough to keep his mouth shut so he called us instead.'

'Wow. Loyalty with a price tag,' Ruben said. 'So they stole it from themselves?'

'Exactly,' Sara said, nodding. 'We've been monitoring the other companies since yesterday because we suspect it's the same thing. Especially since we discovered that they're all part of the same corporate group.'

'So you think the order to move the explosives came from higher up?'

'It's too soon to say. And now the mulled wine is apparently boiling over.'

She ran into the kitchen and turned off the hob while Ruben went into the living room to put the presents under the tree. She heard Leah and Zachary jumping about, full of exuberance. Then she heard a fearsome roar.

'What if I'm the Grinch come to steal all your presents?'

She hurried into the living room and saw Ruben making a lunge towards the parcels, his hands in the air. The children screamed with terrified delight.

'Oh, not the presents …? I see. Well, in that case the Grinch wants to take two small Christmas children with him instead!'

He swept them both up into his arms and began to carry them away.

'Oh no! Not Leah and Zachary!' Sara cried out, playing along. 'Please Mr Grinch, these children have been ever so good.'

Ruben came to a halt. He stared wide-eyed at the children in his arms.

'Huh? You're telling me these are two good kids? Two good kids who should get to meet Santa Claus?'

Sara gave him a warning look. She hadn't made any arrangements for a Santa visit; she didn't have any family locally who could help, and all her friends were busy. It wasn't his fault, but Ruben was promising something he couldn't deliver.

'Ruben …' she said, slashing her index finger across her throat.

But he just grinned at her and glanced towards the hall. Sara looked in the same direction and saw the big bag he'd brought with him. Then she understood. Santa *would* be coming this year. An emotionally immature, middle-aged Santa with a sunbed tan – but still a wonderful Santa, somehow.

It was going to be a good Christmas Eve. Perhaps the best in a very long time.

85

Vincent could already tell from the outside that someone had damaged the door leading to Milda's lab. Loke opened it, looking anxiously around. He was startled when he realized that Nathalie was with them.

'I agreed to Mina coming,' he said. 'Why are there more of you?'

'She can't stay at home on her own on Christmas Eve,' Mina said.

'Sure I can,' Nathalie said. 'But I didn't want to. This sounded more fun.'

Vincent couldn't help smiling.

'It *is* more fun,' he said, turning back to Loke. 'You called right in the middle of Chip and Dale.'

Loke looked completely flummoxed and rather unhappy.

'As I said, I thought only Vincent need know about this,' he said, turning to Mina. 'And perhaps you. But I suppose the cat's out of the bag now, as Schrödinger wouldn't have said. Come on in, everybody.'

Loke showed them into the room where they usually came to see Milda and him working together. Everything was a mess. Whoever had broken in had obviously been looking for something. The mortal remains of Erika Sävelden, Marcus Eriksson and Jon Langseth were all still neatly laid out in skeleton shapes on their respective steel tables. The fourth table was empty.

'Were the Odenplan bones there?' Mina said, pointing to the table. 'The unidentified ones?'

Vincent felt the energy radiating from her now that she was concentrating. It was as if life wasn't in colour unless he was in proximity to her.

He glanced towards Nathalie, who had stopped just inside the door and seemed to be completely absorbed by her phone. She didn't seem to be having *that* much fun.

'Whoever it was swiped the lot,' Loke said, nodding gloomily. 'Not just the bones, but also all the samples and photographs. All the documentation we had on them is gone. I'm so going to be fired when this comes out.'

'You've got to report it right away,' Mina said.

'Remember that it wasn't your fault,' Vincent said.

'Tell that to the people in charge,' Loke muttered.

The fourth table.

The fourth set of bones.

'*Find the fourth one*,' Vincent suddenly said eagerly, looking at Mina. 'I knew it meant something. Someone sent me a kind of challenge a few days ago. It contained four hourglasses and a message. *Find the fourth one before time runs out*, it said. I didn't understand what it meant. In fact, I'd almost forgotten about it – until now. At the beginning of the investigation we only had Jon Langseth. But we've found the bones of four people, and one set is now missing. *Find the fourth one*. Doesn't that sound like it's to do with the victims?'

'You mean your admirer broke in and stole human remains just to play some kind of game with you?' she said with obvious disgust. 'What kind of sick fans do you have?'

'We had the fourth one,' Loke said, pointing to the empty table. 'What's the point of finding the bones again?'

'You're right,' Vincent said. 'It does sound a little odd. But I still have a feeling that it's connected somehow.'

He fell silent and then he saw the same thought occur to all of them.

'If it isn't referring to the older bones …' he said slowly, and Mina nodded. 'Might Niklas be the fourth one? Were the hourglasses sent to me by … the killer?'

'Find the fourth one before time runs out,' Mina said, suddenly looking paler than before. 'What on earth is going on?'

'I've got absolutely no idea,' Vincent said. 'But we've got to find out. And in the meantime, I suggest, Loke, that you call the police.'

86

Niklas was sitting on the only chair in the room with his back against the wall. There was also a mattress on the floor and a small table in the confined space. Apart from that it was mostly rubbish. He'd been in this tiny room for two days. Of course, the perception of time worked differently when there were no windows. The battery in his phone had run out on the first day and ironically he had forgotten to put on his wristwatch on his final morning at home.

But unless he was much mistaken, today was Christmas Eve. If that were the case, then he had seven days to go. One miserable week of existence. And then an eternity of non-existence. Nathalie was surely beside herself with worry. He closed his eyes to shut out the misery, but it was futile. He was so incredibly ashamed that he wasn't there with them.

With Nathalie and with Mina … Had he been too hard on Mina by not letting her into their lives sooner than he did? She had admittedly been the one who made the choice to leave them so long ago, but it was he who had forced her to keep her promise. Was it his fault that she had missed out on so many years with her daughter and vice versa – years when he could have seen them together and when he might even have been together with them?

He just wanted to hug Nathalie, shower her with gifts and wish her the merriest Christmas ever. Instead, Nathalie was having to spend Christmas wondering where her father was. No sixteen-year-old should have to go through that.

He had known all along that his job entailed risk. Being minister of justice had become an increasingly vulnerable position. The attack in the summer had confirmed that. And no matter how shocking it was each time it happened, Swedish politicians had put their lives on the line before. He knew all this. He had chosen to continue anyway.

But his daughter hadn't made that choice. She hadn't signed a deal with the state whereby she consented to her dad risking going missing one day. She deserved to have a father, and very soon he'd no longer be that.

The ceiling above him creaked. Footsteps. He opened his eyes and stared intently at the steps leading up to the ground floor of the building. No feet came into sight. No one was coming downstairs. He exhaled and closed his eyes again.

Then there was Tor.

His poor press secretary had probably lost five kilos in sweat alone by now. And he would probably be shouldering the blame too, given that Niklas had vanished right under the noses of Tor's security detail. He would presumably have kept Niklas's disappearance secret from the public for a while, but that couldn't go on indefinitely. Tor would call a press conference soon. Probably tomorrow – on Christmas Day. It wasn't common for a press secretary to hold their own press conference, but it wasn't unheard of either. And if Tor waited any longer there was a risk that it would all leak and then the ministry would lose control of the narrative. Tor was too polished to let that happen.

After the press conference, absolutely everyone would know that the minister was missing. The search for him would escalate, but it would make no difference.

It would make not the slightest bit of difference.

87

This time Dad had been gone for even longer. Each time he disappeared, it took more days. He knew that because he kept count with marks on the wall. Seven days. He'd been gone for seven more days this time. Almost two months.

'Dad!'

He ran towards him so fast that he almost tripped over the rails. His heart was pounding when he finally felt the soft leather of Dad's jacket against his face.

'My treasure.'

Dad's voice was just as warm as ever – it radiated with love.

'My treasure.'

Dad held him tightly. His arms were strong. Strong enough to protect him from the world. It wasn't until Dad returned that he realized how much he had missed him.

'Have you been guarding my crown for me?'

Dad's big hands held his face. He nodded eagerly.

'Yes. Of course I have. I'll run and fetch it.'

Moving as quickly as his legs would carry him, he ran back to the camp, rooted through the sack in the corner behind the barrels and then carefully pulled out the crown. The golden-yellow metal shone in the firelight cast by the barrel, and he gently polished it with his sleeve before running back to Dad.

'Here!'

He eagerly held the crown out and Dad took it. With a solemn expression, Dad placed the crown on his own head, settling it on his bushy hair.

'Where are the others?'

'They're up gathering food. I had a sore throat, so I had to stay behind.'

'Then we can have a little time to ourselves,' Dad said, taking his hand in his as they walked towards the camp.

'Where've you been?'

He knew the question was forbidden, but this time he couldn't stop himself.

'You know that's a question that has no place in our life,' Dad said quietly.

He was embarrassed – he wanted to explain.

'You were gone for so long this time,' he said quietly, staring down at his feet, balanced on the rails.

He wobbled and Dad caught him.

'But I came back – and that's all that counts. Coming back.'

He turned his face to look up at Dad and smiled. As usual, Dad was right. He was back. Now everything was as it should be.

88

When Vincent returned home, the house was just as empty as it had been when he'd left it. He didn't know what he'd been expecting. Maybe that his family would be back, as if by magic. But reality wasn't magical – in reality, he was alone. Not even Benjamin was to be seen.

Vincent pulled out his phone and attempted to reach his son, wherever he might be, but Benjamin's phone was off.

The text on the Shadow's note that Vincent had received that morning was running through his head alongside the riddle of the hourglasses, which was why he didn't hear the faint beeping coming from the bedroom at first. When he did, he went in and realized it was his alarm clock ringing. It was set for 16.30 and had been going for half an hour. The batteries were almost dead. He turned off the alarm and frowned. He only used it in the morning. There was no reason for him to set it for the afternoon.

There was only one conclusion to be drawn: he wasn't the one who'd set the alarm.

While he had been gone, someone had been into his house and reset his alarm clock. He felt sick at the very thought. The question was what else his invisible antagonist had got up to. Or, for that matter, whether he was actually alone in the house right now.

Vincent moved quickly and quietly through the house, constantly on his guard for anyone who might suddenly jump out and attack him. But the house was empty. And everything was just as he'd left it. Nothing was missing.

Except the obvious.

When he reached the living room, he stopped in the middle of the floor. The ravens on the snowy lawn outside had returned, but this time there were only two of them. And they were just as immobile as last time. They were sitting at a respectable distance from each other, staring up at him. There were two indentations in the snow between them, and a third to the side of the right-hand bird – as if three of their friends had just flown away. Vincent felt a strong compulsion to go outside and check whether they were real. No … That would be to surrender to madness. He was Vincent Walder – the Master Mentalist, the man who was the best there was at controlling his own mind.

Wasn't he?

He fled into the kitchen before the headache caused by the living room became too overwhelming.

89

SIX DAYS TO GO

The room they used for press conferences was packed with journalists. Tor looked around, nodding to the odd face he knew, while waiting for the hubbub to settle down. He hadn't been expecting so many people to turn up – after all, it was Christmas Day. But the number of journalists indicated that this was of significant interest. Good. This was a crucial moment. Niklas's disappearance had hitherto only been known to those inside the ministry and the police, although rumours had begun to spread in the media. Now the public would be informed. Every word would be of great importance, and he had carefully prepared his remarks.

Tor cleared his throat.

'Is everyone here? If so, let's get started.'

'Where's the prime minister?' said a journalist from *Svenska Dagbladet*. 'Shouldn't she be here?'

'I have the full backing of the prime minister to hold this press conference,' Tor said, smiling. 'But she sends her greetings to you all, of course. Anyway – at the top of today's agenda are the rumours that some of you have already contacted us about, and that we have until now chosen not to confirm, since doing so might interfere with an ongoing police investigation. But we have now reached the point where the gravity of the situation means we need the public's help. What you have heard is true. I hereby confirm that the Swedish minister of justice, Niklas Stockenberg, is missing.'

The room exploded into a cacophony of noise and voices. The journalists were shouting to try to drown each other out, and waving their hands frantically in the air to try to catch Tor's attention. He gestured to them to quieten down, and to his surprise it worked immediately. In the silence that followed, all the journalists kept their hands raised.

'Jan?' Tor said, nodding to the reporter from *Dagens Nyheter*.

'When was the minister last heard from?'

'On December 22nd. So three days ago. Vanja?'

A woman with a shock of red hair spoke. She was from *Expressen*. *Aftonbladet*'s reporter glared at Tor.

'Is there any information about how he disappeared?' the woman said. 'Are there indications of an abduction? Is the police's theory that the minister has been kidnapped?'

'I can't comment about which theories the police are basing their investigation on at this juncture. Joakim?'

The reporter from *Aftonbladet* finally got to speak. He gazed at Tor with tremendous intensity as he formulated his question.

'Will you be taking on the role of minister of justice during Niklas's absence?' he said, weighing up every word. 'Many people were surprised when you took time out from your own highly promising political career to work as the minister's press secretary. Is this the moment you've been waiting for?'

Tor pursed his lips, clearly demonstrating his displeasure.

'Joakim, that question is just shameless. You're implying that I had an agenda when I agreed to work with the minister. In practice, it was an excellent opportunity to help a friend of many years' standing while also doing my bit for my country. Of course, it is greatly beneficial to be so close to the heart of power, and I will certainly derive benefits from it in my future political career. But as I said, that is still in the future. I have many years left in me and a lot to do before I reach retirement.'

There was the sound of scattered laughter.

'But to answer your actual question,' Tor said, 'no, I won't be taking on the role of temporary minister. That's not how it works. While we do not have a specific procedure in place for an event like this, we are able to draw upon our experiences following the murder of Anna Lindh and indeed the attack on Niklas last summer. There is some preparation in place for all eventualities. I'm afraid I can't say any more than that. Above all, we hope that Niklas will be found soon. This is our top priority.'

'Do the police have any suspects?' said a reporter from TV4 news, holding out a microphone while the camera beside him zoomed in on Tor's face.

He shook his head.

'Since we don't know what has happened we can't use the word suspect. We're simply asking the public to help by keeping their eyes peeled. If they see the minister of justice or they have any information regarding his disappearance, we would like them to get in touch with the police.'

'His ex-wife is a police detective – is she involved in the case?'

Bodil from the women's weekly *Svensk Damtidning* gazed at him hopefully, presumably desperate for a heart-rending personal angle on the woman feverishly searching for her former husband. Tor made an effort to avoid rolling his eyes. He had no time for the gossip rags.

'I can't comment on ongoing police operations,' he said drily.

There was still a sea of raised hands in front of him, but he knew that from now it would just be the same questions over and over again. The most important ones had already been asked. He'd said what he wanted to say. And it wouldn't hurt the journalists to be reminded of his own career in politics; after all, he had always regarded his time by Niklas's side as limited. However, what mattered now was finding his boss – by any means necessary. His own plans would have to wait.

Under protests from the assembled media, he declared the press conference at an end and hurried into the corridor. The hubbub inside the room continued. The news would be explosive – and not just on home turf. The disappearance of Sweden's minister of justice would spread around the world. The circus was up and running.

Tor returned to his office and slumped into his chair. There was a pen lying at an angle and he automatically adjusted it so that everything on his desk was perfectly positioned. Just the way he wanted it. He glanced at the door leading into Niklas's office. The anxiety was gnawing away at his stomach. Where the hell had he gone? The minister had to be found – now. Anything else was unthinkable.

90

When Mina arrived at police headquarters, she found Loke in the foyer reading a noticeboard. He looked bewildered – and he was inadequately dressed, given the cold weather.

'Hi Loke,' she said. 'What are you doing here?'

Loke started and turned around.

'Oh, hi Mina. Julia Hammarsten invited me to some kind of meeting, but I don't know where I'm supposed to go. Do you think they're going to sack me?'

'I don't think so,' Mina said. 'Julia isn't your boss as far as I know. But I think we're going to the same place.'

She took out her swipe card.

'Were you given one of these?'

Loke nodded and put his hand in his jacket pocket. Suddenly he beamed. 'Oh yes, there was something I wanted to show you,' he said. 'I'd prefer to show Vincent too. Is he here?'

'He's coming,' she said. 'What is it?'

Loke pulled two sealed ziplock bags from his pocket. There was a big piece of bone in each. Mina looked around automatically. Skeletal remains were not typically waved around in the foyer of police headquarters. Fortunately, no one else was in sight.

'Do you remember the pig?' Loke said.

Mina groaned quietly to herself. This was definitely more up Vincent's street.

'In the end, I didn't boil a whole pig,' he said. 'I went to a farm and bought some leftovers from a slaughtered carcass. But look at this. Look at this bone.'

He handed the bag to Mina, who reluctantly took it. Even though she was wearing gloves and the bag was presumably hermetically sealed, its contents still made her feel slightly nauseous.

'What am I supposed to be looking at?' she said queasily.

'It's the front leg of a pig that's been boiled in water and vinegar until the skin and flesh fell away. Do you see those small spots?'

Mina held the bag up to the light. There were small grey patches visible in places on the bone.

'Those are tissue scraps that didn't come loose,' Loke said, swapping bags with her. 'Now look at the other bone. I boiled it the same way. But after it had cooled down, I put it in a terrarium with skin beetles.'

'How did you get hold of them?' Vincent said enthusiastically from behind her.

Mina jumped so hard that she almost dropped the plastic bag containing the bone.

'Don't scare me like that!' she said irritably.

'Apparently my ninja training has paid off,' Vincent said, winking at her. 'But I was asking about the skin beetles …'

'The Museum of Natural History lent me a few,' Loke said.

Mina could tell how proud he was.

'Wow, I didn't know they had a dermestarium,' Vincent said.

'Anyway, can you see any difference between the bones?' Loke said, pointing to the bag in Mina's hand.

Mina could see right away what he was referring to. The bone that had received the attention of the beetles had none of the grey stains. It was as gleaming and clean as the bones that had belonged to Jon, Erika and Marcus. The thought that masses of tiny creepy-crawlies had nibbled them clean made her feel sick.

'They must have been pretty peckish,' Vincent said. 'How long did it take them?'

'Not that long, but it obviously depends on how many beetles you've got,' Loke said, taking back the bags. 'They're not that big, so it's better if you've got plenty of them. I'm not exactly sure how many I borrowed. I suppose it must have been a few thousand.'

Mina pictured a glass box overflowing with tiny, fat, glistening larvae and full-sized beetles crawling all over each other. In their thousands. She swallowed hard.

'I think we're late for the meeting,' she said, quickly heading to the barriers.

91

Julia was almost inordinately happy to be back at police headquarters already. After returning home from her parents', they had tried to celebrate Christmas on their own too, but that had been a bad idea. They hadn't said a word about the things they actually needed to discuss. After all, it had been Christmas Eve. A time of reconciliation and family harmony. Oh, to hell with reconciliation. The mere sight of Torkel was enough to make her skin crawl.

Nonetheless, they'd done their best for Harry's sake. But as soon as Harry had fallen asleep, Torkel had left the house. Or perhaps Julia had effectively forced him out. She couldn't imagine a whole evening at home with Tinder-Torkel and *Love Actually* on the TV.

But today was better. At least this morning she would be spared her husband and, as a bonus, she would get to see Adam – even if they were together with all the others. She felt like an encyclopaedia illustration depicting 'emotional chaos'.

She looked up from her laptop and saw that everyone had already gathered in the conference room. Out of the corner of her eye, she saw Adam, but she didn't react. Vincent gave her a look that was far too searching from his side of the room, and she dared not be anything but her most formal self.

Christer was in his usual seat and Bosse had, for a change, settled down by his bowl in the corner. On the other side of Peder's empty chair was Ruben, who appeared not to have slept at all. Julia noted that Mina was sitting unusually close to Vincent. Perhaps he had bathed in lemon-scented washing-up liquid or something.

The door opened and Loke entered with an air of mild confusion.

'Hello, I'm sorry I'm late,' he said. 'I went to the loo and then I couldn't find my way back, and it's not like there are many people in the building to ask for directions …'

Vincent smiled broadly at him.

'This is Loke,' Julia said. 'He works with Milda and the National Board of Forensic Medicine, in case that's escaped anyone. I've invited him here today since he's contributed such invaluable knowledge about our victims. He's to be considered an official member of the investigative team from now on.'

'It's an honour to be able to help out,' Loke said, nodding to the others.

He looked around the room uncertainly and then went over towards Christer and Ruben. Loke pulled out the vacant chair between the two of them and sat down. Julia froze and stared at him like everyone else was doing.

Loke was sitting on Peder's chair.

The room collectively held its breath for a few seconds, but nothing happened. The world didn't end. Peder's ghost didn't bring the ceiling crashing down on top of them. The clock on the wall ticked on from 08:59 to 09:00. Life moved on.

'OK, let's get started,' Julia said. 'Since the minister of justice's disappearance may be connected to the deaths we're investigating, the top brass are breathing down our necks. The Security Service is leading the search efforts for the minister, but it's up to us to provide them with all the information we can to make that process easier.'

'How are they connected?' Christer said.

'Very loosely at this stage,' Mina said. 'I spoke to Niklas's father. There are similarities between events in Niklas's past and his behaviour before his disappearance to what we've heard about our other victims. But it's nothing more than that.'

'We can't afford to take any chances,' Julia said. 'That brings me to my first point. Ruben, I've been contacted by NOA. Sara Temeric has been given approval to share all relevant information about the Manojlovic family with you. It's a blessing of sorts that they're looking at Peter Kronlund's family right now. And you're obviously to give her a full briefing on our own work. I suggest you liaise with her once we're done here and see where it goes. If the Manojlovics are involved, then it's of the utmost importance that we find out.'

'I've already spoken to Peter and he denies any involvement,' Ruben said. 'He also denies being aware of the fact that Gustaf was paid by Dragan. But I'll get in touch with Sara and see where it … goes.'

Julia paused. Her eyes were surely deceiving her, but it looked like Ruben was blushing.

'Mina,' she said. 'You got an approximate age on the unidentified bones that suggested they belonged to a forty-year-old male who died around the year 2000. That's a step in the right direction. But I gather the bones have gone missing?'

'Gone missing?' Christer exclaimed. 'What the hell's going on? Why haven't we heard about this?'

Julia quietened him with a gesture.

'There was a break-in at the lab yesterday,' Loke said unhappily, looking down at the table. 'But we'd taken DNA samples from the bones, although we haven't got the results yet. We've only been able to search the police database so far, but we've applied for permission to search the commercial DNA databases too.'

'The what?' said Adam.

'You know, the companies you can send a DNA sample to,' said Vincent. 'And then you find out you're twelve per cent Teuton, have a cousin in Chicago, and that you're related to Genghis Khan. It's a very interesting approach to genealogy, although it does entail some risks. You see, one in twenty-five finds out that their father isn't their actual father.'

'Exactly,' said Loke. 'If there are any relatives in any DNA databases out there, we'll get a match. We just need permission to run those searches.'

Bosse stood up and padded over to Christer, before lying down at his feet. Julia saw that Bosse was wearing a red and green collar with plastic bells attached to it.

'Do we know when the bones were put into the tunnels?' she said.

'The forensic anthropologist's dating couldn't give us an exact time,' Mina said, shaking her head. 'But she said that the moss on the bones was at least twenty years old.'

'We'll have to start from the beginning,' Christer sighed. 'I can check whether there are any relevant incidents in the files from the metro in 2000, if that's the year of death, and onwards. I dare say it'll take the whole of Christmas to get through that amount of material. Lasse's going to kill me.'

'But we'll be eternally grateful,' Julia said. 'We'll send Lasse a Christmas present.'

'Good idea. He likes white chocolate.'

Julia glanced at her own notes on the laptop. She knew that what she was going to ask Mina for wouldn't make her the world's most popular boss. But that couldn't be helped.

'There was something that caught my attention in Mina's recording of your chat with the tunnel dwellers,' Vincent said before she managed to speak. 'I wasn't able to be there myself, but …'

'Exactly – thanks so much for the aversion therapy,' Mina interjected, facing Julia. 'I'm super done with those tunnels.'

'One of the people you met spoke about someone called the King,' Vincent continued.

'That OP guy,' Adam said. 'He was banging on about the murder of Olof Palme and the royal family. If we'd stayed any longer he would probably have moved onto the Freemasons and the Bilderberg group too.'

'I don't think he was referring to our Swedish king,' Vincent said. 'In the recording, he said that this king "sacrificed himself" and "died in vain". I think "the King" was one of them. Someone who died. You're investigating dead people found in metro tunnels, and this may be a death that occurred in a metro tunnel. I'm well aware it's a weak connection and may not turn anything up, but it's worth exploring every angle.'

'Vincent's right,' said Julia. 'I want us to find out who this "king" was – and above all, how and why he died.'

'I think Adam should go back down there,' said Mina. 'After all, he's the expert in negotiations. It's getting pretty expensive for me to throw away all my clothes after every visit to the tunnels.'

'Adam's going to meet the graffiti artist who found Jon's bones,' said Julia. 'He's finally agreed to talk. But Vincent can go down into the tunnels instead. He's a good replacement for

Adam. Of course, he can't go alone since he's not a police officer and they don't know him either, but they know you, Mina.'

'Don't even think about it,' Mina said sternly. 'I've got my hands full investigating whether our victims consulted the same psychologist twenty years ago. I've got lots of interviews to do.'

'And you'll do them,' said Julia. 'Right after you've been back down to the tunnels.'

'Er, I don't know whether I can go either,' Vincent said. 'I think I have to focus my efforts on some hourglasses I've been sent. Tunnels aren't really ... What is it?'

Mina gripped his arm tightly.

'The deal,' she said.

'The deal,' he said gloomily. 'OK, we'll do it.'

'I apologize on behalf of my colleagues,' Julia said, turning to Loke. 'But they're often like this. Anyway, it's great that we've got you here today. If I square it with Milda, would you be willing to join our small team as a more permanent addition? You've got knowledge that I think may continue to be useful to us even beyond this investigation.'

'Of course,' Loke said, smiling weakly. 'It would be an honour.'

'Well then,' Julia said, closing her laptop, 'let's get to work.'

Mina let the others leave the room first. Vincent stayed behind too. She had guessed he would. He had been acting strangely ever since he had come round to her apartment. On several occasions he had been about to say something but had then stopped himself at the last moment. She had never seen him so troubled and distracted before.

Loke was the last to leave. She noticed him glancing at Vincent as he left, but Vincent stayed. Mina closed the door and then turned to face the mentalist.

'So, what is it?' she said, folding her arms. 'Are you angry with me or what? You've been acting weird since yesterday.'

'Am I ...?' Vincent said, his eyes wide. 'No, on the contrary.'

Mina studied him. There was stubble on his chin and cheeks. It wasn't like him to be unshaven. His usually neat hair was also in disarray.

She hesitated for a moment, trying to block out the thoughts about which bacteria might be in that stubble, and then she took his face between her hands. Touching his skin made her fingers feel as if they were buzzing with electricity.

'Vincent,' she said.

He took hold of her hands and let out something that sounded like a combination of a sigh and a sob. His touch made the buzzing feel like a more violent shock. She drew breath.

'It's … I really can't say anything,' Vincent said. 'This has to stay a secret between us. OK?'

He let go of her hands and pulled a crumpled piece of paper out of his pocket.

'This was lying on my kitchen table yesterday morning. I got up to make breakfast but Benjamin wasn't … I found this instead of him.'

'I don't understand,' she said.

'You'd better read it. It's from the same person who has been sending me presents all autumn – presents relating to me and my mother.'

'Your mum? What does your mother have to do with …'

Mina fell silent as she unfolded the sheet of paper and saw what it said.

Merry Christmas Vincent!

We have now finally reached your omega.

You may have figured it out by now, but there's a reason why you can't get hold of Ulrika. Maria and Aston are not at Maria's parents'. And Rebecka never did make it onto her trip. And, as you may have noticed, Benjamin is not at home.

I have them. All of them.

You have lived a whole life in denial, but now it's time for you to realize who you actually are. It's time to stop running and face yourself.

If you choose not to, you will never see your family again.

> You cannot be allowed to assume responsibility for others while you persist in running away from your own.
>
> Either way, Vincent Walder will cease to exist. The only question is whether you intend to take your family with you or not. You have a few days to take responsibility for what you did.
>
> The next move is yours. I'm waiting.
>
> Merry Christmas!
>
> PS If you go to the police then it will be over right away for both you and your family. But you already knew that.

'You've kept this to yourself for more than twenty-four hours?' she exclaimed. 'Vincent! Why didn't you say anything?'

The letter felt warm in her hands – she realized that her blood was beginning to race through her body.

'I can't handle this on my own any more,' Vincent said unsteadily.

'But Vincent – this is kidnapping and criminal threats. We have to act immediately. We'll give you police protection as soon as you leave here. We can have someone posted outside your house around the clock, and as for your family … Don't worry, we'll think of a plan. Do you have any idea who the letter is from?'

'You don't understand,' he said, beginning to pace back and forth across the room.

He was like a trapped animal. Mina was anguished to see him like this, but she didn't know how to make things better.

'It won't help,' he said. 'This letter was lying on my *kitchen table*. That means whoever left it there came into my house the night before last. He – for I believe it to be a he – not only left the letter, he also kidnapped Benjamin. All without me noticing a thing. And that's despite the fact that I was awake for most of the night. I can't think of any explanation other than that he must have keys to my house.'

Vincent stopped moving. He slumped down hard onto the floor, with his back to the wall.

'This is the same person who sent the newspaper cutting to Ruben two and a half years ago,' he said. 'I know it. The one who sent me all sorts of puzzles and riddles in the summer that said I was guilty of something – even though I thought at the time that they were from Nova. This has been in the works for years. Whatever the police could do for me, this person has had a long time to plan their countermoves. And now we've reached some kind of finale. But I don't have any idea who he is or what he wants.'

'I can have a word with the Security Service,' she said. 'And with Julia's dad – the police commissioner. We'll come up with a plan. Right away.'

Vincent shook his head fiercely.

'No. No plan,' he said. 'You can't say a word to anyone. You have to promise. It says "if you go to the police then it will be over right away". I'm taking the threat to my family *very* seriously.'

Mina sank down beside him. She had no idea what to say.

92

Ruben went around to Sara's without calling ahead. It had been a late night for her kids the evening before, and even later for him and Sara, so he guessed they would still be at home – probably wearing their pyjamas. He didn't really want to intrude on their family time with a work matter, but he didn't have much choice. Sara would understand.

He stood outside the terraced house in Sickla and peered through the living-room windows. They'd spent most of the evening on the big blue velvet sofa inside. Nothing had actually happened between them – at least nothing physical. Yet there was so much that *had* happened. He'd had no idea how satisfying it could be simply to talk to someone. They had talked about everything and nothing until well past midnight. It had been better than sex with any twenty-year-old out there.

Nevertheless, he couldn't help wondering: if merely talking to Sara was that exciting, what would it be like to … Nope. Absolutely not. He could not allow his thoughts to wander off in that direction right now.

He walked around the house and was about to ring the doorbell when he heard Sara's voice from inside. It sounded as if she was on the phone. The agitated tone of her voice meant that he could hear every word as if she were by his side.

'How sure are you?' she said from the other side of the door. 'If Manojlovic is involved in abduction then there's a real risk that the individual will be abused or even tortured. We really can't wait long before we act. Where are they right now?'

Ruben stopped with his hand halfway towards the door. Had Peter Manojlovic's family kidnapped someone? At the very same time that the minister of justice had gone missing? It couldn't be a coincidence.

'The industrial area in Tyresö?' Sara said. 'Yes, I know the place. The one on Vindkraftsvägen on the right-hand side before the bend in the road. We've had eyes on it for a long time. How soon can we have the task force there?'

Ruben quietly moved away from the door. He knew exactly what to do. He would be there long before the task force was mobilized. He would be able to scope out the area and provide them with invaluable information once they arrived on the scene. He would be a hero in Sara's eyes.

He jogged back to the car, got in and put his foot down. He would be at that address in Tyresö in ten minutes flat.

93

Mina's anxiety was contagious. To Christer, the minister of justice was no more than a serious man on the television who was always going on about crime as if they were in the midst of a blazing war. But to Mina, he was the father of her daughter. Her ex-husband, no matter how odd that thought was.

Christer pushed away the thoughts of Mina. No job was ever made better by personal emotions getting in the way. Nor had he been tasked with finding Niklas. His job was to keep searching for something that might help them in the hunt for the killer who left the bones of their victims in Stockholm's metro tunnels.

Having the screen in front of him always provided a sense of security. He was increasingly reluctant to work in the field. On the one hand, he felt a little hurt when he wasn't asked, but on the other, it had become far more appealing to search for needles in haystacks through the thousands upon thousands of pages in the DurTvå database. Not infrequently, crimes were solved at a desk. He would be the first to attest to that.

Christer entered the year 2000 into the search field and pulled up far too many hits from the archived police reports. He refined the search by limiting it to reports that were related to the metro. There were far fewer hits, but it was still a considerable number. The Stockholm metro generated reports on a daily basis relating to robberies, threats, unconscious people and all manner of other issues.

In his early years on the force, he'd often patrolled the metro, and he had hated every minute of it.

After an hour's searching, he still hadn't found anything that seemed relevant. His work was made more difficult by the fact that he didn't know exactly what he was looking for.

A man had died around the year 2000 and his bones had

been found some twenty years later in the tunnel. That didn't have to mean that something had happened to him there. The bones might simply have been moved there. Christer might be searching for something that couldn't be found. But he was used to that. The reward for his toil – the gold at the end of the rainbow – was the fluttering feeling of delight in his stomach when, from time to time and against all the odds, he found something decisive.

There was a slight breeze on his neck. The winter chill had made its way inside police headquarters. He stood up to do some exercises that he had learned to relax his neck and back. It was something that Lasse had made him take up. Christer had reluctantly been forced to admit that Lasse was right – the exercises did make it easier to cope with the endless hours spent sitting.

He glanced at the desk next to his, where a female colleague from another department had built some kind of Christmas orgy out of ornaments. Santas, trees ... there was even a reindeer. Merry bloody Christmas. After glancing over his shoulder and concluding that his colleague wasn't around, he picked up two of the Santas and positioned them doggy style. After all, they needed to have fun too.

Chuckling, he sat back down and resumed his search. Time passed. Just as the letters were beginning to dance before his eyes on the screen and he was considering whether to get another coffee, he saw something that made him focus. He pulled out his phone and dialled the number in the report. It was two decades old, but if he was lucky the man he was trying to reach wouldn't have changed numbers. Most people didn't.

'Bengt Svensson,' said a raspy voice that clearly belonged to an elderly man.

Christer silently crossed himself. He had reached the right person. Now he just hoped there wasn't any dementia to deal with. By his own calculations, Bengt Svensson would be in his eighties by now.

'This is Christer Bengtsson from Stockholm Police. I'm calling you about a case from the year 2000.'

'Oh my. Well, you do hear that the police are short-staffed

these days, but this must be some kind of record,' Bengt said with a chuckle.

Christer declined to comment. The police and their staffing resources was rarely a fruitful conversation on which to embark.

'Do you remember anything about the incident?' Christer asked carefully.

Bengt snorted.

'You think I'm cuckoo, don't you? I can tell you that my memory is just as razor sharp now as it was when I was a lad.'

'Wonderful,' Christer said apologetically. 'Would you please tell me what you remember?'

'Of course. I was driving on the green line in the afternoon; I think it must have been around two o'clock since it was just ahead of the afternoon rush. But at the time my train was only half-full. It wasn't packed like it is from three onwards. I was somewhere between Rådmansgatan and Odenplan. He was just standing there on the tracks. Arms outstretched like he was bloody Christ himself. And then we hit him.'

'What happened next?' Christer said, feeling his heart pounding harder.

All his instincts as a detective were screaming at him that this was important.

'Well, I followed protocol. Called control. Didn't move the train. I suppose it was ten minutes before people arrived. But that was when it got strange.'

'Yes?' Christer said urgently, even though he already knew what Bengt was going to say.

It was right there on the screen in front of him.

'They didn't find a body. There was blood on the front of the train and blood on the tracks where I must have hit the poor bastard. But no body. Nowhere between the point of impact and where I stopped. It was gone. Vanished into thin air.'

'What was your theory?'

'They reckoned I couldn't have hit him that hard – he'd probably only been slightly injured and then limped away. They assumed it was one of the tunnel people – it might sound horrible, but no one was all that fussed about them. No one bothered to make any further enquiries.'

'But you don't think it's true that he left under his own steam?'

Bengt snorted again.

'I'd already done twenty-five years as a driver by then. I'd had my fair share of blighters deciding to end it all in front of a train doing 80 kilometres an hour. I know what it sounds like when the train hits a body head on. And I know what happens to that body. It ain't pretty. There's no way he survived. Someone or someones must have taken away what was left of him in the time it took for the emergency services to arrive.'

'Why would anyone want to do that?'

'Well, no one knows, and no one was that interested in finding out either. Why do you ask? How come the police are taking this sudden interest more than twenty years later?'

'I'm afraid I can't say,' Christer said.

Out of the corner of his eye, he saw his Christmas-loving colleague approaching her desk clutching a cup of coffee.

'You said you saw the man on the tracks?' he said. 'Can you describe him?'

'We're talking about a fraction of a second. And my memory will have been fresher at the time. You can probably get more out of the report.'

'I'm interested in what you remember now,' Christer said, stifling a chuckle as his colleague sat down without noticing the copulating mini Santas.

'Well ...'

Bengt strung out his words and really did seem to be searching his memory.

'I suppose I've thought about this sometimes ... over the years. And what I remember is that he seemed to be a big man. Hefty chap. But it might have been an illusion. Things are easily distorted at speed and by the headlights in the dark tunnels. But my feeling is, he was a big man. I'm seeing dark hair. Bushy. And a beard too. And ... you've really got to take this with a pinch of salt. It sounded weird when I said it back then and it sounds even weirder now. But I thought there was something shiny on his head. Gold, maybe.'

'Shiny?' Christer said thoughtfully.

Bengt was silent.

'Promise me you'll let me know if you solve this,' the train driver said. 'I've thought about it so often over the years. I didn't encounter many mysteries in my years on the metro, but I've never been able to stop wondering about this one.'

'I'll do my best,' Christer said, ending the call after wishing the man a merry Christmas and a happy new year.

He leaned back and clasped his hands behind his neck. His colleague still hadn't spotted the improper activity taking place on her desk.

94

'Are you OK?'

Vincent gave her a pensive look. Mina shrugged nonchalantly. She always found it difficult to talk about her daily struggles, even with Vincent. And now that he had confided in her about his missing family, and with Niklas missing too, it felt too trivial to talk about her own manias. Besides, she had spent her whole adult life trying to hide them away. Now she was fully focused on coping with another visit to the tunnels.

'There's a difference between my personal and professional lives,' she said. 'I've always known that I can't let my brain play the same pranks on me at work that it does when I'm ... just being me. I wouldn't be able to keep working as a police officer. And I love my job too much to let that happen.'

Vincent looked at her with respect in his eyes.

'And how about you?' she said.

Vincent was struggling to put on a big pair of boots. They looked utterly ridiculous in combination with his otherwise elegant attire.

'If I can just get these on ...' he murmured.

'You don't own a pair of jeans and a T-shirt?' she said, surveying his pressed trousers and neatly ironed shirt.

'No sensible person wears jeans,' said Vincent. 'They discovered back in 2009 that denim contains high levels of toxins like lead and mercury, as well as other highly allergenic substances. Why would I wrap my body in that?'

Mina shook her head.

'Forget about it,' she said. 'I was actually wondering how you're feeling, given ... everything.'

'I'm trying to think about it as little as possible right now,' Vincent said, stamping his feet to get his boots in place. 'We're here because Christer found a report that's probably about the King. Apparently he got hit by a train. Julia won't let us out of the tunnels until we can bring her more information, so it's probably best that we get on with it.'

They walked next to each other towards the entrance to the tunnels, each clutching a torch in their hand. As soon as they stepped onto the rubbish and dirt on the ground, Mina felt her heart begin to beat faster. She cast an eye at Vincent.

'How's the claustrophobia?' she said.

'Probably doing just as well as your fear of bacteria,' he said.

Neither of them was in their element in this setting, but each would have to handle their own demons for the time being.

There were two tunnel openings, and Mina pondered which to choose as she read the graffiti on the wall, including *Fuck your mum* and *Die bastard*. She considered whether to add *Carpe diem* as a counterweight, but refrained. There was nothing about this environment that inspired upbeat sayings.

'The one on the left,' she said at last, pointing at a tunnel that seemed to lead into eternal darkness.

'How charming,' Vincent said in a strained tone.

Mina gave him a gently encouraging nudge to his upper arm. Her sense of mild superiority over Vincent and his phobia quickly disappeared the moment she felt something briskly scuttling across her boot. The tunnel echoed as she screamed and she almost dropped the bag from the bakery that she was carrying.

'Rat,' Vincent said, pointing the beam of his torch at an incredibly large rodent running along the left-hand tunnel.

'Aha, and here I was thinking it might be a Jack Russell,' Mina said tersely. 'Or a Siamese. Come on. Let's keep going. Standing here just stresses me out.'

Her gait far more determined than she felt, she took the lead and headed into the darkness of the tunnel.

'You know that paint you gave me?' she said.

'Yes? Have you used it?'

'Are you out of your mind? But what was that word? The Latin for shadow? It feels like it would be a good fit for these tunnels.'

'Umber,' he said. 'The darkest shadow.'

She nodded, tasting the word.

'Umber. It's beautiful.'

Vincent nodded too.

'It's actually one of my favourite words,' he said.

As they moved further in, their eyes adjusted to the dark. Just like last time, there were occasional lights on the ceiling, which meant they could see more than just what their torches illuminated. Mina felt her heart pounding in her chest and when she looked towards Vincent his face looked paler than usual. Which was saying something.

'Just how far in are they?' Vincent said faintly.

Mina put a gloved hand on his shoulder. It was unusual for her to be the one who was more calm and collected.

'If I remember correctly, they're just around this corner.'

She pointed with her torch. A hard metallic sound cut through the air and made them jump.

'Hello?' Mina called out, and heard her own voice bounce back between the walls. 'Hello! We're from the police. You talked to me the other day. My name's Mina. We just want to ask a few more questions. OK?'

No reply. They continued to move forward slowly while watching where they put their feet. Neither of them was keen to have a broken bottle or needle go straight through their sole.

'Hello?' she called out again, this time a little more softly.

She saw a faint flicker of light ahead of them. It was a warm glow – as if it came from a fire rather than electric lighting.

'We're over here,' said a friendly female voice.

Mina recognized it as Vivian's. Suddenly there was a big figure in front of them and she had to master herself not to scream again. It was Johnny, Vivian's son, and he was beaming at them.

'You came back,' he said cheerfully. Mina nodded. 'Did you bring buns?'

'Yes, I came back,' said Mina, handing the bag of cinnamon buns to Johnny. 'And I've brought a friend. This is Vincent.'

Johnny hooted with joy as he took the bag. Then he proffered his other big fist, took Vincent's hand in his and eagerly pumped it.

'Come on.'

He spun on his heel and led them towards the glow of the fire.

Nothing seemed to have changed since the last time that Mina was here. In addition to Johnny and Vivian, Kjelle, Natasa and OP were gathered around the fire.

'Is this about Palme? Have you come to arrest me for the murder?' OP muttered as he stood up, his gaze suspicious.

Mina shook her head.

'No, no, we're still not interested in talking about the Palme murder.'

OP didn't look as though he fully believed her, but he seemed to settle for the answer and sat down by the fire again.

'Come on, sit down.'

Vivian extended her hands towards them as if she were the hostess at an elegant dinner, before gesturing them towards sheets of cardboard.

Mina noted that Vincent was watching her with wide eyes as she sat down on one of the dirty pieces of card without batting an eyelid. She felt happy and a little proud being able to demonstrate some of the strength that she knew she possessed somewhere, deep down.

'I recognize you,' Natasa said morosely, pointing to Vincent, who looked decidedly out of place in his tailored trousers and shirt.

His white shirt had already acquired several stains and the smoke from the fire looked like it was consciously being drawn towards the white fabric.

'Where would you recognize him from? You don't hang out with posh geezers like him,' Kjelle snorted, glaring at Vincent.

'He's the guy off the posters up there.'

Everyone looked at Vincent in concentrated silence. Then Vivian clapped her hands.

'Yes! Now I know what you mean! He does those … shows, right?'

'I am your humble servant,' Vincent said, smiling.

Kjelle snorted again.

'What's a celeb doing down here?'

'I sometimes assist the police with their enquiries,' Vincent said self-consciously. 'Including one they're working on at the moment.'

'The one with the bones?' OP said. 'Are you sure it's not connected to the Palme murder? The government is still covering it up. There are so many supposed accidents and murders happening to cover up the truth about what happened at the corner of Sveavägen and Tunnelgatan at 11.21 p.m. on 28th February 1986.'

'The most likely scenario is actually that Christer Pettersson ...'

Mina elbowed Vincent in the side, and he stopped. This was not the time to embark on a lengthy discussion about the Palme murder and its many mysteries.

'We need your help to find out more. The killer seems to have a connection to the metro, but no, we don't think it's any of you,' said Mina. 'However, we would like to hear more about the man you mentioned – the one you called the King.'

'"Cos I'm the king, king, king in the bar ..."' Johnny began to sing happily while Natasa giggled.

'You were barely born when the King was here,' she said, laughing.

Natasa got a stern look from Vivian, who, after adding more wood to the fire, appeared to be considering what to say. Or *whether* to say anything at all. They let her ponder.

Mina was unsure how much any of them really knew or could tell. The question was whether any information or knowledge about the King had lived on, here in the darkness.

'I knew him,' said Vivian. 'OP knew him too. And then there was Crazy-Tom, obviously.'

Mina sat up straighter on her piece of cardboard. Something small – not as big as a rat – strolled past at the edge of the light and she had to make an effort not to scream and get to her feet. She didn't want to disrupt the fragile trust she felt she had built up with the group.

'You knew him?' she said carefully.

Johnny continued to hum along to Magnus Uggla, while Natasa watched Vincent with undisguised curiosity.

'Who was he?' said Mina.

OP furrowed his brow as if he didn't understand the question. 'He was the King. What do you mean?'

'Didn't he have a name? You don't know what he was called?'

Vincent blinked in reaction to the smoke, which seemed to be having a love affair with his white shirt.

'We didn't have any names. That was the King's idea. We all left our names up there. We left our selves up top. It was me, Vivian, Crazy-Tom, Svala, Knivas, Järven and Bisse. Everyone apart from me and Vivian's dead now.'

'You have no idea who he was or where he came from?' Vincent said, coughing gently.

'No,' OP said. 'Aren't you listening to me? We left our selves up top.'

'Tell us what he was like,' Mina said softly.

She could see out of the corner of her eye that Vincent was listening intently.

'Oh, the King was incredible,' OP said, his voice filled with equal parts sorrow and admiration. 'He always knew what we should do. And he knew everything. Especially about history. There wasn't anything about history he didn't know. Years, wars, castles, princes and princesses, Sweden, China, America. You could ask him about anything and he had an answer. And he was happy. Always happy and positive. Except … when he wasn't …'

'What do you mean by that?'

Vincent seemed untroubled by the fact that his shirt, just like his face, was now covered in soot.

'"There's no one who can bring you down. Cos you're king, king, king of the bar. That's something that you really know. On the twenty-fifth it hits!"'

Johnny was really belting out the Magnus Uggla song, which created a rather strange association with nights spent in bars in the days before she'd met Niklas.

Mina jumped. She had managed to repress thoughts of Niklas for a while, but now they returned with full force. She should have been looking for him right then, instead of sitting here talking about someone who had lived in the tunnels decades ago.

'The King became …' Vivian said, appearing to search for the right words. 'Sometimes he wasn't happy. But he never wanted to trouble us with that. So when he felt the happiness disappearing, he would disappear for a while too. I don't know where he went.

Then, when he was happier again, he came back. And the rest of us all pitched in with looking after the Prince.'

'The Prince?' Mina said uncertainly.

Vincent opened his mouth to say something, but she held up a finger to stop him. This was new information and she didn't want to mess up the chance to find out more.

'Who was the Prince?' she asked.

OP rolled his eyes. Natasa and Johnny laughed, but stopped after Vivian gave them a look.

'What's a prince? A prince is, per definition, the son of a king,' OP said, sneering at their stupid question.

'The King had a son?' Mina said. 'Is that what you're saying? A boy? How old?'

Deep creases appeared in OP's forehead. Vivian began to talk, but OP shushed her.

'I know this,' he said.

'How tall?' Vincent asked. 'How tall was the Prince?'

OP brightened up. He pointed towards part of the tunnel wall.

'There. You can see there.'

Mina quickly got to her feet. She shone the torch against the graffiti-covered wall, helping the firelight. There it was. A line of dashes. The ones that were often found on door frames. Lines drawn on to mark the height of a child. She stood next to it to compare the top line with her own height. The top line was the same height as her chest. She was 165 centimetres. What did that mean … 130 or perhaps 140 centimetres? Like an eight- or nine-year-old, she guessed.

'Last time you said that the King didn't want to die, but that the darkness eventually took over. So did he die? What happened to the Prince?'

After a moment's hesitation, Vivian replied.

'The Prince went topside. The King had left instructions. I don't know any more than that. We never saw him again. He … A child … A little boy didn't belong down here. But that was such a long time ago now.'

The fire crackled. None of them said anything. But Mina couldn't help thinking about the child who had lived down here in the dark.

95

Adam took a step back to see what Akai was painting. Or more accurately, spraying. Or whatever they called it.

It had surprised him to discover that they were about the same age. In Adam's world, only teenagers did this sort of thing. On the other hand, Akai's work on the wall was rather more than what would have been expected from an angry and frustrated fifteen-year-old who just wanted to destroy public property.

When you stood close to the grey concrete wall, all that was visible were seemingly random orange stripes, clearly painted using cut-out stencils. It almost looked like abstract art.

But if you stepped back two metres then it suddenly transformed into a vivid image of a lion.

'I'm impressed,' Adam said.

'Thanks. The lion's my spirit animal.'

'Cool. I think I was born in the year of the rat or something.'

The tall, pale man smiled.

'It's not quite the same thing.'

'I guess not. So why do you do it? Spraying in public places and risking hassle from the police? You can paint, why …'

'Why don't I paint properly?'

Akai adjusted his knitted blue hat and pointed at the lion on the wall.

'Because of this. Because of the freedom. Because of the ability to create without having to live up to the demands of the establishment. I've done all that. If only you knew where some of my other art is on display. But doing that killed me on the inside. For each expensive painting I sold to a bored, wealthy person looking for something "nice" to hang on their wall to go with their sofa, I died a little bit more. This way I'm free.'

'But how … I know this may seem rude, but how do you support yourself?'

Akai screwed up his eyes, which sparkled above his bushy beard.

'In case it wasn't clear, I sold my paintings for a lot of money. And I live cheaply. If I keep doing that, I can live on my savings for the rest of my life. I suppose I'll just have to do another show if I'm in a real pinch. There might not be much lobster and champagne, but who needs that when you've got this?'

He inhaled deeply and closed his eyes. Then he slowly exhaled, seemingly harmoniously.

Adam was reluctantly fascinated by Akai's outlook on life. Was it really that simple? Lower the demands, jump off the consumption bandwagon, do what you really wanted to do and enjoy the freedom …

'Why do you paint in the tunnels then? No one can see them in there.'

Akai continued to spray on the wall as he replied, adding more and more detail to what Adam now realized was the lion's mane.

'Oh no. People do see. I think the people who live down here also need a little beauty. Life has been hard on them, but they're good folk. And whatever you think, they don't have a bad life. They have each other. They're a family. And they accept me. Have you seen the wall painting I did of them?'

Adam shook his head.

'No, where is it?'

'Over here. Come with me.'

Akai led him eagerly down towards the culvert near the metro station. Adam followed curiously. There was something about Akai's art that drew him in.

'Here!' Akai said, pointing proudly at a concrete wall looming above them. Adam's jaw dropped. The painting was incredibly beautiful in its simplicity. With a few strokes, Akai had caught the people just as he had seen them, gathered around a fire. Someone had destroyed a small part of the artwork, but it had mostly been left untouched.

'Incredible,' Adam said, and he meant it.

Akai's eyes lit up and he pointed at the wall with the canister. His hand was stained orange with paint.

'You can't hang this on a wall,' he said. 'And that's the whole point. It's an experience. Here. Now. Everyone can experience it. It doesn't cost anything to look at it. You don't need an invitation. It's art and it's free. For everyone. Just the way art was supposed to be.'

'I could talk to you about art all day,' Adam said, unable to tear his gaze away from the picture. 'But I've got a job to do. On your outings into the tunnels, have you seen anything that might help us? Perhaps you've heard something from one of the people living down here? Maybe about the bones you found?'

Akai gazed at the family portrait on the wall as he thought. Then he shook his head slowly.

'I would help you if I could. I don't believe in hiding the truth. That's not how I live. But no, I don't actually know anything. On the other hand, I haven't asked. There are some things you don't talk about here.'

'OK, thank you anyway,' Adam said, trying to disguise his disappointment.

Another dead end. But at least he'd had a chance to see Akai's art. He wouldn't forget about that in a hurry. He glanced at Akai questioningly as he raised his phone towards the wall.

'Do you mind if I take a picture?'

Akai responded by holding out his hands and grinning.

'Go for it,' he said. 'That's one of the things that's so great about what I do. You can't take my art with you, but you can. Take as many pictures as you want. Art is free.'

Adam nodded in gratitude and took a few photos.

As he headed back towards the metro station, he saw that Akai was on his way back to the wall with the lion on it. Adam wondered what it would look like when it was done.

96

Mina and Vincent inhaled deep breaths, savouring them. Compared to the dusty air down in the tunnels, the wintry Stockholm air felt fresh and breezy. For a moment, Mina could ignore all the dirt and exhaust particles it doubtless contained.

Vincent went over to a bin and threw away the wet wipes she had given him to wipe the soot off his face. They had considered taking the metro all the way back to police headquarters, but had decided to walk instead. It wasn't all that far, and Vincent said that he thought better when he was exercising at the same time. She suspected that remaining in the tunnels would also have been very unappealing to him, even if they had got on a train instead. Frankly, she agreed.

'How bad did it get?' Mina said, glancing at him. 'Did you have to start counting prime numbers?'

'The tunnels were actually bigger than I expected,' he said. 'The claustrophobia wasn't all that bad – I managed to keep it in check. The interesting conversation helped in its own way too. But I won't be rushing down there again any time soon.'

Mina laughed and her breath made smoke in the air.

'Interesting conversation,' she said. 'Typical of you to put it like that. What did you take from that interesting conversation? Is there anything I might have missed?'

A man came walking towards them along the pavement with seven dogs on leads that were all attached to a belt around his waist. The passage between the shovelled heaps of snow on the pavement was far too narrow for them all, so she and Vincent quickly moved aside. He took her hand and they jumped across a dyke of snow and into the road so that the dogs could pass. Mina swore silently to herself. They ought to prohibit dogs in the city. Actually, they ought to prohibit dog *owners* in the city.

As they were passing, two of the dogs stopped to urinate against a lamp post.

'I was thinking about something Natasa said in passing,' Vincent said, once the dogs had moved on. 'She commented that Johnny had barely been born when the King died.'

Mina nodded. She realized that she was still holding Vincent's hand. It felt so natural, but now that she had become conscious of it she felt embarrassed, so she let go and climbed back over the heap of snow and onto the pavement.

'I do remember her saying words to that effect,' she said. 'What of it?'

'How old would you say Johnny is?'

Mina pondered that. Johnny really was an unusual man. He seemed to harbour so many different ages simultaneously.

'Hard to say what's behind all the dirt and the beard,' she said. 'But he's probably about … twenty-five?'

Vincent nodded.

'I think so too. But let's add a bigger margin to that. If the King died about a year after Johnny was born, that means the King died twenty to twenty-five years ago. That would agree with the date of death for the unidentified bones we found in the tunnels. Combine that with the information that Christer dug up about the accident on the metro – the one where the man was hit while wearing something shiny on his head. I'm thinking it was a crown. That would also fit in time terms. If we only had Christer's interview with the retired metro driver to go on then it would be too uncertain. But I'm absolutely convinced that the bones we found belong to the King.'

Mina smiled and looked up at the sky, which had briefly turned clear and blue. A few birds flew past above them. A small piece of the puzzle had fallen into place. She didn't know whether it was important, but it felt as if it was. And Vincent had found it by listening to what had been said in passing, rather than focusing on the parts of the conversation that she had devoted her own attention to. She glanced at the grimy man who was walking by her side and felt a sudden warmth welling up within her. But she tried to focus on the conversation.

'So we think we know who the bones belong to,' she said, 'but we've no idea who the King actually was. We don't know what he was called or where he came from. Or whether he had anything to do with the other victims.'

'There's something else too,' Vincent said. 'The King died just before Erika, Marcus and Jon went through their spells of depression. I'm only speculating here, but what if there is actually a connection between the old bones and what happened two decades later? Might the victims and the King have known each other? Might it even have been his death that triggered those depressive episodes? Normally I wouldn't back such a loose connection, but their remains were all found in the same condition as his.'

Vincent fell silent. He stopped and looked thoughtfully ahead.

'I'd like to retract that last bit,' he said, scratching his face. 'It doesn't feel quite right that they knew each other personally. There's a missing link between them. But I'm pretty sure that Erika, Marcus and Jon were somehow connected to a homeless man who was mowed down by a metro train around the turn of the millennium. A man with a crown. And if that's correct, then the same must be true of your ex-husband.'

Mina looked at him. For the first time, there was something resembling an answer rather than just more questions – and all it had taken was a sooty shirt.

'We've got to find the connection,' she said.

97

The coffee was out of the question – he only drank coffee made from real beans and prepared by a trained barista. The coffee in the ministry had always been left to stew in the pot for far too long and was not a substance with which he intended to sully his taste buds. It would have to be a cup of tea instead. And most definitely not one made with one of those tragic teabags paid for by the taxpayer. It would have to be made using his secret tin of Ceylon tea leaves. He also kept a jar of honey in the small compartment where he stashed his tea. The plastic squeezy bottle of honey for general use wasn't worthy of the name.

'Tor, the prime minister is on the line, asking for you.'

One of the younger assistants had run into the break room, sounding a little short of breath. Tor stopped with the teaspoon halfway to his cup, still laden with honey.

'Tell her I'll call her back in five minutes' time,' he said. He intended to make his tea in accordance with the rules of the art.

'But, but, but … it's the prime minister! Don't you want to take it now?'

The assistant's face was bright red with stress and, for a moment, Tor felt a twinge of sympathy. This assistant wouldn't last long in the government offices with such a low level of stress tolerance.

'I said, I'll call her in five minutes,' he repeated, his voice a little steelier this time.

The assistant grasped the message and disappeared as quickly as he had arrived. Tor sipped from his cup. Perfect. Absolutely perfect.

Without rushing, he walked down the corridor back to his office. He didn't want to spill the tea; honey would only make his hands sticky, and if there was one thing he hated it was sticky hands.

He carefully set the cup down on his desk, but not until he had put a coaster out first. The desk had been in the government offices for an eternity, and he was not going to be the one to leave rings on it.

He checked that everything on the desk was straight, drank a few sips of the hot tea, and then reached for the phone. His calm exterior didn't quite match what he felt as he placed the call. What did the prime minister want from him? He realized that it must be to do with Niklas's disappearance – there was no other issue that trumped it in terms of significance. But from what point of view? Anger? Support? New information?

The prime minister's private secretary answered, as he always did, but Tor was put straight through, as his call was expected.

He and the prime minister had known each other for many years. Their political careers had tracked one another, crossing paths, and occasionally even colliding ever since their days in the youth party. Prime Minister Hjortén had even taken him to one side and asked – with unexpected consideration – whether he really wanted to step back and serve as press secretary to the minister of justice instead of continuing to pursue other, higher profile pathways.

He had assured her that he knew what he was doing. Tor always had a plan. Nothing happened by chance, and accepting what might upon first glance seem a foolhardy offer in career terms had its reasons. As his father had always said.

'Hi Anna, it's Tor. You called?'

'Hello Tor. No news yet?'

Prime Minister Anna Hjortén's voice sounded harried and he could only imagine the pressure she was facing from every direction.

'No, no news,' he said, well aware that she was grasping for the tiniest of straws.

But what would he know that she hadn't already heard, given that the majority of the Swedish police and the Security Service were under her command?

'We've got to solve this,' she said. 'We have to find him. The assorted media and governments of the world are watching. We'll look like a banana republic if our minister of justice turns up murdered.'

'There's no reason to believe the worst,' Tor said soothingly. 'No one has been found dead yet.'

He concealed his own concern about Niklas's disappearance. The prime minister would not benefit from him telling her about his own personal emotions. The most important thing was to remain calm and controlled.

'What can I do for you?' he said.

He knew from experience that the prime minister could be long-winded.

'I want you to talk to *Expressen*,' she said. 'I'm sure you've seen their series of articles "Powers Behind the Throne", where they interview people in the corridors of power who the general public might not be aware of. I've asked my press secretary to speak to them about using you for their next interview.'

'With respect, Anna,' Tor said, 'is that really the right thing to focus on? All my time at present is being spent on the search for Niklas.'

'Exactly,' the prime minister said. 'And that is precisely what I want you to talk about. *We* need to own the narrative of Niklas's disappearance. Not the media. We need to show that the Ministry of Justice is strong. So you need to show yourself as resourceful and the ministry's strong outward face. Besides, it wouldn't do you any harm to get a spot of personal attention would it? Everyone knows you climbed down a couple of rungs when you took on the job. Mind you, you did a good job at this morning's press conference.'

Tor sighed in response.

'But strictly *entre nous*,' the prime minister continued, 'how was Niklas when you last saw him? Are we dealing with – I don't know – burn out? An existential crisis? PTSD from what happened last summer? Or just a plain old midlife crisis?'

'Niklas was in splendid form before Christmas,' Tor said drily. 'Physically and mentally.'

'I don't know whether to feel reassured or even more troubled by that,' Anna said. 'Anyway – *Expressen*?'

As a press secretary, he understood what she was getting at. It was absolutely the right thing to do at this time. He took a sip of the tea, which had begun to cool down.

'Sure,' he said. 'I'll do the interview.'

'Good. It's scheduled for tomorrow.'

After he'd ended the call, he went to make a fresh cup of tea. He hated cold tea.

98

Vincent was sitting with his elbows on the kitchen table and his head in his hands. He would have preferred not to go home after visiting the tunnels, but Mina had needed to go home to take a shower as usual. They had parted ways in the police headquarters basement car park. He couldn't very well have asked to go with her. He stank of smoke, and he really needed to change his clothes. Still … he just wanted to be with her.

Instead, he was sitting in his kitchen. It was the only place in the house where he could be, except for the bedroom. He hadn't gone into the living room since the day before. The headaches were at their worst in there, and he wanted to avoid the big wall. He was well aware how irrational it was to be afraid of a wall, but that didn't matter. Anyway, there wasn't anyone left in the house to notice.

The emptiness was almost physical. The echo of Aston's shouts and Maria's scolding were still embedded in the walls. The sofa in front of the TV was still a little flatter in the spot where Rebecka always liked to sit. If he made an effort, he could practically hear Benjamin going on about share prices. But they were all no more than echoes. They were like ghosts in his brain reminding him that no one was actually there.

Which reminded him that the Shadow had his family.

He rubbed his chin.

Thoughts like that didn't help. He didn't know what the Shadow wanted from him in tangible terms, and until he found out, he would have to stay active. Right now, his greatest enemy was apathy.

He tried to focus on the things he had scattered across the table in front of him. There were notes from the encounter they'd just had in the tunnels, and copies of the other documents in the investigation. He'd been permitted to borrow them on the condition that he didn't tell anyone – as if there was anyone in the house he *could* tell.

The frame containing the four hourglasses stood among the papers. At the bottom of the frame there was a strip of tape on which he had written underneath each hourglass how long it took for the sand to run through. Seventeen minutes and thirteen seconds for the first. Thirteen minutes and five seconds for the second. Ten minutes and three seconds for the third, and sixteen minutes and three seconds for the fourth. It was probably only the tally of minutes that mattered, but he had written it all down, just in case.

He had been right that they were all measuring different spans of time, but completely wrong about their relationship to one another. Seventeen, thirteen, ten and sixteen. He had searched high and low, but had been unable to work out what that might be an expression of. And that was where his ideas about the hourglasses had ended.

He could see the aquarium from the corner of his eye.

The mudminnows needed feeding. But perhaps he could feed them without going too far into the living room. After all, physical movement while trying to solve a problem was a good thing – and that was exactly what he was trying to do. Expressions like 'get a new perspective' and 'find a different starting point' weren't just metaphors – they were real problem-solving methods.

He stood up and went over to the aquarium, dispensed a little fish food into his hand and then held it just above the water's surface. As usual, the mudminnows swam up and ate from his hand. Aston had given them names, but Vincent couldn't recall a single one of them right now. He kept looking down into the aquarium all the time, taking care not to look at the wall.

He shifted his gaze towards the table in the kitchen where the hourglasses still stood. He hadn't seen them from this distance or from this precise angle before. Hopefully it might dislodge some idea or other in his head.

Find the fourth one before time runs out, it had said on the note.

When the fish had finished eating, he returned to the kitchen and sat back down at the table.

He wished Mina was there. He could always think better when she was there. But his home wasn't safe for anyone any longer.

The fourth one.

Vincent opened the files containing the documents relating to Jon Langseth, Erika Sävelden and Marcus Eriksson. He already knew what they contained. The three victims hadn't known each other and hadn't shared any mutual friends or colleagues. Only a few similarities had been noted.

He went through them in his head again.

One: the victims had all had meteoric careers.

Two: all of them had hit rock bottom twenty years ago.

Three: they all seemed to be aware that something was going to happen to them immediately before their disappearance.

Four: their remains had been found in different tunnels on the metro network. Jon had been found at Stadshagen on the blue line, Erika at Karlaplan on the red line, and – if Crazy-Tom had been telling the truth – Marcus had been found at Bagarmossen on the green line.

That was it.

Almost.

There were also the King's bones at Odenplan. Perhaps they were the clue that tied all the others together. Or perhaps they weren't.

And somewhere in all of this was Niklas Stockenberg, Mina's missing ex-husband. He matched the first three points applicable to the other victims.

Vincent wanted to throw the files across the room in frustration. It was all so ... woolly. The whole thing.

In addition to the files, he had laid out a map of Stockholm, marked with the locations where the victims had been found. He also had a map of the metro network with the stations in question marked on it. He had tried to find a geographical connection between the stations or places, in the same way he'd done with Nova's chess game in the summer, but that hadn't turned anything up.

Hang on.

He looked at the metro map again.

Marcus's skeleton had been found on the green line. But there was actually more than one green line. The green lines mostly ran along the same stretch, which made them look like the same thing. But at Gullmarplan they split into three branches. With three different line numbers.

It was the same with the red and blue lines. When they left the city centre, they divided into two lines each, both of which were assigned different numbers.

He returned to the reports.

Marcus had been found at Bagarmossen. That placed him on the green line, on line number seventeen. Erika's remains had been found at Karlaplan, the red line, on line number thirteen. And Jon had been at Stadshagen, which was on the blue line, on either line number ten or line number eleven.

Seventeen.

Thirteen.

Ten or eleven.

Vincent looked back at the hourglasses again, and then at the notes of how long it took for the sand in each one to run through.

17 mins (13 secs)
13 mins (5 secs)
10 mins (3 secs)
16 mins (3 secs)

He slapped his forehead. The answer had been right in front of him all along. The minutes for the first three hourglasses all matched the line numbers where the skeletons had been found – in the very order in which the victims had disappeared.

Marcus, 17.

Erika, 13.

Jon, 10.

Vincent swore silently to himself. He should have spotted this long ago. But the line numbers had never been the focus of the investigation – it had been about the stations nearest the finds. That, however, was no excuse. He was the Master Mentalist – this was supposed to be his thing.

The fourth and final hourglass must symbolize *the fourth one*. The older, unidentified bones that probably belonged to the

King had been found at Odenplan. That could be line seventeen or eighteen or nineteen. But the hourglass indicated the line in question was line *sixteen*. That meant the King was not 'the fourth one'. And there were no more heaps of bones in the metro system. They had searched. Therefore, it had to be referring to Niklas Stockenberg. The only question was, where line sixteen was.

He examined the network but couldn't find it. The lines were numbered in ascending order, but after line fourteen – the red line between Mörby and Fruängen – there was a jump in numbering to seventeen, which was the green line between Åkeshov and Skarpnäck. Lines fifteen and sixteen simply didn't feature.

Find the fourth one before time runs out.

The headache began to gnaw away at him again.

The good news was that he knew which metro line Niklas Stockenberg would be found on. And the clue seemed to suggest that they could save his life.

The bad news was: it was a metro line that didn't exist.

99

Ruben drove at a crawl through the industrial estate. Someone had cooked up the ingenious idea of building it in the middle of the forest. Despite the comings and goings in the area, it was the perfect spot if you wanted to stay away from prying eyes. Inside the large industrial and warehouse buildings he was passing, anything could be happening without anyone being aware of it. He pulled onto Vindkraftsvägen. Ruben had taken his own Chevrolet Camaro – which he had secretly christened Ellinor – instead of a police car, to avoid drawing attention to himself.

He quickly spotted which building Sara must have meant. It was on the right-hand side, just before a small car park under some trees. It was the last building on the road before there was a sharp bend to the left. The perfect hideout. He followed the road left and parked not far away before strolling back, trying to look as though he was associated with one of the neighbouring businesses.

The car park on the corner was empty. A metal staircase led up to a loading bay. On the wall beside the goods-in area there was a white sign covered in green writing, but the light above the sign was off and the sign itself looked old. He guessed that the technology company in question hadn't been there for some time.

There was also a door and a small window. He was in luck, since most of the warehouses didn't have any windows at all, but he could already tell from a distance that it was dark on the inside while it was daylight outside. The risk was too great that someone would spot his silhouette if he tried to look through the window. He crept up the stairs and pressed his ear to the wide loading door. It could be hoisted up and down like a garage door, and it didn't seem to be especially thick. There were no sounds to be heard from within.

He needed to know what was in there without being discovered. The question was, how he could pull that off. He looked around and spotted a wooden stick protruding from the snow by the lower edge of the door. He kicked the snow away from around the stick. It must have got stuck when the door had been lowered, creating a small crack between the door and the ground. The crack had then been covered in snow and become invisible. This was exactly what he needed. If Ruben had believed in any higher powers, he would have been thanking them now.

He shovelled the snow away with his hands to allow him to gain access. Then he lay down as quietly as he could and peered through the crack. Beyond the door was a large warehouse space with the roof at least eight metres high. A dozen people could work in there without any problems, but there was no one working right now. The place was deserted. There was no furniture, no shelving, no people. Nothing. Definitely no Niklas.

Sara's sources were wrong.

They weren't there.

Ruben stood up and brushed the snow off himself. Sara's bosses were about to send the task force to the wrong place. He had to figure out where the Manojlovics had taken Niklas, and quickly, so that he could tell Sara where to go. He returned to the car and got into the driver's seat before pausing to think.

The Manojlovics were a big family. They hailed from Södertälje, although not all members of the clan lived there these days. They would hardly be so stupid as to take the minister of justice to their own home. But, he thought, they might take him to someone else's ...

He had a crazy idea. It was a gamble, but it wouldn't do any harm to check. He pulled out his phone and went to check the population register online.

Jackpot. Peter Kronlund – the man who had done everything to hide his past – still owned a second home not far from Södertälje. Ruben started the engine, quickly checked the rear-view mirror, and then floored it as he headed out of the industrial area. It would probably take him half an hour to reach Södertälje. He could still make it there first. He would still be able to help Sara.

100

When Mina emerged from the shower, she found a drowsy Nathalie in the kitchen eating cereal. Mina glanced at the time. It was afternoon. Much of her daughter's Christmas holidays were clearly based on sleeping as long as possible. Although perhaps that was perfectly normal.

Mina really had no idea how the holidays worked. Were they supposed to go away together? Wasn't that the sort of thing people did during the holidays? Not that she had the time for it, since she was in the middle of an investigation. But perhaps she ought to ask, just so she knew for next time.

'Hi sweetie,' she said, entering the kitchen.

'Morning,' Nathalie said through a mouth filled with cereal.

Mina caught a glimpse of them in the hall mirror. Nathalie was wearing a white bathrobe and she had a towel wrapped around her body and another around her hair. If it had been a painting, it could have been called *Mother and Daughter*. She smiled to herself. She also noticed that there wasn't so much as a crumb on the table by Nathalie's bowl. She knew that was utter care and consideration on her daughter's part, and she felt so much love for the girl that she could barely breathe.

'What are your plans for today?' she said.

'I don't have any. Thought I might meet a friend. I've got to do *something*, so that I don't spend all my time worrying about Dad. Maybe listening to someone else's problems is just what I need. Or I might go back to bed again. I'm shattered.'

Mina shook her head. Had she slept that much when she had been sixteen? Probably. And Nathalie had gone through a lot in the last few days.

Her phone rang in the living room. She quickly went to answer it and left Nathalie to her breakfast. Or was it lunch?

'Hi, it's Josephine,' a voice said.

Josephine Langseth. Before Mina had got into the shower, she had sent a text to Josephine saying she wanted to talk. Josephine sounded slightly out of breath.

'Thanks for getting back to me so quickly,' Mina said. 'Are you outside?'

'I'm out for a run. I've got to channel all this anger and disappointment somehow. It was too bloody expensive to do it with champagne. Better for the kids if I head out for a run too. I've stopped for a breather, but I'll be getting going again soon. What did you want?'

Mina turned on the speakerphone so that she could towel her hair dry simultaneously.

'I'll get straight to the point,' she said, massaging her scalp with the towel. 'We gather that Jon had a … mental health slump about twenty years ago. Do you know if he consulted a psychologist at the time?'

There was a few seconds' silence.

'Twenty years ago?' Josephine said. 'I was twelve years old at the time. You'd have to ask his last wife about that.'

'Do you have her number?'

'Sure, I'll send you Carina's number right away,' Josephine said, letting out a rather strange and hoarse laugh. 'Good luck. You may need it. And don't pass on my regards to Gustaf if you speak to him. Got to run.'

Mina hung up and immediately dialled the number that Josephine had sent over.

'Carina Langseth? My name's Mina Dabiri and I'm from the police. I'm calling about Jon.'

'*Now* you call, huh?' said a voice dripping with sarcasm. 'Can't Josephine help you?'

Mina had apparently roused a wasps' nest, although that wasn't always a bad thing. Stirred-up emotions could sometimes shake interesting facts loose.

'Well, I'd like to start by saying how sorry I am for your loss.'

Carina snorted loudly, but Mina ignored this.

'And I have a question about Jon's mental health twenty years ago. In particular, I'd like to know whether he consulted a psychologist at that time?'

Carina laughed hard.

'Jon was a wreck twenty years ago,' she said. 'His parents really did fuck him up good and proper. He'd never got to grips with anything, and to be honest he was pretty much ready to throw himself off a bridge at that point. Literally. With the benefit of hindsight, I should have let him.'

Mina didn't quite know how to reply.

'But ... you're saying he went to see someone?' she said.

'Yes, he went to see someone. But that ended just as abruptly as his depression. All of a sudden he was like a new man. All by himself. It's just a pity that the new man was a complete arsehole.'

Mina went over to the desk and flipped through Beata's address book. She knew the name by heart, but she wanted to be sure. Niklas's psychologist had been called Esbjörn. Esbjörn Andersson. The man who had – for whatever reason – opted to celebrate Christmas in Rwanda of all places.

'Do you know what the psychologist was called?'

'Are you kidding? It was twenty years ago.'

'I understand,' Mina said. 'I assume you don't have any contact details either.'

'Damn right.'

'If you think of anything that seems important, please don't hesitate to give me a call. You'll have my number on your phone now.'

She hoped Carina cared enough to take note, but she doubted she would. Jon had clearly not been Carina Langseth's favourite person.

After Mina had ended the call, she finished drying her hair while thoughts scurried around her brain like rats in a maze. There was something gnawing away at her – something she ought to have cottoned onto. But she couldn't capture the thought. The rat couldn't find the way out.

101

Milda knew she ought to change something about her living situation. She wasn't stupid – she was well aware that she buried herself in her work to avoid dealing with what was going on in her life outside working hours. At the same time, it was a blessing to have a job that she loved going to. The bones case had become something of an obsession for both her and Loke. She knew he had spent just as many hours as she had on trying to solve it, and the theft of the oldest bones felt like a personal loss to both of them.

As if he had read her thoughts, Loke appeared in the doorway. Milda jumped in her chair. He had an ability to move noiselessly, and now he was suddenly there.

'I made the security guys review the CCTV footage one more time,' he said. 'They're pretty sick of me now. But there's nothing. And there's no one recorded going into the building apart from you and me. It's as if a ghost flew in and stole the bones.'

Milda shook her head in frustration.

'I don't get it,' she said. 'How can someone come in, steal the bones, get out, and not be visible at any point?'

'Perhaps we ought to ask Vincent, given he knows everything about magic,' Loke said.

Milda smiled wryly.

'You're just looking for an excuse to hang out with him. There's a bit of a bromance there, isn't there?'

Loke blushed.

'Stop it. I just think it's incredible to be able to talk to someone of Vincent Walder's intellectual stature.'

'Really …?' Milda said with feigned surprise.

Loke laughed.

'So says a woman whose favourite song is "Eloise".'

'What do you know? It might be Vincent's favourite too.'

Milda stifled a laugh when she saw Loke's affronted expression. If she were honest, she didn't think Vincent was all that fond of Arvingarna.

Both of them jumped when her phone rang.

Loke made as if to leave, but Milda picked up and gestured at him to stay.

'Yes? That soon? Well, yes, it is a special case … No, I can't comment on whether there is any connection to the minister's disappearance, no matter what rumours you've heard. But … I can say that it was very much a priority to move this to the top of the agenda.'

She could see that Loke was listening intently.

'Yes? OK? I see … OK. You have my email address. Thank you.'

She could tell from Loke's frustrated expression that he was trying to interpret her answers without any success. She grinned as she hung up.

'You remember we were given access to the commercial genealogy databases?' she said. 'So we could try to find a DNA match for the older bones? Even if it's a bit dodgy from a GDPR point of view …'

She saw the zeal in Loke's eyes.

'Yes, I was hoping that the Family Tree database might turn something up, given that it's so popular in Scandinavia,' he said. 'Was that them?'

'That was one of the others,' she said. 'Ancestry. They found a match.'

Loke looked as if he was about to start jumping up and down on the spot. Milda couldn't resist stringing the answer out to torment her assistant just a little.

'Everything suggests it's a nephew of our guy,' she said. 'So they're close relatives. They've emailed me all the data, but I actually recognized the name they gave me. I just can't quite place it.'

Milda opened the browser on her computer and typed in the name as she was talking. You never knew. Sometimes you got lucky. There was a handful of people in Sweden with the same name as the one she was searching for, but only one matched with the other information she'd been given.

An unfamiliar face was staring at her from the screen. Oddly enough, there was even a Wikipedia entry on the man.

She began to read it aloud to Loke, but quickly stopped. She stared at him and he stared back at her as if he couldn't believe what he'd just heard. She understood exactly how he felt.

'I've got to call Julia,' she said.

'I'm going there now,' Loke said. 'She called a meeting. I can go through the Ancestry documentation with her in person. They'll never believe us otherwise.'

The man on the screen continued to stare at them.

It couldn't be a coincidence.

102

Ruben drove back towards town, taking the motorway. That provided him with better room for manoeuvre among all the hungover Christmas motorists compared to crossing paths with them on the country roads. Ellinor's engine was humming. She was doing her job, carrying him to Södertälje faster than he had dared hope. He considered once or twice whether to call Sara, but decided it was better to wait until he had all the facts. It would probably take NOA at least an hour to coordinate their operation.

Once he'd passed Södertälje, he left the motorway. After a while the narrow country road turned into a snow-covered gravel track. He was back in the woods. His phone satnav said that he was just two kilometres away. He had to crawl along, but this time it was because the road was winding its way between small, snow-covered summer cottages that no one had visited in months. The snow on the track was untouched apart from the single fresh set of tyre tracks he was following. A couple of hundred metres before he reached Peter Kronlund's cabin, he stopped. The other set of tracks continued.

He walked the last bit on foot, the snow crunching beneath his boots. A little further ahead, he saw the tracks leave the road and enter a garden. Ruben entered the woods and made his way forward under cover of the trees. He checked his map again. There was no doubt about it. The tracks led to Peter Kronlund's cabin. When he reached it, he saw a black RAM pickup and a BMW parked outside. They were there. It was time to call Sara. He was about to pull out his phone when he was suddenly struck to the ground. Ruben cried out in surprise and pain.

The phone flew in a wide arc through the air and landed in the snow.

'What the fuck?' he said, spitting snow from his mouth.

He turned onto his back in the snow. There was a man stooping over him, a smile playing across his lips. Ruben recognized him right away. Dragan Manojlovic – the leader of the Serbian mafia. A man legendarily happy to get his hands dirty when necessary.

Dragan was bigger than any man Ruben had ever met. The shit had hit the fan very fast indeed.

'You seem to have dropped something,' Dragan said. 'I'm afraid it's gone now.'

Dragan stamped his foot on the spot where the mobile had landed.

'You do know you're on private property, right? We thank you for not making telephone calls here.'

Dragan looked at him.

Ruben looked back. He was desperate not to appear weak, but didn't dare seem too cocky either. Both were liable to get him into even more trouble.

'What am I thinking?' Dragan said after a few long moments of silence. 'You'll get wet lying there in the snow. Come with me and warm up.'

Ruben stood up slowly. If Dragan knew that Ruben was a police officer then it was already over.

'I really am sorry,' Ruben said, trying to sound like a clueless tourist from Stockholm. 'I was just out for a walk. I suppose I must have tripped. But I'll be fine now. Thanks for your concern.'

The burly man blocked his path.

'I insist,' he said, pointing towards the cabin with a hefty arm.

Ruben had no choice. With Dragan following him, he stepped out of the woods and walked down towards the cabin. Dragan wouldn't let him go – that much was clear. And he couldn't escape either. The slightest misstep would probably mean a bullet in his back. Dragan was notorious for his brutality and his short temper.

Another man emerged from the cabin. Ruben recognized him as Victor Manojlovic – Peter's brother. It seemed the whole family had come together for Christmas.

'Who's this?' said Victor.

'A belated Santa Claus,' said Dragan. 'Let's see what presents he's brought with him.'

Victor held the door open for Ruben.

He hesitated but saw no alternative. Every second that he remained alive was a good second, so he stepped inside and found himself in the living room.

There was plastic sheeting spread across the dining table, and on top of it he saw a hammer, pliers, a knife and a drill. Tools that could be found in any ordinary workshop. The plastic underneath them, however, told Ruben that they were for a completely different purpose. A knot formed in his stomach.

On one of the chairs by the table there was a man. His hands and feet were bound, but he wasn't wearing a gag. The Manojlovics evidently knew that there were no other people nearby, which meant there was no need to worry about silencing the man if he screamed.

But the man wasn't Niklas Stockenberg.

It was Ted Hansson – the leader of the xenophobic Sweden's Future party.

103

'Thank you for coming with me. I needed to get out of the office for a while,' said Mina.

'I always jump at the chance to drink coffee that isn't made on police premises,' Vincent said with a wry smile.

He stood up when the barista called out his name and returned with two paper cups bearing the café's logo with his name added in sloppy handwriting.

'I hope you don't mind that I touched it,' he said, nodding at her cup.

Mina raised it in a toast to him.

'In some strange way I've grown accustomed to your germs.'

'That might be the best compliment I've ever received,' Vincent said, sitting down opposite her.

Dejection enveloped Mina like a wet blanket. Every passing second that Niklas was missing felt like tiny pinpricks all over her body. She hadn't thought that worry could be a physical sensation – not until Nathalie had wound up in trouble the previous summer. Now she felt the same physical anxiety in relation to Nathalie's father. The worry was threatening to paralyse her, but she had to find a way to use that energy to move forward – towards a result and towards finding him. She also knew she had to stop for a while, change environment and have a coffee like this. She also wanted to convince Vincent to change his mind. She took a sip of coffee.

'Have you changed your mind?' she said. 'Please say you have. Tell me that I can call the commissioner and get a plan in place to find your family.'

Vincent looked around in panic.

'Not so loud,' he said. 'We don't know who the Shadow is. He might be here. And no, I haven't changed my mind. No police. Not yet.'

Mina sighed in frustration. She so badly wanted to help him, and it was insane that she wasn't allowed to. It went against every professional instinct she had. At the same time, she understood his reasoning. The Shadow had been crystal clear in the letter about what would happen if the police became involved.

'But ... I actually think I've found another piece of the puzzle,' Vincent said. 'In the investigation, I mean. There's a connection between the location of the heaps of bones and the hourglasses I was sent. You see, hourglasses are about time. An hourglass *is* time. And the riddle was "Find the fourth one before time runs out". That was confusing at first. We had four heaps of bones and we thought we'd worked out who person number four was. But what if the King isn't the fourth one?'

'Well, his bones come from a different era to the other victims – there's a gap of about twenty years,' said Mina.

'Exactly,' Vincent said. 'That gives us three victims and three locations. When I compared how long it took for the sand to run through each hourglass, the number of minutes matched exactly with the numbers on the metro lines where the three victims were found.'

'Metro line numbers?' Mina said, leaning forward with interest. 'And you just came up with that yourself?'

'It's obvious when you think about it,' Vincent said, smiling wryly. 'If we assume the fourth hourglass symbolizes a fourth victim, then it refers to a fourth location on the metro. A fourth line. And that's where he is. Or will be.'

Mina half rose from her chair.

'And you're only saying this now?! Given all the similarities we've identified between Niklas and the other three, he's guaranteed to be the fourth victim.'

'I agree,' said Vincent.

'He might be being held captive somewhere close by right now. Where is it? Which line?'

'That's what's so strange. The fourth location is on a line that doesn't exist.'

Mina opened her mouth incredulously. Then she closed it again and sat back down.

'What do you mean, it doesn't exist?' she said.

'Stockholm's metro is missing two line numbers. Fifteen and sixteen. And "the fourth one" – Niklas – is supposed to be on line sixteen. If we believe the hourglass. But given that the metro has been expanding for more than seventy years, perhaps it's no surprise that the numbering hasn't always been consistent.'

'Perhaps,' she said. 'But I have to tell Julia about this, because it might be the key to the whole thing.'

Then she lowered her voice.

'Have you heard any more?' she said. 'About your family? You haven't thought of some crazy fan who might have taken them? Even if you don't want to involve the police, you can involve me.'

Vincent looked down at the table and pushed his mug away.

'Sometimes I wonder whether I've had a nervous breakdown and imagined the whole thing,' he said. 'And that I'll get home to find them all there. But they're not there. And I still have no idea who has taken them. Or what I have to do.'

The way he looked at her almost broke her heart.

'It's going to be all right?' he said. 'Surely it's going to be all right?'

She placed a hand on his and looked him in the eyes.

'I'm here,' she said. 'I'm with you all the way. As much or as little as you'll let me be.'

It wasn't much of an answer to his question. But any other words of comfort would have been hollow – and they both knew it.

104

It was icy cold inside Peter Kronlund's cabin. Ruben could see his breath when he exhaled, and Ted Hansson on the chair opposite him was shivering with cold. Dragan and Victor hadn't bothered to put on the heating. Fortunately, Ruben had been allowed to keep his coat on after they had emptied his pockets, but he still glanced longingly towards a heap of outdoor clothes in the corner. A scarf wouldn't have gone amiss. They had also tied him to a chair. He tugged gently at the ropes to see whether there was any chance of freeing himself, but he soon gave up. He was well and truly tied down. The knots were far too good.

Ruben had met Ted before, and not in the best of circumstances. On that occasion, Ted had been leading a demonstration in Mynttorget along with Jenny Holmgren, the mother of a child who had disappeared and been murdered in mysterious circumstances. Ruben and Julia had had the pleasure of interrupting the demonstration when they arrived to bring Jenny in for questioning. Ted had become very upset.

He looked much smaller now than he had as a puffed-up demagogue in Mynttorget. Ted was looking down at the floor and appeared to be slipping in and out of consciousness. Ruben desperately hoped that Ted wouldn't remember him – and that if he did, he would be smart enough to keep his mouth shut about Ruben's status as a police officer.

'Where did you find him?' said Victor Manojlovic from the kitchen.

'In the woods,' Dragan said.

'Looks like a cop if you ask me,' said Victor.

'Well, he ain't one of Teddy's mates.'

Teddy. Ted. What on earth did the Manojlovic family want

Ted Hansson for? The man on the other chair was a racist brute, but that didn't mean he deserved to be treated like this.

Ted looked up.

He seemed to perceive the question in Ruben's eyes, because he smiled grimly.

'And people say I'm exaggerating when I say we import criminals,' the party leader said in a low voice. 'Those two don't seem to appreciate my message. Ironically, it turns out I've been right all along. If Sweden's Future were in charge we would have deported their sort long ago.'

Sweden's Future. Ruben sighed. Ted's political party thrived on cultivating uncertainty and fear. It would play right into their hands if it came out that their party leader was being held captive by the Serbian mafia. Whipping up a lynch mob on social media targeting all people of non-Swedish origin wouldn't be difficult after this. It had happened before and innocent people had been hurt. Ruben had to make sure it didn't happen again, but that was a problem for later. First he had to survive.

'Shut up in there!' Victor bellowed from the kitchen.

'I'll go and see if we've got any more of Santa's elves in the woods,' Dragan said, opening the front door.

If possible, it became even colder in the cabin. Ruben saw that Ted's entire body was tensed. His thin jacket was obviously offering him no protection against the cold.

'Hang on, what should we do with the guy in there?' said Victor. 'We can't let him go. But if we kill him it's another body to deal with. I haven't got time for that. Not today. I'm supposed to be picking Milan up soon.'

Dragan closed the door again.

'Maybe we don't need to do anything,' he said. 'We can just leave him behind when we leave. The cold will do the rest. He only has himself to blame for coming here.'

'And Teddy?'

'That bastard has it coming. We'll deal with him as soon as I'm back.'

'I'll go and have a look in the opposite direction,' said Victor. 'That way it'll be quicker. Those two aren't going anywhere.'

The two men went outside and the cabin became silent.

Ted looked at Ruben.

'If you're here to rescue me then I'm afraid you've failed,' he whispered angrily between chattering teeth.

'You're the one who's always going on about police incompetence,' Ruben said sourly. 'So it must be nice to be right for once?'

Dragan and Victor would soon be back. Ruben didn't have long to come up with a plan to ensure that he and Ted survived – but he had no ideas. None at all.

105

She weighed the ballistic helmet in her hands. It had a camera mount on the top, but it was empty at the moment. The last time she'd had anything like it on her head had been a skiing trip to the Rockies. Well, not so much skiing. The kids had been so little they'd gone sledging. But she and her husband had had an amazing week. That had been only a few months before she had moved back to Sweden and it had all fallen apart. It was funny how quickly life could change. But she would introduce Zachary and Leah to the Swedish mountains just as soon as she got the chance.

'Is that the right size?' Wilhelm asked at her side.

'Sorry, I was a million miles away,' Sara said. 'This isn't exactly the Analysis Department, which is where I started when I came back.'

The flying squad van they were inside jolted and she automatically grabbed a handle. At least there were some reflexes still there.

'Surely you didn't think we'd let those paper pushers hang onto you for ever?' Wilhelm said, laughing. 'It's a little overdue, but welcome back.'

'Thanks,' she said, pulling a balaclava over her head. She put on her helmet and checked that her bulletproof vest was properly fitted.

'I know you're the boss,' Wilhelm said, putting on his own helmet. 'But as you just said, you've mostly been working on admin since you got back. So when we go in, I want you to stay at the back. It's been a while. Let the guys at the front do their job.'

'Do you really think we need shields?'

'I don't think anything. But it can't do any harm. We don't know what resistance we're going to encounter.'

The van jolted again. This time Sara managed to maintain her balance without any support.

'At any rate, this is a long way from going skiing,' she said, laughing to herself.

Wilhelm looked at her quizzically and then adjusted his Heckler & Koch MP5.

She looked around at her colleagues in their full gear. She was incredibly proud of them. For the first time since she had left the USA, she felt as if she had come home. This was her place. And the men in the van were what had made that possible. She cleared her throat and the whole squad turned to face her.

'You already know what the situation is,' she said. 'I don't have to tell you that we need to be ready for anything. As Wilhelm just reminded me, we don't know what kind of resistance we'll encounter. We expect them to be armed. What we don't know is whether they'll be stupid enough to try shooting us. So keep your eyes peeled.'

The van stopped.

'We're here,' came a grunt from the driver's seat.

Sara looked around. She made eye contact with each of them to see whether anyone had any questions or had suddenly become nervous. It could happen to anyone – even the most practised. Nerves were natural. The real problem were the people who never got nervous. Over-amped cops were not a good thing. But a nervous officer could pose a safety risk and had to stay behind in the van.

She met nothing but determined pairs of eyes.

Sara nodded in satisfaction.

'Let's take these bastards down,' she said, opening the back doors and jumping out.

Wilhelm meant well, but she was the boss. If he thought she was going to stay in the background he had another think coming.

106

His thoughts kept returning to Sara. His completely idiotic plan to go and reconnoitre Peter Kronlund's cabin had been about playing the hero in front of her. Where Sara was concerned, he always felt acutely aware of his own shortcomings. When he looked at her, it was as if he saw himself in a mirror of truth. He saw his irresponsibility, his vanity and his self-absorption. So he wanted to be a better man for her. And for Astrid. He probably had some catching up to do with Granny too.

Sara made him realize with excruciating lucidity that he had spent most of his adult life chasing the wrong things. Emptiness. He had been chasing emptiness. And now he was stuck in a cold cabin along with a tortured racist who was sobbing with self-pity, and facing a future that probably consisted of an unmarked grave in the woods outside.

He wouldn't be found until the berry and mushroom pickers stumbled upon his skeletal remains after some animal had dug them up. His Camaro would probably be shipped out of the country for parts or to be sold on with fake plates.

Ruben shook his head. Perhaps he ought to devote a little more time to thinking about how to get out of this mess, instead of how Dragan and his henchmen would deal with the practicalities.

'Hey?' he said, lightly tapping Ted with his foot. 'You still there?'

The party leader didn't answer – he just kept crying. A large damp spot had spread across the front of his beige chinos.

Ruben wondered whether Sara would mourn him. It wasn't as if they were a couple. And now they would probably never have the chance to be one, either. He realized that it was something he had been hoping for, more than he had wanted to admit.

But there, in the cabin, with the cold rising from his mouth in clouds and his life hanging by a thread, there was no time for lies. The truth was that he wanted everything with Sara. He wanted the house, the Volvo, the dog. He wanted dinner parties with chat about scandalous house prices and rising interest rates. He wanted to bicker about whose turn it was to put the kids to bed, who was going to do the laundry and who last did the shopping.

He wanted a wedding, with Sara in a white dress, in a church, with a priest. The whole caboodle. Astrid, together with Leah and Zachary, would walk ahead of them into the church, scattering rose petals. There would be a massive party full of relatives they didn't really want to invite. He wanted it all and then some. Just as long as it was with Sara.

There were low voices outside and Ruben screwed his eyes shut. He kicked Ted again – the man appeared to be slipping into unconsciousness. No matter how much he disliked the man, he didn't want him to die right before his very eyes.

There was a scrape and a door creaked. Loud voices. They were back. Ruben caught himself silently praying. A gust of wind swept over his face and he shivered. It was even colder than it had been before.

He wondered how they would kill him – would they really leave him to freeze to death, or would it be a bullet to the head? Other possibilities included suffocating him with a plastic bag over his head, strangulation with a rope, or just breaking his neck. If he had a choice, he would definitely opt for the bullet. That was the quickest and most painless option. Asphyxiation with a bag came at the bottom of the list. He wasn't as claustrophobic as Vincent, but the mere thought of being unable to breathe and slowly suffocating made the panic rise within him.

There was the sound of rapidly moving feet outside the door behind his back. And there was some kind of muffled tumult. What the hell were they playing at? He kicked Ted again – the man grunted without raising his head. The politician was still alive then.

A crash made Ruben start. What the? He hopped around in a semi-circle on his chair to get a view of the door. There were several people barging through it with their weapons drawn, and he could see even more people behind them.

Police uniforms.

They were wearing police uniforms.

Then he saw who had come through the door first.

It was Sara.

She stopped in the middle of the room in the light streaming through the wrecked door. It was the sexiest thing he had ever seen. He was saved. She had saved him.

It was very far from the scenario he had envisioned. He probably looked like the most pathetic man in the world, sitting there helplessly tied to a rickety kitchen chair. His dreams of Sara in a bridal dress slowly began to dissolve and disappear.

Someone used a knife to cut the ropes holding him down. Ruben stood up and massaged his wrists. He didn't dare look Sara in the eyes. Instead he stared down at the floor.

'Secure the cabin and the area outside,' he heard her say to her colleagues. 'Wilhelm, get Ted Hansson out of here. I'll deal with this washed-out specimen.'

Ruben despondently followed her to the door, limping slightly as the circulation had disappeared from his legs and feet. When they passed the bundle of clothes in the corner, he started. Something didn't feel right about the way they were positioned.

'Wait,' he said, kneeling beside them.

He carefully lifted the top-most coat, a dark blue Canada Goose with a fur-lined hood. Underneath the coat, he found the dead eyes of Gustaf Brons staring back at him.

107

He was hungry. And cold. They had been topside searching for food, but the chill meant that people were reluctant to go out, which meant there wasn't much to find. The chill had also found its way down to them. Dad had found a discarded duvet in a skip and given it to him. It kept the very worst of the chill out, but it was still so cold that he was shivering.

There was also something different about Dad. He was quiet. So quiet. Where the words had always flowed, seemingly endlessly, he was now silent. He had tried to get Dad to talk, tried to bring up subjects that he liked. Old Swedish kings. Struggles for territory and power. The assassination of Gustav III. What had happened when a French lieutenant by the name of Bernadotte had been made King of Sweden. He'd heard Dad talk about that kind of thing a thousand times. Always with the same enthusiasm. Now there was none of that left.

He knew that Vivi was worried about him but that she didn't want to show it. But he could still see it. He saw everything. The dark made everything clear.

Dad always lay close to him when it was time to go to sleep – especially now they needed to keep warm. He felt Dad's breathing as his ribs slowly rose and fell. The breathing of sleep. He carefully laid a hand against Dad's back, which was turned towards him. He didn't want to wake him. Dad's sleep had been restless for a long time now. He needed his sleep. The crown lay on Dad's other side, carefully placed on a piece of cardboard. In his sleep, Dad was mumbling Mum's name – over and over again. He had begun to do it more and more often.

The ground shook as a train passed by. It was probably almost empty at this time of night. He wondered what the people on the train would think if they knew how close by they were. People they wouldn't dignify with so much as a glance topside. The invisible ones. That was why they called the people on the trains the 'visible ones'. Because they saw each other – and they saw themselves. Perhaps above all they saw themselves. He didn't want to be one of them. He thrived on invisibility; on floating between dream and reality. Floating in darkness.

As Dad said Mum's name again in a tone of pain, he stroked his back gently. He crawled closer and pulled his duvet over Dad too. With his cheek against Dad's leather jacket, he fell asleep to the sound of the rails singing. Tomorrow, things would probably be better. Tomorrow, Dad would put on his crown and tell them about all the kings who came before him.

Tomorrow.

108

'Have a space blanket.'

Sara leaned over to wrap the foil emergency blanket around him. It was cramped and a little difficult for her to reach him in the back seat of the car, but she did her best. As if he were a child.

Ruben felt his humiliation growing by the second. He was supposed to be the hero. He was supposed to be the one who found Dragan and brought the villain to Sara. She was supposed to have swooned and fallen into his arms. Instead he was sitting here wrapped in foil like a burrito. And he was freezing.

'Thanks,' he muttered, avoiding looking her in the eye.

Damn it, he still thought she was the most gorgeous thing he'd ever seen. Her sumptuous curves, her uniform, and the way she calmly issued orders to the other officers.

Sara seemed to hesitate for a moment. Then she got into the back seat next to him and closed the car door behind her.

'Seriously,' she said, with a look that burned straight through him. 'What are you doing here?'

Ruben swallowed. This was worse than facing the head teacher in high school. He considered a plethora of answers. All of them were better than the truth, but in the end he decided it was just as well he got it over with. It was all over anyway.

'I … I heard you on the phone,' he said. 'About the raid on Dragan. That they had kidnapped someone.'

'When?' Sara said, furrowing her brow. 'And where? At mine?'

'I was o-on my way to see you,' he stammered. 'But then I heard you through the door …'

'And then you thought …?' Sara said, her tone neutral.

This was worse than if she had been barking at him like a watchdog. Her calm was eerie.

'I went there and realized that he wasn't in the place where you were going to strike. So I ... I thought of Peter Kronlund and figured he might have a cabin somewhere. You know how it is. No matter how much he says he's out of the family business, there's no such thing as out. They'll always consider Peter's stuff as their own, and at their disposal. Like a cabin. If they need somewhere to lie low.'

'Smart thinking,' Sara said in that same neutral tone. 'We realized they couldn't be in Tyresö. But it took us much longer to make the other connection.'

Ruben squirmed miserably in the blanket, making it rustle.

'Well, yes ... It turned out I was right. And I only came to observe – to see whether they really were here. Then I was going to get in touch with you and give you the address.'

'But?' said Sara.

Her tone was so neutral she sounded like a robot.

'But they saw me. And they put me in the house with Ted. He's a bloody cry-baby. And why was he there anyway? All he does is talk a load of shit.'

'Ted Hansson has been using the Manojlovics to threaten journalists who have been critical of Sweden's Future,' she said. 'We've been tracking him for some time now – as I told you. But when the time came to pay for their services, Ted played dumb. Denied he'd ever given them a job in the first place. And when he refused to pay ...'

She nodded towards the cabin.

'And Gustaf Brons?'

He fidgeted uneasily at the memory of the dead eyes staring at him from underneath the coat. You never got used to that sort of thing.

'He burned through the cash from Dragan very quickly,' Sara said. 'And then he made the mistake of borrowing more. He's been in hiding since before Christmas, and both we and Manojlovic's guys have been looking for him. But they got the jump on us, thanks to Josephine.'

'Josephine?' Ruben said, his eyes widening.

'We've been tapping her phone in the hope that we might find Gustaf. And she did reveal his hiding place – but she revealed it to Manojlovic. In exchange for a few hundred thousand kronor.'

'Shit. There go all my illusions about true love.'

'I know – and when it all started out so well,' Sara said, smiling ironically. 'I'm afraid they got there before we did. And that brings us here. We have to be grateful there aren't any more people like Gustaf Brons who have to leave in body bags.'

'Sorry,' Ruben said, squirming yet again and making the blanket rustle. 'This was so fucking stupid – I don't even know where to start. I wanted to …'

He steeled himself. Honesty wasn't something that came naturally to him in these situations, but after his brush with death he couldn't stick to his old ways. He didn't dare look Sara in the eyes as he continued.

'I completely threw my judgement out of the window,' he said. 'Because I wanted to impress you. I know I'm a pathetic bastard, so I wanted to show you another side to me. I wanted to make you proud of me. I wanted to be your hero.'

The silence that followed felt loud enough to shatter the car windows. His cheeks felt hot and flushed, and he continued to stare at the headrest in front of him, trying not to turn towards Sara again, no matter how much he wanted to. The rustle of the blanket would only compound his misery. Cool guys didn't rustle.

Finally, he dared to turn his head and look at her. What he saw was anything but the contempt he was dreading. It looked almost like love. Without saying a word, she leaned forward and kissed him.

And Ruben kissed her back as only a man wrapped in a tin foil blanket could.

109

FIVE DAYS TO GO

The journalist from *Expressen* had wanted to meet Tor at home, but he had refused. There were limits – they could just as well interview him at his place of work. After all, it was all supposed to be about people in the corridors of power. The photographer, however, had not been at all satisfied so a compromise had been reached.

The interview would be conducted in his office, but the pictures would be taken on a rooftop in the old town. Apparently the photographer had a vision of wintry Stockholm unfolding below Tor as if the city were under his command. The symbolism was appealing – not that he would admit that to anyone.

But the photographer was coming later. For the time being, it was just Tor and the journalist, Matilda. They had met on several previous occasions, but Tor had always been on duty as press secretary.

'I'm afraid I don't have much time,' Tor said. 'The search for the minister is still in full swing.'

'I understand,' Matilda said, placing her mobile phone on the table. 'I promise to be as efficient as possible. But this is a fairly significant profile we're doing, so I hope you've got an hour or two for me. Do you mind if I record this?'

Tor nodded. Significant profile. He liked the way it sounded. 'So what do you want to know?' he said.

He tried placing his hands behind his neck, but that felt far too macho. He put them in his lap instead.

'Everything,' said Matilda. 'Of course, we need to talk about the disappearance of Niklas Stockenberg and how that's affected the ministry and your work at the moment. I know there will be information you can't share for security reasons, but I'd like as much as possible. I'd also like to discuss who you are when Niklas is around. And who you were before you started working for him.'

Tor cleared his throat.

'As the minister of justice, Niklas Stockenberg does what may be the most important job in Sweden,' he began.

He then described his close cooperation with Niklas and what a privilege he thought it was to work with such a far-sighted minister. He explained that the search was continuing but that it was too early to draw any hasty conclusions. He had rehearsed what he would say the night before so that he was able to include the maximum amount of information without seeming too stressed. He didn't want to disappoint the prime minister.

Matilda nodded encouragingly as he spoke, but without interrupting him.

'Working as a politician is unfortunately a risky job these days,' Tor said. 'But Niklas is one of the bravest people I know. We'll find him.'

Matilda nodded one last time. Then she looked at her mobile on the table and adjusted the volume on the recording.

'Thanks,' she said. 'And now, if you don't mind, I'd like to hear about Tor Svensson the politician. You haven't always been a press secretary. You had a political career of your own, didn't you?'

'Well, I was drawn to politics because I wanted to make a difference,' Tor said with a smile. 'As a young man, I saw the serious structural and societal issues that we face in Sweden. These are problems that most people don't seem to see in the same way, or that they weren't interested in solving.'

'You almost make it sound as if you were an activist in your youth?'

'Like Greta Thunberg?' Tor said, laughing. 'No, on the contrary. I was always of the opinion that real change could only be achieved from the inside. That's why I became a politician – even if I'm currently taking a break from that kind of work. Greta tries to exert influence from the outside and it's more visible. I have to admit that after spending a few years in these corridors, I do find myself wondering whether her tactics aren't more effective if you want to achieve change.'

Matilda smiled back at him.

'Politics runs in the family,' she said. 'Your grandfather was politically active, wasn't he?'

That was an accusation rather than a question. Tor glared at her. She ought to have known better than to bring that up, but she was young and eager. He had known it would come up sooner or later in their conversation – that was why he always declined interviews. He was simply surprised that she had asked about it so early.

'My grandfather's political interests were a reflection of the time in which he lived,' he said, with an edge to his voice. 'And they weren't particularly different to those of many other people in Sweden at the time. I met my grandfather just twice before he died. On the second occasion I was four years old, so I don't remember him. You must understand that for me, it's like talking about a complete stranger. As for my own political awakening, it was more the result of being in a politically aware sixth form with classmates who thought those things mattered. But if you'd like to write about my grandfather, then I suggest you take a look at the newspaper archive at the national library. That way I won't have to waste any more of your time.'

He made as if to stand up, to indicate that the interview was over.

'No, I'm sorry!' the journalist exclaimed, her voice tinged with panic. 'I didn't mean to … My editor said I had to ask that question. Of course we're here to talk about you.'

Tor sat down again, making an arch with his fingertips. He smiled at Matilda.

'The challenge that Sweden faces is to maintain what was once called "law and order",' he continued. 'That's why someone like the minister is so important. Because right now we have neither. Our laws are inadequate and we haven't had any order in a long time. We've all read about the rise in violence in our suburbs. Shootings in which both the perpetrators and the victims are barely more than children. The escalating drug trade in schools and places of employment. But the problem runs deeper than that. It's structural. We have to start from scratch. We have to build a new society based on respect and equality. A society in which criminal gangs cannot gain a foothold. In that respect, our minister of justice is a crucial instrument and I am proud to be able to support him in that work.'

'And what role are you going to play in that work in a few years' time?' Matilda said, her admiration clearly audible.

Tor smiled broadly at her.

'I envisage an opportunity to be involved in leading it.'

110

'I hear Sara came and saved you?'

Ruben snorted and strongly considered ignoring Christer altogether. However, that option was tricky because they were sitting opposite each other in the canteen, each with a sandwich and a cup of coffee.

'Oh, I was just unlucky,' Ruben said.

'I love the picture of you in the police car with that foil blanket on you.'

'Where did you see that?'

Ruben stared at Christer in amazement. He had thought what happened in the police car stayed in the police car.

'Apparently it's all over Twitter or whatever it is they call it. Adam showed me this morning. One of the officers took it and posted it. I think he said it was a virus?'

'Viral,' Ruben said testily, taking a big bite from his cheese and ham sandwich. 'It's viral.'

Then he put the sandwich down on the worn white plate.

'How did you pluck up the courage to get with Lasse?' he said.

Christer paused in astonishment, his sandwich halfway to his mouth.

'Why do you ask?'

'Oh, I'm just wondering …'

Ruben immediately regretted his question. The most emotional conversation he and Christer had ever had was when they had both grieved over AIK's defeat by Djurgården the previous summer.

'Aha,' Christer said, taking a bite from his sandwich, a big smile on his face.

'What do you mean, *aha*?' Ruben said, squirming wretchedly. He was so stupid. He should have kept his mouth shut.

'It's Sara, isn't it? Who – I would like to point out again – saved you.'

'For the last time, she didn't save me.'

'Aha, so it *is* her then!' Christer said, unable to conceal his glee at his colleague's obvious discomfort.

'Do we have to talk about this?' said Ruben, still squirming.

'You started it.'

'Yes, but …' Ruben said, sighing. 'Damn it.'

Christer suddenly looked at him seriously. Then he put down his sandwich on his plate and leaned forward.

'It's like a bungee jump.'

'A bungee jump? What do you mean?'

'Well, I mean that love is like a bungee jump.'

'What are you on about? Have you been drinking?'

Ruben gazed suspiciously at his colleague across the table.

'No, I mean it. It's like a bungee jump. You can't stand around thinking about it for too long – that gives you time to get scared. And then you might not do it. Looking back, it scares me how close I came to bottling it. The trick is not to think. Just do it.'

'Just do it,' Ruben repeated. 'That's the best advice you have when it comes to love? "Just do it"?'

'Yep,' said Christer cheerfully, picking up his sandwich.

Disgusted, he removed the top layer from his sandwich and extracted the green lettuce leaf from underneath it.

'Does anyone know what this is for?' he said. 'Who came up with the idea of adding a dirty great piece of lettuce to an otherwise perfectly decent sandwich? If they stopped putting them in, would anyone ever ask why they hadn't been given a piece of lettuce in their sandwich?'

'I've already taken mine out,' Ruben said, pointing to a sad-looking green leaf on his plate. Then he sighed. 'You say I've just got to jump?'

'Just jump.'

Ruben shook his head.

'I would never have thought it: that you've been bungee jumping.'

Christer laughed.

'Me?' he said, wiping his eyes. 'Go bungee jumping? I think maybe you're the one who's been drinking. Not on my life.'

111

Nathalie knocked on the door of Tor's office and then went in without waiting for an answer. Mina shook her head as she followed. Her daughter had obviously inherited her father's determination. Tor was standing by his desk, speaking into the phone.

'I'll talk to you later,' he said when he spotted Mina and Nathalie. 'I have to go.'

'How's it going?' Nathalie said. 'Have you found Dad yet?'

Tor leaned against the edge of the desk and sighed.

'Nathalie, I know this must be the worst Christmas ever for you,' he said gently. 'It's not the ministry who are doing the searching – it's the Security Service – but they … we still don't have anything. I wanted the two of you to come in because I wanted to find out how you were doing. How are you feeling? Is there anything I can do?'

There was a bowl of boiled sweets on Tor's desk, wrapped in paper adorned with the logo of the government offices. Nathalie helped herself, tore off the wrapper and popped the sweet into her mouth.

'How do you think I'm feeling?' she said. 'According to that awful message, Dad's only got a few days left to live. Surely you or the Security Service have a way to track down people who go missing? Why don't you do that? Since you want to know what you can do. And once you've found him, put him inside a kryptonite box with ten thousand security guards outside it.'

Mina could hear how close to tears her daughter was – and there was nothing she could do about it. Except be a mother. She went over to her and softly patted Nathalie's back. Outside the window, the snow had begun to fall again, but it was the wet snow of the inner city that quickly turned to slush as soon as it touched the ground.

'That was exactly my plan,' Tor said, waving his index finger in the air. 'He's going to have more security than … the president of the USA when this is all over. And to answer your question about tracking people, we've been able to locate his mobile phone. If only he had taken it with him …'

Tor waved towards the desk, where there was a mobile phone lying by the computer.

'That's your dad's,' he said. 'We found it in a desk drawer.'

Mina glanced at Nathalie, whose shoulders slumped.

'We've also talked to Granddad,' Nathalie said in a low voice, sitting down on one of the chairs in front of the desk. 'But he didn't know anything either.'

'Walther?' Tor said, perking up. 'How was he? I've always liked him. Did you know he was the first person in your family that I ever met – long before I started working with Niklas. I did an internship with him. Well, he wasn't in the Supreme Court back then, obviously. But … Oh, I'm sorry. I'm rambling. When did you talk to him?'

Tor had said *your family*. Mina was still unaccustomed to being part of a family. But she had little difficulty imagining that Walther had got along with the austere man who inhabited this office.

'We went there the day before Christmas Eve,' Mina said. 'He mentioned you too.'

'He seemed well,' Nathalie said. 'We had some coffee and he had nut cookies and toffee cookies. Like a real granddad. But he hadn't heard anything about Dad.'

Tor frowned.

'Nut cookies?' he said. 'Are you sure?'

Nathalie nodded and opened her mouth to say something. Then she closed it again with a snap.

That was it. That was what Mina had known was wrong when they had been in Äppelviken. She cursed herself. She should have realized at once. It had been so long since she'd seen Walther that she could be excused for not remembering his preferences. Nonetheless, she should have. Walther's. And Niklas's.

'Because …' Tor began.

'Because Granddad is allergic to nuts,' Nathalie said, and Tor nodded. 'But how come you know that?'

'It was probably ten years before you were born,' Tor said. 'When Walther was in the Supreme Court. He and his colleagues went out for their Christmas meal at … I think it was Operakällaren. There were nuts in Walther's meal. He nearly died. It wouldn't have made the headlines normally, but it was Christmas. The newspapers loved the whole scenario, and Walther's health was national news for days.'

'I remember that,' Mina said. 'When Niklas and I were married, there was only one time when Walther permitted anything that he was allergic to into his home. That was when his son came to visit. Nut cookies were always served. They were Niklas's favourite. Walther wasn't so allergic that he couldn't be in the same room. I remember it well.'

Then she gasped and struggled to speak before she continued.

'Walther had a plate of biscuits out because he'd just had coffee with someone else when we arrived. It must have been Niklas. I'd bet anything that Walther is hiding him in the house.'

Nathalie stared at her for several seconds, then she turned to Tor.

'It's probably best that you call all those guards and police officers and soldiers that you have. They need to be at my granddad's in the next thirty seconds.'

Tor grabbed his phone but then he stopped.

'I agree that we need to look into this,' he said. 'But it needs to be done carefully. While it's heroic of Walther to hide his son – if he really has – it also means that Walther could be in danger. Whoever recorded that message might also hurt him. We don't want anyone to get wind of the fact that we have a theory about where Niklas is. It's going to take a while to coordinate everything discreetly.'

Nathalie looked as if she wanted to object, but Mina placed a soothing hand on her arm.

'If your father is at Walther's then he must have asked for his protection for a very good reason,' she said. 'If lots of police show up in all their gear, he might just run for it. He's never liked having guards around him – as you know. And he managed to give his own security detail the slip.'

She glanced at Tor, who was shuffling awkwardly even though

she knew it wasn't his fault. Her ex-husband was very strong-willed, but his escape from his security detail would probably have consequences for someone, somewhere, who might not be in their job much longer.

'If Walther has managed to hide him for this long, then he can keep on doing it for another hour or so,' she said. 'Niklas is obviously safe there, given that no one has found him yet. Don't forget that I'm a police officer too. We've got to let Tor and the Security Service handle this.'

Nathalie folded her arms and pouted.

'Well, I'm going there,' she said. 'I want Dad to tell me why he left without saying anything to us.'

'That's … not actually a bad idea,' Tor said. 'A granddaughter and a former daughter-in-law paying a visit to an elderly relative at Christmas? Nothing strange about that. You go there and talk to Niklas – if he is there – and ask him to come back here with you. If he refuses, try to make him understand that he at least needs his core security detail. He knows they're discreet.'

Nathalie turned on her heel and left. Mina was about to follow her when Tor stopped her. He waited until Nathalie was safely in the corridor.

'Take your own car,' he said in a low voice. 'And take the long way – as if you only decide spontaneously that you're going to visit dear old Walther. Just in case you're being watched.'

He paused and glanced towards the corridor. Then he lowered his voice even more.

'I don't know who can be trusted any more. I'm sure Niklas is fine, but make sure you take your service weapon. Just to be on the safe side.'

112

The closer to the house in Äppelviken they got, the angrier Nathalie became. How could her grandfather have lied to her like that? She knew it was good of Walther to protect his son, but Niklas didn't need protecting from his own daughter. She was going to give Walther a piece of her mind.

'I should have thought of it when we were there!'

Nathalie thumped the dashboard.

'Take it easy,' Mina said, indicating to turn right. 'It's brilliant that you thought of it at all. And Niklas is safe – no one knows he's there apart from us and Tor. Well, I say *know*. But I'm pretty sure.'

'What's up with this weird route?' Nathalie said. 'This isn't the normal way to Granddad's.'

'It pays to be careful,' Mina said, glancing in the rear-view mirror.

She drew a sigh of relief. She hadn't seen anyone who seemed to be following them at any point during the drive.

'We're almost there.'

Nathalie stared at the road as if she could make the car go faster by willing it to. The two of them were silent for the final stretch up to the house. The snow had continued to fall and lay on the road in a thin layer. It looked very Christmassy, but Nathalie couldn't have cared less.

Nut cookies.

How incredibly stupid.

She'd always been told that her grandfather was probably one of Sweden's most intelligent people. She almost burst into laughter at the stupidity of it all. There was no way that Dad was getting the Christmas present she had bought for him.

Her mother pulled onto the driveway and parked beside

Granddad's car just like last time. It was still in the same place. Nathalie guessed that he didn't go out driving very often.

They pressed the doorbell. The last time they had been there, they had been expected, but they were now unannounced. It might take Walther a while to open up.

Nothing happened.

Mina rang the bell again. There was nothing audible from within. Nathalie reached forward and pressed the bell hard for a third time.

'He doesn't seem to be at home,' she said, looking around. 'Why don't we check the windows? Dad might be in the basement.'

'There's a large attic too, if I recall correctly,' Mina said, nodding. 'Walther must have kept him out of sight of that woman who comes to help out, so I think you're right. The basement or the attic.'

Nathalie tried the door handle. To her surprise, the door opened. She and her mother exchanged a look. They both knew that Walther never ever left his front door unlocked. Mina nudged it open.

Something was wrong. Nathalie could feel it with every fibre of her being.

'Mum,' she whispered anxiously.

'I know,' Mina whispered in reply. 'Stay here.'

'No way.'

She took her mother's hand and together they crossed the threshold. The hallway was completely silent. Mina pressed the switch on the wall just inside the door but the lights did not come on.

'Walther?'

Mina called out cautiously but was met with resounding silence.

'Granddad? Dad?' Nathalie shouted, unable to disguise the panic in her voice.

Mina took a few more steps into the dark hall, before shouting again.

'Walther? It's Mina and Nathalie.'

They proceeded with caution. Mina turned on the torch

on her mobile phone. The beautiful old floorboards creaked beneath Nathalie's feet. She felt her pulse quicken. Her mother seemed to be just as nervous as Nathalie felt. Her mother – the detective who could do everything.

'Dad!' she shouted as loudly as she could.

The noise made Mina jump. She turned around and shushed Nathalie. 'Don't shout like that – we don't know what's happened.'

'Do you think something has happened to Dad?' Nathalie said, not feeling at all brave any longer. She should have stayed outside, but it was too late now.

'It's probably fine,' Mina said. 'Your grandfather is probably just having a nap. And your father will be here somewhere.'

Nathalie shook her head.

'No,' she said. 'Can't you feel it? There's something very wrong in here. It smells weird. It's sort of metallic.'

A few metres ahead of them in the hall, the door leading down to the basement was open. It was hard to see in the dark, but there seemed to be something lying on the floor in the doorway. Nathalie pointed. Mina unholstered her gun and gestured to Nathalie to stay where she was. When Mina reached the doorway, she shone her mobile downwards. Then she crouched. Nathalie heard a strange sound come from her mother.

'Stay where you are,' Mina shouted vehemently. 'Don't come here. Wait there. I'll only be gone for a second.'

Mina disappeared down the stairs to the basement, but the light from her phone had already shown Nathalie what had happened. It was her grandfather who was lying in the doorway.

'Granddad!' she shrieked, rushing towards him.

Walther was lying with his feet in the doorway and his upper body on the steps, as if he had tripped on his way down. He wasn't moving.

'Has he hurt himself?' she said. 'Is he injured? Or is it a heart attack? I've heard …'

She stopped short when she saw the blood. It was coming from the back of Walther's head and trickling down the steps. She instinctively took two steps back.

'Nathalie,' her mother said as she quickly climbed the stairs, taking care not to stand in the blood.

Mina put her hands on Nathalie's shoulders and led her backwards into the hall.

'Nathalie, look at me.'

Nathalie had difficulty concentrating. That was her *grandfather*.

'Look at me, Nathalie.'

Nathalie did as she was told and looked her mother in the eyes. Mina had an expression that Nathalie had never seen before.

'Walther's dead,' Mina said baldly. 'It was not an accident. Someone has killed him. And it happened recently – in the last half hour. Can you smell that? It's gunpowder. We might have passed the murderer on our way here.'

'And Dad?' said Nathalie, muffling a sob.

'I think he was here – in the basement. I saw a mattress on the floor down there. But he's not here now. Whoever killed Walther has taken Niklas.'

113

Three months. Three months without Dad. No one said anything to him, but he could see it in their eyes. He'd searched for him every time he'd gone topside. Today he'd thought he'd seen him. Dad's bushy hair, his brown leather jacket. He'd seen him from behind, walking away, but when he'd run to catch up with him and tugged at his sleeve, the man had turned around and it hadn't been Dad.

Three months.

The longest he had been gone before had been two months, but before he had left – while he had still been there – he had withdrawn. Into the silence. Into a place where he couldn't reach Dad. He had tried. He never cried normally because the darkness didn't allow you to cry. No one who was invisible could allow themselves to cry. But the week before Dad disappeared again, he hadn't been able to stop the tears. Yet Dad had remained silent. His hand was no longer warm; it was no longer strong. It no longer sought his. And when he took it in his, the hand no longer felt like Dad's.

'Look! I'm the kiiiing!'

The new guy who had turned up out of nowhere a few days earlier had put on Dad's crown. He capered around, expecting laughter from the others. No one laughed.

The rage rose within him – quickly and hotly – and made his ears ring. Without thinking, he rushed forward with a roar that came from deep within. He threw himself at the guy's skinny, heroin-addled body with all his might, causing them both to crash to the ground. He tore the crown from the guy's head and pressed it to his chest. The guy got up slowly. There was something dangerous in his eyes, but that didn't matter – he wasn't scared. He had Dad's crown.

'I'd go if I were you. Before something happens.'

Crazy-Tom's calm voice. One by one, the others got to their feet. They did nothing. There was nothing more to say. They stared at the guy with the same expressions on their faces. He got the message. Angrily, he grabbed his rucksack and sleeping bag and stalked off towards one of the other tunnels.

'What's all this fuss?'

Dad's voice. He wasn't sure whether he was imagining it – whether the crown in his arms was summoning Dad's voice. But when he turned around, there he was. Dad. The King. Yet not. He had slumped into a pale imitation of himself. His cheekbones protruded prominently from a face that had lost its accustomed shape, and his big brown jacket hung limply from his body like loose skin.

'Give it to me,' Dad said softly, reaching out for the crown.

He slowly handed it over. He wanted to throw himself into Dad's arms like he always did, but something held him back. Something that was different, something alien. There was no Dad in that gaze any more. There was no sparkle, no light dancing in the glow of the fire. The eyes were dark. Dead.

'I've come to say goodbye,' he said, bowing slightly.

Vivian made to step forward, but out of the corner of his eye, he saw Crazy-Tom extend an arm to hold her back. Something was going on – something he didn't understand.

Slowly, Dad raised his hands and placed the crown onto his head. It shone gold and Dad closed his eyes as he removed his hands, letting the crown rest on his head. Then he turned to them. He held out his hands. For a moment, he resembled Jesus – it was as if the crown on his head were made from thorns.

'I was wrong. She was right. This isn't life. Life is with her. Life is in the sun.'

'Don't do it. Think of the boy,' Vivian said gently.

What did she mean? He frowned as he tried to understand. But he understood nothing of what was happening. Vivian came over and stood behind him with her arms around his chest. It felt more as if she was restraining him than an embrace.

Dad slowly began to back away, the crown still glittering on his head. The ground began to shake as a train approached.

He kept looking at Dad and writhing in Vivian's embrace, but that only made her tighten her grip.

'I love you – don't forget that,' Dad said.

For just a moment, some of the sparkle returned to his eyes. Then it was gone again and they were black and bottomless.

The ground shook more and he could hear the train close by. Dad was standing in the middle of the track. He needed to move.

Dad needed to move.

He tried to shout but not a sound came out. Not a peep. Vivian clutched him even tighter – so tightly that he could barely breathe.

'I'll tell your mum all about you,' Dad said.

The train was even louder now. Their gazes were locked together. And then a tiny, tiny light was illuminated in Dad's eyes. Or perhaps it was just the reflection of the crown. The train was visible in the distance. Dad raised his arms even higher without averting his gaze. They were locked together – connected for all eternity. Then he was gone. The sound of the impact echoed off the train and seconds later there was the scream of brakes in his ears. The train slowly came to a halt. Then silence.

Nothing but silence.

Vivian loosened her grip. She turned towards him and took his face in her hands.

'You've got to be a big boy now,' she said gently. 'And you have to trust us. You're our prince. Go into the left-hand tunnel and stay there until I come to fetch you. Do you promise?'

He nodded. He didn't know what they were going to do, but it didn't matter. He knew that Dad was gone. And that was the only thing that mattered.

He slowly walked towards the left-hand tunnel.

The King was dead.

114

Julia glanced at Adam and saw his concentration as he piloted the police car along the snowy Bromma roads at high speed. If it hadn't been for the gravity of the situation, Julia would have made him pull over so that she could straddle him then and there. He was extremely sexy in his freshly pressed uniform. What most people didn't realize was that even police officers were turned on by uniforms. But there wasn't time for that. They were playing catch-up with the Swedish media.

She had barely got off the phone with Tor from the Ministry of Justice when the first journalist had called. If there was one thing that not all police officers were good at, it was keeping quiet. The news of the murder of a former Supreme Court judge had spread at the speed of light – especially when it had turned out to be the father of the missing minister of justice.

Walther's death was the shot in the arm that the newspapers needed to keep the headlines about Niklas relevant just a little while longer. The assembled masses from the Swedish media were probably already en route to the same house in Äppelviken as she and Adam were. As well as Tor Svensson.

When they arrived at Walther Stockenberg's house, Adam parked behind Mina's car. Julia asked him to stay there and got out, giving him a yearning look. Mina was sitting on the steps leading up to the house with her arm around her daughter.

'First things first,' Julia said as she jogged towards the house. 'She needs to get out of here right now.'

She pointed at Nathalie.

'Unless we want the tear-streaked face of the minister's daughter on the front pages of the tabloids tomorrow.'

Nathalie started and shook Mina's arm off her.

'What do you mean?' Nathalie said, looking confused. 'What tabloids? We only just called the police.'

'Which means that every single photographer and reporter with a half decent phone camera is heading here right now,' Julia said. 'Adam's in the car – he'll drive you home and make sure you've got company until Mina gets back.'

Nathalie rose on unsteady legs. Mina nodded to her daughter and squeezed her hand.

'I'll be back as soon as I can,' Mina said. 'I promise.'

Nathalie walked over to the police car. After opening the door, she turned around and took one last look at Walther's house. Then she sobbed loudly before getting into the car. Adam floored the accelerator.

Julia turned to Mina, who was surveying the lawn and its apple trees in front of the house.

'I can't believe we used to sit here in the summer in peace and quiet having a coffee with Walther and Beata,' Mina said. 'The garden furniture under that tree hasn't changed at all.'

Even though it was still only the afternoon, the garden was already shrouded in darkness. It was incomprehensible how anyone got through December. The sun went down almost before it had risen. But Julia could imagine what an idyll this must be on summer evenings. She could see that Mina's eyes had moistened, but there were no tears. Julia guessed they would follow later. Right now, they were both in work mode.

'Tor told me how you worked out where Niklas was,' she said. 'That's one smart kid you have.'

'Niklas owes Nathalie an explanation for why he just upped and left her,' Mina said, looking at her. 'She's been so worried about him. We thought he was safe with his father. I wanted him to have time to talk to her before the inevitable media storm kicked off. How could I have predicted … this? It turns out he was just at Walther's in safe, leafy Bromma.'

'Have you found anything indicating where he might be now?'

Mina shook her head.

'I've searched the whole house,' she said. 'He's not here now. But the basement is in a right state and there's a mattress on the floor. Wherever he is, I don't think it's of his own volition. We might have been wrong before when we thought someone had taken him – but this time it seems he really has been abducted. And Walther must have got in the way.'

They were interrupted by a car stopping outside the low hedge that separated the garden from the road beyond.

'That's probably Tor,' Julia said, nodding towards the car.

A moment later, the car doors opened and Tor and his entourage got out. Tor nodded in her direction, adjusted his collar under his jacket, and set off towards them.

'The press will be here at any moment,' Julia said to Mina, more gently than before. 'But don't say a word to them. OK? I'll handle this. And get off that cold step before you freeze to death.'

115

Adam had been very succinct on the phone, but Vincent had grasped the essentials. Nathalie's grandfather – Mina's former father-in-law – was dead.

When Adam asked if Vincent could keep Nathalie company until Mina got home, he said yes right away. Adam had suggested bringing Nathalie to Vincent's house in Tyresö, but that felt like an extremely bad idea. The house felt more and more like a bear trap that might snap around him at any moment – and anyone else who happened to be in the house at that time. So Vincent had suggested they meet at Mina's apartment instead, since that was a place where Nathalie would feel safe.

He had set off immediately and had managed to arrive before Adam and Nathalie, which meant he had been waiting in the cold outside the main door in Årsta. He had never been there without Mina before. It felt strange to be there now – as if he were a trespasser. But Mina had a family now.

Unlike him.

He tried to block out thoughts of where his family might be. He was afraid that the panic would paralyse him completely if he let it in. But being unable to do anything was driving him mad. If only he understood what it was the Shadow expected of him. But the thoughts and ideas of crazy people could never be predicted. He would have liked to stand on the roof of police headquarters and cry out for help. The only thing stopping him was the threat, which he was taking deadly seriously. If the police got involved, things would go badly. All he could do was wait for the Shadow to get in touch again and in the meantime try to keep busy. He had to trust that the Shadow was treating his family well.

Keeping Nathalie company was therefore not only something he wanted to do, but also a necessary and welcome distraction.

A police car pulled around the corner and approached the building. At first, he thought it was Adam and Mina, but then he realized it was actually Nathalie sitting beside Adam. She really was becoming more and more like her mother, at least in terms of appearance.

The car stopped and Vincent opened the door for Nathalie.

'Thanks for your help, Vincent,' Adam said from inside the car. 'I've got to head straight to police headquarters now.'

'Of course,' Vincent said. 'Nathalie and I will stay here until Mina gets back.'

Nathalie quietly got out of the car. She didn't say anything as she entered the building or as she climbed the stairs to the apartment. Vincent knew better than to push her. She had a lot to process. All he could do was make sure it wasn't too overwhelming for her.

They went into the apartment. Nathalie took off her shoes and dropped her coat on the floor before making her way into the living room. She sat down stiffly on the sofa and stared at the wall in front of her. Vincent sat down next to her, taking care not to get too close.

'It's so scary,' she said at last.

Her voice was barely audible. More silence followed.

Vincent waited.

'He was in his own home,' she said suddenly with a sob. 'Aren't you supposed to be safe in your own home? What if someone got in here and killed us? It's just as unthinkable. Who would want to kill my granddad? He was the kindest man in the world. I mean, he was really strict. But he was still the kindest.'

Vincent nodded. An intrusion into their own home was a harrowing experience for the majority of people. He knew exactly how it felt when a place where you thought you were always safe no longer offered any protection. But he had to try to make Nathalie feel safe nonetheless.

'I don't think it was a regular burglar who killed Walth— your grandfather,' he said. 'Whoever did it was probably looking for your father. He clearly has more dangerous enemies than anyone has realized.'

Nathalie snuffled.

'Because he's the minister of justice?' she said. 'That's crazy.'

'Because of that, or because of something else,' Vincent said. 'No one knows who sent that business card.'

'Did you think that hearing that would make me feel better?' she said, smiling feebly at him. 'Turns out you're not very good at this.'

Vincent laughed.

'I've done worse,' he said. 'I tried to comfort your mother once. First I googled how to do it.'

'You're weird,' Nathalie said, curling up in the corner of the sofa. 'I want Dad to come home now. I'm freezing.'

'That's the shock,' Vincent said. 'You'll feel strange and out of sorts for a while. It's quite normal – and it does stop, even if it doesn't seem like it will now.'

He got up and hesitated for a moment before going to Mina's bedroom. He wouldn't normally have dared to go in there, but needs must.

'I'll get you a blanket,' he said. 'Sleep for a while if you can. If you want to talk or make gingerbread houses or anything else then I'll be here.'

Nathalie nodded listlessly.

'I think I'm going to rest for a bit,' she said quietly.

Vincent took the blanket off Mina's bed and returned to the living room to find that Nathalie had already fallen asleep on the sofa.

116

Both TV4 and SVT had set up portable lighting to make Julia and Tor more visible in the garden, and the journalists who were using their mobile phones to film them were grateful for the boost. Darkness had fallen completely, even though it was only half past three in the afternoon. Mina desperately longed for the light of spring. At least the snow made it lighter than it would otherwise have been, but she hated the December darkness.

Right now, however, it was her friend. Mina was standing immediately behind Tor and Julia, present, but just beyond the light. No one would think to ask her a question. The impromptu press conference had already got off to a shaky start. The reporters reminded Mina of dogs that had found a scent.

'Isn't this a disastrous failure for the police?' said the TV4 reporter. 'First you've been unable to find the minister of justice, and then you've been unable to prevent an attack on Walther Stockenberg, the minister's father. This is appalling. Who is in charge? How does the Police Authority intend to proceed?'

'I'm afraid we can't divine people's actions,' Julia said, and paused. 'It would be great if we were all mind-readers, but in reality people will regrettably continue to be unpredictable,' she said, pausing again.

It was a tactic Mina recognized. It was the kind of pause her boss also deployed before telling her something unwelcome. But the dogs needed a bone.

'This is a very serious situation,' Julia said. 'We haven't disclosed this until now, but we have reason to believe that there is a new threat against the minister of justice. This is likely to be the reason why Niklas Stockenberg went into hiding of his own volition. We had no reason to believe that the threat extended to his family, or his father in particular. That was an error of judgement. Naturally, we will carry out an internal review to examine this.'

The journalists began to talk over each other. A woman with a mobile phone raised as a microphone pushed her way forward. The phone was emblazoned with the logo of *Aftonbladet*.

'I have a question for Mina,' she called out. 'That is Mina Dabiri standing behind you Julia, isn't it?'

Mina froze. This was completely against the rules. Julia was leading the press conference and it was to her that all questions were to be posed. There was no reason for Mina to answer questions. But the woman smiled coldly at Mina.

'Does this threat extend to you and your daughter? Because the minister is your ex-husband, isn't he? And you have a daughter? How do you feel about that? Are you able to do your job under these conditions? How afraid is your daughter?'

The journalists erupted with questions and the cameras turned towards Mina. She saw nothing but dazzling beams of light shining towards her face. Suddenly she knew how deer felt when they were on a motorway. There was nowhere to escape to. All she could do was stand still.

'May I have your attention,' Tor said.

He cleared his throat and then repeated himself more loudly.

'May I have your attention! A little professionalism on your part is desirable, given the circumstances. Otherwise this press conference is over.'

The cameras swung in his direction.

'To go back to the first question, this is not a policing failure,' he said. 'This is a *political* failure. The police have done the best they can with their limited resources. I must emphasize the word limited, and personally apologize in that regard. That is something we must change. We cannot have a society that allows this kind of thing to happen. Violence and a lack of respect have escalated uncontrollably. And as you can see, this is no longer confined to the suburbs. While it may be true that the police are powerless, this is because *society* is powerless. The rule of law in this country is in free fall.'

'Is that the official view of the Ministry of Justice?' said SVT's reporter, raising her eyebrows.

'No,' said Tor. 'I'm not here today as Niklas Stockenberg's press secretary. Today I'm here as a politician. I had intended to wait to return to that role, but having seen what the minister – who happens to be a close friend – is facing, I feel that I must act. No one else is. It's been barely six months since a serious attack on the minister, and we all know that several other Swedish politicians have paid with their lives in the past. Enough is enough.'

All the journalists began to talk across each other. Tor pointed to the reporter from TV4. Their camera also had the brightest light.

'That's very fine rhetoric,' the reporter said. 'But it's rhetoric that we've heard before from other politicians. How are you going to make a difference?'

'I have a tangible plan of action,' said Tor. 'As soon as I've had a chance to brief parliament on it – and I will – it will be communicated to the Swedish public. You won't miss it.'

'But you aren't a member of parliament ...' the reporter said.

'Yet. I'm not a member of parliament *yet*.'

All the lights were now shining on Tor in the dark garden. And while Mina was standing diagonally behind him and could only see his back, she could have sworn that he was loving every moment of it.

117

He had never really imagined how he would feel when the world no longer contained his own father. For as long as he could remember, Walther had been a kind of constant primordial force – an omniscient entity who was constantly watching and constantly judging. But one that also loved.

Now, more than ever, Niklas remembered the moments when his father had shown him love, given him security, taught him things that could never be taken from him.

But Walther had been taken from him. Niklas could still hear the shot ringing in his ears. He could still see the blood in his mind's eye. It had been for ever imprinted upon him. The only question was how long 'for ever' would last. Five days, if the voice on the telephone was to be believed.

Five days to live.

Niklas shivered. He was freezing cold. His coat was still in his father's basement, and he was wearing nothing but chinos and a thin shirt. The cold and wet had begun to creep inside his clothes, and he jumped up and down on the spot to keep warm. There was a rustling in the gravel as something scurried away, having been disturbed by his movements. He tried not to think about what it might be.

So much regret. And yet not. He had made the best decision he could at the time, and he really had made the most of it. He had lived the very best life he could.

He pictured the dinner with Nathalie and Mina. It felt like an eternity ago, even if it had only been a week or so. A dinner he had never thought would happen. Yet they had sat there, all three of them, around the table. As a family.

He knew they could never be a traditional family again – too much water had passed under the bridge for that. Both he and Mina were not the same as they had been when they lived together. But it had still been clear to him that there was love between them, even if it was a different kind of love to what they had shared before. The love that existed now centred on Nathalie and united them for ever. It was a strong and unbreakable bond.

Or so he had believed.

That was when he had naively believed that they had the rest of their lives to share the joys of their daughter's life. It had been comfortable but foolhardy to allow himself to forget the truth.

There was so much he would miss. Nathalie's first sweetheart. Her first heartbreak. Graduation from senior high school. Going to university, her choice of course. Her partner, her wedding, her kids. All the things that formed the patchwork that was life. He had taken it for granted that he would be there for all of that. But now he was trying to cling to the idea that Nathalie would at least have her mother by her side.

He couldn't remember how he had got to the place he now found himself in. There had been a sting – a smarting feeling under the skin – and then darkness. The wheelchair lying on the ground next to him explained how he had been transported.

At least he knew roughly where he was. The first time he had heard the sound rumbling past on the other side of the locked door, he had realized. But there was no way out. He had chosen his fate on that occasion long ago. Now it was time to pay the price. The problem was that the price suddenly seemed far too great.

118

Julia was so exhausted that she couldn't even bring herself to take off her coat after returning from the media scrum at Walther Stockenberg's house. She slumped down into the chair in front of her father's desk and watched him pacing back and forth across the room. The commissioner's brow was furrowed.

'It's as if I'm stuck in a vice that's being constantly tightened,' he said. 'It was bad enough when the minister went missing. And now this business with Walther … It's only a matter of time before the press call for my resignation. Or a politician from some minor party spots their chance to beat their chest. It's happened to government ministers before – so why not a police commissioner?'

'Just tell me what you need,' Julia said. 'I'll do my best to sort it out.'

He stopped moving.

'It's very simple,' he said, turning to her. 'I need this case solved. No more, no less. If I have understood things correctly, there is a threat towards Niklas Stockenberg which is similar to what happened to Jon Langseth. Which has also, I gather, happened on a further two occasions. That you know of. And yet you are no closer to a solution than the last time I saw you.'

Julia considered mentioning that the last time they had met, her father had insisted that Gustaf Brons was behind all of it, but she held her tongue. Instead she sighed deeply and gazed out of the window.

What if life could be as black and white as a police investigation? Guilty, not guilty. Murdered, not murdered. Married, not married.

'Julia?'

She looked up at her father.

'How are you?' he said, more gently than before. 'I know I don't ask that often, but how are things at home?'

That was the thing: she was no longer sure of anything.

Torkel, Harry and Adam filled her thoughts every waking minute, every second of every day. One moment she knew what to do, the next she changed her mind. Could she and Torkel save their wounded marriage? Did she even want that? Did Torkel? And what about Adam? What did she want from him? The sex was good. No, it was better than that. It was incredible. But was there anything beyond that?

All of these thoughts flashed through her mind in just a few seconds. They were well-worn thoughts that often gnawed away at her. She knew she had to make some kind of decision. But whatever decision she took, it would have wide-ranging consequences not just for her, but for Torkel, Harry and Adam.

They were like a row of dominoes, just waiting for her to nudge the first one.

Her father was waiting for an answer, his face puzzled.

'I know you're counting on me and the team,' she said, avoiding the question. 'And we'll crack this. I know it might seem as if we're not on it, but I'm sure we are.'

On it. She needed to be on it. Everyone expected her to be on it. They always did. Julia always stayed cool and composed. But life had become complicated. Perhaps she ought to take a break and go and gossip with some colleagues whose names she barely knew. She could drink coffee in the break room, eat ginger biscuits, ask people how they'd celebrated Christmas. But she quickly let go of that thought. She had to work. Somewhere in the jumble of information, data, evidence and statements, there was an answer. She knew that. There always was.

'Good,' said the commissioner. 'Because if I lose my job then I'll hold you directly responsible. That would make for a really bad atmosphere at our next family Christmas—'

He was interrupted by a loud ringing sound. It was Julia's phone. The display showed the caller to be the National Board of Forensic Medicine. She gave her father a look and he nodded grimly, so she answered.

'Hi Julia, hope you had a good Christmas,' Milda said. 'Sorry to bother you, and I'm sure it's nothing, but I'd still like to check with you.'

'What's it about?' said Julia. 'And thank you, I had a good Christmas. I hope you did too.'

'Well, it's just that Loke hasn't shown up for work today,' said Milda. 'And I can't get hold of him on the phone either.'

'I'm sure there's a natural explanation. Maybe he's just ill?'

'This is Loke we're talking about. The world's most reliable person. He hasn't missed a day's work since he started here, and he always lets me know if he's going to be more than about ninety seconds late. So I just wanted to check that he didn't say anything to you yesterday about going away or anything like that? I've been a little ... distracted lately, so I might have forgotten about it.'

Julia frowned.

'To me? I didn't see Loke yesterday.'

'That's strange. He was supposed to take the documents to you. Didn't he—'

Milda was interrupted by a shrill ringing sound. Julia held her mobile away from her ear to avoid being deafened.

'Hang on Julia,' Milda said, talking more quickly than before. 'I'm sorry, that's the hospital calling me on my private number. I need to take it right away, but do call me if you hear anything about Loke.'

Milda hung up before Julia even managed to say goodbye. The commissioner looked at her with a quizzical expression.

'What was that all about?' he said.

'I'm not quite sure,' Julia said. 'It was about Loke.'

'The most recent addition to your team?'

'Yes. Apparently he didn't turn up for work today.'

119

Vincent hadn't heard anything from Mina since she had relieved him at her apartment. She hadn't asked him to stay, but that wasn't particularly strange. She needed to be alone with her daughter.

He hadn't tried to reach her since then either, but he had still been thinking about her. In fact, he couldn't think about anything else.

It felt as if he was drowning, and Mina was his lifebuoy. But he didn't dare reach out his hand to ask to be saved. That wasn't something one could ask of anyone.

He wanted to avoid the empty house in the evening as much as possible – there were far too many ghosts there. So he had gone out for a walk in the woods to clear his head. But as usual, he'd been hopelessly inappropriately dressed. The snow had penetrated into his loafers in just a few minutes and he'd stumbled several times on tree roots hidden in the darkness by the white blanket of snow. His headache, however, was absent for the time being.

He stayed out in the woods for as long as he could, no matter how unsteady and cold he was.

However, he eventually gave up when he stopped to lean against a fir tree which immediately dropped all the snow off its branches straight down his neck and inside his clothing. Mina would probably have laughed her head off if she had been there to see his discomfort.

After his soggy walk in the woods, he took a long, hot shower. Then he fetched a bottle of whisky – an Akkeshi Single Malt Peated from Japan – that he kept for very special occasions.

He took the bottle and a glass into his study where the timeline of his 'Christmas presents' was still attached to the wall. He poured a little whisky into the glass and set down the bottle. The Akkeshi was perfectly balanced and one of the few whiskies that required no extra water to adjust the molecular composition and flavour. He stared into the glass to avoid the threats on his wall.

After sipping his way through three glasses, he looked at the time. It was half past nine. He shook his head. How could time have disappeared so quickly? It seemed impossible that he had been there for several hours. Not only was he losing his mind, but he was apparently also losing his grasp of time.

At least the late hour meant that he could get in touch with Mina again without disrupting the work that Walther's murder had doubtless created. And Nathalie might be asleep by now. He picked up his phone.

Hi, been thinking about you all evening, he wrote.

Then he quickly deleted all of that apart from the first word. What the hell was wrong with him?

Instead he wrote: *Hi, thinking of you. Hope Nathalie is as OK as can be hoped for. Get in touch when you have time.*

He sent the text message and then stood up. He felt dizzy. Apparently he was sensitive to alcohol today. He probably should have eaten some dinner. Or breakfast, for that matter. Perhaps he should have eaten anything at all in the last twenty-four hours, now that he came to think about it.

Bloody hell.

But it was too late now. He wasn't hungry. He staggered into the bedroom and lay down on the bed. The phone in his hand buzzed. It was a reply from Mina.

It's all still dreadful. Niklas still missing. Nathalie's grandfather still dead. But Nathalie will be OK. She's a tough girl. Can we meet early tomorrow at police HQ? Bring the letter. I know you have objections, but for once please trust me.

Vincent wanted to ask a hundred questions about Nathalie's grandfather and how Mina was feeling and whether she needed him. Especially the last one.

Do you need me?

But he didn't follow up on the impulse. He sent a reply saying that he would arrive as early as he could and bade her goodnight. Then he closed his eyes and began to float away.

A sound wrenched him out of his light sleep. The alarm clock on the nightstand was beeping furiously. He turned it off and took note of the time. 22:19. He knew with absolute certainty that he hadn't set the alarm. But he no longer had the strength even to feel surprised. The Shadow was playing his own game and he could only follow along until he understood what it was all about.

He turned his head and looked out of the bedroom window. For a change, the clouds had disappeared and the moon was casting its light. The snow on the trees and lawn outside shimmered in the moonlight – it looked almost phosphorescent. It was beautiful but also a little frightening. The moon and the trees didn't care one bit about him. The fact that his family was missing wasn't something the snow had a view on. The world outside the window carried on completely separately from what was happening to Vincent Walder.

There were two shadows on the lawn. The moonlight revealed their feathers. The ravens were back, as he had somehow known they would be. Just like last time, there were only two of them. Now they were sitting a little further apart, as if waiting for three friends to settle down between them.

If they hadn't been birds then he would have thought that someone was trying to communicate with him in code. But they were birds. They couldn't communicate. Or at least not in code. He sighed and turned his head again. The clock now said it was 22:25. He already knew that he wasn't going to sleep another wink tonight.

120

FOUR DAYS TO GO

Just as Vincent was about to enter the foyer of police headquarters, he saw Julia coming along the pavement. The sun wasn't due to rise for several hours yet, but the street lights formed puddles of light that made the snow appear luminescent in the dark. Julia's face was like a storm cloud. She had dark bags under her eyes. Vincent waited for her to catch up so they could walk inside together.

'Good morning,' he said. 'And happy third day of Christmas.'

'Happy ... You've just made that up, haven't you?' she said. 'I'm so sick of Christmas.'

'Not at all,' he said, feigning indignation. 'Until the holiday reforms of 1772, today – three days after Christmas – was also a public holiday. As indeed was the fourth day of Christmas.'

They went inside and passed through the barriers. The foyer was silent and deserted. There were no school trips waiting to be admitted. No shivering cops clutching paper cups of coffee by the noticeboard. They waved to the man behind the reception desk, who was stifling a yawn.

'You're here early,' Julia said to Vincent. 'I didn't even know you were coming in. What does your family have to say about you being gone so much over Christmas?'

He came close to telling her. He so badly wanted to explain why he was avoiding his home. To tell her about the headaches that were always worst at home. About the wall in the living room that he was so afraid of. And above all, about the fact that his entire family was missing, that he'd received death threats and that he was terrified of what would happen next.

'I'm seeing Mina,' was all he said.

Which was also true.

'But I might ask you the same thing,' he said. 'What do your family say? You and I seem to be the very first people to arrive in the whole building.'

Julia was silent for a while. The bags under her eyes suddenly seemed very prominent.

'It's … complicated,' she said. 'My family, that is.'

Vincent nodded.

'If you promise not to ask, then I won't either,' she added.

They proceeded towards the lifts in silence. Vincent would have preferred to take the stairs, but he had started to get to grips with the lifts in police headquarters. It wasn't as bad as it had been that spring almost three years earlier. But it was still far from his favourite place on earth.

'By the way, Mina told me about metro line sixteen – the one you discovered doesn't exist,' Julia said as the lift doors opened. 'Something about an hourglass?'

Good. Continuing to talk was the distraction he needed.

'Yes. I don't understand it,' he said. 'I know I'm not wrong. It's too neat a match with the riddle of the hourglasses not to be—'

'I spoke to the metro press office yesterday,' Julia said, interrupting. 'There was a line sixteen. It was a temporary line that ran parallel to two others. It started in Vällingby on the green line but ended in Liljeholmen on the red line. Exactly where it switched from one to the other I don't know, but that's the situation.'

Vincent felt a weight lift off his shoulders. Perhaps his sanity wasn't in question after all. He had been right.

'Interesting,' he said. 'Then we know something more about the person who gave me the hourglasses. Whoever it was, they have detailed knowledge of the metro. It's worth pondering why. But whatever the reason, it may be where Niklas is now.'

'You think he's already dead?' Julia said, staring at him.

'I don't know,' Vincent said with a shake of the head. 'I hope not. According to the countdown, he's still got four days to go. But four days is a long time to stay hidden, given the forces out looking for him. The tunnels would be ideal in that respect. It's a maze down there.'

The lift doors opened. They stepped out, but then Julia came to a halt and turned towards him.

'And you can't be more precise than saying it's line sixteen? There isn't a particular station you can point us towards?'

Vincent shook his head.

'I thought so at first,' he said. 'I thought the number of minutes in the hourglass represented the line number and that the seconds might be the stations. But that didn't tally with the places where you found the other bones, no matter how I counted. So I'm afraid not. I don't know any more than that right now.'

Julia sighed and pulled her phone from her pocket.

'There's a total of forty-seven underground metro stations in Stockholm,' she said. 'Line sixteen passes twenty-five of them. I'll request eleven pairs of officers to check out two stations each. Ruben and Adam will have to do the other three. It's going to be a logistical nightmare. Another one. I think the people at the metro are going to be sick of us. But I don't think we have a choice.'

She called a number and put her phone to her ear.

'This is going to be a long day,' she said with another sigh.

121

Mina looked at her reflection in the mirror. She barely recognized the pale face staring back at her with its red, swollen eyes. For once, she was the one who was late rather than Vincent, but she was unable to bring herself to move any faster. It had been a long night. She had been up talking to her daughter about Walther for hours. She had tried to remember his good side. His marriage to Beata.

Nathalie had been asleep for the last hour or so, and Mina didn't want to wake her. But she had been fine when she had gone to sleep. Mina had been right in her assumption that Nathalie was a resilient girl. She would get over this. And she most definitely didn't need a babysitter now that the initial shock had subsided.

Mina just hoped that Vincent would think she'd had an allergic reaction when he saw her. She left a note on the kitchen table and then crept out quietly so as not to wake Nathalie, before driving to police headquarters as quickly as the morning traffic allowed.

Vincent wasn't waiting for her at the main entrance as she expected. She looked around the deserted reception area in case he had sat down, but he wasn't there. Had she arrived before him? She went over to the man behind the glass partition.

'Morning,' she said. 'Have you seen Vincent Walder? If you know who that is?'

'The mind-reader?' the man said. He appeared to have slept as badly as she had. 'He arrived a while ago together with Julia Hammarsten. I think they went upstairs.'

Mina thanked him and went through the barriers. She had just reached the lifts when the doors opened and Vincent hurried out, looking over his shoulder. They collided head-on, but he caught her in his arms before she fell.

'Mina?'

'Vincent!' she said. 'What … what are you doing?'

'I … well, I …' he stammered, glancing over his shoulder again. 'Um … Do you remember what you said about practising taking the lift? I may have been … having a few goes.'

She laughed. He still hadn't let her go.

'You're doing cognitive behavioural therapy training using police resources?' she said.

'I might be.'

He was holding her close enough that she could make out his familiar scent.

'Vincent?'

'Yes.'

'You're still holding me.'

Silence.

'I know.'

They remained in that position a little longer. She wasn't quite sure what to do. She didn't want him to let go. His warmth was radiating into her and she hoped that he felt the same thing, but they couldn't stand there for ever.

'People will talk,' she said at last. 'They'll testify that they saw you kidnapping me.'

Vincent slowly let go of her.

'Why did you want to meet so early?' he said. 'And is Nathalie OK on her own?'

'Nathalie's as resilient as her mother,' she said. 'She's meeting up with friends today. It'll be good for her to do something else. And I had an idea. Did you bring the letter?'

Vincent nodded.

'We can send it off to the National Forensic Centre in Linköping and get them to check it for fingerprints,' she said. 'We can do it anonymously – we can remove everything from the letter that's personally connected to you before we send it.'

'Fingerprints?' Vincent said in surprise.

But he pulled out the letter and handed it over.

She shook her head.

'I don't want to touch it,' she said. 'It's fairly common for people who send threats to do so more than once, and to more than one person. You get professional trolls online, but letters are still used occasionally – as you've found out. If your letter was sent by anyone who has a criminal record, then we'll be able to find them. We just need to take your fingerprints and send them along so that NFC know which ones to exclude when analysing the letter.'

Vincent held the letter gingerly between two fingertips and put it back in his pocket.

'That's not such a bad idea,' he said. 'Especially since I still don't have any leads on who they might be. I suppose it is involving the police, but only indirectly. I doubt the Shadow would find out.'

'Let's take your fingerprints right away,' Mina said, setting off down the corridor towards the lab.

122

Christer was standing by the coffee machine. He heaved a deep sigh. The date was glowing on the machine's display. The twenty-seventh of December. Four days of the year left. It seemed as if there wasn't going to be any leave over the Christmas holiday this year. Not that it mattered much. Lasse was going through an intense period of work because of the many festive bookings at the Ulla Winbladh restaurant, which meant he was working long hours.

But a few days at home in front of the goggle box with a good detective series would have been nice. There hadn't been much of that since Lasse had come into his life. Not that he was complaining … Lasse's company was even better than his personal favourite Harry Bosch. More handsome too.

Julia came around the corner. She was clutching an empty coffee cup and her hollow-eyed gaze was like a laser sight trained on the coffee machine.

'You look knackered,' he said. 'Shouldn't you go home to Torkel and Harry?'

'Harry? Sure,' she said. 'Each second I spend in this place makes me feel like a crappier mother. Thanks for the reminder.'

'And Torkel?'

'Not quite the same pang of guilty conscience there. You done or what?'

She nodded at Christer's mug, which had been filled long ago but was still in position under the nozzle. He removed it and Julia almost aggressively inserted her own. Sometime he was going to ask her about what was going on in her life – but this wasn't the right occasion.

'You coming then?' said Julia. 'We've got a meeting now. I've got a great job for you that'll take the rest of Christmas.'

He sighed, ditched the coffee in the sink and put his mug back under the nozzle. This required an absolutely fresh cup of piping hot coffee.

123

'I know you're all tired and worn out right now, but I really appreciate the incredible work that you're doing. We've got the eyes of the world on us in the search for the minister, and it's not a cliché in this context to say that the clock is ticking. Rather loudly.'

Julia surveyed her motley group and couldn't help but feel pride at what they had accomplished in their few years together. Above all, she was certain that they would continue to deliver in future.

'Ruben, could you update us on what's happened with the Serbian mafia angle?'

It was mean, but she couldn't help herself. There were titters from around the room, and Julia struggled not to start laughing. The photo of Ruben in his space blanket and the story about him being rescued by Sara from NOA two days ago had spread like wildfire through police headquarters.

'Nice,' Ruben said grumpily. 'That's just great. But to answer your question, Ted Hansson is at home safe and sound and we've concluded that the Serbs have nothing whatsoever to do with our case, despite the connection to Peter Kronlund and Gustaf Brons. Nothing but an unfortunate coincidence.'

'Thanks Ruben,' Julia said with a nod. 'I hope you've all reflected on how inappropriate it is to go off on your own adventures when on police business … It's great to see initiative being used, but please ensure that common sense is also part of the calculation.'

'Yes, miss,' Ruben said irritably. 'We don't need to talk about this any more.'

'Well then, let's focus on the angles we still have. We have a few tangibles. Thanks to Vincent, we have a specific location to search for Niklas. It might be that he's somewhere in the metro tunnel system along line sixteen.'

'The line that doesn't exist? That's what I heard …' Christer said.

'That's right,' said Vincent, who was sitting next to Mina. 'According to Julia, it was a temporary line that ran in parallel to two others. But the problem is that it passed through a total of twenty-five metro stations.'

'How sure are we that he's there?' Ruben said.

'Not at all sure,' said Julia. 'But it's all that we've got to go on. So until we have something better, I've requested a search of the tunnels along the line. A number of officers will go over the stations systematically, one by one, today. Ruben and Adam, you're also on the list.'

'I saw that,' Adam said with a nod. 'We'll go right after this meeting ends.'

'Great. We've also got the connection that we've identified between the victims – all of them had a depressive episode around twenty years ago. That matches with the minister of justice's backstory, according to his father. We still haven't been able to find the unifying factor, but we're looking into whether they might have consulted with the same psychologist and whether there's any connection to "the King", whose remains we believe we had in our possession until they were stolen. How are we doing on getting hold of Niklas's psychologist?'

'He's still in Rwanda and I haven't managed to reach him yet,' Christer said, slipping a piece of gingerbread to Bosse, who noisily gobbled it up.

'Then we'll have to look for a different way in. I'm tired of waiting for him. If all our victims went to see a shrink twenty years ago then we should be able to see that in their banking records. They must all have made regular payments to the same person or company.'

A piece of gingerbread caught in Christer's throat and he coughed.

'So …' he said slowly, 'you want me to find out what bank accounts our victims had twenty years ago, contact the banks and ask them to find old statements? During twixmas? Without me knowing which account they paid the money to?'

'Yep,' Julia said, nodding. 'I told you it would be a great job.'

'Do you realize how many transactions I'll have to go through? And what if they saw the psychologist through the public health service? If so, we'll only see that they occasionally paid consultation fees at their health clinic. Which might as well have been for blood tests with the GP. Sisyphus had it easy by comparison.'

'I know,' Julia said. 'But we've got a missing government minister. I'm fairly certain that most people are going to be eager to help. That includes the banks. However, I'm all ears if you have a better suggestion.'

Christer shook his head.

'I'll get started right away,' he said.

Julia consulted the list she had made before the meeting to check she hadn't forgotten anything, but was interrupted by a gentle tap on the glass door. This attracted everyone's attention and Julia gestured at her colleague outside to open the door.

'Yes? We're in the middle of a meeting here.'

'You've got to call Milda,' the woman said.

'Do you know what it's about? Can I call after the meeting?'

'She said it was about Loke. They've found him. And he's in hospital.'

Julia stared at her. Then she got out her phone. There were fourteen missed calls from Milda.

124

He was with Mina at Il caffè just a stone's throw from police headquarters. Julia had brought the meeting to an abrupt close but had asked them to stay nearby before rushing off. Despite the fact that it was still early, the café was already full of thirty-somethings hunched over their laptops. Vincent and Mina had managed to bag the last table at the back of the room. He had bought a bun while she had bought a sandwich made from crispbread that he guessed she had no intention of eating.

'I realize that you're frustrated at not being able to do anything right now,' he said in a low voice, 'but sometimes it's good to focus on something else for a while. Like when you go to play pool. Distracting yourself with something completely different is the best way to recharge your brain.'

'Vincent,' she said firmly, 'we are not going pottery, in case that's what you're getting at. Nor are we going to paint with the umber. Just so you know.'

He held up his hands in a defensive gesture.

'That wasn't …'

'But I appreciate the thought,' she said, applying pressure to the crispbread with her finger so that it split into three parts. 'Not the clay. That's not appreciated. But that you haven't given up on the idea of doing things with me. I know … I know I can be difficult like that. But why don't we just talk instead – while we wait?'

She reached across the table and put her hand on his arm.

'How are you?' she said. 'I know how I felt when Epicura had Nathalie. But at least I knew where she was. Your family – I can't even imagine … And please tell me you've changed your mind about involving the police. At least a little bit. I know you're worried for your family, but that threat to you was nothing less than a death threat.'

How was he feeling? That was a very good question. The truth was that he didn't dare think about that too much, in case it floored him so hard that he couldn't get back up. Concerns for his family had to be kept at arm's length – preferably further, in fact. Otherwise he would be of no use to anyone. Not to Mina, and least of all to himself.

'I agreed to checking for fingerprints,' he said. 'But any more involvement from the police would be too easy to find out about. I need to solve this on my own. And as for the death threat … that was only if I don't meet the Shadow's demands.'

That was a white lie. It had said in the letter that Vincent Walder would cease to exist regardless of what he did, but he hoped that Mina wouldn't remember that. She was worried enough about him as it was.

'I know it doesn't help in the slightest to say it,' Mina said, 'but I would be in a total panic. I can't understand how you've managed to remain so calm.'

Vincent took her hand off his arm and squeezed it between his own. He would have preferred to hold her, but he was afraid he would break down if he did.

'I've got to stay rational so that I can keep functioning,' he said. 'So I'm trying to see the whole thing from the outside, as if I were a stranger looking back at what's happening from twenty years in the future. It's a way for me to gain distance and shut down my emotions.'

'Does it work?' said Mina.

'Not one bit.'

125

She found the emergency department at the Karolinska hospital without any trouble. Sooner or later, all police officers on active duty got to know the emergency departments in the city like the back of their hand. Memories of various tragedies assailed her at the mere sight of the sign, but after years in the line of duty, Julia was used to processing memories of the dead, wounded and mangled.

'Where is he?'

She nodded briefly at the officers waiting for her by the doors.

'He's gone in to see the doctor,' one of them said. 'Thankfully it's a quiet day here so he was able to get help quickly. All we know right now is that it isn't life-threatening. I did a basic examination when we found him and the injuries appear to be superficial. That was what the paramedics thought too. But obviously I can't be sure. He might have internal injuries, and he'd taken several blows to the head.'

'I'll go in and see what I can find out. Thank you for doing such a good job.'

Julia's tone was curt, but she knew that her gratitude would go a long way. Many commanding officers hadn't used the words *thank you* in their entire careers.

She hurried inside. After flashing her credentials at the reception desk, she was allowed into the corridor and asked to wait until a doctor could speak to her. It didn't take more than five minutes before a dark and handsome physician appeared. She looked at his name badge.

'Hello Mehmet, my name's Julia Hammarsten. I head up the police team that Loke is part of. How's he doing?' she said.

As a police officer, it always touched her more deeply when a colleague was hurt – and that wasn't confined to those colleagues who were also in the police. There was a strong protective instinct that applied to everyone in justice and law enforcement. Going after one of them was akin to going after all of them.

'The injuries are superficial,' the doctor said. He had a slight accent. 'Physically, Loke won't suffer any permanent effects, but mentally this will have been a traumatic experience. He will probably require professional help in order to process it.'

'Can I talk to him?'

Mehmet hesitated for a moment, but then nodded.

'If you promise not to wear him out.'

'Loke is on my team – I won't do anything that would harm him.'

'Then you have my permission.'

The doctor pointed to one of the doors on the seemingly endless corridor and Julia briskly set off. With her hand on the door handle, she paused for a moment and took a deep breath before opening it.

Loke looked pitiful lying in the hospital bed. He had bandages around his head and a big black eye. His arms lying on top of the yellow hospital blanket were covered in large bruises.

'I wouldn't like to see the other guy ...' Julia said, closing the door behind her.

Loke laughed, but the laughter quickly turned into a fit of coughing and he put his hands to his ribs.

'Oh no, are you in pain?'

'Only when I laugh,' he said, smiling wryly.

Julia got a chair from the other end of the room and carried it to the side of his bed. She immediately felt overwhelming tenderness for the young man lying there. On the few occasions she had met Loke, he had made an effort to take up as little space as possible – as if he thought he didn't have the same rights as anyone else to exist or be heard. In the hospital bed he appeared to be fading away into the white sheet under him.

'Have you got any relatives that we or the hospital should get in touch with?' she said, resisting the impulse to pat Loke's hand.

For some reason, she was convinced that he would perceive that as too much of an intrusion into his personal space.

Loke shook his head.

'No, there's no one. My job is my family.'

'Well, Milda is on her way,' Julia said. 'She's probably running every red light in town to get here.'

Loke laughed but then began to cough again.

'I told you not to make me laugh.'

'I can't make any promises – I'm inherently hysterically funny,' Julia said, shrugging.

She didn't really know this man, but she realized that she liked him. She understood why Milda had such a protective instinct towards him and why Vincent had taken such a liking to him. Beneath the timid surface she could discern a shining intellect.

'Can I ask what happened?' she said cautiously.

Loke nodded.

'You can ask, but I'm afraid I won't be much use. I didn't see anything. I was going to head down to you lot with the documentation – I wanted to show it to you personally. I was putting on my coat and then everything went black. When I came to, everything hurt and I was chained to the handle of a cabinet down in the basement. Luckily for me the handle wasn't attached to the cabinet very well otherwise I'd probably still be down there.'

'So you didn't see who attacked you?' Julia said, feeling her heart sink.

She had hoped that Loke would be able to provide them with some useful information, but the man in the bed shook his head again.

'Ouch. I think I probably ought to keep my head still too. No, I didn't see anything. I reached for my coat and then: bang, gone. Until I woke up and found myself chained up. I've no idea how they got in.'

'They?'

'A person or persons unknown. I don't know.'

'Do you think it's the same people who stole the old bones?'

Loke made a grimace of despair but didn't answer.

'It's OK, we're going to do a thorough investigation.'

She hesitated. Then she placed her hand on his anyway. He blinked but didn't withdraw his hand. She patted it a few times and then she stood up.

'If you think of anything, just call me,' she said. 'But make sure you get some rest. We'll do everything we can. That much I promise.'

'Thanks,' Loke said weakly, wincing with pain. 'Did Milda tell you about the DNA match?'

Julia came to a halt.

'What DNA match?'

'I suspected it might fall between the cracks,' Loke said with a sigh. 'It's all my fault – I was the one who took it upon myself to tell you about it. And Milda has been very stressed lately. It wouldn't surprise me if she assumed you already knew. Better late than never, I suppose.'

'What are you talking about?'

'We should be happy that there are so many people who want to do their family trees. The nephew of the heap of bones registered with one of those genealogy sites where you submit a saliva sample. He's called Tor Svensson. Milda googled him, and apparently he works with Niklas Stockenberg.'

Julia stared at him. She could almost hear the cogs spinning in some invisible machine. Somehow, this was all connected. The only question was how.

126

Christer ended the call. He had just spoken to Handelsbanken. In order to pull account history from more than ten years ago for Marcus Eriksson, he needed not only Marcus's name and personal identification number, but also the account number that Marcus had held at the time. The same was true for Erika Sävelden and Jon Langseth.

The chances of Marcus's mother remembering a twenty-year-old account number were vanishingly small, and that was assuming she had even known it at the time. And while Christer might get lucky once, he needed to get lucky three times for it to yield anything. It felt much easier to wait until that shrink came home from Rwanda. However, he supposed he might be able to turn something else up, since Julia had sent him on this wild goose chase anyway. Her idea had at least got the cogs turning. There was a thought taking shape somewhere deep down in his brain, but it wasn't quite ready yet. He knew it wouldn't show itself until it was done.

Mark Eric – Marcus Eriksson's alter ago – was making an obscene gesture at Christer from the monitor in front of him. He had clicked his way to Mark's Wikipedia page while he had been on the phone to the bank. The page told him that Mark's first single had been released by the then-fledgling record label Not Loud Enough Records – to an enormous media buzz.

Christer read about the release of Mark's record again and then clicked on the link to an article from *Expressen*. It was by a music writer criticizing the heavy marketing campaign for the unknown Mark Eric, and questioning whether it was just a cynical record company ploy.

But Mark's records had kept on coming. A few years later, the same writer had written an article with the headline 'Mark Eric is here to stay' in which he paid tribute to the label's faith in their artist.

Christer went to the label's website. It turned out that Mark was their first and biggest artist. They had released some other records too, but they seemed to be rather half-hearted ventures by some of Mark's friends. Mark himself had presumably engineered their signings. The record company had been founded by a handful of enthusiasts and an obliging venture capitalist who had launched a public relations agency at the same time.

Hmm. That was some investment.

He continued to search online, looking for the people who had been named and then for the company that had injected funding. It was a family-owned company. It was a family whose name he had seen on several occasions in recent days.

That might, of course, be a coincidence. It could just be someone with a similar name. But the contours of the unfinished thought at the back of his mind were beginning to become clearer.

He opened a new tab and searched for Erika Sävelden. Several hits led to articles about prizes and awards she had received for her lectures, but he also found links to a booking page on the website of a talent agency called Talking Minds. They appeared to have been responsible for securing most of Erika's bookings.

He picked up the phone and dialled their number. A woman answered immediately.

'Hello, this is Talking Minds. Louise speaking. How may I help you?'

'Hello, my name is Christer Bengtsson. I'm calling from the police,' he said. 'We're looking into the disappearance of Erika Sävelden – I'm afraid I can't really comment on why at present – and I gather that you used to represent her. Would you mind telling me a bit about your working relationship?'

'Erika?' the woman said with a laugh. 'Well, that was actually before my time at the agency. But I've obviously heard about her. Erika's first year on the speaking circuit was unlike anything we've seen in the industry – before or since. The huge amount of requests she received formed the basis of the rest of her success.'

'How do you mean?' Christer said, looking for a pencil.

'For some reason, public speakers always become more attractive when they already have a lot of bookings in the diary,'

Louise said. 'The fact that the first hundred requests came in from the same company wasn't something we needed to advertise.'

'Do you remember what the company was called?'

He listened quietly to what Louise at Talking Minds had to say, taking notes on a Post-it. Then he thanked her before ending the call.

The idea was clear now. He looked at what he had written down about Marcus and Erika. There was a connection, but he needed to find another. Jon was next in line. Christer had begun to discern a pattern and knew what to look for, so he didn't bother calling Josephine Langseth. Instead, he contacted the Companies Registration Office to find out which companies Jon Langseth had been involved in for the last twenty years.

It transpired that Jon had started out small and taken some risks that had paid off, before selling the companies when they were prosperous and using the profits to start bigger and better companies. But Jon's money – even though he'd ended up with a sizeable amount – hadn't been enough on its own. He'd needed investors for his ventures.

In a fifteen-year-old article from *Dagens Nyheter*, Christer found an interview with a number of Swedish and foreign angel investors. Jon's company at the time was mentioned in passing as an example of the kind of business they were funding.

The investment company backing Jon was mentioned by name.

And there, on the screen in front of Christer, was the final connection.

The information hadn't even been difficult to track down once he knew what he was looking for. No one had bothered to hide it, since it was already concealed in so many other layers of documentation. And on its own it was completely meaningless. You had to be looking for all the connections at the same time.

Christer picked up his pencil. He had found the common denominator for all three victims. Julia had been right – it was about money. Just not in the way she had thought. He stared at the name he had jotted down on the Post-it note. The same name, three times. He found it hard to believe there wasn't a connection between that name and Niklas Stockenberg too. And if that were the case, then Niklas was in even greater danger than any of them had imagined.

127

Ruben kicked the gravel in frustration. He was sick of the tunnels. He hadn't liked the metro before, and the frequent visits to the dirty darkness over the past week hadn't done much to change his mind. He and Adam had been tasked with supplementing the officers inspecting the former line sixteen by taking the last three stations: Zinkensdamm, Hornstull and Liljeholmen.

He supposed they ought to be grateful it wasn't more, but three was three too many. The representatives from the metro company hadn't even bothered to continue chaperoning them. Fortunately, they had already dealt with Zinkensdamm and were almost done with Hornstull.

Frankly, it seemed rather unlikely that Niklas Stockenberg was being held captive underground – or at least in proximity to any of the metro stations. Firstly, it was deadly. Trains were rushing past every five minutes and he and Adam were forced to step well back each time to avoid being pulled over by the suction. Secondly, there was nowhere to hide someone. There were various nooks and crannies, but nowhere you wouldn't quickly be found.

'I think Vincent is way off the mark,' he said as they sought shelter from another passing train. 'As usual. Who's to say that Niklas hasn't been locked up somewhere above ground? He might still be close to one of the stations. That seems much more likely to me.'

'I agree,' Adam said, shining his torch down a service tunnel that ran away from the tracks at an angle. 'The problem with that is that we have no idea where he might be. At least down here the possibilities are … limited.'

'And thank fuck for that,' said Ruben, following Adam into the smaller tunnel.

The service tunnel was a dead end where tools and pallets were kept. Just like every other space they had found and checked out. Empty. Nothing. There was nowhere you could hide a minister of justice.

'I think we're done here,' said Adam. 'That just leaves Liljeholmen.'

They followed the tunnel back to the station where they climbed up onto the platform to wait for the next train. The easiest way to travel between two stations on the metro was to take the train.

'From Liljeholmen, the metro is mostly above ground,' Ruben said as they got onto a train on the red line 14 service to Fruängen. 'So we only need to search one end of the station, where the train goes through the tunnel. I bet we won't find anything there either. Have you heard anything from the others?'

Adam looked at his phone.

They had started a group chat with the other pairs of officers who were out searching so that they could provide ongoing reports of anything they found. IT would doubtless have something to say about that arrangement from a purely security-focused point of view, but no one wanted to work unnecessarily in the final days of December. If anyone found anything there was no point in the others continuing to search.

'All the groups are done apart from one,' said Adam. 'And us. No one has anything to report.'

'I told you,' Ruben said gloomily. 'Waste of time.'

Adam raised an eyebrow and smiled.

'Is there somewhere you'd rather be? Correct me if I'm wrong, but have you and Sara Temeric …?'

The question hung unspoken in the air.

Ruben glared at him. The train jolted, forcing him to grab a pole.

'Correct me if I'm wrong,' Ruben said in the same tone as Adam. 'But have you and Julia Hammarsten …?'

Adam gaped. He looked completely shocked.

Ruben smiled smugly. Fair was fair. It was probably a good thing for Adam to realize that his and the boss's little secret wasn't quite as secret as they seemed to believe.

The train stopped at Liljeholmen and they got off. Ruben began to walk towards the rear end of the platform where there was supposed to be a small ladder to admit them to the tunnel.

Another dark, boring tunnel. In his mind's eye, he saw Sara. He saw her incredible smile.

'Waste of time,' he muttered as he clambered down into the tunnel with Adam following. 'My God, what a fucking waste of time.'

128

They shook hands with Tor as he showed them in. This meeting room was one of the most austere rooms Milda had ever seen. An oblong, dark grey table stood in the centre of the room with pale grey upholstered chairs around it. The art on the walls, from the state collections, was not likely to raise a smile either. This was a room where middle-aged men in dark suits sat about frowning.

That was all prejudice, of course. But the sight of Tor Svensson in his impeccable dark blue suit didn't do anything to change her mind.

Milda and Julia both sat down.

'Thank you for coming,' Tor said to them. 'I know your time is precious, so I really do appreciate it. I simply have so much to do right now with everything that's happened and I can't get away.'

Tor laced his fingers together around a black coffee mug. Milda noted that he hadn't asked whether they wanted any coffee. This was clearly not going to be a long meeting.

'Not at all,' said Julia. 'We thought you should hear this from us personally. Milda, do you mind taking over?'

Milda adjusted her chair and cleared her throat.

'Yes, of course. I work at the National Board of Forensic Medicine,' she said. 'You're probably aware that the police are investigating a case that may be connected to the threat to Niklas Stockenberg.'

'The three murder victims found in the metro tunnels,' Tor said, nodding.

'Exactly,' said Julia. 'But when we were searching, we also found a heap of bones that was much older and that doesn't seem to be related to the other three victims.'

Tor raised his eyebrows.

'The police were able to identify the three contemporary victims fairly quickly,' Milda said. 'But the other skeleton has been something of a mystery. That was until we got a hit in the DNA database of a genealogy company and traced the deceased's nephew. There's no easy way to say this, but ... Tor, I'm afraid the bones were your uncle's.'

Tor's eyes widened and he spilled a little coffee on the table.

'Björn?' he said in surprise. 'You've found Björn?'

'It would seem so,' Julia said. 'We were wondering if you could tell us a bit about him. We don't know anything. Until you just told us his name, we didn't even know that.'

Tor sighed deeply and lowered his head. Then he looked up at the ceiling for a few seconds before he began to talk. His voice was not as steady as it had been before.

'I always liked Björn when I was little,' he said. 'He was a teacher and everyone loved him. But he was a manic depressive. Not that I understood that at the time – it's something I realized later on. There were spells in his life where he drank too much and talked about killing himself. But life is ironic that way. Linda beat him to it.'

'Linda?' said Julia.

'His wife. It was a shock to everyone. She was always so happy and carefree. Especially in the run-up to when it happened. But we should have seen the signs. Isn't it the case that people who are planning to take their own lives sometimes seem to be at their best just before it happens? Because they've already made up their minds?'

He was looking at them now and there were tears in his eyes. Julia looked as if she wanted to say something, but she refrained from doing so.

'Björn came home one day to find a farewell note,' Tor said. 'By then she was gone. They found the body two days later on the shoreline at Hornstull. Björn blamed himself. He said it was his fault for being impossible to live with. After that, his own dark spells became longer and deeper. And then one day he was gone too. Everyone assumed he must have jumped off the Västerbron bridge, just like she did. The worst part is that he took their little boy with him. The whole family wiped out. Dreadful. But now you say you've found his remains?'

Milda nodded quietly, moved by his story.

'Then I'd like to arrange a decent burial for him,' Tor said. 'I assume there won't be any problems releasing his remains to me, since I'm his closest living relative?'

Milda glanced unhappily at Julia. She really did wish she'd been given a cup of coffee. Or anything that would allow her to busy herself and avoid answering Tor's question.

'We have … we no longer have them,' she said in a low voice, fidgeting. 'They're … It seems they've …'

'His remains have been stolen,' Julia said. 'It happened the night before Christmas Eve.'

Tor stared at them for a few seconds while his face became increasingly red. Then he slapped the palm of his hand against the dark grey tabletop, making the rest of the coffee in his mug splash out.

'I might have guessed as much,' he said. 'Are you lot capable of doing anything right? Alongside everything else that's happened, you can't even keep track of some bones? I'm going to talk to your superiors. This incompetent team cannot be allowed to remain in existence.'

'I understand that you're upset and that this is dragging up old memories,' Julia said. 'But our team is very competent. I'm very sorry about the theft of your relative's bones, and we're doing everything we can to retrieve them. But I should add that the theft took place at the National Board of Forensic Medicine. However, I do have some questions for you that might help us in our investigation.'

'I don't see how I can help you. You said that Björn's remains weren't connected to the other three victims,' Tor said, standing up.

He grabbed some napkins and began to mop up the coffee on the table.

'We'll have to look into that,' Julia said. 'It seems that Björn died around the year 2000. Do you remember in which year he disappeared?'

'Oh, it must have been in the early nineties if I remember correctly,' Tor said, throwing the soggy napkins in the bin.

'Ninety-one or ninety-two ... Hang on a second. Are you saying that he may have spent ten years homeless in the tunnels?'

'It seems that way. Björn's son – your cousin – was with him. We've heard stories about a boy who grew up down in the tunnels.'

Tor shook his head as if he was unwilling to take in what he was hearing. Milda felt for him. She tried and failed to imagine what it would be like to receive news like this herself. The sombre colour palette in the room felt more and more fitting.

'How is this connected to your murders?' Tor asked with a sigh. 'And to Niklas? I don't understand.'

'It may not be connected at all,' Julia said. 'But your uncle's date of death matches other events that took place in our victims' pasts. We don't know what it means – if it means anything at all. But we'd very much like to reach your cousin. In the tunnels he went by the nickname "the Prince". If you have any information that can help us find him, we'd be keen to hear it. Other relatives? Someone who might have been in contact with him? I'm guessing you're also interested in seeing him, now that you know he's potentially still alive.'

Tor stared into space for a few seconds.

'Who else knows about this?' he said. 'It would be an unnecessary distraction to my current work if the media caught wind of this.'

'I agree,' Julia said. 'We want to keep the media out at all costs. We don't want a repeat of Walther Stockenberg. Right now, the only people who know are in this room – plus the rest of our team.'

Tor nodded as if he had made a decision. He picked up his phone and dialled.

'Hi Anna, it's me,' he said when he got through. 'I need a favour.'

He quickly repeated what Milda and Julia had just told him. He nodded a few times, then offered his thanks before ending the call. He turned to Julia again.

'That was the prime minister,' Tor said. 'She's offered her personal guarantee that you'll get all the resources you need to find Björn's son. Or the Prince, if you like ... But if anyone asks, he isn't my cousin.'

129

He visited Dad's grave every day for two years. He had been allowed to help make the mound. The others had prepared it the way that Dad had taught them to. A royal burial. A burial worthy of a king.

It wasn't possible to tell what the mound of gravel contained from the outside, but he could feel the bones when he placed his hand on the mound. He felt Dad.

He often talked to him, telling him what was going on in the world of the invisible. Who was still there. Who had gone. Who had arrived.

But with each passing month, it felt less and less like a home. Without Dad, there was no family. There was no home in the darkness.

Without Dad, he was just invisible.

The decision slowly took shape in the time that followed. It was time to become visible. It was time to leave the darkness. Perhaps he would find a family in the sunshine – the sunshine that had shone on him when he had been little. He had almost forgotten how it felt. The light, the rays, the warmth spreading through him. Perhaps he could find that again.

He slowly ran his hand over the mound of gravel.

'I'll be back,' he said quietly, knowing as he stood up that he meant it.

He came from two worlds. He could belong in either.

He didn't say anything to the others when he left.

He was going to visit them again – they weren't losing him. But he could no longer belong to them.

Odenplan station was full of people. The spring sunshine was high in the clear blue sky and had brought out makeshift seating at the city's cafés and restaurants. These were full of people raising their faces towards the sky.

The phone booth was a few hundred metres away and in his trouser pocket he had a collection of coins he had found. He knew the number by heart. Dad had taught it to him, but he had also taught him that it could only be used in emergencies.

This was an emergency. He had been invisible, but now he was becoming visible.

He inserted the coins, dialled the number he had memorized and listened as it rang. It was time now. Time to leave the darkness.

130

'Knock knock?'

Julia didn't wait for a reply before opening the door and stepping through it. The first things she noticed were her father's rosy cheeks and his excited look.

'The prime minister,' he said hoarsely.

Julia sat down on the uncomfortable chair in front of her father's desk and looked at him quizzically.

'Yes? What about her?'

'She called!'

'Called who?'

'Me!'

'Oh come on, it's hardly the first time you've spoken to a prime minister. Didn't you even play the odd round of golf with the last one?'

'Yes, but there's something about Hjortén. She's so … vigorous!'

'Dad, please. Talk to one woman with power and you're all flushed. Be careful I don't let on to Mum that you're in love with the prime minister.'

'Nonsense. I don't know what you mean!'

Julia grinned.

Her father – the commissioner of Stockholm police – looked down.

'You won't say anything to your mother will you? That would be unnecessary.'

Julia put her fingers to her lips, made a locking gesture with her hand and pretended to throw away the key.

'So what did she say?' she asked eventually.

'Who? Your mother?' said Egil Hammarsten, staring at his daughter in confusion.

'No Dad,' Julia sighed. 'The prime minister. Anna Hjortén.'

'Oh, yes. Of course. Well, she praised us for the incredible work she thinks we're doing, and said she wanted to show her clear support for the investigation. She assured me that we'll have all the resources we need put at our disposal. The eyes of the world are on Sweden – we can't lose another government minister. It'd make us look like a banana republic.'

'Did she say that? That we'd look like a banana republic?'

Egil ran a hand over his bald pate, which was still covered in small beads of sweat following his call with the prime minister.

'Perhaps not in those words. Actually, I think she did. Anyway, the message was quite clear. We've got to find the justice minister – alive.'

'So we need to find the justice minister? Alive? It's a good job you clarified that – I've been wondering for days what I'm supposed to be doing.'

'I see you have the same sense of humour as your mother.'

'I'll take that as a compliment,' Julia said, standing up. 'But joking aside, I just wanted to pop in and say that we've eliminated lots of avenues of enquiry, as you may have heard. That's progress of a kind.'

'Yes, I told you that Gustaf Brons chap was a dead end. You ought to listen to your old father a little more often.'

Julia rolled her eyes but refrained from commenting. It was hard to teach old dogs new tricks. And she could always get her own back by revealing to her mother that her father had a crush on the prime minister.

131

'Sorry I'm late!'

Milda dashed into her lab, her heart in her mouth. Loke was hunched over a microscope at the far end of the room. He looked up and nodded when she entered. She caught sight of the large wall clock, which showed the time was 2.30 p.m. Oh no! She was later than she thought.

'You're already out of hospital?' she said to Loke. 'I'm so sorry. You definitely don't need to be here today.'

Loke straightened up and turned off the microscope.

'It's fine,' he said. 'I'm just a little sore. And that's mostly my pride. I'm happy to work. But do you have a moment?'

He pointed to the corner of the room they had set up as their own break area since they rarely had time to go to the actual canteen. Milda sank down onto one of the chairs. She shook the Thermos on the table and found it empty. Obviously. Loke took the other seat.

'It's none of my business,' he said cautiously, 'but I can't help noticing that something is wrong. You're late for work almost every day. You look like you haven't slept in a week. And to be honest, you're pretty distracted even when you're here. Is there anything I can do?'

Milda swallowed hard so that she wouldn't start crying. She had been trying to make sure that she did the right thing by everyone while also being professional at work, but the result was that she felt like an elastic band that was about to break. Loke's unexpected kindness had dispersed the tension a little.

'Thanks,' she said, shaking her head vigorously. 'It's Mykolas. My grandfather. He's in hospital. It came out of nowhere. Well, I suppose it didn't, actually. But he hasn't been letting on how much pain he's in. That means the cancer had spread throughout his body before it was found. They say he doesn't have long left. I'm visiting him in hospital as often as I can – that's why I'm not always here. I'm trying to find times when he has the energy and is awake.'

She looked at Loke. It was becoming harder and harder to hold back the tears.

'I don't know what I'll do without him,' she said.

Loke took her hand.

'Look, you should take care of your grandfather. The people in our families are the most important thing we have. We have them for a while and then we don't have them any more. But they still influence us for the rest of our lives. I'll man the fort here. No one needs to know. It's not as if the bodies are going to let on. I mean, come on, three of them are actual skeletons.'

Milda began to laugh even though tears were running down her cheeks. The relief of talking to someone who listened and understood was huge.

'Visit him as much as they'll let you,' Loke said. 'And I want to rephrase my question from "is there anything I can do?" to "is there anything I can do for you?"'

Milda wiped away the tears with her hand and nodded.

'There is actually one thing you can do,' she said, pulling out her phone.

She switched on the Bluetooth speaker on the table and connected to it while searching for her playlist in Spotify. Then she hit play on the Arvingarna song 'Eloise' at top volume.

'It's Grandpa's favourite,' she said. 'And mine. Make sure you really give it some welly.'

They screeched along with mingled tears and laughter.

132

'Julia!' Christer called out, storming through the door with his face bright red and his eyes sparkling with excitement. 'Good! You're back!'

'Yes, I am. And apparently you've given up knocking,' she said.

It wasn't like Christer to move with such speed, let alone without knocking, so whatever he had come to tell her was surely important.

'I've found a financial connection. Like they say in the movie, follow the money!'

Julia had no idea what film he was referencing and she didn't bother to ask. She was far more interested in the money connection.

'So you found something while going through the bank accounts?' she said, hearing the eagerness in her own voice. 'Or have you tracked down our adventurous psychologist?'

'No, no, not the accounts,' Christer said. 'If I'd gone down that line I'd still be working on it. But I've found something else which I think means we can drop the shrink as an idea.'

'How do you make that out? If it turns out they all consulted the same guy, then that's a strong connection between our victims.'

'It's possible, but we still don't have any evidence for that. And I've found something much more compelling. Something that is more than just a hypothesis – this is tangible. I've discovered that all three victims got a major boost in life about twenty years ago. At first they were all deeply depressed – and for all I know they might all have seen the same psychologist. Although I'm more inclined to think they didn't. The boost came from an entirely different place. Mark Eric benefitted from a huge and unusually costly marketing campaign provided by his brand new record label. Erika Sävelden went from being an unknown to an established lecturer in a year by securing more than a hundred gigs. The vast majority of those bookings came from the same company. And Jon Langseth's start-ups benefitted from private investment all along.'

'And?' Julia said, baffled. 'It's no surprise they all had help – isn't that necessary in most cases to achieve success? They're not alone in that.'

'Sure,' Christer said, his eyes triumphant. 'But in this case they all had the same benefactor. He's been hiding in the background thanks to his family firm, but it isn't hard to track him down. He probably didn't think anyone would look for him, and you probably won't believe me when I tell you who it is.'

Julia stared at Christer as he told her the name of the person who had set Mark, Erika and Jon on the track to success – the person who had laid the foundations for so many years of stellar performance by the trio. When she heard the name, she grabbed the edge of her desk tightly.

'I suppose he might just be a philanthropist,' she said, more because she had to say it than because she believed it. 'Someone who happened to have lots of money and the desire to selflessly help people who were struggling.'

Christer nodded.

'He certainly could be,' he said. 'Except for the minor detail that everyone whose careers he launched has subsequently been found in skeletal form in a metro tunnel. That can't possibly be a coincidence. And I promise you that if we look closely, we'll find him skulking in the shadows of Niklas Stockenberg's past too.'

'We can't scare him off,' Julia said. 'We have to proceed with caution. I'll call to schedule a meeting with him tomorrow. That's good work, Christer.'

The jigsaw pieces were slowly falling into place, one by one. The only problem was that Julia still couldn't make out any kind of motif for the puzzle – there was no picture there, nor any rhyme or reason to it all.

133

THREE DAYS TO GO

Vincent went out early in the morning to get the newspaper from the mailbox. Just as he didn't want his music to be digital, so he preferred to read his news in print. When he had the time. When he opened the lid of the mailbox, he saw there was a letter inside as well as the newspaper.

It was a new message from the Shadow, written on an anonymous sheet of A4 paper.

He grabbed the letter and the newspaper and trudged back through the snow to the front door. He hadn't bothered to clear the path since Christmas Eve and it now looked like a shovel had never been anywhere near it. His shoes filled with cold snow, but he didn't care in the slightest. The message was more important. He stopped by the front door and read it in the glow of the external lighting on the house.

> You still haven't got it.
>
> I didn't think it would be so hard,
>
> but you can have another day.
>
> One more day.
>
> Meet me at the Gondolen restaurant at 6 p.m. tonight.
>
> This is your last chance.

* * *

The Shadow wanted to meet him! He would finally find out who it was. The thought filled him with a degree of excitement, but also nausea. He had just a day to work out what the Shadow wanted and he didn't dare think what would happen to his family if he failed.

But the encounter at the restaurant would be the perfect opportunity to capture his tormentor. He just had to ask Mina and Ruben to be there. Or … perhaps not. The Shadow would doubtless have thought about that. He or she wouldn't have agreed to meet at a location where there was any risk of apprehension.

The Shadow still held a trump card: Ulrika, Maria, Aston, Benjamin, Rebecka. They were still at stake. Even if the Shadow had asked to meet Vincent at police headquarters, Vincent wouldn't have dared say a word about it to the police. But he supposed he would have to tell Mina that he was meeting the Shadow, just in case something happened to him.

He opened the front door, went into the desolate house and took off his snow-filled shoes. He turned on the main light in the kitchen and put the newspaper on the side before making his way into the living room. He never went in there any longer – the last time it had felt as if someone had put a hornets' nest in his head. The walls were screaming at him and his eyes ached. But he still turned on the main light – he had enough shadows as it was. He stopped with his hand on the light switch and gazed automatically out of the window that overlooked the garden to the rear of the house. He wasn't at all surprised to see that the ravens were back.

This time there were four of them – just like there had been the first time he saw them. Once again, they weren't sitting in an even row. There was a gap between the third and fourth birds.

He had concluded that they must be stuffed. The Shadow was putting them in his garden when Vincent wasn't there. Of course, he could go outside and take a closer look, but if they were to fly away – if they actually were real – then his brain would probably explode.

Maybe they were just in his head. He thought about the study he had told Umberto about on his last visit to his agent. Overexertion and stress led to a build-up of toxic substances in the brain's frontal lobe where rational thought took place. Given the messages, the insinuations and the threats he had received all autumn, it was perhaps not surprising that he had begun to hallucinate.

He shook himself. These types of thoughts were not helping at all. He had to do something.

He went back into the kitchen, found a pen and sat down at the table. He was convinced that the Shadow was responsible for all the peculiar things that had happened to him in recent days. The cut-up Christmas card, the alarm clock, the birds. And the hourglasses too? No, they were something else. Whoever the Shadow was, it wasn't someone who wanted to help him with the murder enquiry. The hourglasses had come from the killer, or from someone who knew what the killer was going to do. He was sure of it. Vincent pushed thoughts of them aside and focused on the other things.

He wrote down what he knew on the back of the letter. If he could find a common denominator then he might be able to understand what the Shadow was after.

Firstly, the Christmas card. Benjamin had discovered that the inscriptions on the cards were Bible quotes from the Book of Proverbs, verses 27:15 and 20:25. He wrote them down on the paper.

27 15 20 25

Then there was the alarm clock. It had gone off at 16:30 and 22:19. At first, he had thought that he was supposed to see something then, but it was probably the precise times that mattered. He noted them beneath the Bible verses.

27 15 20 25

16 30 22 19

And then the ravens. Odin's messengers. Associated with lost souls in many mythologies around the world. Was the message that Vincent was a lost soul? Maybe. But it couldn't just be that. The Bible quotes and the alarm clock could be reduced to two-figure numbers. Was the same thing possible with the birds? He closed his eyes and summoned the images of their positions in the snow on the four occasions he had seen them.

The first time there had been four birds with a gap between the first and the second.

The second time, it had been two birds, two empty holes between them and another hole to the right-hand side.

The third time he saw them, there had once again been two birds but with space for three more between them.

And this final time there were four birds with a space between the third and the fourth birds.

Once those images were clear in his mind, he simplified them by replacing the birds with black squares. The gaps between them – the holes in the snow – became white squares. In his mind's eye, he now saw four rows of black and white squares.

Black – white – black – black – black.

Black – white – white – black – white.

Black – white – white – white – black.

Black – black – black – white – black.

That was good, but they still weren't numbers. But black and white were opposites. They were like yes and no; on and off. Alive and dead.

They were binary.

The ravens were a binary code.

He opened his eyes and picked up the pen. He translated the black squares into ones and the white squares into zeros on the page.

10111 10010 10001 11101.

Four binary numbers. He wrote the sequence of numbers 16 8 4 2 1 underneath each binary number. By adding up the numbers with a one on top of them and ignoring the ones with a zero, he was able to convert the binary numbers into ordinary denary numbers.

23 18 17 29

He wrote the new numbers underneath the ones relating to the Bible verses and from the alarm clock. Now he had three rows.

27 15 20 25

16 30 22 19

23 18 17 29

He had a strong suspicion of where this was all going, but there needed to be a fourth row for it to work. What had he missed?

He stood up and went into his study. Was there something hidden in the presents sent to him by the Shadow during the autumn? No, he had already solved those challenges. It had to be something else.

He went back into the kitchen and his eye was caught by the calendar on the wall, still displaying Fermat's Last Theorem. He had forgotten to ask Maria who had circled 21, 24 and 28 December. And now he could no longer ask.

21, 24 and 28.

Oh crap!

He turned over to January. His suspicions were confirmed. January 14 was also circled. The Shadow had given him the first four numbers in the calendar long ago, but Vincent had missed it. His hand trembling, he wrote down the four numbers from the calendar above the others, since they were chronologically the first ones he had received.

21 24 28 14

27 15 20 25

16 30 22 19

23 18 17 29

He knew exactly what he was looking at, but he refused to work it out. He couldn't do this any more. The Shadow could mock him however much he wanted. Vincent closed his eyes. Outside, the sun had just begun to rise, but within him the darkness was creeping ever closer.

134

'Of course I want to do everything I can to help, but it would have been more practical if we had gone over this when we last met.'

Tor held his hands out in frustration while steadily looking Julia in the eyes.

'We appreciate you taking the time to come to us on this occasion,' Julia said, scrutinizing him carefully as she sat opposite him in the interview room. 'I'm afraid we weren't in possession of this information the last time we met.'

The word that spontaneously sprang to mind as she studied the man before her was *immaculate*. Tor Svensson did not have a single hair out of place.

'Is Mina here?' he said.

'Not right now. I know you've had some contact through Niklas, so it's best to avoid any personal connection while we are questioning you.'

'Questioning me?' Tor said, looking indignant. 'Am I under suspicion for something? If so, I need to call my lawyer.'

Julia shook her head. She cursed herself for her choice of words – it was unusually clumsy of her. The investigation had begun to wear her down, while the chaos at home was hardly improving matters. She was tired. So utterly, utterly tired.

'Sorry, that was a poor choice of words,' she said. 'It's just that I often question people in this room. But in your case, it's simply that something has come up and we need your help to resolve it.'

'Like I said, I'll be as helpful as I can. Niklas's absence is dreadful on every level. Both for me personally and for the country as a whole.'

Julia leaned forward and lowered her voice.

'Then I suppose you can imagine the pressure we're under,' she said. 'The prime minister called us not long ago.'

'Yes, Anna is very worried about Niklas,' Tor said, nodding. 'I spoke to her about the matter just this morning. She and Niklas are … close.'

'So can we run through my questions?' Julia said casually.

This was something she had learned early on as an interrogator. The less interested she sounded in the answers to her questions, the more incautious people became in their replies.

'Go on,' Tor said with another gesture of his hands. 'The sooner we're done, the sooner I can get back to trying to get Swedish society on an even keel.'

Julia did a double-take. Tor really did think about himself in grandiose terms.

'We've finally found a connection between the people whose bones were found in the metro tunnels,' she said.

Tor appeared to be waiting for her to continue.

'Twenty years ago, all three victims faced certain … difficulties.'

'Difficulties?'

The man in front of her looked confused. Immaculate but confused.

'They weren't in a good place in life. But we've discovered that they were lucky enough to receive help that enabled them to move on.'

She paused. Tor didn't look as if he knew what she was talking about. She glanced discreetly towards the camera in the corner to check that it was still recording.

'What do you mean, they received help?' he said.

'Well, the help came in different forms. Financial. Contacts. And it came from different sources. But behind all of those there's a company that is a common denominator in all this. Are you familiar with the company Hird AB?'

Tor looked startled.

'It was my father's … well, my grandfather's company,' he said. 'But how … What are you getting at?'

'Are you at all involved in the company?'

'No, I've never taken much interest in business. I became

politically engaged from an early stage. It all started in the young conservatives for me, as it happens. Although I can't deny that my family's business dealings have given me a comfortable life, I've never been involved in the company at all. Not that one, nor any other of my family's companies.'

'This took place after your father passed away,' Julia said calmly, fixing her gaze on him. 'And your grandfather died in 1983.'

'I still don't know anything,' Tor said, now looking very clearly baffled. 'It's all managed one way or another. I'm hopeless about business. I receive a monthly deposit. And there are a few accounts for different purposes – for instance, there's one for maintenance of the house.'

'So you don't know anything about investments made twenty years ago to support Jon Langseth, Erika Sävelden or Marcus Eriksson? Or Niklas Stockenberg, for that matter?'

Tor reacted strongly when she mentioned his boss.

'What's Niklas got to do with this?' he said. 'Niklas has never mentioned anything about a time when he was … how did you put it? When he wasn't in a good place in life. And are you implying that some sort of payment was made to Niklas by my family? No. I would have heard about that. That's the kind of thing the media sniff out right away.'

'Do you mind if we take a closer look at Hird's financial dealings?'

'Look away. I've got nothing to hide. I've never been bothered about money. My goal has always been to bring about change. To improve the world.'

'How have you related to … your family's background? Given that you've chosen not to play an active role in the family business?'

'I assume you're referring to Grandpa Harald?' Tor sighed and shook his head. 'I'll be the first to admit that it's not the finest hour in our family history. But I barely met the man. I wasn't very old when he died, so I've only heard the stories at second-hand. But we mustn't forget that those were different times. People quite seriously believed that you could distinguish between the races based on their craniums. Although I don't know for sure, maybe that played the same sort of role in the popular imagination as those DNA tests that are now available so that people can discover their own origins. Niklas gave them to everyone on the staff for Christmas last year and encouraged us all to send in our DNA because he thought it was intriguing and, well ... I suppose that's just a version of defining "us and them". Humanity has been busy categorizing and grouping itself since time immemorial.'

'You aren't aware of a connection between your father Rune or your grandfather Harald and the victims, or Niklas?'

'I'd never even heard their names before you said them. Are you absolutely sure that Niklas and the metro bones are connected?'

'Are you saying you have a better theory?'

'Personally, I believe the motive for Niklas's abduction is political.'

'Political? In what way?'

Julia discreetly checked the camera again. It still said *Record* in red lettering on the display.

'Chaos. It's the cornerstone of all political change. Chaos,' Tor said emphatically.

'I'm not very politically savvy. I'm afraid you'll have to explain that one to me.'

'You have order. And you have chaos. They're counterpoles. Two things that sound like constants with a clear meaning. Yet they can be viewed from completely different perspectives depending on who the observer is. After the two World Wars, the idea of democracy emerged in the West based on political freedom and legitimate opposition. In China, however, that's perceived as an inability to act, and inefficiency. Order or chaos? China distinguishes between economic and political liberalism. Market liberalism is good, but legitimate opposition, religious freedom, freedom of association and free speech are all bad. In Sweden we think democracy is the norm and that it's the obvious goal for all nations. But as early as 1933, Herbert Tingsten wrote that it's far from clear that democracy will survive. Is democracy order? Or is democracy chaos?'

'And what do you think this has to do with Niklas's disappearance?' Julia asked.

Tor leaned across the table.

'I think someone wants to create chaos,' he said emphatically. 'By kidnapping and perhaps killing our minister of justice. There might be other attacks against political dignitaries. Like I said, chaos. We're already well on the way if you look at how the country is doing right now. I know you're doing your best in the police, but it's already too late. Fatal shootings. Drug smuggling. Honour-based violence. This country is teetering on the edge of the abyss, and a dead government minister might be one of the things that causes us to fall into the darkness of chaos. And if someone wants to push us down, then it's likely to be because they want to create something else. A new thing that would hitherto have been unthinkable. Many believe that Tingsten was right and that democracy has had its day. They think a strong hand is best suited to leading our country through the challenges that the world currently faces. I think this is the perspective that we're dealing with, and it's got very little to do with how a Swedish rock star got started in his career or who booked a lecturer for public speaking engagements.'

He snorted as he said the last bit.

Julia stood up.

'I have a couple more questions,' she said. 'But I'm afraid that nature calls.'

'I'll be waiting here,' Tor said, reaching for the glass of water on the table.

Julia left the interview room and headed for the ladies. Once she had gone around the corner, she pulled out her phone and called one of the prosecutors she had saved to her contacts.

'Hello, this is Julia Hammarsten. I need a quick decision on an arrest warrant. Tor Svensson. Yes, *that* Tor Svensson. I'll send over the documentation shortly. Thank you. And this is about the minister of justice, so I don't have to tell you how important it is that we act quickly. Thank you.'

She rang off, her expression severe. Tor might be immaculate, but he wasn't completely perfect. He was lying. She didn't know *why* he was lying, but she knew that he was. He'd committed exactly the mistake that Julia had hoped he would. He'd said too much.

135

Adam looked at the note on which he'd written the name of the social worker. Mandy Wall. He walked slowly down the corridor in the social services office, scrutinizing the names on the doors. He found the right one on the final door and knocked.

'Come in!' a voice shouted from the other side.

There was a smell of cinnamon and pine when he entered the small office, and he quickly located the source of the smell to a scented candle that was burning. The wick gave off a crackling sound, almost like a fire, and together with the candle bridge in the window and some strings of fairy lights, the office seemed unexpectedly cosy.

He stepped forward and greeted the social worker. He was expected.

'Do you want me to turn on the main light?' said Mandy Wall. 'I'm on the computer so much and I prefer not to have too much light. Anyway, if you're going to be stuck working over Christmas you might as well make it a bit cosier. Here, have a ginger biscuit.'

Mandy Wall was a large and buxom woman clad in a red tunic. She pointed to a tin in front of her, but Adam shook his head.

'Where are you from?' she said.

Her gaze drew an answer from him.

'My parents were from Uganda,' Adam said.

It still felt strange to talk about his mother in the past tense. He wasn't sure that he would ever get used to it.

'But my mother came here alone when she was pregnant with me,' he added. 'She'd got a job at Uppsala University.'

'I'm from Somalia myself,' Mandy said. 'I met Anders, that's my husband, when he was there on business. And here we are, more than thirty years and three beautiful kids later.'

She pointed proudly to a framed family photo on her desk.

'Do you have kids?'

'No, not yet,' Adam said, picturing Julia. And Harry. He quickly changed the subject.

'I've got a few questions for you about a family that you were the case worker for, according to the files.'

'Files? So someone filed their concerns formally?'

'Yes. Family acquaintances did so on several occasions. This family has just cropped up in a live investigation and my boss thought it would be worth looking into it. And that's when I found these reports. Social services and the police were both involved back then.'

'Back then?'

'Yes, I've got to warn you that this took place more than thirty years ago.'

Mandy grimaced as if he had just dropped something foul smelling into her lap. He guessed that the social services archives were just as far behind as the police's records when it came to digitization. She pointed to an empty chair and he sat down. The aroma of gingerbread was irresistible and he helped himself to a heart-shaped biscuit.

'Oh gosh, that must have been just after I started here,' she said. 'I've worked with thousands of families since then. Do you have their names?'

Adam nodded. He began to speak, but his mouth was full of ginger biscuit, so he finished chewing before he continued.

'Svensson. Björn and Linda Svensson. And they had a son. I've got the case number here.'

'Brilliant. That'll help.'

Mandy put on a pair of glasses that were hanging around her neck, took Adam's note and began to key the details into her computer. She hummed quietly as she studied the screen and the sound mingled pleasantly with the crackling of the scented candle.

'Here we are,' Mandy said, leaning towards her monitor. 'Yes, I remember them well. Both parents had mental health problems. Björn was admitted to the psych ward several times for the treatment of manic depression – I suppose we'd call that bipolar disorder nowadays. And Linda suffered from depression. I recall meetings about the boy – Mattias – where we considered whether to take him into care. But the problem, if that's the right word to use, is that during their good periods, Björn and Linda were great parents. That kind of thing is tricky. We opted not to take Mattias away from them – instead we tried to help Mum and Dad as best we could. But … well, that wasn't enough.'

'I gather the mother committed suicide?'

Julia had told him what little she'd found out about the family's tragic fate from Tor. That was bad enough. But Mandy frowned.

'You're right about the suicide. Linda jumped off the Västerbron bridge. After that, Björn went AWOL with the boy. We always assumed he killed his son and then himself, but the bodies were never found. Tragic. Just so tragic. And he had such sterling support from his family as well. Björn, that is. I was in touch with his brother a fair bit. Let me see, what was he called …? Oh, here it is. Rune. Rune Svensson. The families mixed a lot. Rune tried to help them as much as he could.'

She took off her glasses and turned towards him.

'Why are you asking about this family?' she said, interrupting his train of thought. 'Have you found them?'

'I'm afraid I can't say anything right now,' Adam said.

Mandy nodded briefly. This was clearly not the first time she'd heard those words from an officer of the law.

'I'll print this off for you,' she said. 'I hope it's of use.'

Then she brightened up.

'Here you go – and have another biscuit!'

Adam hesitated.

'If you don't take another heart then I'll give you the slipper.'

Adam held his hands up disarmingly. He felt a smile spreading from ear to ear. His mother had always threatened him with the slipper. He happily helped himself to another gingerbread heart.

136

Vincent glanced towards Mina's living room to make sure that Nathalie wasn't within earshot, but she seemed to be absorbed in whatever Netflix series young people were watching these days. He'd suggested she watch *Doom Patrol* on HBO Max, but all she'd done was give him an odd look.

'Thanks for having me,' he said.

'You're always welcome here – I thought you knew that,' Mina said, smiling. 'The whole keeping people at a distance thing hasn't exactly worked out for me.'

She put the leftovers from her and Nathalie's lunch into the fridge. Vincent didn't say a word, but Mina appeared to be keeping food. That was a huge step forward. He guessed the leftovers were for Nathalie rather than Mina – that was as far as she was going. But it was still progress.

'You sounded worried on the phone,' Mina said.

He nodded, pulled out the new message left by the Shadow in his mailbox and handed it over.

'I don't know whether worried is the right word,' he said. 'The Shadow wants to meet me tonight.'

She read the brief message, her eyes wide.

'At Gondolen?' she said. 'OK. We can fill the place with plainclothes—'

'No,' Vincent interrupted. 'Please don't. My … my family might get hurt.'

Mournful music drifted through from the living room and someone in the show called out a name.

'Idiot!' Nathalie said loudly. 'So unrealistic.'

'Have you heard from them at all?' Mina said, lowering her voice. 'Your family, I mean?'

Vincent shook his head and leaned against the kitchen table.

'Not a thing,' he said. 'I'm trying not to think about them too much. Instead I'm concentrating on trying to give the Shadow what he wants. And on the bones case. This may sound terrible, but … if I started thinking about my family, I'd turn into a quivering wreck. I wouldn't be able to stand on my own two feet, and that wouldn't help anyone. I just have to trust that they're being reasonably well looked after. The Shadow has no reason to hurt them – it's me he's after.'

Mina turned over the sheet of paper.

'What's this?' she said in surprise when she saw the numbers on the reverse.

Vincent looked at the matrix he had created using the Shadow's numbers.

21 24 28 14

27 15 20 25

16 30 22 19

23 18 17 29

'It's another message from the Shadow,' he said. 'These numbers were taken from the calendar in my kitchen, a Christmas card sent to me, my alarm clock and my garden. I think the Shadow wants to show that their meaning runs through everything I do. That it's all around me.'

'And what meaning is that?'

The music in the living room was replaced by a pulsating bass. Something in Nathalie's show was clearly exciting.

'The same thing the Shadow has been reminding me of all autumn,' Vincent said. 'Come and sit down.'

He handed her a pen.

'If you add up each row, what do you get?'

Mina fell silent for a few seconds as she pointed at each number with her pen.

'All the rows add up to the same number,' she said. 'They add up to eighty-seven.'

'That's right. Try adding them up top to bottom instead.'

Mina concentrated. He could see her quickly doing the sums in her head.

'What the …?' she said. 'Each column adds up to eighty-seven as well.'

Vincent took the pen from her hand and pointed at the rows and the columns using the end.

'So it adds up to eighty-seven in both directions,' he said.

Then he drew a horizontal line between rows two and three, and a vertical one between the second and third columns. The numbers were now divided into four equally sized fields, each containing four figures. He pointed to the upper left-hand field.

'Twenty-one – twenty-four – twenty-seven – fifteen,' he said. 'That also makes eighty-seven. And take a look at the field next to it. Twenty-eight – fourteen – twenty – twenty-five. Eighty-seven again. It's the same with the other two. All four of these add up to eighty-seven.'

'But how do you even figure out …' Mina began to say.

'Oh, we're not done yet. Look at the numbers in the four corners. Twenty-one – fourteen – twenty-three – twenty-nine. That's eighty-seven. And now take a look at the two diagonals, twenty-one – fifteen – twenty-two – twenty-nine and fourteen – twenty – thirty – twenty-three. They're also both eighty-seven. And there are even more ways to arrive at eighty-seven.'

Mina shook her head as if she couldn't believe her eyes.

'It's known as a magic square,' Vincent said. 'It's an old mathematical problem. It was also the finale in my very first show, when the world first heard about Vincent Walder the master mentalist. Everything goes around in circles for the Shadow. My beginning and my end. My alpha and my omega. My grand finale. And whichever way I turn, everything comes back to this.'

He scrunched the paper into a ball. He didn't want to look at it any more.

'Mum, have we got any gingerbread left?' Nathalie called from the living room.

'Check yourself,' Mina shouted back.

The television fell silent as Nathalie paused her show. She came into the kitchen and began to rummage around in the cupboard. Eventually she found a red plastic container and carefully shook it. It sounded more than half full.

'How come you're being so weird?' she said. 'This place went as silent as a graveyard when I came in. What's the big secret?'

'We're doing our jobs,' said Mina. 'But you're welcome to stay and listen.'

'Do you know any more about Dad or Granddad?'

'I'm afraid not, sweetheart. We're doing maths. Want to join in?'

'Are you nuts? I'm on my Christmas holidays.'

Nathalie went back to the living room, taking the container of biscuits with her. It was good to see her behaving like a normal teenager even though she was in the middle of a traumatic experience involving her missing father and her murdered grandfather.

'I don't understand,' Mina said, turning to Vincent after they'd heard the television show start up again. 'Why eighty-seven? What does it stand for?'

'Don't you remember?' he said. 'No, of course you don't. Why would you? The numbers eight and seven stand for the eighth day of the seventh month. The eighth of July. It's my mother's birthday. That was something Jane reminded me of with her leopard book. According to the Shadow, the summer when my mother died is my alpha. My beginning. He actually pointed it out in the newspaper cutting he sent to Ruben. Not that any of us noticed at the time. And this Christmas is … well, it's clearly my end.'

Mina took the scrunched-up piece of paper from his hand, unfolded it and stared at the numbers that had been hidden throughout his daily life.

'We're dealing with one sick person,' she said.

Vincent nodded slowly.

'Perhaps now you understand why I've got to meet the Shadow alone,' he said. 'You can't say a word to Julia and the others when we see them.'

Mina gazed at him silently.

'But would you do me a favour?' he said. 'If you haven't heard from me by eight o'clock this evening, please start searching for me with every person in uniform and all the blue lights you can get hold of.'

137

Mina tried to find the right words to describe the atmosphere in the conference room. Elevated was the best she could muster. They had reached the point in the investigation where everything that had been at a standstill or moving far too slowly suddenly began to accelerate towards the goal – towards the solution. Even if that was still unclear.

'Where's Loke?' Ruben said, looking around.

'Milda couldn't spare him at the moment,' said Julia. 'Apparently she had an important visit to make to someone sick, or something like that.'

'Oh, just when we were getting used to him,' he said.

'I'm sure he'll be back,' Julia said. 'Now, let's start with you, Adam.'

Adam cleared his throat and nodded.

'I've spoken to the social worker who was attached to the Svensson family,' he said. 'Both Björn and Linda had issues with their mental health, and social services considered whether to take their son, Mattias, into care on several occasions. But Linda took her own life by jumping off the Västerbron bridge, and Björn and Mattias disappeared not long afterwards. It was assumed that they were dead – that Björn had also committed suicide, just as Tor said, and that he'd taken the boy with him.'

Adam grimaced.

'But it turns out they were living down in the tunnels instead,' Ruben said. 'Bloody hell. What a fate.'

'And you're saying that Tor Svensson is cousins with the boy? With Mattias?' Mina said, trying to straighten it all out in her head.

'Tor arrived here two hours ago,' said Julia. 'Just to answer some questions. And as a result of that chat, I requested his detention with immediate effect.'

Everyone around the table looked shocked.

'It won't work for long,' she said. 'And we're still waiting for the prosecutor's approval on it, so we've currently offered Tor lunch and we're doing everything we can to delay him. I'd prefer it if he didn't leave the building if at all possible.'

'Excuse the stupid question,' said Ruben. 'But ... what the fuck? If I may speak plainly. What happened?'

'You'll have to be patient. I'm not ready to share yet. Not until Vincent has watched the recording of our conversation and given us his own conclusions based on Tor's behaviour. I don't want to colour his perception.'

'You weren't there?' Ruben said, turning to Vincent.

'No, and that's probably for the best,' said Vincent. 'After all, I've been in several interviews with suspects over the years. There's a risk that Tor is aware of that. If I had been in the room when he arrived, it might have sent the wrong signal and resulted in him raising his defences. I suspect Julia wanted to avoid that. But I'll be happy to review the footage once we're done here.'

Julia nodded. Mina was still having a hard time taking in what Julia had said – she was wrestling with the idea of the prim, dry as dust Tor being in custody. It was practically absurd to think of it. She was as bewildered as the others.

'We've also taken a look at Tor's and Mattias's shared background,' Julia said, nodding at Christer. 'You've pulled together some information on the family. Can you explain what you've found?'

Christer frowned and then picked up a sheaf of papers from the table.

'Björn, Mattias's father, was brothers with Tor's father Rune,' he said. 'Their father, Harald, was the very devil. He was one of the few Swedes known to have been in Germany during the Second World War, fighting for Hitler. He reportedly served at Dachau – one of the concentration camps.'

'I didn't know there were Swedes who fought for the Nazis,' Ruben said, wide-eyed.

'There were plenty of Swedes who were Nazis during the war,' Christer said with a snort. 'Some of them were mad enough to head for Germany and take up arms on behalf of the Third Reich.'

'Didn't Harald face any consequences?' Adam asked.

Christer shook his head.

'Harald came from a very wealthy family with a background in banking. When he returned, he was given a fancy job in the family firm, Hird AB. Little more was heard from him. The rich always get by.'

'Were the sons Nazis too?' Mina said, leaning forward with interest.

'There's no suggestion of that. Rune continued to manage the family businesses and assets. Björn became a school teacher – he taught Swedish and history. Well, until he … until he didn't.'

'And once they were down in the tunnels, Björn and Mattias became the King and the Prince,' Julia added. 'Mina, you went down there and spoke to Vivian and the others. Did they say when the Prince left?'

'No, not exactly,' Mina said. 'But they talked about him as a child and they'd measured his height, and it was definitely a child's. So I assumed he hadn't been there since he was little.'

'This whole thing is still very messy,' Julia said. 'According to the countdown on the answering machine, we've got three days left to find Niklas Stockenberg. We probably won't be able to put together all the pieces of the jigsaw before then. The important thing is that we understand enough to work out where he is. Or who is holding him.'

Vincent let out a sudden loud groan and Mina jumped.

'Are you OK?' she said, looking at him anxiously.

'The business card with the phone number on it that Niklas was given,' he said. 'Jon, Marcus and Erika obviously received them too. That's why their behaviour changed – albeit in different ways. They all knew that they were going to die two weeks before it happened.'

'Jesus Christ,' Ruben said. 'And then they ended up down in the tunnels.'

They sat in silence for a while.

'I don't know if this is the right moment, but I met up with Akai,' Adam said. 'The guy who found Jon Langseth's bones. He showed me an incredible mural that he did last year. It depicts the whole group that we met down in the tunnels. He really is good.'

Adam pulled out his phone and scrolled through his photos. Once he'd found the right image, he passed his phone around the room.

'"Don't swipe right, don't swipe left, just look," as they say on Instagram,' Ruben chuckled, before passing the phone to Mina.

Mina looked at the phone that Ruben was holding out to her. Other people's phones were something she detested; they were crawling with bacteria. However, she sucked it up and took the phone since her curiosity outweighed her paranoia. She would drench her hands in sanitizer later.

Adam was right. The painting was incomparable. She recognized each and every one of them. Vivian. Kjelle. OP. Natasa. There was only one face that was unfamiliar. Additionally, someone had sprayed *Sussi was here* over a large part of the unknown individual's face, so it wasn't possible to discern their features. But there was something painted above the figure's head. She pointed to that part of the photo and turned the mobile towards Adam.

'What's this? Your flash is really bright just there, so it's not quite visible. But you saw the painting in real life – do you remember what it was?'

Adam looked for a moment in silence.

'I'm not quite sure. I suppose I thought it was a halo of some kind. The person might be someone who died down there. I don't know.'

He shrugged. Mina continued to examine the picture in deep concentration before realizing what she was looking at.

'That's not a halo. It's a crown. Like a king wears. Or … a prince.'

The room fell silent. Julia hurried over to look at the screen.

'Mina's right,' she said. 'But that's an adult – not a child. And this painting was done last year?'

Adam nodded.

'And it's supposed to depict the people living in the tunnels now?' Julia said, her voice grave. 'If so, that can't be the King. If this shows his son, that means Tor's cousin is still down in the tunnels. And if the Prince gave his father a royal burial …'

'… then he might be the one who buried the others in the same way,' said Vincent. 'We've got to find Mattias.'

138

The small camera that Julia had positioned in the interview room had recorded her conversation with Tor in 4K high resolution. This meant that Vincent was able to zoom in on Tor's face in tremendous detail. Not that this was necessary – most things were obvious if you knew what you were looking for, and Vincent did.

He had paused the video on the laptop just before Julia said that the victims had faced difficulties earlier in life.

'Look at this,' he said to Mina, who was sitting beside him. 'What do you see?'

He glanced at Mina out of the corner of his eye and felt as if his heart had taken an extra beat. Even when he was fully focused on work, he couldn't help but be affected by her. She was so incredibly beautiful when she was concentrating.

He realized that she was waiting for him, and hurried to play the video again.

They heard Julia say her line and Tor reply by repeating the word *difficulties* as a question. Vincent paused again.

'He looks surprised,' Mina said. 'As if he doesn't quite understand what she means.'

'That's right,' said Vincent. 'But watch just before that.'

He went back a few seconds and tried to pause just after Julia had said *difficulties*. The expression on Tor's face was only there for a fraction of a second before it vanished. Vincent had to do the same thing several more times before he found a frame in which it was clearly visible.

'Micro expressions,' he said, nodding at the screen. 'According to the psychologist Paul Ekman, we have seven basic emotions: happiness, sadness, anger, disgust, contempt, fear and surprise. These emotions are clearly visible in distinctive facial expressions. It's incredibly difficult to completely hide an emotional reaction because emotions are automatic and they happen more quickly than our conscious reactions. As I say, Ekman's term for them is micro expressions. These are quick, fleeting reactions that show a genuine emotion before consciousness takes over and tries to control the facial expression – for example, by showing confusion, as in this case. But what did you see just before that?'

On the screen, the corner of Tor's mouth had tensed and moved upwards. It was only a few millimetres, but that was all it took. What appeared was not a smile.

'He looks … superior,' Mina said.

'Exactly. This is the facial expression for contempt. But in Tor's case, it only lasts for a split second. That's why it's a micro expression. Then we get the feigned confusion that you saw.'

Vincent played the entire sequence without pausing. He hoped that Mina would spot the change in Tor even though it was quicker than the blink of an eye. She nodded enthusiastically.

'There!' she said. 'Wow. Now I know what to look for, it's super obvious. But I wouldn't ever have spotted it if you hadn't pointed it out. What does it mean?'

'Two things,' Vincent said, turning to face her.

That was a stupid move. He felt self-conscious sitting so close to her and looking into her eyes, but she was merely gazing back at him questioningly. He had to pull himself together.

'Firstly,' he said, clearing his throat, 'it means that he knows exactly which difficulties Julia is referring to. You don't react that forcefully without having something tangible to react to. In other words, he already knows about the victims' prior history. Why would he know about that if he didn't know who they were?'

'So he's lying when he says he doesn't know Erika, Jon and Marcus,' Mina said slowly.

'It's the only reasonable explanation. And secondly, he also exhibits disdain for the "difficulties" that the victims faced. That is to say, that Erika, Marcus and Jon were depressed and verging on suicidal, if I've understood correctly from the interviews with their relatives. I doubt Tor has much time for people he regards as weak.'

'So Tor knew the victims and knew what they went through,' Mina said.

She sat back in her chair and closed her eyes.

'And he hates them for it,' she added. 'He also knows Niklas went through the same phase in his life. Tor must despise him too.'

She suddenly opened her eyes and gazed at him in horror.

'Vincent, is everyone ... am I ... that easily read? Do I have those micro expressions too?'

'I've never given that a moment's thought,' Vincent said, trying to maintain an air of innocence.

At the same time, he realized that he had just taught Mina that she could read *him*. Oh dear.

'But how sure are you about this with Tor?' she said. 'I still haven't seen or heard anything in the interview that's good enough grounds to hold him.'

Vincent nodded and moved the cursor in the play bar to the final seconds of the footage. Then he hit play again.

'*I think this is the perspective that we're dealing with,*' said Tor on-screen, '*and it's got very little to do with how a Swedish rock star got started in his career or who booked a lecturer for public speaking engagements.*'

'I saw that micro expression again,' Mina said. 'Contempt. When he said "rock star".'

'Very good. But did you think about the words too? All Julia mentioned was investments. How does Tor know that they were used to fund people's careers? And she didn't say a word about public speaking, so where did he get that from? I'll bet that's what Julia reacted to. He's talking about things he shouldn't know about. Julia's reaction was quite right. Tor is far better informed than he's letting on. He's created three fantastic careers for others – four if we count Niklas. Right when they were at their lowest ebb. That's an incredible and selfless thing to do. So why is he lying about it? Shouldn't he be proud of it, if that's all he did? And why does he hate them? I'm guessing that if we can find out why, we'll also find out why they're now dead.'

Mina remained silent for a long time. He liked the silence. But he also longed to hear her stimulating voice again.

'Look at him,' Mina said in a low voice, pointing at the screen. 'Those well-manicured nails. There's not a speck of dirt on his cuffs, even though he must have been wearing that shirt all day. And his shoes are always polished to within an inch of their lives. I can't really see him building burial mounds out of gravel in a metro tunnel. I'm more inclined to believe what you said in the meeting – that the Prince was the one who built them.'

'I agree,' Vincent said, nodding. 'But Tor is definitely the brain behind the … well, whatever this is. If we look at the evidence found by Christer, it's obvious that Tor is operating behind the scenes. The muscles and perhaps even the outward face belong to his cousin. And it gets even worse.'

Everything that they had seen so far had only been a warm-up for what Vincent had to show her next. He'd needed to make Mina aware of the importance of small behavioural changes so that she would understand what was coming next. Not just understand, but also *feel*. It was the next part that had really scared Vincent.

He dragged the cursor back and stopped just before Tor began to talk about the person who had kidnapped Niklas probably having political intentions.

'Have you seen this part of the interview?' he said.

'No, I didn't have time to watch it all before.'

'Good,' Vincent said, muting the sound. 'Watch his body language and facial expressions, and then tell me what he's talking about.' Vincent started the video and let it run to the end in silence. Mina watched Tor attentively. After a while, she began to nod imperceptibly, as if she were agreeing with something inaudible that Tor was saying. When the video reached its end, she took a few seconds to collect herself.

'Let's see,' she said. 'He was leaning forward and making a lot of eye contact. A smile came and went at the right-hand corner of his mouth … You know, it's not easy breaking it down into details like you do. If feels as if the meaning gets lost. Somehow, the sum is greater than all the parts. Can I tell you how it felt instead?'

'A very good suggestion,' Vincent said. 'Our feelings are often shortcuts to things that we already know in purely rational terms. The brain saves time and energy by skipping the rational approach and instead gives us a "feeling" about what the situation is. That's intuition. But real intuition is based on us having previous evidence to indicate that our thinking is right. Otherwise we're simply reacting based on whims and prejudices. Unfortunately, most people who talk about "gut feeling" don't understand that there's a difference between—'

'Vincent,' Mina said sharply.

'Oh, sorry. Your impression of Tor. Go on.'

Mina looked at the man on-screen again as he sat leaning forward over the table with both palms on the table top.

'It's clear that he's passionate about whatever he's talking about,' she said. 'It feels like he's pitching an idea on *Dragon's Den*. And his commitment is infectious. More than that, it's compelling. I'll buy lots of whatever he's selling.'

'Don't be so sure of that,' Vincent said, playing the sequence again from the beginning but this time with sound.

They listened in silence as Tor outlined his thoughts on democracy being in terminal decline and his belief that someone might be trying to plunge the country into chaos.

Mina was pale by the time the video ended.

'The whole thing about creating a new order out of chaos,' said Vincent. 'That's Tor's own idea. *He* is the one who's passionate about that. And I don't think he's talking about Niklas any more. You don't create a new social order by killing four individuals. Not even if one of them happens to be the minister of justice. I think Tor is planning something else – something much bigger. I'm afraid we've seriously underestimated how far he's willing to go.'

139

'Julia! Wait!'

Sara ran down the corridor as fast as she could. Julia was getting into the lift at the other end, but she got out again when she heard Sara's voice.

Sara reached the lift and inhaled hard as she sought to catch her breath.

'Hi Sara,' Julia said, smiling. 'Nicely done with Manojlovic and Ted Hansson. And finding Gustaf Brons.'

The doors closed behind Julia and the lift departed.

'Yes, it all ended up being a bit rushed,' Sara said. 'We would have preferred to spend longer looking into the gang first, but honestly, it was pretty liberating to pull Ted Hansson's pants down.'

'Is that an official NOA position?' Julia said, chuckling. 'I've got a colleague who is rather grateful for your urgency.'

Sara felt her cheeks begin to flush. The truth was that she and Ruben had effectively been inseparable in their spare time since she had found him in that cold cabin three days earlier, but they hadn't told anyone that yet. She wasn't quite sure how the world would handle the shock. She barely understood it herself.

'Anyway, I've got an urgent question for you,' she said. 'You brought Tor Svensson in for questioning this morning, right? Please tell me you've still got him.'

Julia raised her eyebrows.

'Yes, it was something of a surprise,' she said. 'When he arrived, all we really had was circumstantial evidence. But he managed to give himself away to the extent that I requested a warrant to detain him right away. I haven't heard anything, so I assume he's in the Kronoberg remand prison. Of course, his lawyers will probably appeal in the strongest possible terms, but these things don't move fast, so he should be there for at least another day. What's up?'

'Can we …?' Sara said, pointing to Julia's office.

Julia nodded. They went into her office and Julia closed the door behind them.

'We've been tracking suspected terrorist activity for some time,' Sara said. 'Someone has stolen large quantities of ammonium nitrate. Enough to make one hell of a bomb. We received a tip that helped us to find the chemicals at various locations, but we haven't let on that we know where they are. Instead, we've been keeping the warehouses under surveillance. And almost all of them have been visited over the last forty-eight hours. He was admittedly disguised in a cap and sunglasses, and wore different clothes, but it's incredible how far these modern facial recognition software packages have come on. The same person visited every one.'

'Tor Svensson?' Julia said, staring at her.

'Yes. We think he's planning something terrible.'

Julia grabbed her coat.

'Let's get over to the cells right away,' she said. 'It'll only take us three minutes to get there. I'll call ahead to let them know we're coming.'

She grabbed her phone, dialled a number and wedged it between her shoulder and her ear.

'It's Julia Hammarsten,' she said when someone picked up at the other end. She was wriggling into her coat at the same time. 'We're coming over to talk to Tor Svensson. Right away. It's urgent.'

Julia stopped mid-movement. She listened, then she hung up. Then she looked at Sara.

'How could I have been so stupid as to think it would be that simple?' she said. 'I should have known better than to try to take down the Ministry of Justice.'

'What do you mean?' said Sara.

'Our request to detain him was rejected. Tor left the building two hours ago.'

140

Julia chose to stand up even though her father had asked them to sit down. Sara Temeric was still on her feet too. For once, Julia wasn't freezing cold while inside police headquarters – probably the result of running all the way to the commissioner's office.

'Now we have to be very careful,' her father said, also standing as he gazed out of the window. 'How sure are you that you can tie Tor Svensson to the murders?'

'We still only have circumstantial evidence,' Julia said. 'But we have a lot of it. We also believe that Tor lied about his cousin, and he's also involved in this somehow.'

'However, NOA has evidence directly pointing to Tor's involvement in the theft of the chemicals,' Sara said.

Julia looked appreciatively at her colleague. Sara exhibited none of the fear that the commissioner usually instilled in people. He turned towards them.

'You've already provoked him,' he said thoughtfully. 'He's likely to be on his guard. And the accuracy of the computer insisting that someone in different disguises is the same person will be a contentious issue when it goes to court. Especially when that someone is the minister of justice's press secretary. I'm afraid that you face a long legal process before you can put him behind bars. How long do you have?'

Julia glanced at Sara. How on earth was she managing to remain unaffected by their dash? Julia was sweating buckets and could feel her heart pounding. Sara probably spent a lot of time in the gym. She supposed she ought to start going again too. Adam might say she was perfect as she was, but …

'If Tor is involved in the murders of Jon, Marcus and Erika then it's reasonable to assume that he was also involved in the threats to Niklas, since it seems to follow the same pattern.

According to the recorded message, Niklas is going to die in three days' time,' she said.

'That's quite a big "if", given that we're talking about Tor Svensson,' the commissioner said.

'We also don't know whether he's actually building a bomb,' said Julia. 'But *if* he is and *if* he's involved in the murders, then I would guess he's going to detonate the bomb at the same time as Niklas is killed. He can't wait much longer – he must be aware that the noose has begun to tighten. If he's going to act, then he has to go now. *If* it's him. The question is – do we dare take any chances?'

'Remind me what quantity of explosives we're talking about?'

'I'm convinced that it's him and not anyone else in those pictures,' Sara said. 'And if that's the case, he's got his hands on around ten tonnes of ammonium nitrate. That's what we know about – he might have more. That would be the biggest ever civilian explosion to take place in Sweden, if he were successful. Much of Stockholm city centre would be reduced to dust. In the worst-case scenario, it would leave thousands dead and injured.'

Her father ran his hands over his face. He suddenly looked very old despite his uniform.

'Then I suggest we move forward with caution,' he said. 'But quickly. Because you're right – we can't take any chances. Take the rest of the day to compile your evidence – whether it's concrete or circumstantial. Make the most compelling presentation you can. Ensure that you eliminate all those "ifs". Tomorrow morning we'll take it to the prosecutor to request Tor Svensson's immediate detention. I'll write to the prosecutor personally to emphasize the importance of this happening.'

Julia looked at her father. She wanted to thank him for not opposing her for once, but instead she nodded briefly.

'Well? Why are you standing here?' said the commissioner. 'Get a move on.'

141

The Gondolen restaurant was full. The restaurant had recently re-opened following an extensive refurbishment, and the people of Stockholm were evidently delighted to be back, judging by the number of patrons. Vincent was surprised that the Shadow wanted to meet in such a crowded place, but the Shadow didn't do anything by accident. There would be a reason why they were meeting there of all places.

'Walder?' the maître d' said in surprise when Vincent approached her lectern. 'It's been a while. Then again, it's been a while since most people have been here. Welcome back. Booking for two, wasn't it?'

'If you say so,' Vincent said.

The maître d' gave him a slightly strange look but beckoned him to follow her.

'We've had to put you at the bar,' she said apologetically as they entered the main dining room. 'You would not believe how many bookings we've had since we opened. You were lucky that …'

'That'll be fine,' Vincent said. 'The bar has the best seats as far as I'm concerned.'

He sat down on the seat indicated and smiled warmly at the maître d' to show how happy he was. She smiled back, clearly relieved, and dashed off to greet the next patron.

There were two menus lying on the bar. The seat beside Vincent was empty; the Shadow hadn't yet arrived. Vincent had no idea what to expect. Would it be someone old or young? Would it be a man or a woman? It occurred to him that it might be someone he knew. He really hoped not. It was most probably, as Mina had guessed, a stalker. He hadn't encountered any more of those with serious problems since Anna, the woman who'd had a tattoo of him on her back. But Anna was totally harmless compared to the Shadow. It was as well to be prepared for everything.

A man emerged from the gents. He caught sight of Vincent and smiled broadly, before heading towards him.

Was that the Shadow? Vincent vaguely recognized him. He couldn't immediately place the man, but he knew he'd seen him somewhere before. There was something about the way he moved as he approached Vincent that was very familiar.

'Vincent!' the man said, enthusiastically shaking his hand. 'You came!'

There was no doubt about it – this was the Shadow. At last Vincent was able to put a face to his tormentor. If only he could recall where he'd seen him before.

'I didn't exactly have much choice,' Vincent said. 'Where's my family?'

The Shadow shrugged and sat down.

'There's no cause for concern,' he said. 'I haven't done anything to them that you haven't already done yourself. But you needed space to think by yourself for a while.'

'If you've hurt them …'

The man held up a hand and looked affronted.

'Vincent, Vincent,' he said. 'Let's not be vulgar. You should be focusing on the task at hand. You don't have long left.'

Vincent gazed across the packed dining room. Were any of the patrons plain-clothes police officers? If he gave a signal or shouted for help, would they apprehend the Shadow? But no one seemed to be paying them any attention. Mina had kept her promise.

'What do you want from me?' he said. 'And who are you? You said I have to take responsibility for what I did and stop living in denial. I assume you're referring to … what happened … to my mother.'

'You see?' the man said with a disapproving shake of the head. 'You still can't even say what actually happened!'

'It was forty years ago. And it was an accident. A tragic accident.'

The Shadow began to flip through the menu.

'Langoustine gratin or veal topside,' he said aloud. 'What do you think? Porcini mushroom confit sounds like a good side.'

'Just tell me what you want me to do,' Vincent said tersely.

'What do you mean by me having to take responsibility? What does that even mean? And why are you interfering in my life?'

'It's a pity they don't do black pudding in the evenings,' the man said as he closed the menu. 'I really didn't think you were so slow on the uptake, Vincent. You've been given all the clues. Read the letters again. Carefully. It's all in there.'

He glanced at Vincent and then leaned in close as if he were going to impart a secret.

'You do still have them, don't you? The letters?' he said. 'You haven't given them to the police or anything like that?'

Vincent didn't reply.

'All I want is for you to start taking responsibility for your actions,' the Shadow said. 'That's it.'

'But you're not going to say what you mean by that any more specifically?'

The Shadow smiled and shook his head.

'It's not that hard,' he said. 'But since you still don't seem to understand I'll give you one more chance. Just like I wrote. One last chance. I'm not a bad man, Vincent.'

He produced a padded envelope and handed it to Vincent. Inside there was a piece of black elasticated material with a fastener on it. On the strap there was a rectangular piece of plastic the size of a matchbox.

'We'll meet again tomorrow. Until then, I'd like you to wear this. It's a microphone and GPS transmitter. You wear it on your ankle. The whole business of taping microphones to your chest only happens on television these days. But this will mean that I know exactly where you are and I'll hear everything you say over the next day. I don't want to see you tomorrow and only find out afterwards that you blew your chance. Have a good evening, Vincent.'

The man stood up as if to leave.

'Wait,' Vincent said. 'You still haven't told me who you are or why you're doing this. And why are we here at Gondolen? What's …'

The Shadow shook his head.

'You really aren't that smart any more,' he said, adjusting his jacket. 'You ought to know who I am by now. But I promise that tomorrow all will become clear. Now enjoy your dinner. The bill's on me.'

142

TWO DAYS TO GO

Vincent arrived early. It almost felt as if police headquarters had become his place of work. He could no longer sleep at home. Granted, he had returned home from the restaurant by half past six and had texted Mina to say that he was OK, but the Shadow's words had kept him awake for the rest of the night. Concentrating on the investigation was the only thing he could do to keep his sanity – what little of it he still had.

He was going to put the map of the metro tunnel network on the conference room wall. The map of Stockholm that had been there previously had been taken down after Vincent had turned it into a huge chessboard six months earlier. Since then, the wall had been empty. Until now.

Vincent stuck pins in all four corners so that the map wouldn't roll up. Just as he was finishing, Ruben popped his head around the door.

'Time for that stuff again, eh?' he said, nodding at the map. 'What is it this time? Ludo? Don't answer that – I don't want to know. Have you seen Adam?'

'No, I haven't actually seen anyone here yet,' Vincent said.

Ruben nodded and disappeared. Vincent retrieved the hourglasses from his bag. He turned the frame containing them and watched the sand begin to fall. The symbol of the hourglass was to be found everywhere in this investigation. The four in his hands were really a map to the burial mounds. They were also marked around the heaps themselves in the tunnels. And there was an hourglass on the business card with the phone number printed on it that had been handed to Niklas. Vincent still remembered what the voice sounded like – the one saying how long Niklas had left. There were only two days left until his time was up.

Vincent had really hoped that they would already have found Niklas in the tunnel somewhere along line sixteen. It would have made everything so much easier. In retrospect that seemed naive. Just because something would be convenient for the investigation didn't make it any more likely.

At the same time, they hadn't come across any other leads on where Niklas might be. However, unless he had totally misunderstood the message accompanying the hourglasses, there was a way to save Niklas before it was too late.

Find the fourth one before time runs out.

But where? As Julia had said, line sixteen was long. And once Niklas was in place in the tunnel in two days' time, they wouldn't have much time.

But why would whoever had sent the hourglasses to Vincent say which line it was, rather than which station? It seemed odd to leave it so vague. He looked at the numbers that he had written underneath the four hourglasses.

17 mins (13 secs)
13 mins (5 secs)
10 mins (3 secs)
16 mins (3 secs)

He'd thought that the minute counts for each one revealed the metro lines and that the seconds would therefore indicate the stations themselves, somehow. In the hourglass representing Marcus Eriksson, it took seventeen minutes and thirteen seconds for the sand to run through. Line seventeen was right. But thirteen stations didn't get him to Bagarmossen, where Crazy-Tom had found Marcus, regardless of which end of the line he started counting from.

The same was true for Erika and Jon. It didn't matter which end he started from – the seconds didn't lead him to the stations where the bones had been found.

But what if there was another starting point? One that mattered to the person who had sent the hourglasses? Vincent was now convinced that the hourglasses and the other puzzles sent to him had come from the Prince. The skeleton of the King – the Prince's father – had been found at Odenplan.

What if the King was the root of it all?

Vincent put his finger on the map on the wall and counted thirteen stations from Odenplan. That took him right to Bagarmossen, where Marcus's bones had been found.

He tried it again. Erika had been found on the red line thirteen. Her hourglass said five seconds. Vincent started again from Odenplan. It was five stations from Odenplan to Karlaplan where Erika had been found, via a change at T-centralen. The third hourglass was for Jon. Blue line ten. Two stations from Odenplan took him to Fridhemsplan. There he changed onto the blue line and after one stop he ended up at Stadshagen, where Akai had found Jon.

He had solved it.

The final hourglass – Niklas's hourglass – took sixteen minutes and three seconds. From Odenplan that meant either Thorildsplan in one direction or T-centralen in the other. But the station at Thorildsplan was above ground, and the bones were always found in the tunnels. That left just T-centralen.

He knew where Niklas would be. Finally. He ought to have been celebrating, but he knew that Julia wouldn't be pleased. T-centralen was the most complex station on the entire subterranean network, with trains and platforms across several different levels. It was the one point in the network where all the lines on the system intersected, where more than three hundred thousand passengers got on or off each day. And it was there, somewhere in the myriad of tunnels, that they would have to find Niklas in two days' time.

Find the fourth one before time runs out.

Vincent hoped that meant they would have an hour or so to find Niklas – that he would be taken into the tunnels before time ran out. But he didn't dare be that naive again. They would have to prepare for the possibility that there would be very little time. So they needed to know exactly when, down to the minute, Niklas was going to die. He would have to ask Mina to call the number and check.

As if she had heard his thoughts, Mina came into the room carrying two mugs.

'Sorry I'm late,' she said. 'The coffee machine was broken. I had to get hot chocolate instead.'

'Perfect,' he said, accepting a mug. 'It's almost as cold inside as it is out.'

He blew on the drink.

'And perfect timing, by the way,' he said. 'I've solved it. I know where Niklas is. Or rather, I know where he will be. I was right about line sixteen – he's just not there yet.'

'Vincent, I'm not following you,' she said.

'It was simple, actually,' he continued, pointing to the map. 'I just had to count the stations on line sixteen. Well, it isn't there, but the stations are. The trick was to count from Odenplan since that's where the King was buried. The hourglasses tell us that it's all based on the King.'

'Sometimes I'm scared about what goes on in your head when it *isn't* simple,' Mina said, carefully sipping her hot chocolate.

'The point is that Niklas will be in one of the tunnels at T-centralen,' Vincent said. 'In two days, when his time runs out.'

Mina fell silent for a few seconds.

'T-centralen,' she said. 'My God. And we know that Tor is preparing a bomb that's probably going to detonate at the same time as Niklas … dies.'

'But the recorded message tells us when he's going to die – down to the minute. We just have to make sure we're in the right place before it happens. Can you call it again so that we can check the exact time?'

'Sure, just a second,' Mina said, pulling out her phone.

She dialled the number and put it on speakerphone.

'Hello Niklas Stockenberg,' said the familiar voice. 'We hope you have been satisfied with our services during this period which has now reached its end. You have … zero days … three hours … and … fifteen minutes … left to live.'

Mina stared at him.

'They've changed the message,' she said. 'Niklas is going to die in three hours' time.'

143

~~TWO DAYS TO GO~~

THE FINAL DAY

Vincent's phone was ringing. His display told him that it was Loke. Vincent pushed aside all thoughts of Niklas and T-centralen – there was no need to frighten Loke unnecessarily. He took a deep breath and answered as neutrally as he could.

'Hi Vincent – it's Loke. Do you have a minute?' Loke said eagerly.

'Of course,' Vincent said, quickly flashing his screen to Mina to show her Loke's name.

'I'll go and brief Julia,' she whispered. 'We need to get to T-centralen and find Niklas right away.'

Vincent watched her dash off.

'There's something I've been thinking about in relation to the skin beetles,' Loke said as Vincent put his phone back to his ear. 'About how hard it is to keep those kinds of beetles in controlled circumstances, especially once the larvae become full beetles. So I went out on a limb and reviewed the last two years of reports from the Health and Environmental Board.'

'Good thinking,' Vincent said, realizing what Loke was getting at.

This bone expert was no slouch.

'I'd almost given up,' Loke said. 'But then I found a pest report from just last week. Despite being in a public place, the pests were found in such quantities that a report was filed. Can you guess what they were?'

'Skin beetles,' Vincent said, nodding.

'Exactly. Found on the platform at Hötorget metro station, of all places. That can't be a coincidence. I should think there's a large terrarium of skin beetles somewhere in the tunnels not far from Hötorget. Warm, slightly damp and dark. It's the perfect environment for them. That's where the bones have been cleaned. I thought you'd want to know.'

Loke sounded as if he was about to hang up.

'Just a moment!' Vincent said. 'The team have their hands full preparing to launch the search for Niklas. It suddenly became very urgent. There isn't time to search for a terrarium too, but I could go down and take a look. I'm only in their way here. In fact, I think we should both go.'

'I don't know,' Loke said hesitantly. 'Dirty tunnels aren't really my kind of place.'

'I understand that more than you can know, but aren't you curious? After all, you were the one who figured it out.'

'OK ... fine. You've convinced me. Meet you on the platform at Hötorget in ... say half an hour?'

'I'll be there in fifteen minutes,' Vincent said, ending the call.

He retrieved his jacket and hurried down the corridor. He stopped when he saw Mina and Julia in the latter's office.

'Loke has found the place where the bones were cleaned,' he said. 'I'm going to head over there to check it out with him. I'm not exactly much use in your rescue efforts.'

'Well done, Loke,' said Julia. 'Where is it?'

'Take a guess,' Vincent said, sighing. 'Why can't anything ever be above ground? What's wrong with people?'

'You're going down into the tunnels?' Julia said sceptically. 'Haven't you heard about the bomb?'

'Yes, Mina told me.'

'It's probably somewhere at T-centralen – in the same place as Niklas. Sara says that's what NOA think too. If you want to detonate a bomb in Stockholm then T-centralen is the best strategic location to ensure maximum damage. Tor has got his hands on more than ten tonnes of ammonium nitrate, so the tunnels won't be safe, and if something goes wrong ...'

She fell silent.

'I know,' said Vincent. 'But there are still a few hours left on

Niklas's countdown. And I'll be back here in forty minutes. Tops. I promise. Best-case scenario, Loke and I have found something important.'

'I don't want to have to worry about you too,' Mina said.

Vincent stopped. He suddenly wanted to give Mina a hug. He knew, however, that he would probably be unable to let go of her afterwards. Instead he nodded curtly at them and dashed off.

There was a metro station just around the corner from police headquarters, so he got on a train for T-centralen where he could change for Hötorget. T-centralen was rammed as usual, with commuters and tourists everywhere. Of course, none of them had any idea what was about to happen. He pushed aside those thoughts and got onto the next train.

After one stop, he got off. Loke was already waiting for him on the platform.

'A colleague gave me a lift,' he said. 'But I wanted to wait for you so that we can go in together.'

Vincent looked around the platform. There weren't any skin beetles that he could see. They had obviously been dealt with. The city tended to deal with some tasks rather more quickly than others.

'The skin beetles were found at the north end of the platform,' Loke said. 'So I assume they came from the north tunnel. I've already arranged permission for us to go in.'

'As for me, I've worked out where Niklas is going to be,' Vincent said, following Loke to the end of the platform. 'At T-centralen. With almost three hours to go, Julia's team are guaranteed to find him. The Prince isn't playing fair by changing the countdown – but the challenge was to find the fourth one before time ran out. And they will.'

'The Prince?'

'Oh yes, you weren't at that meeting. I'll explain later.'

'T-centralen, you say?' Loke said, letting Vincent walk ahead of him as they left the platform and entered the tunnel. 'My oh my. That's only one station along.'

The light from the platform quickly disappeared behind

them as Vincent walked further into the tunnel. He considered turning on the torch on his mobile, but thought it was better for his eyes to adjust to the dark. Loke was following him.

'Where do you think we're going to find the terrarium?' Vincent said.

Suddenly he felt something pricking his throat. It was as sharp as a needle.

'I'm disappointed in you, Vincent,' Loke said into his ear. 'You completely misunderstood the riddle. Niklas isn't at T-centralen.'

'Loke …?' Vincent said in confusion. What the …?

'Don't move unnecessarily – you've got a syringe against your throat. Keep moving. And give me your phone.'

He did as Loke told him.

Loke took the phone from his hand and Vincent grimaced when he heard Loke smash it against the stone wall.

'What did you think of my presents?' Loke said. 'All those puzzles and riddles for almost two years. Did they amuse you?'

A jolt passed through Vincent.

'You're the one who's been sending them?' he said, clearing his throat. 'They've been incredible. But what do you mean, I misunderstood the riddle?'

'I thought I had found someone like-minded,' Loke said with an air of disappointment. 'That you of all people would appreciate the challenge. You should know that some of those things weren't at all easy to get hold of. So I decided to give you a chance to find Niklas. Tor was against it, but it's not often that I find someone I respect – and I like you, Vincent. But in the end, it seems I overestimated your abilities. It's a pity you didn't manage to save him.'

They continued to walk in silence. Loke led him further and further into the tunnels. They veered off on several occasions until the rumbling of the trains was only audible in the distance.

'Loke … are you the Prince?'

No reply.

The needle was extremely sharp. But as long as the area around it didn't start to tense, it meant that Loke hadn't injected him with whatever was inside the syringe. Which was a silver lining of sorts.

'I'm guessing there aren't any skin beetles down here,' Vincent said.

Loke laughed heartily.

'I knew you could be smart,' he said. 'And since you're wondering, the syringe at your throat contains a combination of pancuronium and potassium chloride. They really are fascinating substances. Pancuronium used to be marketed as Pavulon – it's a drug used for anaesthesia in the healthcare sector. It hasn't been for sale for more than a decade, although it's not that hard for someone in my line of work to get hold of it and keep a stock. This dose will cause your muscles to relax so much that you'll stop breathing. You can make potassium chloride yourself – all it takes is a little lye and some hydrochloric acid. Both are of course highly corrosive, but they neutralize each other. The result is usually mixed with salt for use in cooking. There's enough in this syringe to make your heart stop.'

'Is that what you gave Erika, Marcus and Jon?' Vincent said, staring dead ahead of him in the dark tunnel.

'I'm not a physically strong person, as you know,' Loke said. 'But when I offered to draw a line through the whole thing and let them live as if they had learned their lesson, they all came to my home of their own volition. They promised me money, shares in their company, sex … They were desperate. I gave them thiopental-laced champagne.'

'My God. They must have been out almost immediately,' Vincent said.

'Yes, you can find some quick-acting stuff in our hospitals,' Loke said, laughing. 'I could have cut them up then and there to boil their bones, but I'm not a monster. I gave them a lethal injection first before I got to work. Stop! We've arrived.'

To their right was a deeper space. It ended in a concrete wall in which there was a door.

The needle disappeared and Loke appeared in front of him. In his other hand he was holding a gun. It looked almost antique and completely out of place in Loke's long slender hands.

'It was my grandfather's,' Loke said when he saw Vincent's look. 'I don't like guns – they're so vulgar. And I'm not good at using them. But don't think I won't shoot if I have to. I won't miss at this distance.'

Loke dropped the syringe on the floor and pulled out a key. He unlocked the door while keeping the gun aimed at Vincent. The tunnel wasn't very light and it was pitch black beyond the door. Loke gestured for Vincent to go into the room. When Vincent entered, he dimly made out a figure slumped over on a chair.

It was Niklas.

144

Julia surveyed her team. Christer and Ruben were at the table, while Adam and Mina were leaning against the wall of the conference room. Milda was there too. Julia had asked her to attend their hastily convened meeting and take Loke's place while he was out with Vincent.

'I don't think Tor is in hiding – his ego is too big for that,' she said. 'After all, we didn't manage to get the thumbs-up to detain him. If I were Tor and insisting on my innocence, I would go home, stay visible, act normally. He knows that we don't have any concrete evidence tying him to the murders. But he doesn't know that we know about the bomb.'

'Tor's constant refrain about Sweden needing to be shaken from the ground up suddenly takes on a whole new meaning,' Christer said, with a shiver.

'But if he's sure we can't get him, why did he bring forward Niklas's countdown?' Mina said.

'I think he's under pressure,' Julia said. 'He hadn't counted on us getting a DNA match. He knows we don't have anything else, but he also knows that might change. If he wants to detonate the bomb, he has to do it before it's too late. And I'm guessing that he wants to do it at the same time as he kills Niklas.'

'You keep saying "he",' Mina said thoughtfully. 'But I think it's the Prince who is doing all the legwork, while Tor is staying visible, with the perfect alibi.'

'I'll bet the bastard is at home sipping a cup of tea right now,' Ruben said, hunched over his laptop.

'That's actually what I was about to get to,' Julia said. 'I suggest we pay him a visit. We don't have time to wait for a decision from the prosecutor. Tor shouldn't suspect anything – he doesn't know that we know his plans. Thanks to Vincent, we've got the best guess we can about where Niklas will be in two and a half hours. But I'd prefer it if we found him sooner than that. And I bet Tor knows where he is right now.'

'Let me pull up a map of the area where Tor lives,' Ruben said, typing on his keyboard. 'So that we know what to expect. Let's see. Here's the address …'

He whistled.

'Posh people really do live on some swanky streets,' he said. 'Tor lives on Strandvägen – I suppose he must have a view of Djurgården and likes to pretend it's his own garden.'

'Strandvägen?' Milda said. 'That's where Loke lives. Although not the Strandvägen in town – he lives on the one in Djursholm. There's a road with the same name there. I went to the wrong one on my first visit.'

Ruben frowned and leaned closer to his laptop.

'Well, I'll be damned,' he said. 'The post code doesn't match … Hang on. Tor doesn't live in town either. He seems to live in Djursholm too. Let me just …'

He tapped away and then turned the screen to show the others. Ruben had gone to Google earth and it was already zooming in on Sweden. After a few seconds, Stockholm was visible, then Djursholm, and then the address. There was also a small street view showing a huge house with its own gates and a short avenue leading to the main door.

'Swanky as hell, like I said,' Ruben said.

'But … that's Loke's house,' Milda said.

The others stared at her.

'What on earth are you saying?' Julia said.

'That's Loke's house. I've been there. But how can that be? Are you sure you put in the right address? Loke's surname is Svensson too – maybe there's been a mix-up. It's such a common name.'

Ruben double-checked the address and nodded. Julia experienced a sinking feeling in her stomach. They had missed something incredibly important.

'What's Loke's real first name?' she said in a low voice. 'I assume he isn't really called Loke?'

'Well, he is, actually,' Milda said. 'But it's a middle name. He prefers it – so no one has ever called him anything else. But his actual first name is Mattias. Mattias Svensson.'

The room was filled with deathly silence as the import of Milda's words dawned on them all.

'Why didn't you say anything?' Ruben exclaimed.

'About what?' Milda said. 'What are you talking about?'

'Loke's the Prince,' said Mina. 'Tor's cousin. And they live together.'

'Could it … could it really be Loke who committed the murders?' Christer said.

Julia nodded slowly.

'But why?' Christer said, shaking his head.

'There's far too much that we don't understand right now,' Julia said.

She felt as if she was inside a snow globe that someone had just shaken. All the parts of their investigation that she had thought were neatly in place were now spinning around her in absolute chaos.

'What on earth are you talking about?' Milda said, looking completely bewildered.

'Vincent is alone with Loke right now,' Mina said, panic rising in her voice. 'He was only meant to be gone for forty minutes.'

She checked her watch.

'I'll call him,' she said, pulling out her phone.

But it didn't ring. Vincent's phone was switched off.

'Shit,' Ruben snapped. 'Looks like Loke's going to finish Vincent off as well as killing Niklas and detonating the bomb.'

'Three birds with one stone,' said Christer. 'One hell of a stone though.'

'We've got to find them *now*,' Julia said.

They all stood up and raced out of the conference room.

145

'Is he alive?'

Vincent tried to adjust his eyes to the darkness in the small room. It was a service room, unused and forgotten. The perfect place to hide someone.

'I'm alive.'

The faint voice in the darkness quickly became a face when Loke turned on the torch on his phone.

'So ... what happens now?' Vincent said.

He deliberately kept his tone as flat as possible. Loke's mental state was still unknown to him. Vincent had no idea how Loke was affected by emotions such as fear or anger. Until he'd had time to gain an understanding of Loke's psyche, he needed to remain as emotionally neutral as possible.

'We wait,' Loke said, sitting down.

He waved the gun at Vincent to indicate that he should sit down next to Niklas. Vincent obeyed. The concrete was cold through the fabric of his trousers, and the floor was grimy. Niklas was little more than a ghostly figure in the glow of the mobile phone. He looked tired and haggard. There was dirt smeared across his face, in his hair and on his clothes.

'While we wait, explain to me how I was supposed to find Niklas here,' Vincent said in the same neutral voice as before. 'I may have misunderstood the riddle, as you put it. But the police searched all of line sixteen and found nothing.'

'The plan was obviously to move him to a location closer to the platform when the time came,' Loke said in irritation. 'But I didn't have time. It was all such a rush. But don't worry. We're very close to Hötorget. There are more tunnels than just the metro down here.'

'And here we are to wait,' Vincent said neutrally.

He mustn't affect Loke by betraying an emotional reaction to the situation. He had to keep his equilibrium.

'We're waiting for the fall – didn't I say?' Loke said. 'Do you know that my name comes from the Old Norse word meaning to close or complete? My role is to be the one who brings about the fall and the end. Ragnarök.'

Loke slowly turned the torch to show the rest of the room. It was bigger than Vincent had first thought. At first he didn't understand what was filling the rest of the room – then he realized that it was a mass of holdalls stacked on top of each other in multiple rows. They extended all the way up to the ceiling. He estimated that there were several hundred of them. It was hard to see in the semi-darkness, but they all looked well-filled. He realized that they had also passed others like them in the tunnel on their way here, but he had thought they were rubbish.

It wasn't difficult to guess what was in them. The bags were Tor's bomb. All it would take was the detonation of one to trigger a chain reaction. The pressure and heat from the first bag would cause all the others to explode.

Tor had almost ten tonnes of ammonium nitrate here. Vincent estimated the total quantity of explosives to be at least double that. His mouth went dry.

Loke glanced nervously at his wristwatch. Vincent guessed that the appointed hour was approaching.

'Since we're all just sitting here waiting to die, it'd be nice to have an explanation,' he said, trying to speak lightly, although he was terrified.

Vincent knew that Loke liked him – that had always been clear in his body language, and he had also expressed admiration. With luck, Vincent could exploit that. But if he lost the connection between them, that opportunity would be gone.

Niklas was still silent, his head bowed. Vincent patted him gently on the leg but got no reaction. Niklas had given up. He would be of no help.

It was up to Vincent to find a way out of this situation. Getting Loke to talk was the key to that – unless the Shadow, who was guaranteed to be listening in via the microphone attached to

Vincent's ankle, was a decent enough man to call the police and fire brigade. Vincent doubted it.

'Well then,' Loke said, with a shrug. 'I assume you already know that Tor and I have been working together.'

Vincent said nothing. He didn't want to reveal that he didn't have a handle on all the details. That might make Loke clam up again. So he nodded as if what Loke had said was already obvious. Most of all, he wanted to ask how long they had left – but it was too soon for that.

'Help me to understand why,' he said. 'What do the hourglasses mean? On the business cards and around the heaps of bones?'

Loke sat in silence for a while. Vincent waited patiently. He wondered whether they could be overheard – was there anyone outside the door? Probably not. It was just him, Loke and Niklas. There was no one else in the world now. They were the universe. They were life and death.

'My mother was the most beautiful person I've ever seen,' Loke said. 'When she was happy it was as if the sun was shining through the windows of our little flat in Kungsholmen. And Dad loved her so much. But when she jumped off that bridge, the sun went out. For Dad. For me. It all crumbled. When Dad didn't pay the rent we got evicted. And I guess Dad felt that since the sun would never shine again, we might as well live down here in the darkness. It might sound unlikely, but we were actually happy down here – at least, most of the time. We had our own little world with a family and a home. A kingdom where my father was king. Everyone loved Dad. And when he felt the darkness coming for him – the darkness from within – he would disappear for a while. That way I didn't have to see him when he was like that. But even when he was happy, he was still filled with sorrow that Mum had chosen to leave us. That was how he saw it – that she had abandoned us. In the end, he did the same thing. He abandoned me.'

Loke gazed into another corner of the room. Vincent was able to make out a mound of gravel about a metre high and realized instantly what it was.

'Is that …?' he said.

Loke nodded.

'So you were the one who stole the bones from your own lab,' Vincent said calmly. 'But why did you call me about it?'

'Dad belongs down here,' Loke said, looking tenderly towards the mound. 'He shouldn't be spread out on a cold metal table. That wasn't worthy of a king. But I knew there would be a commotion when I took the bones. I called you because I thought you might be able to help me keep a lid on it, but I was wrong.'

'And the others received the same kind of VIP burial in the tunnels because …'

'Because they had all become kings in their own way. Even if it was on borrowed time. And the King was buried down here. What was good enough for him was good enough for them.'

Vincent glanced at the heap of gravel containing Loke's father.

'So after your father … disappeared … you moved in with Tor and Rune?' he asked.

'I would have liked to stay here,' Loke said with a nod. 'But I couldn't any more. Dad had taught me Rune's phone number so I knew it off by heart. I called him and said that his brother was dead. He was thrown at first – everyone thought we had died long before. But I was able to live with them.'

'How old were you then?'

Vincent squirmed a little. His behind had started to ache and the chill was penetrating further and further into his flesh.

'Ten. And Tor was twenty. He took me under his wing right from the start, and taught me all the stuff I'd missed out on while I'd been down in the tunnels. Rune died not long afterwards. Then it was just me and Tor.'

Vincent shifted position on the floor. He glanced towards the bags. When Loke heard him moving, he swung the torch towards him. In the beam, Vincent had a better view of Niklas. He was in exactly the same position as before. Vincent wasn't sure whether he had heard any of their conversation. Or even whether he was alive.

'What are you up to?' Loke said suspiciously.

'Sorry. I'm not as young as I once was. I'm stiff.'

'Like I said, I'm disappointed in you.'

'I haven't been myself lately. But to get back to you – it sounds as if things worked out. I can't quite see how your story ends in murder.'

Vincent heard Loke snort in the dark, but they evidently had enough time that he could continue to tell his story. As long as he didn't seem to be in a hurry, everything was still fine.

'Tor understood my anger about Mum and Dad,' he said. 'Dad always said that life was a gift. It wasn't something you threw away without a second thought. That went against everything that life stood for. And then he did it anyway. Tor told me that Grandpa Harald always said our family was descended from the Vikings. And the Vikings didn't sacrifice their lives unless it was in battle. Life wasn't something you had the right to give up of your own volition. And that's right. So Tor was interested to see what would happen if someone who had given up was offered the chance to start over. You asked what the hourglass stands for. Isn't it obvious? It's a reminder that everything has an end. But what happens if you get the chance to turn over your hourglass? That's what Tor wanted to know. If someone could go from absolute rock bottom and achieve their wildest dreams, what would they aim for? He wasn't all that impressed by the results. A lecturer? A rock star? Are those humankind's greatest desires? It was somewhere in the midst of all this that the idea of shaking people up properly was born. Starting over from scratch.'

'Harald. Rune. Björn. Tor. Loke,' Vincent said with a nod. 'All Viking names.'

'Loke was my middle name, not my first name, but Tor said it should be my given name instead of Mattias. Loke, the one who brings about the fall.'

Vincent glanced at the piles of holdalls again.

146

Mina stops the police car outside the gates to the large house in Djursholm.

'Damn it,' Christer mutters beside her. 'How do we get in? Those gates look sturdier than our car.'

Christer insisted on coming along this time. There is a video intercom attached to the wall beside the gates. Mina is doubtful that Tor will let them in, but with a little luck he doesn't know why they're here. They have no choice but to try. Adam and Ruben took it upon themselves to go into the tunnels and lead the search for Niklas, Vincent and Loke, while she, Julia and Christer went to the house to bring in Tor.

Mina gets out of the car and presses the intercom button. After a few seconds, it crackles into life.

'Yes?'

'This is the police,' she says. 'We're here to see Tor Svensson.'

'Sorry, Mister Svensson not here right now,' says the woman's voice on the speaker. 'I just clean house.'

Switching to English, Mina repeats her statement: 'This is the police. Would you please let us in?'

The intercom is silent. Then they hear a click and the gates begin to open inwards. Mina gets into the car to find Christer staring at her, wide-eyed.

'Well, that's a stroke of good luck,' he says.

'Skill,' Mina replies.

She pulls onto the driveway and, once she has parked up, she gets out of the car along with Julia and Christer.

Julia climbs the steps and rings the doorbell. A woman with long black hair opens the door.

'Please come in,' she says, looking uncertainly at them. 'But I don't know when Mister Svensson will be back. And I am just leaving.'

'I'm sorry,' Julia says, showing her credentials. 'But we need to search the house.'

'I don't know,' the woman says hesitantly. 'I just cleaned.'

'We promise to take off our shoes,' Christer says, stepping neatly past her.

'I was on the bridge.'

The voice suddenly speaking makes Vincent jump. It's Niklas. His voice is dry and feeble. Vincent can hear him gathering saliva and swallowing before he continues.

'I was on Västerbron bridge,' Niklas repeats, 'when a young boy came over to me. One cold autumn day. There was something about that boy and how innocent he was that made me explain why I was standing there and how I was going to end my life. To this day, I don't know why I spoke to him. I suppose I was buying time before taking the final leap. After I had finished talking, he offered me a solution. A deal. If I postponed my death by a few years, he could solve all my problems. If I had set my heart on death, then the boy could first help me live for real.'

'Loke?' Vincent says, and Loke nods.

'At first it seemed ludicrous,' Niklas says. 'What could a young boy do about my worries? But he called someone on his phone. I spoke to an adult, and he told me the deal was for real. That all my problems would go away immediately if I agreed to them giving me at least ten years. It piqued my curiosity. It was so crazy that it seemed real just for that reason – and I didn't have anything to lose, given what I was about to do. So I said yes. If it turned out they were bluffing, I could always jump the next day. I remember thinking that. But it wasn't a bluff. They stuck to their word. All my problems were solved.'

'Why twenty years?' Vincent says to Loke.

'There wasn't any specific rule,' Loke says with a shrug. 'Niklas got twenty years. It was only seventeen for Marcus. He was the last one we picked up from the bridge and the first we left in the tunnels. Erika and Jon both got eighteen years. The important thing wasn't the time, but that they had to realize their dreams. After all, they'd already decided to end their lives. They'd all taken the easy way out and turned down the gift of life. They'd thrown away what they'd been given. We wanted to be sure that they really understood what they'd chosen to lose, by letting them first experience everything they could have had. The same goes for Niklas.'

'And I have so very much to lose,' Niklas says quietly.

The bomb dog is a Labrador who goes by the name of Radar. He's walking ahead of Ruben in the tunnel. There are three different levels in T-centralen – four if you count the commuter train platforms. There are multiple tunnel portals on each. That makes for fourteen tunnel openings to be searched, not counting escape routes and staff quarters. The commissioner has given them all the reinforcements available at short notice, as well as dogs from the national bomb squad. But the search is slow. Far too slow.

The bomb technicians suggested sending robots into the tunnels, but that won't help them find Loke and Vincent. Or Niklas. They need to clear the tunnels manually. But the officers are spread out thinly, and it's a huge area to search, with so many tunnels to be checked in such a short time. Fortunately for Ruben, he has completed his dog handling training, which means he's able to walk with his own dog.

The tunnel is almost unnaturally quiet. Ruben barely dares contemplate the chaos above ground. T-centralen is connected to Stockholm's central station and is the subject of regular bomb threats, but almost all of them are false. However, this is a serious threat, and the prime minister has more than delivered on her promise of resources. Efforts to coordinate between the Security Service, the police, the emergency response centre, the metro operator and the rail operator were concluded in record time. The decision to cordon off T-centralen – thus effectively shutting down all metro traffic across Stockholm, since all lines pass through it – is not at all popular, however. To top it off, they have been forced to stop all the long-distance and commuter trains which leave from the mainline station above, as well as the Arlanda Express carrying tourists to and from the airport. The hub of the entire city – indeed the country – is at a standstill and has to be evacuated. All available patrolmen have been summoned to assist, while

NOA is providing support with helicopter surveillance and the national bomb squad.

Ruben suspects that right now there are hundreds if not thousands of people shouting indignantly at his colleagues above ground as they are refused entry to the station.

The task force is helping to search the tunnels alongside Julia's team, and he wonders whether anyone will find anything soon. They won't be able to keep the place cordoned off indefinitely. Not that they have much time – once Niklas's time runs out, Loke is guaranteed to activate Tor's bomb. And then it'll all be over.

'Just close the door after you,' says Tor's cleaner, rushing down the steps as if she's suddenly in a hurry.

Mina watches her disappearing towards the gate and then follows Christer into the house. The hallway is at least the same size as her apartment. Hanging from the ceiling is a large crystal chandelier.

'Tor!' Julia calls out. 'This is the police.'

'Do you think he's at home?' Mina asks.

Julia nods.

'I don't think the cleaner was telling the truth,' she says. 'She was too nervous for that.'

Julia draws her weapon, keeping it trained on the floor. Mina and Christer do likewise.

'I'll take up position here,' Christer says, standing by the front door. 'In case Tor is here and tries to sneak out.'

Mina looks at him in amazement. She's never seen Christer this active before, but she likes it. The veteran policeman blocking the front door isn't someone to be messed with.

Julia and Mina proceed beyond the hallway. A staircase leads them upstairs, where they find a study and two bedrooms with separate bathrooms. One bedroom for Tor and another for Loke. But Tor isn't there. They go downstairs again.

'Have you seen him?' Julia says to Christer, who replies with a shake of the head.

Downstairs there is a dining room which is mostly taken up by a huge walnut table. There's also a living room with an open fire and a grand piano, as well as an adjacent kitchen. The size of the kitchen implies that Tor must have kitchen staff. But Tor isn't there either. Even so, Mina agrees with Julia – it doesn't feel as if they're alone in the house.

'I thought less and less about the deal as time passed,' Niklas says. 'Things just worked out for me. I chose to forget that there was always someone pulling strings for me in the background.'

Vincent can feel the dust tickling his nose and he has to make an effort not to sneeze. He doesn't think that a sneeze will trigger the bomb in the corner, but he can't be sure.

'But didn't you recognize Tor when you started working together?' he says. 'His voice?'

'No, not at all. How would I have? He came into my life many years after that moment on the bridge. Who remembers a voice?'

'Faust,' Vincent says. 'You were Faust.'

The pieces were slowly falling into place.

'Yes,' Niklas said quietly. 'I sold my soul to the devil.'

'That's not true!' Loke says in a shrill, angry voice. 'Tor isn't the devil. It's the other way around – we did you all a favour!'

'All?' says Vincent.

'Erika, Jon, Marcus. It was the same with all of you,' Loke says. 'I found them on the bridge, every one of them. All of them about to throw their lives away. Instead, they got years and years more and they realized their dreams. We gave them a gift! *You*, Niklas, chose to end your life at that moment. That hasn't changed. Tor and I have simply ensured that you actually appreciate the life you've chosen to end. If you don't want to die any more, that isn't our problem. A deal's a deal. You had already made up your mind to die on that bridge.'

It's never occurred to Ruben before how vulnerable Stockholm is. But the lockdown of T-centralen affects the entire city's infrastructure. Striking at the right point is all it takes to paralyse a city of millions. Tor knows what he's doing.

The comms radio clipped to his belt crackles into life.

'We've searched as far as we can along the northbound blue line,' Adam says. 'Nothing here either. Just like at the south end.'

Ruben sweeps his torch beam across the tunnel walls. The old detective's instinct that he's learned to rely on is telling him that something is wrong. They should have found them by now. There can't be much time left. What did it say in the clue that was sent to Vincent?

Find the fourth one before time runs out.

That's no help.

He continues walking along the southbound green line and reaches a large opening parallel to the track. It appears to be a staging area for repair materials. Radar the bomb dog suddenly barks. The canine stops and tenses.

'What's up boy?' Ruben says, grabbing the microphone on his comms radio. 'Have you found something?'

He activates the radio.

'Possible traces of explosives,' he says into the microphone. 'All teams stand by.'

The Labrador seems to be pondering it, then he relaxes and starts walking again.

'False alarm,' Ruben says in disappointment, returning the radio to his belt. 'They don't seem to be here either. I don't understand ... There can't be that many places to hide.'

'I'm going to check upstairs again,' Julia says. 'Just to be sure we didn't miss a wardrobe or anything. Not that Tor seems like the kind of person to hide in a wardrobe, but you never know.'

'I'll do down here again,' Mina says with a nod.

Both the living and dining rooms are open enough that she can see he isn't there immediately. Unless he's hidden behind the curtains – but he isn't.

The kitchen is built like the kind found in a restaurant, with worktops around the sides, and a kitchen island with a gas hob in the centre. There are two closed doors in the kitchen. She's already checked them, but she opens them again.

One goes into a pantry so big she can walk inside it. The other goes into a similar room in which Tor stores wine. The tall shelves on the walls are filled with bottles, each of which probably costs more than a month's pay for her.

She's about to close the door to the wine room when she

notices something – the left-hand shelf is on castors. That's odd, given that it isn't that big a room. She holsters her gun and tugs at the shelf. It rolls smoothly forward by a metre to reveal an opening behind it. The covered reverse of the shelf acts as a door. She's assailed by the sharp smell of vinegar.

'Mina, we're going outside to check the house,' Julia calls from the hallway.

'I'm coming,' she calls back, peering into the room behind the shelf. 'I'm just going to check something.'

'May I guess?' Vincent says. 'You were never attacked in your lab either? When you suddenly went missing it was actually because you needed to beat Mina and Nathalie to Walther Stockenberg's to retrieve Niklas, because he'd gone into hiding there.'

Loke nods in the dark.

'We had to improvise,' he says. 'Tor called before Mina and Nathalie had even got out of the lift on their way out of the building after visiting him. He couldn't leave – that would have looked suspicious. I didn't have time to think of a decent excuse – I just had to do a bunk for a few hours. At least he asked Mina to take the long way. It was a close-run thing. I barely made it. I passed them on the road as I was leaving. Looking back, it wasn't the best thought-through plan. But at least they believed me in hospital when I went there to get an alibi. I had to stage some injuries to myself. And that dealt with another problem of ours too, in that it delayed the news about the DNA match for almost twenty-four hours.'

'What about Walther?' Vincent says. 'You say you give people a choice. Did he agree to die? Did you do a deal with him where he chose this? And what about all the people who will die when that bomb goes off? Have they chosen that?'

'That's … the price I have to pay for doing the right thing,' Loke says. But Vincent can tell his answers are no longer as self-assured.

Vincent suspects that the words coming from Loke's mouth are no longer his own – it sounds more like Tor speaking. Thus it is Tor's logic that Vincent must seek to understand. His motives. Loke was the young and pliable disciple. And perhaps it really did begin just as Loke said, with the two of them trying to show people who had already given up, what life actually had to offer. As well as teaching them a lesson.

But Tor's plan seems to have changed over the years. It's metamorphosed into something far worse. The rows of black bags along the wall indicate that much. Tor has gone from seemingly supporting Loke, to exploiting him, and Loke finally seems to have cottoned on to that, now that he is inside the tunnels – not that he would ever admit it. But that's the crack that Vincent has to pry open if they're to have a chance of getting out of here.

Ruben is about to give up and go back when he spots a metal door down a passageway to his left. He shines his torch at it. The lock has been broken and the door is slightly ajar. If Loke and Vincent are anywhere down here, then it's guaranteed to be in there. There isn't anywhere else they can be.

He draws his weapon while grabbing Radar's collar to ensure that the dog doesn't give him away. He approaches as quietly as he can. There's nothing audible from beyond the door. But that doesn't have to mean anything. He takes a moment to collect himself and then pushes the door open with his foot while staying back.

Nothing happens.

He crouches to minimize himself as a target in case Loke is armed, and then he enters. The torch beam reveals a small storeroom, which is empty apart from some mattresses on the floor and a row of empty vodka bottles. It's probably no more than a sleeping space for Vivian's mates. But there's no Vincent, no Loke, and no Niklas.

There's no bomb.

Find the fourth one before time runs out.

Before time …

Ruben comes to a halt.

Before time runs out.

It's impossible. Can it be? Vincent hasn't solved the puzzle properly. The Master Mentalist has it all wrong.

The room behind the wine rack is as big as Tor's entire kitchen, and it looks like one too. And yet not. Unlike the kitchen, it's fully tiled. There are worktops along two of the walls, along with hotplates. There are big stainless-steel pots on the hotplates with a strong smell of vinegar emanating from them. On the far wall, there are two metal doors that bring to mind cold stores. Mina enters. As she gets closer, she sees that the grout between the white tiles is discoloured in places, speckled with rusty brown spots. It's reminiscent of umber – the paint Vincent gave her. She brushes her hand along a tile before yanking it away when she realizes what the substance must be: blood. The discolouration is blood.

She spins on her heel and takes a second look at the pots. This is where Loke and Tor boiled the bodies. Of course, they must have dismembered them first. Hence the blood. Suddenly her phone rings. The sound makes her jump. After she's fumbled it out of her pocket, she sees a number on the display that she doesn't recognize.

'Detective Mina Dabiri,' she says.

'Hello there. My name's Sebastian Bugh. I'm actually trying to reach Vincent Walder, but I can't get hold of him and he left me your number when we met, so …'

'Bugh?' Mina interrupts. 'The entomologist?'

'One and the same,' Bugh says with satisfaction. 'I just wanted to find out how you're getting on with those skin beetles.'

'Vincent isn't … he's not here right now,' she says. 'But as for the beetles, we found out that it's possible to get thousands from the Museum of Natural History.'

'Is it? They can rarely spare more than a handful. You have to let them multiply on their own. It can take a while before you have a full-sized colony.'

At that moment, she spots it in the corner of the room, on the floor by one of the worktops. The terrarium is the size of a bathtub and seems to be filled with soil.

No, please …

'Hello?' says Sebastian Bugh.

She hangs up and walks closer. The soil is moving against the glass walls. When she is up close, she realizes that it isn't soil. The dark mass is in fact made up of small, black and brown beetles that are a little less than a centimetre long. They're fat and oily and very, very numerous. The terrarium is almost full to the brim. The only thing stopping them from crawling out is the glass lid.

Mina puts her hand to her mouth so as not to vomit.

'How do you mean, it's "the price for doing the right thing",' Vincent says, taking a risk and asking for Loke's justification. 'How is this bomb "doing the right thing"?'

'My grandpa knew what was right,' Loke says loudly, as if trying to convince the walls themselves of what he is saying. 'He's been judged harshly by history, but no one understands what he wanted to do. Germany needed to go through a baptism of fire. Blood may have been spilled – including innocent blood – but that's the price of bringing about change. Tor knows that. Tor sees clearly, where others only have clouded, short-sighted vision. He knows that order comes from chaos. The innocents who will die in the chaos are sacrificing their lives for something better. There's nothing more beautiful than that, is there? Anyway, no one is ever truly innocent – least of all a man like Walther. He was a symbol of the old ways – of the putrefaction.'

'Those aren't your words,' Vincent says. 'They're Tor's. Loke – you value life. Everyone's lives. That's why you've done all this. That's why you helped people who were struggling, who weren't in a good place. It was to remind them about the gift of life when they had forgotten about it. You said so yourself. But now you're talking about sacrificing innocents as if they have no value. There's no difference between you and the people you're trying to teach a lesson. Remember who you are.'

Loke's gaze wavers. He opens and closes his mouth a few times, but is suddenly interrupted by Niklas.

'Is that what Tor said when he told you to go to my father's to get me?' Niklas snaps. 'That my father had to die because he was rotten? Let me tell you this: Walther Stockenberg stood for justice. Everyone knew that. What do you stand for?'

Niklas's previous apathy is gone. Loke averts his gaze, but Vincent spots the tears on his cheeks in the darkness.

'Because of who you are,' Loke says at last, 'your sacrifice is more important than the others'. You're even more of a symbol of everything that's wrong with society, given your role. My dad – the King – need never have ended up down here in the tunnels if society had worked properly. He needn't have died. But you failed at your job. So you're going to die down here when the old world burns.'

Find the fourth one before time runs out.

Ruben realizes that the message is not referring to Niklas's time, as Vincent thinks. The message is connected to the hourglasses. So that means the time in the hourglass itself. The time, that according to Vincent, indicated T-centralen was where Niklas would be found. But the message said they had to find the fourth one *before* time ran out. The riddle wasn't a statement of time. It's a place.

Niklas is at the station *before* time runs out. He's at the station *before* T-centralen. According to the details they have about the former, temporary line sixteen, that would be Hötorget.

Vincent missed it.

Ruben has managed to work out what the famous mentalist failed to see. Ha! He winks at Radar. The dog's tongue hangs out as he looks quizzically up at him.

Ruben grabs the radio and composes himself to avoid shouting.

'We're in the wrong place,' he says urgently. 'It's the station before. Hötorget. We all need to get there right away.'

Hötorget. That station isn't cordoned off above or below ground. Ruben feels chilled to the core when he realizes what that means. Immediately above the metro station is the Hötorget square where hundreds of people are passing by at any given moment. It's also where the Stockholm Concert Hall is – there's probably a Christmas concert on right now. There are more than seventeen hundred seats in the place. Not to mention a few more hundred people in the cafés and shops below ground. And all the buildings lining the square. He quickly counts in his head.

At least three thousand people will perish if Tor's bomb goes off – including Niklas and Vincent.

Ruben pulls out his phone and opens the clock app, where time is counting down inexorably. All the officers down in the tunnels have set their times by that abominable recorded message so they can see how long is left until Loke detonates the bomb.

The timer shows seventeen minutes and forty-two seconds. They aren't going to make it.

'I know you're in here.'

Tor's voice is coming from the kitchen.

'And ... I see you've found Loke's workspace.'

Mina holds her breath. She needs to hide. Tor hasn't come into the room – he hasn't seen her yet. The chillers. She creeps towards them and tugs gently at the metal doors, but they're locked.

'That's a pity,' Tor says.

His voice is closer now.

'Without that room, you don't really have any evidence. The legal process will be strung out for years and you will probably all get the sack. But in there you might find traces of DNA. And we can't have that.'

She has to overpower him. She'll probably only get one chance, but there's no good spot for her to surprise him.

'So you'll have to be the police detective who disappeared,' Tor continues, still in the kitchen. 'Your friends are outside. It's going to take them a few minutes before they wonder what became of you and they come back. A few minutes is all I need.'

There's a metallic sound in the kitchen and Tor rattles something that sounds heavy.

'Speaking of minutes, it can't be long until Niklas's time is up,' he says. 'I don't want to spoil the surprise for you, but if the wind is blowing in the right direction then we ought to hear the blast all the way out here. Any moment now. And then it really will be time for a new order. Grandpa Harald was right. We can't go on coddling people like we do in this country. The herd must be led. The weak must be weeded out – those who take everything for granted and complain about society without doing anything about it, not realizing how privileged they are. Since Harald, I'm the only one who can hold his head high and see the weaklings for what they are. Do you know what it's like to have to work with them? To smile at them? To pretend that the whiners' opinions matter one bloody bit? They're vermin. I hate them. I'm going to kill them all and then build a world of proud Vikings – just as it was always meant to be. And you'll all thank me for it.'

The air in the room is thick. She has to cough into the crook of her arm so she does so as quietly as she can, praying that Tor doesn't hear her.

'Although not you personally, of course,' he adds. 'You'll have the honour of being the mystery talked about for years. The ex-wife of the kidnapped minister of justice who had a breakdown in the middle of the investigation and disappeared without trace. Of course they'll search for you, but they won't find the room you're in. Once the shelf is closed, the room is fully sealed. And I won't be a suspect. After all, I'm not even here. Your colleagues have already noted that. Damn this extension cord.'

There's the sound of an engine starting in the kitchen. The motor pulsates. It sounds like a saw. Mina coughs into the crook of her arm again. Something is wrong with the air.

'I'd like to boil your bones afterwards, just like Loke does,' Tor shouts over the racket. 'But I'm afraid there probably won't be time for that. I'll just have to settle for the dismemberment part.'

Tor is clearly raving mad. Mina draws her weapon slowly so as not to be heard. In the worst-case scenario, she'll have to shoot him.

'I'm just coming,' he says. 'This saw is a little tricky to carry around. The bloody cord keeps getting tangled around my feet. By the way, I don't know whether you've given any thought to that hissing sound that's been going on for a while? Look down and you'll see the hose that's sticking into the room. That's gas from the kitchen. I've switched on the fan too, so by now it's probably started to fill up the room quite nicely.'

She coughs a third time and realizes why. She hasn't been able to smell the gas because of the stench of vinegar from the pots.

'I assume you're armed,' says Tor. 'But you should think hard about firing your weapon. It'll be quite an explosion. What would your daughter say if you sacrificed your life to take mine?'

He's right. Her gun is of no use. Mina looks around in a

panic. There's nowhere she can hide. The doors to the chillers are locked. The pots on top of the hob are too small.

The terrarium.

No.

Anything but that.

She's going to die.

Loke gazes at them silently. By the light of his mobile phone, Vincent can see the tears running steadily down Loke's cheeks.

'I know what I've done,' he sobs. 'I'm part of the problem. I have to burn with you.'

Vincent begins to applaud ironically. Loke is vulnerable now. No matter what it takes, Vincent has to break him down even more to be able to get him onside.

'Magnificent,' he says as sarcastically as he can manage. 'Tor is going to be so very pleased with his little suicide bomber. He hasn't had to lift a finger. He's probably at home watching Netflix right now and not giving you a second thought. And you're going to die for him.'

'No, no,' Loke stammers, sobbing again. 'It's not like that at all. Tor's going to emerge from the shadows and lead the country in a new, better direction. He says this is going to be a country we can be proud of again. Like it was for the Vikings. Life mattered then. Everyone's going to realize. Tor promised me … He's going to make sure I'm remembered as the person who made it all possible.'

'You bastard,' Niklas says quietly, wiping his eyes with his sleeve. 'You bastard.'

He makes as if to get to his feet, but Vincent gently stops him and makes him sit down again.

'Of course you'll be remembered,' Vincent says. 'But not in the way you think. Tor's plan can only work if you're an awful terrorist, the likes of which the country must be protected from. He's going to throw your memory into hellfire. You'll be hated for ever. Your name will be spat on. And Tor will be the first to ensure that that happens.'

He sees the realization slowly dawning on Loke as he quickly glances at the stack of holdalls. Loke checks his watch again, then looks at Vincent. The panic in his eyes is there to see. It's now or never.

'It doesn't have to be like that,' Vincent says slowly and clearly. 'Help us to save all the people up there. You're my friend. You don't deserve this. You're the Prince. You can be the hero – instead of Tor.'

Loke doesn't answer. But Vincent can see the panic slowly draining from Loke's gaze, to be replaced by a cold-headed calm.

Loke has chosen his path.

'Maybe you're right,' he says. 'Tor has other plans and he hasn't told me the whole truth. But he's also helped me. I have no choice. Tor took care of me and saved my life. The Prince's life. I owe him. He can do as he pleases with my life. Dad would agree.'

Vincent's shoulders slump – it hasn't worked. There's nothing more he can do. A dirty, subterranean concrete room will soon be his grave, while the blood of innocents trickles down from above.

'How long is there left?' he asks quietly.

Loke doesn't answer.

Vincent closes his eyes and pictures his family. And then Mina. He wishes he'd touched her one last time.

Mina can't stay where she is – she has to do something. She runs over to the terrarium in the corner, tugging three wet wipes out of the pack in her pocket. She stuffs two of them into her ears. The third one she tears in half and shoves into her nostrils. Then she pushes the lid aside and climbs over the high glass side. Tropical heat strikes her. If she moves quickly, she won't have time to think about what she's doing.

As she stands inside the terrarium, the skin beetles come up to her thighs. They press against her legs in a swelling tide. She sits down so that they come up to above chest height. They crawl excitedly across each other and around her.

'Here I come!' Tor shouts.

Mina screws her eyes shut and screams silently inside herself. Then she leans back in the terrarium until the beetles cover her whole body and face. Part of her sanity shatters, but she keeps leaning backwards into the sea of skin beetles. She prays that the wet wipes remain intact, otherwise she'll soon have hundreds of beetles crawling into her nose and ears.

Through the wipes and the mass of live things, she hears the pulsating sound of Tor's saw as he runs around the room.

'Where are you?' he shouts angrily.

There's a twitch at her eyelashes. The beetles are trying to crawl underneath her eyelids.

She screws them even more tightly shut.

'Have you hidden in the chiller? No?'

The wet wipe in one of her nostrils suddenly comes free and something begins to explore Mina's nose. Her brain begins to shut down. This is too much. She can't possibly survive it. The beetles find their way inside her top and start to crawl across her skin. There's a tickling sensation between her lips.

It's becoming increasingly difficult to think clearly. She consists of nothing but pure and unmitigated panic, which is shutting down all her defence mechanisms. Her will to live. The terror is too much. She just wants to die. To give up. To glide into a merciful escape from the rustling, crunching, dreadful things covering her body. She can feel them moving up the insides of her legs inside her trousers. Die. She wants to die.

Then she sees Nathalie – just as clearly as if her daughter were standing before her. A rapid sequence of memories follows, like an old slide show. Nathalie as a newborn. Red, slimy, screaming furiously. Nathalie's first steps. Wobbly, her arms outstretched for balance, heading into her mother's arms.

Their daughter in Niklas's arms. His wounded, accusatory look. Change slide. She sees the day when she left Nathalie on the floor, occupied with her colourful toy horses and merrily waving to Mina, completely oblivious that her mother was leaving her for good.

Mina moves on quickly through the slides. The pictures are too painful. Nathalie now, as a teenager. So beautiful. At home on her sofa. In the kitchen. Building a gingerbread house together covered in disgusting sweets in wonky lines. Nathalie's smile. The gaze meeting her own. For a split second she sees Vincent. At home. In her apartment. Vincent and Nathalie.

Mina forces herself to breathe surreptitiously. The vile beetles are crawling all over her thighs, her back, her stomach. She can hear the rustling of their movement through the wipes stuffed in her ears. They want to get in. They are trying to penetrate her defences all over her and get past her shield.

She can't give up. Can't succumb to death. She needs more pictures, more memories of Nathalie to cling on to. And of Vincent too. Mina focuses on controlling her breathing just like Vincent taught her. In. Out.

She has no idea where Tor is.

She's been buried alive.

Buried in a living cocoon.

But it is a cocoon

and cocoons protect.

A thought occurs to her. She's still holding the gun. She tries to aim it towards the sound of Tor. He seems to have stopped moving because she can no longer hear him. Now the saw has been turned off.

'Hmm. I really did think you were in here,' he says, sounding puzzled. 'Strange.'

She hears nothing but his voice, dull and distant. But that's enough to give her her bearings.

This has to work – she has no choice. Mina aims the gun towards his voice and fires blindly.

The chill is penetrating all the way into his bones. Beside Vincent, Niklas is sobbing almost inaudibly. Loke glances at his watch.

'It's time,' he says.

He wipes his eyes and takes something from his pocket. It looks like a key fob – it's a piece of black plastic with a few buttons on it. Vincent recognizes it. He has one like it on his car keys – it's the remote control for a garage door. He assumes that the receiver is located somewhere in one of the bomb-laden holdalls. He tenses his entire body. One small click on the black fob and Hötorget will be transformed into a crater.

Loke stops all of a sudden, as if he is listening for something.

At first Vincent hears nothing. But then he is able to discern a faint female voice through the walls. Mina? No. Someone else. The voice is calling for the Prince.

'Vivian?' Loke says. 'What's she doing here? They were supposed to stay away.'

He brandishes the gun at them as he stands up.

'Don't try anything,' he says. 'There's only one way out of here and I'll be covering it – with this.'

He waves the remote control with his other hand.

'The signal is strong enough to reach the detonators in all the bags simultaneously, and I won't be taking my thumb off it.'

Loke gives them a hard look before backing towards the door with the gun still trained on Niklas and Vincent. He turns the key in the lock and slowly pushes open the door. It opens outwards, to the right. The faint light from the tunnel is a welcome addition to the dark room.

'Prince?'

The voice can be heard from the left-hand side of the doorway. Loke turns in that direction while using his back to push the door further towards the right. Suddenly, the door flies open the whole way. Loke loses his balance and falls over. Vincent gets to his feet just as a big hand reaches from behind the door and wrenches the gun from Loke's hands. It's the huge hand of Johnny. Vincent hurries to the doorway. Loke is lying on his back just outside.

'Grab that!' Vincent yells, pointing to the fob in Loke's other hand. 'It's the trigger for the bomb!'

'Bomb?!' Johnny cries out in terror, and stamps on Loke's wrist.

Loke screams in pain and unfurls his fingers. Vincent takes aim with his foot and kicks the fob out of his hand.

'Why?' Loke whimpers. 'What are you doing?'

Vincent bends down and carefully picks up the remote control from the ground. He opens the battery compartment on the reverse and removes the power source so that it can no longer transmit a signal. Then he places the fob back on the ground and smashes it with his heel. Only then does he realize that he has been holding his breath ever since Loke took it from his pocket.

The glass around Mina is shattered by the bullet from her gun. She tumbles out of the terrarium in a sea of beetles onto the floor. She's holding her breath, ready. But the firestorm never comes. There were enough beetles surrounding the muzzle of the gun that the brief blast didn't reach and ignite the gas.

The beetles are crawling across the entire floor. Lying next to her is an electric bone saw. And lying in a pool of blood beside it is Tor. The tide of beetles has covered half of him already and they move greedily across him while he clutches his chest and whimpers quietly.

147

'Johnny, give me the gun,' said the man whose name, Vincent vaguely remembered, was Kjelle.

The man stepped forward in the faint light beyond the door with his hand outstretched. Johnny grinned and handed over the pistol. Then he offered a hand to Loke to help him back to his feet. Vincent returned to Niklas. He grabbed him under the arms and led him slowly out of the room.

As they emerged, they found Loke with his arms hanging limply by his sides, staring at Vivian.

'What are you doing here?' he said. 'I'm one of you.'

'This is for your father's sake,' the older woman said, taking a step towards him. 'You don't remember everything about your father. You can't. But your father hated violence above all else. He never hurt another human being. And he would be heartbroken if he knew what you've done.'

'How did you know?' Loke said in a voice that sounded vulnerable and close to breaking.

In that moment, Vincent saw the small child within him – the one who had lived his life down here in the darkness.

'Sorry,' said OP, the man who was always banging on about the murder of Olof Palme. He was standing at Vivian's shoulder, hanging his head.

'You?' Loke said, and Vincent heard how wounded he was. 'I thought you of all people would understand. You've always seen the world for what it is. You were the only one I told, for that very reason. Because you already know.'

'Even I know that most of what I say is bullshit. And it's nowhere near as crazy as what you told me. You said you'd killed three people and were planning to blow us all to kingdom come! All for your cousin's sake? I had to tell Vivian. Bloody hell lad, you're the King's boy. You're *our* boy, Prince. I couldn't let you do this.'

'We suspected it was probably you when we saw the new burial mounds,' Vivian said. 'So we didn't say a word to anyone. But we didn't realize how bad it was.'

Loke's lower lip began to tremble. Vincent could see he was crumbling on the inside.

It had probably been so clear in the beginning. Life was to be valued – your own and that of others. That was just the way it was. Those who didn't value it needed to learn a lesson, so that they understood what they were throwing away. It had been that simple for him.

But at some point during his childhood, Tor had begun to control Loke and exploit him for his own ends, and finally he had managed to transform Loke into what Loke hated the most. Someone who didn't value life. Someone who was prepared to murder thousands of people. Vincent guessed that this had just dawned on Loke.

'Prince,' Vivian said softly. 'You've been misled. But we're here. We're here for you. Your father …'

Before she could finish, a roar erupted from Loke's throat. It grew stronger and stronger and he turned his face towards the roof of the tunnel, like a wolf howling in vain at the moon. He screamed like a hurt child, and the sound reverberated between the walls and echoed in a chorus created by a single voice. Johnny covered his ears, but Loke's howling grew only louder – until it stopped abruptly. Then Loke began to run.

148

He should never have left them. The visible were just as invisible as the people living down in the darkness, if not more so. And he had fooled himself. In his longing for a family – for belonging – he had deluded himself. The only family he needed was down below.

He should never have left them.

The Prince ran quickly and purposefully. They would need substantial reinforcements to find him down here – reinforcements that were doubtless on the way, though right now, he probably didn't need to be looking over his shoulder. They were busy dealing with their oh-so-important minister of justice. And the Prince knew his way around the tunnels blindfolded. He was already halfway to the next station.

He had believed Tor when he had said they were like brothers. That they were equal. That they shared blood and spirit and a legacy that coursed vigorously through their veins. He had never shared Tor's fascination with Grandpa Harald, but he'd understood Tor's needs. Rune hadn't been the father to Tor that Björn had been to him while he'd been alive. Tor hadn't grown up with love; he'd never known what it felt like to be swept up in a big warm hug that smelled of smoke and leather.

He'd never had a dad who was the King.

Instead, Tor had often been shut up in the basement, and he'd lived in a darkness different to the one that Loke had. It had been a cold, lonely darkness where Grandpa Harald's trophies had kept him company. Items that were inextricably linked with Harald's tales of brotherhood, heroic deeds and a society that needed saving.

Tor had understood Loke too. He had listened to everything that had burst forth from him after he'd come to the surface and moved into the big house. During the long nights when he'd been unable to sleep, when the loneliness had scratched at his chest like

Buster the rat had scratched about the tunnels for food, Tor had listened. He'd listened to how his mum had fallen towards the water without anyone seeing it, without anyone being there in her final moments. Tor had listened as he'd spoken of the dull thud when the train had hit Dad's slender body, and how the crown had been flung from his head and to the side, landing seemingly untouched on the ground.

How the invisibles had given his father a worthy burial – a royal burial – by boiling the bones and burying them under a heap of earth.

His small body had harboured so much anger during those long nights – anger that he had roared, while Tor slowly caressed his back. Dad had explained over and over again that life was the most precious gift we had.

He reached Rådmansgatan station and continued to run along the tracks. People on the platform were pointing and shouting at him – they said he wasn't allowed to be on the rails, but he ignored them. It didn't take him long to reach the tunnel at the far end of the station. He was once again enveloped by darkness.

The next station was Odenplan. Dad's favourite.

When Tor had made his suggestion, it had been the answer, the way forward, the way to release what would otherwise have been locked inside for ever. A chance to teach people a lesson. To teach them how fragile and valuable life was. To teach them to appreciate what they had. As those people had stood there on the bridge about to jump, they were invisible. He and Tor had made them visible – but it had all been a lie. He had seen the truth in Vincent's eyes. After all these years, he could tell it was the truth. He had been a pawn in a game, without knowing which game was being played. Tor didn't care about protecting life. All he wanted was to hurt others to secure power.

In the beginning at least, it probably had been no worse than that. But the darkness in Tor had grown and led to further ambitions – ones like their grandpa's. Tor didn't care how many he killed to start building Harald's world order. All Tor cared about was leading. He wanted to be the King. But he would never be king, because the King loved people in the same way that Loke did.

He wasn't even called Loke – that was a name that Tor had given him.

He was called Mattias

– and he was the Prince.

Tor had lied to him. But Tor was wrong. And Dad had been right.

The ground began to quake beneath his feet. He slowed down. He could hear voices, but he knew that they were further away than they sounded and amplified by the echo of the tunnels. A light flashed and went out. It became darker and tall shadows moved along the walls. The vibrations beneath him intensified as he got closer to Odenplan station.

He closed his eyes and saw them together: Mum and Dad. Finally. They were dancing around the kitchen at home, next to the table with its waxed check tablecloth and shabby mismatched chairs. They were dancing and laughing, their gazes fixed on him. He missed them so incredibly much. There was a light shining around them as if they each had their own sun, and neither of them was invisible any more.

They beckoned to him. Dad had his crown again. He was as Loke remembered him when he was happy. When Dad was the King and owned the world.

Oh, how he missed him. With light feet shaking from the vibrations, the Prince walked towards them both.

When he opened his eyes again, he saw the two lights. They were so clear. So radiant. There was a loud fanfare to mark the arrival of his royal inheritance. He spread out his arms.

He was home.

149

Mina was sitting next to Vincent on a bench on the platform. She had ignored Julia's suggestion that she undergo a medical examination following the episode at Tor's mansion – all she had done was change clothes and come to Vincent as quickly as she could once she had heard what had happened. The medics on the scene had established that there were no physical injuries to Niklas or Vincent, and they had wanted to give them sedatives. Niklas had accepted the tablets with gratitude, but Vincent had declined. He was trembling beside her like an aspen leaf.

'Sorry,' he said. 'I'm experiencing a flashover of adrenaline and cortisol right now – hence the tremors and heart palpitations.'

Mina put her hand against his chest. He was right: his heart was racing. Then again, so was hers.

Vincent carefully put his hand on top of hers and squeezed it.

'It'll soon pass,' he said. 'But I don't understand. How could I mistake what the message meant so much that I got the location wrong? How could I be so stupid? I'm supposed to be the one …'

He fell silent. The deserted metro station was almost ghostly. The trains were due to resume service in ten minutes' time, but for now they had the station to themselves. She guessed there would be a lot of angry people waiting outside, stressed and annoyed that they hadn't been able to ride the metro for a while, and completely oblivious to the fact that they could all have been dead by now.

'I wonder what the Shadow makes of all this,' Vincent said. 'I wonder if he's finally satisfied?'

'What do you mean?'

Vincent tugged up his trouser leg to reveal a black strap around his ankle.

'I'm wearing a GPS tracker and microphone,' he said. 'The Shadow has been with me all along. He heard everything. Today was apparently my last chance for penance if I want to see my family again.'

'Saving half the city must be penance enough,' Mina said, taking Vincent by the arm. 'Come on, let's go, before the station fills up with people wondering why the Master Mentalist is sitting here quivering like a leaf.'

They stood up and moved towards the escalator.

'When and where are you going to meet the Shadow?' she said, nodding towards the patrolman at the foot of the escalator. 'I want to make sure every cop in town is there for it. As soon as you have your family back, we'll take him down. I intend to personally ensure that he's put away for a very long time.'

'Thanks,' Vincent said. 'But we both know that won't work. I have to wait for him to contact me, and if I know him, he'll do it in a way that ensures the police can't touch him.'

Mina nodded. As much as she hated not being able to do anything, she knew he was right – they couldn't do anything that risked the safety of his family. She couldn't imagine what Vincent must be going through.

When they exited through the station doors at surface level, the sun broke through the clouds and its rays warmed her face. The snow-blanketed Hötorget square, which was usually a sea of slush no matter how much snow there was elsewhere in town, was sparkling magnificently in the sunshine. Everywhere she saw people talking and laughing while they enjoyed the warmth. As ever, the market stallholders in the square were competing to see who could call out their wares the loudest. A woman walked past and gave Mina a big smile. There was an intensity of hustle and bustle in the square – as if the people there somehow sensed that they had just avoided death.

'Where are we off to?' said Vincent.

'You're coming home with me to Årsta,' she said. 'I might not be able to catch the Shadow, but I'm definitely not leaving you on your own right now. Nathalie will be at Niklas's tonight – she's so relieved to have her dad back, she's refusing to leave his side. And if you think I'm letting you head off to an empty house in Tyresö, you can forget it. I'm going to wait with you until the Shadow gets in touch. You can stay at mine until this is over.'

150

Harry was still with Julia's mother at her house. She had fortunately said yes when asked if she could babysit. Julia hadn't said why she wanted help with Harry – only that things had got messed up that morning. It wasn't a lie … They really had got messed up, although she wasn't thinking about the chaos in the metro tunnels. It was her life and marriage that had got messed up. If they were the same thing …

Torkel ought to be home from work by now. Julia hadn't said anything to him because she didn't know how he would react, but the reason she had arranged for childcare was because they needed to get to grips with the issue they had both been padding around. They needed to sit down and talk. About the future. About them. About Harry.

After she had parked the car on the driveway in front of the house, she lingered behind the wheel for a little while. It would have been easier if she had prepared what she was going to say; the fact that she had finally decided to talk it out with him didn't mean she had formulated a proper plan. It was as if her brain and her heart were in a full-scale war with each other and kept taking turns to have the upper hand.

Harry's little red sledge was leaning against the wall of the house, and this tiny detail made her heart ache.

They had fought so hard for him. They had been so united. There had been so much love in their struggle to ensure that one day there would be a small sledge leaning against the wall of a house. And yet, they had failed. Perhaps she would eventually feel able to go through their relationship, dissecting it and evaluating exactly what had gone wrong. But not now. Did it really matter what had gone wrong? Wasn't it enough to conclude that sometimes things did go wrong? Or would she not be able to learn from her mistakes if she did that?

Gaaaah. Julia thumped her head softly against the steering wheel. Then she took a deep breath and got out of the car.

Light, powdery snow had recently fallen, leaving the white ground outside the front door clean and untouched. There were no footprints. Nor were there any tyre tracks left by Torkel's car, but that didn't mean that he wasn't at home. One of their recurring rows was that he was always lending his car to his brother.

Once she had unlocked the door, she took another deep breath, stamped the snow off onto the doormat and then took off her coat. The house was in darkness, with the only light coming from the electric candle bridges and the Christmas tree lights.

'Hello?'

No reply.

Julia frowned. Torkel was supposed to be at home. She went into the living room, then the bedroom. No Torkel. She turned on the main lights as she searched the house for any explanation of where he might be. Well, that was a little ridiculous. He might just have taken the car to the supermarket. But something told her that wasn't where he was. The atmosphere in the house was different.

When she turned on the kitchen light, she saw the letter propped up against a large white candle on the table. Her heart began thudding in her chest, and for a moment she considered whether to turn around, put her coat and shoes back on, get into the car and drive off somewhere – anywhere – without reading the letter. But she knew that wasn't possible. The letter was there. It couldn't be made to go away through sheer willpower.

Julia sat down heavily on one of the kitchen chairs. The kitchen furniture had been inherited from Torkel's paternal grandmother – it was a beautiful old wooden set that they had spent half a summer sanding down and painting in the proper way. They had been so proud of their work.

She slowly opened the envelope with her index finger. She pulled out the paper inside, unfolded it and read it carefully with her hands shaking. A life. A letter.

An ending.

When she had read the letter, she sat there for a short time staring into space. Then she picked up the lighter from the table and lit the large candle, before holding the letter to the flame. The flame slowly devoured the black writing on the white paper.

When there was only ash remaining and the embers had been completely extinguished, she left them on the table and stood up.

She pulled on her coat, still moist with snow, and went outside to retrieve the red sledge, which she put in the boot of her car. She was going to go and pick up Harry. They were going sledging. That was all that mattered.

151

Vincent was awakened by someone shaking his shoulder. He was lying on his side with his arm around Mina. They'd fallen asleep wearing dressing gowns – she'd found a spare one that only reached down to his knees. But that didn't matter.

Mina had spent more than an hour in the shower when they had got back to hers. Once she had emerged from the boiling hot bathroom, she had cut her hair even shorter than it had been two and a half years ago. He had held her in silence until she stopped crying. Neither of them had felt able to talk about what they had gone through.

The Shadow hadn't made contact all evening.

At some point in the night, they must both have taken off their dressing gowns without him remembering, because Mina was now wearing a vest and pants, while he was in boxer shorts. Her back was warm against his ribs and her soft neck was just a few inches from his face. He could have lain there like that for the rest of his life, but the shaking of his shoulder continued. He turned his head to see who it was, half expecting to see Nathalie.

The Shadow was leaning over him. Vincent started and Mina whimpered as he accidentally squeezed her arm. The Shadow raised a finger to his lips and pointed towards the kitchen.

Vincent carefully let go of Mina and rose from the bed. He found his shirt on the floor and pulled it on before following the Shadow out of the bedroom. He cast one long glance at Mina before pushing the door to. He would have preferred not to close it – he didn't want to lose Mina from his field of vision for even a moment – but he didn't want her to wake up either.

The Shadow sat down on a kitchen chair and gestured to Vincent to sit down opposite him.

'Bravo,' the Shadow whispered, silently applauding. 'I knew you had it in you.'

'What did it take?' Vincent said. 'Saving the whole city? Was that enough lives to satisfy you?'

'Not at all,' the Shadow said, with a shake of the head. 'I'm not remotely interested in what you got up to down there in the tunnels. But this, Vincent. *This*!'

He swept his arm in an arc, indicating Mina's apartment.

'What do you mean?'

'Surely you understand that this … person … that you've built up – this Master Mentalist – is nothing more than a psychological defence? A mental shield? Exactly why do you think you're always counting things and analysing everything?'

'Mum counted too. I've come to suspect she was probably on the autistic spectrum.'

The Shadow nodded earnestly.

'Certainly, and a place on the spectrum is hereditary,' he said. 'You've got a good dose of it yourself. But when you're constantly counting and analysing, when you're Vincent Walder, you overactivate your rational thought. Which in turn means you don't have to process your emotions. You haven't bothered to do that in a long time. Your emotional self is still beside that box containing your dead mother. You haven't processed any of that. Instead, you chose to peel away Vincent Boman and become Vincent Walder. The mentalist who had to control everything. You hid yourself in him, and you've been hiding behind your family.'

Vincent gazed towards the bedroom door, which was slightly ajar. He could just glimpse Mina through the crack. That made him a little calmer.

'My family,' he said. 'Where are they?'

'But now, without being able to hide behind your family and without having the Master Mentalist as your shield, you've finally experienced how it could have been,' the Shadow continued, as if he hadn't heard the question. 'Now you've understood and felt – finally *felt* – what you could have had if you had remained Vincent Boman.'

Vincent felt the tears beginning to form.

'I was a child,' he said in a low voice. 'I had no choice. To not feel was purely a defence mechanism.'

'One that became an identity,' the Shadow said. 'But right now Vincent Walder no longer exists. After all, I wrote in my letter that Walder would cease to exist. You don't need him. Feel everything, Vincent.'

Emotions that had been stored away from the age of seven to the present day suddenly surged forward as if from a broken dam. There were feelings he didn't even know he had. Feelings tied to his mother, to Jane. To himself.

And feelings about Mina.

There were so many emotions about her.

Big emotions, small emotions. Feelings he recognized and feelings that he couldn't put into words. They all washed over him with such force that he thought he might drown. He had no idea how long it went on for.

A few seconds.

An eternity.

But eventually, the most palpable of the feelings had passed. The storm surge was over, but there was still movement under the surface inside him. He didn't think that it would stop moving, either. Was this what it was like for everyone else? Did everyone carry all this around with them day in, day out? It was a new way of being. It was unfamiliar, but not unpleasant.

'Do you feel it?' said the Shadow. 'Do you feel what it's like to exist without your mental shield, when you feel as much as you think?'

'Yes,' Vincent said flatly. 'I feel it. But it's almost too much ...'

'That's because you're not used to it. Welcome to the human condition. One in which we don't count stairs and bottles of water and know everything, but instead we're irrational, led by our emotions, contradictory, but also filled with love. This life – right here, right now with Mina – that could have been yours all along. If only you had dared to be Vincent Boman. If only you had dared to feel.'

Vincent nodded as tears appeared in his eyes again.

'I want this,' he whispered. 'It hurts and I'm afraid. But I want this.'

'Good,' the Shadow said, leaning towards him. 'Because we're not done.'

The smile was gone and the Shadow's gaze darkened.

'You had to understand what you had caused before your punishment was meted out to you.'

'Punishment?' Vincent said, his eyes widening.

'Naturally. Your choice to become Vincent Walder has not only suppressed the memory of your mother – it's also caused people to die. Jane. Kenneth. Tuva. Robert. Agnes. You may not have committed the acts themselves, but you were the catalyst. This cannot go unpunished.'

'What are you going to do?' Vincent said uncertainly.

He gazed at Mina through the crack in the door again. She still appeared to be deeply asleep. It hurt his chest to see her – well, hurt was the wrong word. But it ached. It felt tender. And he was breathing strangely – as if there wasn't enough air in the room.

The Shadow leaned back and arched his fingertips together.

'Your punishment is that you must continue to be Vincent Walder, the Master Mentalist, now that you understand what it would have meant had you dared to be Vincent Boman.'

'What do you mean?'

'How many plug sockets are there in Mina's apartment?'

'Six visible ones,' Vincent said automatically. 'But I moved the sofa to hide one, so there are actually seven. There are also six in the stairwell – two on each landing.'

As he answered, he felt the broken dam in his head beginning to repair itself. The dam that had kept all the emotions – the *real* emotions – at a distance for his whole life. He realized too late and tried desperately to keep the new breach in the dam wide open, but a lifetime of counting things took over.

He was Vincent Walder once again.

The super-rational Master Mentalist.

He closed his eyes. If he had been able to cry, then he would have done so. When he opened his eyes after a while, the door to the bedroom had closed. He could no longer see Mina, and the Shadow had departed just as imperceptibly as he had arrived.

152

THE FIRST DAY

Vincent wasn't there when Mina woke up. She listened for sounds from the kitchen or bathroom, but the whole apartment was silent. She could feel his absence physically. She yawned and got out of bed.

On the floor by her feet there was a messy heap of clothes. Had they …? No, she would have remembered that, no matter how traumatized she had been by the events of the previous day. But she didn't understand why Vincent had left so early. And where had he gone? She took her phone from the nightstand and called him. No reply. Of course – Loke had destroyed his phone.

It didn't feel at all good that he wasn't there. He hadn't been himself the evening before. If he did something stupid then she would never be able to forgive herself.

Vincent seemed at any rate to have taken most of his clothes with him. There was a piece of elasticated material with a black lump on it lying on the floor. It was the microphone given to Vincent by the Shadow. She picked it up and opened the part that Vincent had said contained the GPS transmitter, but instead of electronics all she found were a few pieces of Lego stuck together. She frowned. What was going on?

She pulled out her phone again and called Julia.

'Hi, it's me,' she said as soon as Julia picked up. 'Have you heard from Vincent at all?'

'No? Isn't he at home?'

Of course – Julia didn't know that Vincent had slept over at Mina's. And she would ensure no one did find out, either. It was their own business and nothing the wider world needed to take an interest in.

'I can't get hold of him,' she said. 'He was pretty shaken yesterday. I'm going to head to Tyresö to check up on him. I know where he lives. But can I ask you for one thing?'

'Anything,' Julia said. 'It would be great if you requested a bit of leave, given what you and your family have just been through.'

Mina took a deep breath. She was not sure how what she had to say was going to be received. After all, she had withheld vital information from the police.

'Please don't be angry,' she said. 'But Vincent received a threatening letter on Christmas Eve. Someone kidnapped his whole family. He wasn't allowed to involve the police, so he didn't dare say anything about it to us. I had to promise not to tell you anything.'

'What the hell?' Julia shouted into her ear. 'How can you … And now you think Vincent might be missing too?'

'I don't know. But he met the kidnapper at the Gondolen the day before yesterday. Someone must have seen them there. Can you send someone over to talk to the staff? With a little luck we might at least get a description.'

'I'll call Ruben right away.'

'And I'll call you as soon as I get to Vincent's,' Mina said, hanging up.

153

'The mind-reader bloke?' said the waiter as he laid tables.

The lunch rush was due to begin in an hour's time. Ruben was already hungry, but he had promised Granny that he and Sara would have lunch with her. If he knew his grandmother, she would have hoarded some particularly good almond cookies for dessert.

'Yeah, he was here a few days ago,' the waiter said. 'But I didn't see him with anyone. All I saw was him sitting at the bar on his own, muttering to himself. To be honest, I didn't think he'd come back.'

'What do you mean by that?' said Ruben. 'Why wouldn't he come back?'

The waiter paused in the middle of laying a table and laughed, as if he'd just thought of something funny. Then he shook his head.

'Well, he was here, oh, I don't know. It must have been over two years ago,' he said. 'Before we redid the place. He sat at the bar that time too – all night – and caused a real scene. Ranting and raving. Then he was in the gents and it sounded like he was ripping the bloody toilet out. He embarrassed himself so badly that I didn't think we'd ever see him here again.'

'But you're saying he was on his own that time as well?'

'Spot on. He was alone that time as well.'

154

Vincent's car wasn't on the driveway when Mina arrived – not that it necessarily meant anything. She pulled up to the house and got out of the car. She had rehearsed what she was going to say when Vincent opened the door. He'd get a proper telling off for scaring the life out of her for no good reason.

She trudged through the snow to the front door and rang the bell. It didn't seem like Vincent not to have shovelled the snow, although she supposed he hadn't had the time to deal with that lately.

She rang the bell again.

'Vincent?'

She knocked.

No reply.

She tried the handle and the door opened. Unlocked. This felt even less like Vincent. She regretted not coming in uniform – that way she would at least have had her service weapon. Memories from when she and Nathalie had entered Walther's house flashed through her mind. This was far too similar to that situation. She almost imagined that she could see a bloodied Vincent lying on the hall floor as she entered.

'Vincent? Maria? Hello?'

What were Vincent's children called …? Perhaps they'd returned home if the Shadow had kept his promise? The names came back to her.

'Rebecka? Benjamin? Aston? Are you guys here? It's Mina – I'm a friend of your dad's.'

Silence.

Mina took a few more steps and found the light switch. She had been expecting a hallway stuffed with coats, lots of differently sized shoes and a sledge or two for Aston. But, apart from two pairs of leather shoes that evidently belonged to Vincent, the hall was empty. Odd. She was most definitely an efficient cleaner, but even she had coats in her hall. And there was a whole family living in this house. The Shadow could hardly have taken it all with him.

So where was their stuff?

Something was clearly wrong.

A voice in the back of her head told her that she might not want to know what was wrong. She could still walk away – she needn't think about the peculiarly empty hall. No … She had to find Vincent.

She carried on into the kitchen, finding it just as empty.

Although it wasn't completely empty. She opened several cupboards and found a handful of mismatched plates, two glasses and two mugs. There wasn't much more than that. It was hardly enough kitchenware for a full family. There was a calendar hanging on the wall and a coffee maker on the counter. Documents pertaining to the investigation into Jon Langseth and the other victims were strewn across the kitchen table, but she saw no evidence of the bric-a-brac that usually gathered in any kitchen.

It wasn't just empty, it felt … desolate.

Unnaturally desolate.

The hair on the back of her neck stood on end as Mina moved on through the house. Everything she saw felt wrong, in a way she was unable to put into words. She found Vincent's study and breathed a sigh of relief. At least that looked exactly the way he had described it. The Shadow's presents were pinned to the wall, and in a bookcase there was an assortment of home-made mysteries, riddles and puzzles. She assumed that most of them had been sent by Loke.

'Vincent?' she called. 'Are you here?'

She moved out of the study. She knew him so well, but she didn't know the person who lived in this house at all. Suddenly, what Vincent had said about Jon Langseth echoed in her head.

'It's easy to think you know the reason for a change in behaviour with the benefit of hindsight. When you think you already know what happened. That knowledge changes the memory of what you saw.'

She was moving faster now. She didn't want to stay in the house any longer than was absolutely necessary, but she had to be sure that he wasn't to be found anywhere.

She tried the first door on the right – probably one of the children's rooms. She swallowed hard when she saw that it was as empty as the hallway and kitchen. It didn't look like anyone inhabited it, full stop. There was nothing. No toys, bookcases or even a bed. The walls were in urgent need of fresh paint, and the floor was grey. She went into the room and ran her hand along the windowsill. Her palm turned grey as the dust covered it.

Now it was more than just the hairs on the back of her neck responding – her entire scalp was crawling.

'Vincent,' she whispered. 'What have you done?'

Two other open doors testified to bedrooms just as empty as the first. Vincent had a big family – a wife and three children. There ought to have been signs of them everywhere. Clothing. Luggage. Bags. Knick-knacks. Books. Crumbs. Dirty laundry. Aston's toys. The kinds of things that a family filled its home with. But she could see none of that. Nothing at all.

In a panic, she opened every cupboard and wardrobe she could find, in case Vincent somehow, incredibly, turned out to be even more of a manic cleaner than she was. But they were all empty.

This couldn't be the right house. After all, it had been more than two years since she had been there – and on that occasion it had been summer. She must have made a mistake – this was probably Vincent's neighbour's house. Yes, that was it. Of course.

The only problem was that she'd seen the name Walder on the mailbox. She was sure of it.

It was the right house – it was everything else that was wrong.

Mina went into the living room and stumbled to a halt. She suddenly felt dizzy. She was probably breathing too quickly and oxygenating her brain far too much, but she couldn't help it. The rational part of her knew that it was a reaction to shock, but that knowledge didn't alleviate the feeling that she was in freefall. She supported herself on the back of the sofa to stop herself from falling over. Apart from the sofa and the TV, the living room contained an aquarium with fish in it, but that wasn't what had captured her attention. It was the one-metre-high letters painted over and over to fill an entire wall.

UMBRA

'Vincent,' she whispered, or perhaps she only thought it. She wasn't sure. She could feel her eyes brimming with tears. 'Oh no, Vincent.'

Her phone buzzed and made her jump. She wiped her eyes with her hands several times and then looked at the screen. It was a text message from the National Forensic Centre in Linköping.

We've examined the letter you sent us.

She had completely forgotten about that. The threatening letter that Vincent had received from the Shadow on Christmas Eve that she had sent for analysis.

There aren't any fingerprints on it apart from those of Vincent Walder. If someone else has touched it then they wore gloves. Or he wrote it himself.

The truth hit her so hard that her legs almost buckled. There was a reason why the house was empty.

It always had been.

There was no family.

'Why didn't you say anything?' she whispered, making her way over to the wall where she placed a hand on the letters as if she might be able to feel him through them. 'I could have helped you. Surely you understood that? You didn't have to be alone. Why, Vincent?'

Then she realized that he *had* tried to explain it to her – on multiple occasions. She just hadn't been listening. Perhaps she hadn't wanted to understand what he was trying to say. She dropped her phone and heard it hit the floor. Vincent's words were drowning out everything else in her head.

Dissociative identity disorder … You know – what used to be known as multiple personality disorder. When parts of your own personality are split from one another. People who suffer from it often struggle to understand who they are and feel they have no control over their own actions. It's always rooted in a profound childhood trauma.

He had been living here all alone. Just him and his trauma.

Mina cried out and put her hands over her ears so that she wouldn't have to hear any more, but his voice continued unabated.

The brain is both our greatest friend and our greatest enemy. The things it can do to protect us are … quite remarkable. As I said, Mephistopheles is perhaps just one side of Faust. Sometimes we're our own worst enemies.

She gazed at the letters on the wall again and finally let the tears run down her cheeks without caring any longer.

Sometimes I wonder whether I've just had a nervous breakdown and imagined the whole thing.

Her tears were like a river washing her away with them, but through them she could still see the message on the wall with crystal clarity.

UMBRA

Ulrika Maria Benjamin Rebecka Aston. Latin for the darkest shadow.

155

ONE YEAR LATER

Mina looked out of the window. The snow was late this winter. They had reached the dying days of the year, but the weather apparently thought it was still early November. Much as she liked the cold, it was a relief not to be dealing with the biting chill of the previous winter.

Amanda offered her the bottle of hand sanitizer, but Mina shook her head. She no longer needed it. Amanda put the bottle back on the table next to a miniature Christmas tree that flashed its lights at irregular intervals.

'How are you feeling today?' said Amanda.

Mina turned to her. The upholstered chair she was sitting on was covered in the same shades of beige and brown that adorned all the furnishings in Amanda's office. Did psychologists' training include a section on how they had to furnish their office with nothing but natural wood colours?

'Fine, thanks,' Mina said. 'I received an invitation yesterday from Ruben and Sara – they've got engaged and they're having a party. Kind of crazy, right? Inviting people to a party just because you've decided to get married. But Christer, Lasse, Adam and Julia are going. Adam's bringing … Jessica, I think his girlfriend's called. It didn't work out with Julia after the divorce, but I think it probably did her some good—'

'Mina,' Amanda said, interrupting her briskly. 'We're not here to talk about your colleagues. How are *you*?'

Mina fell silent and gazed out of the window again.

'I'm OK,' she said after a while. 'Things are improving all the time on the cleaning front. In the last month, I've barely washed more than Nathalie does. Obviously twixmas has been a bit odd for us all – Nathalie and Niklas too – because it's almost a year to the day since … it all happened. Nathalie's still grieving for her grandfather. But she's a strong girl. I'm actually having dinner with her and Niklas this evening. Nathalie's cooking, so obviously her father is on tenterhooks because he's basically a cooking fascist. It's going to be entertaining to see how long he can keep himself in check.'

'Almost a year to the day,' Amanda said, jotting something down in her notebook. 'How do you feel about that?'

'Honestly? I can't stop thinking about it. And I still haven't heard anything from Vincent. Not in a whole year. I'm worried about him. Do you know anything? What do your colleagues say?'

'I don't know anything more about Vincent Walder than what I was able to ascertain from your report a year ago,' Amanda said. 'Which is that he needs help. So I hope that he's checked in somewhere and is getting the support that he needs. But even if that were the case, I wouldn't know anything about it. The law is very clear about patient confidentiality – patients are allowed to request secrecy about their whereabouts. That means absolutely no one can find out. It's fairly common in the psychiatric healthcare system.'

'But everyone knows that Tor Svensson's in the high-security psychiatric ward in Huddinge, don't they?'

'Yes, it's lucky that you only grazed him with your shot,' Amanda said. 'Tor's fate is the result of the rapid judgement against him. His megalomania accelerated to problematic levels even during the trial itself. But Vincent is free to do as he pleases. And he's simply disappeared. Vincent's case is … unique.'

'Vincent is unique through and through.'

'Although I work with you all a lot, I'm not a cop, so I can only go by what I've seen on television. But can't you trace him by seeing where he's used his credit cards or something like that? Or his phone?'

Mina shrugged.

'Loke destroyed his phone. His number isn't active and there's no information available to suggest that he's got a new one. As for credit cards, he hasn't done anything wrong, so I can't use police resources to search for him. He's a regular citizen, and the banks aren't keen on handing out information like that about their customers for no good reason.'

'But you've tried.'

It wasn't a question. Of course she had. It had been the first thing she had done. But it hadn't yielded anything then, and she hadn't had better luck when trying her hand on subsequent occasions.

Lying on the table next to her was a week-old copy of *Dagens Nyheter*. There was an article on the front page about the newly-elected leader of Sweden's Future, but Mina didn't think it was worth committing the name to memory. Since Ted Hansson's resignation a year ago, the party had struggled to find a leader they could make stick. Most candidates had only managed a month or two in post before their political ignorance had made it too difficult for them to run a national political party. For now, Sweden's Future was in the doldrums. As far as Mina was concerned, they were welcome to disappear altogether.

'It's hard to believe that it's been a year since I went into his house in Tyresö,' Mina said quietly. 'It feels like it was yesterday. It was just so dreadfully … empty. I still sometimes dream that I'm there. I can't believe that Vincent's entire family was nothing more than a fantasy.'

Amanda nodded slowly and put down her pen.

'I really shouldn't say anything until I've conducted a thorough psychological assessment of Vincent in person,' she said. 'But after listening to you for the last twelve months, I can only reach the same conclusion you have. His family seems to have been a subconscious construct – it was probably his way of dealing with his childhood trauma. I've never seen such a serious case of split personality as Vincent's.'

'I think Vincent's family represented different aspects of himself,' said Mina. 'Aston was his emotional side. Benjamin was his analytical ability. Rebecka was his social self. Maria was the spiritual part of him – something I suppose Vincent was never comfortable about having. And Ulrika was probably his cynicism. Of course, I've said all of this before. But I still don't understand what happened.'

'Perhaps it's time for us to talk about this,' Amanda said, leaning forward. 'My goal with these sessions has been to ensure that you're feeling as well as can be, given everything that's happened. Since our focus has been on you, there's one thing I've deliberately avoided touching on. But perhaps now it's time.'

'What are you talking about?'

'Your role in what happened to Vincent.'

'My role?' said Mina.

She had said no at first, when Julia had said she wanted her to start seeing Amanda. The last thing she needed was a shrink rooting around inside her head – no one had any business being in there. In the end she had given in after Julia had said that it wasn't a request but an order. But she never looked forward to the meetings. And this new topic of conversation was not something she had any desire to tackle. She looked at her watch in the vain hope that time would be up, but wasn't so lucky.

'Yes, yours,' Amanda said, smiling. 'I think Vincent's fantasy world began to unravel when you came into the picture. For the first time, someone was there for him. You. He didn't need his external personalities in the same way as before. No wonder Maria was jealous of you, and that they were always arguing so much. Don't forget that Maria was real to Vincent.'

'But how couldn't we have realized?' Mina said. 'And why didn't he say anything?'

'I think he was trying to free himself from his fantasy in his own way. The fight at the restaurant with "Ulrika" was probably an attempt to rebel against the false reality he had built up. But he didn't succeed. The need to break free gave rise to "the Shadow" – Vincent's subconscious that wanted to hold "our" Vincent to account for the life he had denied himself. And as I've said, I think your presence played an important part in that process. After who knows how many years, he finally wanted to start living in our reality – and it was all thanks to you.'

Mina was silent for a moment. She looked out of the window again, allowing Amanda's words to sink in. She wasn't going to cry.

'I miss him,' she said in a low voice. 'Whoever he is now. Or wherever.'

Amanda nodded silently. There was nothing she could say that would make it better, and she seemed to realize that. Amanda smiled and closed the notebook in her lap. Apparently their time was up.

'By the way, there is one more thing,' Amanda said. 'The thing about umber – umbra – that you mentioned the first time we met. There wasn't much in Vincent's home, but I scrutinized your report in detail in an attempt to get to grips with him psychologically. You know the fish that he had in his aquarium? I don't know whether I ever mentioned it, but I looked them up. They're called mudminnows. But in Latin they're called *Umbra limi*.'

Umbra limi. A weak smile crossed Mina's lips. Typical Vincent.

156

Vincent emerged from the petrol station clutching six ice creams. The family had got out of the car to enjoy the sunshine. This really was an unusually mild winter. He managed to stuff the change into his pocket. It wasn't easy finding shops that still took cash, but there were still some out there if you just put your mind to it.

'Ice cream break!' he said.

'I thought you were going to fill up?' Ulrika said.

'Ice cream in the middle of winter?' Rebecka said. 'Why are you always so weird, Dad?'

'I'll have Aunt Ulrika's!' said Aston.

'Out of the question,' Ulrika said, snaffling two ice creams. Then she turned to her sister.

'Which one do you want, Maria? Dark or milk chocolate?'

Vincent smiled at them and tugged the cap a little lower down his forehead. The assistant inside the shop hadn't recognized him, but it was as well to be careful. In truth, however, it had been a long time since he'd been recognized. It was funny what a little dark hair dye and a bushy beard could do.

'No ice cream in the car,' he said. 'It'll only make a mess on the seats.'

The memory of a car with shrink-wrapped seats flitted through his mind. Mina's car.

Mina.

His heart ached. Even though it had been a year, his longing for her hadn't diminished. In fact, he missed her more than ever. But the Shadow had given him no choice. However his heart felt, he wasn't allowed to think about her too much. Not yet. Not until he was done with what he had to do.

If he ever was.

'Benjamin, do you want to get some driving practice in?' he said.

'No, you keep driving Dad,' said Benjamin. 'It's better when you do it.'

'Are we going to find a new house to live in soon?' Aston said, after finishing his ice cream. 'I'm sick of hotels. It feels like we've been travelling for ever. Where are we actually going?'

Vincent laughed and ruffled Aston's red hair. Red? That wasn't right. He blinked and saw that Aston was blond again.

There was a sign by the exit from the petrol station saying that it was just thirteen kilometres to Kvibille. Thirteen kilometres to the farm where it all began.

'I think we're almost there,' Vincent said. 'We'll know it when we see it.'

Acknowledgements

We authors would be out of a job without you, the reader. So, first of all: thank you for making it all the way here and for sticking with us on this winding adventure.

As usual, we'd like to thank Joakim Hansson, Signe Bedinger, Anna Frankl, Steve White and everyone else at Nordin Agency for their continued endeavours to share our modest works with the world. Many thanks also to Lili Assefa and the rest of the team at Assefa Kommunikation, who are the people responsible for ensuring that you heard of these books in the first place.

Of course, our heartfelt thanks also go to the team at Bokförlaget Forum, headed up by our publisher Ebba Östberg and manuscript consultant John Häggblom, as well as our editor Kerstin Ödeen, all of whom we have, as ever, given far too much to do. Pia-Maria Falk and Clara Lundström's marketing team deserve to have rose petals scattered at their feet.

Special thanks go to the exceptional Marcell Bandicksson for designing the covers for our Swedish editions, to Nicole and the team in SL customer service who answered our many questions about the metro, to Mattias Forshage, entomologist at the Swedish Museum of Natural History, who taught us enough about beetles that we could open our own dermestarium, to Anders Palm of the Greater Stockholm fire service for imparting vital knowledge about gas, and to Teresa Maric at the National Operations Department who didn't report us for asking her for the best way to blow up a popular spot in Stockholm city centre. (We should add that the unmarked black van that's been parked outside the office for the last week has been noted.)

As usual, we have also received invaluable assistance from

Kelda Stagg and Rebecka Teglind in matters ranging from crime scene forensics to dating skeletal remains.

Our profuse thanks to Catharina Enblad, who set us straight on life in the corridors of power.

Additionally, a huge thank you to all those we have omitted by name even though you truly deserve to feature here. We appreciate your understanding.

As always, we've been obliged to take liberties with reality, both in terms of the details around police operations and in relation to the world as a whole. We hope that this hasn't been too obvious.

It would have been impossible to pilot this project safely into port without the understanding of our families, and especially of our respective better halves Linda Ingelman and Simon Sköld. It's bordering on miraculous that they tolerate us – especially as we approach a deadline – but we have decided not to scrutinize this masochism on their part, instead settling for saying: thank you and sorry. Again. We love you.

There are also a few other individuals who merit our thanks on this occasion: Julia Hammarsten. Ruben Höök. Christer Bengtsson. Peder and Anette Jensen. Adam Blom. Sara Temeric. Thank you for letting us into your lives as you solved crimes, got engaged, had children, fell in love, divorced, celebrated Christmas and even died (sorry Peder!). You've been a constant source of surprise to us, and it has been a pleasure getting to know you.

Our greatest thanks go to our stars, Vincent Walder and Mina Dabiri. Knowing that our paths won't cross again hurts a little, but we wish you every success for the future wherever you may go. If we bump into each other in town, perhaps we can buy you a cup of coffee and hear about what you've been up to?

We miss you already.

Camilla and Henrik, July 2023

21	24	28	14
27	15	20	25
16	30	22	19
23	18	17	29

Don't miss the gripping start to the Mina Dabiri and Vincent Walder trilogy, *Trapped*

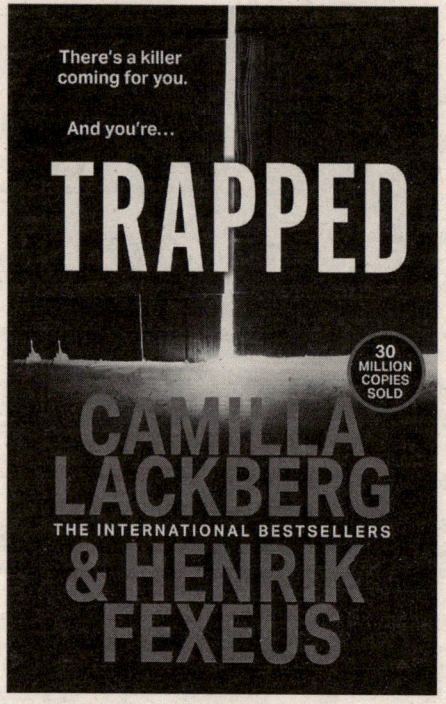

A shocking murder…
It's a case unlike anything detective Mina Dabiri has seen before. A woman trapped inside a magician's box, with swords pierced through. But this time, it's not a magic trick. It's murder.

A case which twists and turns…
Knowing she has a terrifying killer on her hands, Mina enlists the help of celebrity mentalist, Vincent Walder. Only he can give her an insight into the secret world of magic and illusions.

A ticking clock to stop a serial killer…
Mina and Vincent soon discover that the murder victim has the roman numeral III engraved on her leg. The killer is counting down. There are going to be three more murders. And time is running out to stop them.